Bumper Book of
Pony Stories

Bumper Book of Pony Stories

For Love of a Horse
A Devil to Ride
The Summer Riders

Patricia Leitch

This edition produced exclusively for Bookmart by
Armada, an imprint of HarperCollins Children's Books,
part of HarperCollins Publishers Ltd 1990

Printed and bound in Great Britain by HarperCollins
Manufacturing Ltd, Glasgow

Contents

For Love of a Horse

CHAPTER ONE

It all happened suddenly. In a three. The way things do.

"But that's rubbish," thought Jinny, pressing her forehead against the cold glass of the window pane. "It only seems like that to us. Billions and millions and trillion billions of things all happened. We just picked three of them."

She stared down at the busy Stopton street opposite their flat – at the supermarket, the dress shop and the Bingo Hall. In her ears was the growling throb of constant traffic. Throughout all her eleven years, Jinny had never lived anywhere else but in the city. Even at two in the morning the traffic roared and pounded in the street outside their home. All night long, footsteps rang sharp on the pavements. This was the way you lived, caged in by noise – a human sardine packed in with all the others. If you were lucky, you went away for a fortnight in the summer to the country, but that wasn't the way you lived – that was holidays. The city was your real life.

Then, suddenly, the three things happened. Whizz, crash, bang – and tonight was their last night in Stopton. Tomorrow the Manders family were going to live in the Highlands of Scotland. In a grey stone house, Finmory House, that had its own beach, Finmory Bay, its own moors, and even its own mountain, Finmory Beag.

They had looked it up on an Ordnance Survey map in Stopton Library.

"That's our house," Mike had said to the library assistant who came to wag a fat finger at them and point to the SILENCE notice.

"And none of your lies either," she had told him, not believing their wish come true.

"But it *is* true," Jinny breathed. "True tomorrow. Tomorrow night we'll be in Inverburgh, and the next night – Finmory."

Jinny's breath steamed the window pane. She breathed harder, then wrote with her finger nail:

Horses
Ponies
Foals

She stood back from the window to gaze for a second, entranced by the spell she had cast.

"Horses, ponies and foals. Oh my!" she chanted, in a *Wizard of Oz* tune. "Horses, ponies and foals. Oh my!"

For a moment longer, she stood without moving, then she swung away from the window, her mane of straight, red-gold hair flying out from her head, her blue eyes bright with excitement, her wide mouth stretching her sharp, small-featured face into nothing but grin.

"Horses, ponies and foals. Oh my!" she yelled, as she pranced through their flat. "Horses, ponies and foals. Oh my!" Her bare, bony feet stamped out the rhythm as she went dancing through the rooms where she had always lived – and after tomorrow would never see again.

Mr. Manders, packing the last of his books into tea chests, paused and shouted to Jinny to make less noise or old Mrs. Robertson would be banging on the ceiling again. He was a short, thick-set man, with shoulder-length hair that was wearing bald on top, a thick, reddish beard and a face that crinkled into long laughter lines. Really, he was glad that one of his family could plunge into the thought of their new life with such total en-thusiasm. Now that the decision had actually been taken, Mr. Manders was wondering desperately if he was doing the right thing. A middle-aged Stopton probation officer suddenly selling up everything and going off to the High-lands. He was going to write a book and be a potter. At one time, the fact that the only pottery Mr. Manders had ever done in his life had been at evening classes had only made the move seem more of an adventure. But during the last month he had been waking up in the early hours of the morning to lie staring into the darkness, wondering if it was all a mad nonsense. He told himself he had no choice. He had reached the stage where he had to go. He couldn't bear the hopelessness of being a probation officer in a big city for a moment longer.

Mrs. Manders and Petra were in the kitchen, wrapping up dishes in sheets of newspaper.

12

"Watch what you're doing," Mrs. Manders warned, as Jinny's elbow knocked a mug off a shelf. But because she was high with excitement, poised on the knife edge of a new life, Jinny's hand flashed out, caught the mug before it crashed to the floor, and put it back safely on the table.

"You'll end in tears," Petra warned – as if she were fifty, not fourteen. Jinny stuck her tongue out at her without interrupting her chant. "And don't be so childish," Petra snapped.

Petra had short, brown, curly hair like her mother's. Without much washing she stayed clean and tidy. Dirt seemed to fly away from Petra as readily as it seemed drawn to Jinny. When Petra knotted a scarf around her neck, it stayed where Petra put it, its ends twisted attractively, like the scarves in the women's magazines that Petra was always reading. When Jinny tried to improve her appearance by knotting one of Petra's scarves fashionably round her neck, people kept on asking if she had a sore throat. Petra played the piano. She practised every night, working endlessly at scales and exercises. She passed all the exams she sat and was going to be a music teacher. Jinny was tone deaf, but it seemed to her that Petra couldn't play at all. It was all work – not music. If Jinny had been musical, as Petra was supposed to be, she would never have wanted to be a music teacher. She would have been a soloist, playing to vast, silent audiences all over the world, their applause flaming around her and going on for ever.

"Horses, ponies and foals," chanted Jinny, seeing calm bay hunters, shaggy Highland ponies, woolly foals with bottle-brush tails and perhaps, perhaps, the horse of Jinny's dreams – an Arab mare who would come cantering over the moors when Jinny called her name.

"Have you packed your painting things yet?" her mother asked.

Jinny shook her head.

"Well, you won't let me near them, so if you don't do it I suppose they'll be left here."

Jinny supposed her mother was right, and, finding scissors and a ball of string, she went through to her bedroom to get on with it.

13

Mike was sitting on her bed, reading.

"Mind your legs," Jinny said, and crouched down to bring out her boxes from under the bed. She hardly ever let any of her family see her drawings. If they did see them, they always said the wrong things. Even when they praised them, they still said the wrong things. But Mike didn't count.

There were three flat cardboard boxes, overflowing with paintings and drawings, and a folder filled with work from school that Miss Dickson had allowed her to keep when school had broken up last week for the summer holidays.

"Now, whatever else you do in this wilderness that your mad father is taking you to, don't you dare stop drawing, Jinny Manders," Miss Dickson had said as she sat at her desk taking a last look at Jinny's paintings.

"No, Miss Dickson."

"Get a cardboard box."

Jinny had brought a box from the shelf at the back of the classroom, and Miss Dickson had taken her into the walk-in cupboard where none of the class was ever allowed to go.

"Now hold that up and let's see what we can find for you."

Jinny had held the box while Miss Dickson had filled it with plastic tubes of poster paint, most of them almost empty, but some still half full. She had dropped in a new box of pastels, a tin of used wax crayons, four black felt-tipped pens, two thick paint brushes and a paint-encrusted palette. "You can clean that up for yourself. Vim, hot water and elbow grease." Then she had reached up to the top shelf, lifted down a thick wad of drawing paper and laid it on top of the box. "Now, remember, don't you dare stop painting."

"For me!" Jinny had gasped in astonishment.

Miss Dickson had nodded, and marched out of the cupboard before Jinny had even begun to thank her.

Jinny stretched under the bed, wriggling to reach the box at the furthermost corner. She dragged it out and examined her treasures. She felt like a miser fingering her gold. The thick, squidgy tubes of paint, the prim row of

14

brand-new pastels, the cough sweet tin full of shiny bits of wax crayon, and the thick brushes. Jinny spat on the palette, rubbed one of the brushes into it, and tried the effect of saliva and mud-coloured paint along the edge of a sheet of paper.

"You're not starting to paint now?" asked Mike, shutting his book and stretching out on his front, with his face hanging over the edge of the bed as he watched his sister.

"'Course not," said Jinny. "I'm packing them up." And she began to sort the drawings and paintings into piles.

All the animals that Jinny had been able to find in the city were in her drawings, but mostly they were of horses. There were the ponies who still pulled the carts through the city traffic, some plump and well cared for, but some galled and rheumy-eyed. There were police horses, who always seemed to Jinny to be almost a part of the policemen's uniform. Despite their shining tack and well-shod hooves, Jinny couldn't help feeling that nobody loved them. Once, coming home with her family very late on a Sunday night, they had seen a young policeman riding a black horse and leading a bay, galloping them along the deserted street. Jinny looked at her painting of the two galloping police horses, the young man and the high, gloomy buildings. It wasn't very good – the policeman's arms were wrong – but the two horses were alive, being horses again instead of hairy Z-cars.

Most of the drawings of people riding were of pupils from Major Young's riding school. It cost two pounds for an hour's ride. Now and again, Jinny had saved up enough birthday and Christmas money to have two pound notes to give to Major Young. He didn't approve of children who arrived in jeans. Incorrect dress, he called it, and kept Jinny out of sight, tucked away in a back paddock, bumping round and round on a stolid, dark brown cob. "Don't come again until you're properly kitted out," the Major would tell her. But it was such a long time between Jinny's riding lessons that the Major had always forgotten her.

Jinny leafed through her drawings of correctly-dressed riding school pupils. Fat, scared girls, clutching their reins in gloved hands; boys who were bored; chatting ladies who

15

looked as if they should have had their knitting with them, and a superior girl who stabled her showjumpers with Major Young.

"The city's not the place for horses," Jinny thought. "But Finmory will be." And Jinny was swamped by the thought that tomorrow she would have left Stopton for ever; that it was true; that it was real. Sea and mountains and a Highland pony to ride.

"It did happen in a three, didn't it?" she said to Mike.

Mike held up two fingers and a thumb. He was nine, brown-eyed and curly-haired like Petra, but easy company, always pleased to be with you.

"Granny Manders died," he said and tucked down his thumb.

Granny Manders had been eighty-nine and as small as Jinny, her long wisp of white hair always carefully arranged round her pink scalp. High lace collars matched the crêpe skin of her neck, and enormous rings weighted her dry, bony fingers. She had lived with a Miss Simpson in an echoing house full of shadows, oil portraits and mice. She had died in her sleep.

"Two," said Mike. "Daddy sold her house. And three, he packed in being a probation officer. Hey, that's nice." He tried to pick up a pencil drawing of one of the shire horses that pulled the brewers' drays. Jinny whisked it out of his reach and packed it away in a box.

"Why did Dad stop? So suddenly, I mean?" Mike asked.

Jinny wasn't quite sure herself. "Remember Paula Hay?"

Mike screwed up his face. Dimly, he thought he could remember a spotty girl who had giggled a lot. So many of the people Mr. Manders had worked with, and tried to help, had come to their house over the years that they were mixed in Mike's memory.

"Uh, huh," he said vaguely.

"Well, I think," said Jinny, tying up her boxes, "that it was because of her. They sent her to prison because there was no room for her anywhere else. Dad couldn't stop them. She wasn't much older than Petra."

16

"What had she done?"

"Stolen food from a super. That was the last thing she did. Done other things before that."

Jinny pulled the string tightly around her box, knotting it hard. She didn't want to think too much about Paula Hay. She had overheard her mother and father talking about her when Mr. Manders had come home from the court that had sent Paula to prison. If it wasn't so impossible that it could never, never be true, Jinny would have thought her father had been crying. Once, Jinny had gone with her father to the two rooms where the Hays lived. There had been a baby that looked like a wizened old man, who had cried all the time they were there with a thin, whining noise, and four other children lying in a bed under a blanket that was black with dirt. The smell had choked in Jinny's throat for days afterwards, and the baby still haunted her dreams.

"We won't see Ken again," said Mike regretfully.

"No," said Jinny, tugging harder than ever at her knots.

Ken was another thing that she wasn't too keen on thinking about. Ken had been magic. He would have been looking for a winged horse at Finmory, not just an Arab. When Jinny had shown Ken her drawings, he had known what to say. And once he had arrived outside their flat, like a miracle, with a skewbald pony, saddled and bridled, and taken Jinny for a ride through Stopton. His probation had ended over three months ago, and since then they hadn't seen him again. As long as they stayed in Stopton, Jinny was always expecting to open the door and find Ken there. But how would he possibly find them at Finmory?

"Want to see my surprise?" asked Mike.

He led the way to his bedroom, opened his empty wardrobe, and three kittens came fumbling, delicate-pawed, on to the carpet.

"Finmory cats," said Mike. "There were only three left in the pet shop so she gave them to me."

Jinny picked up the black kitten. Its needle claws caught in her shirt. Tiny triangles of ears pricked upright above the flower face. It pushed its head against her hand, twitching its ridiculous scrap of tail.

"They're the first," said Jinny. "Our very first animals."

17

"Supper's ready," called Mrs. Manders. "Come and get it."

But Jinny hardly heard her. "The very first," she repeated, and trooping out of the open wardrobe came dogs and a goat, ducks and hens and all the wild animals that were at Finmory, waiting for them. The animals that Jinny had been longing for all her life were there, but best of all was the promise of ponies. Jinny saw Palominos and Appaloosas, Norwegian ponies, Exmoors and Highlands, retired racehorses, pensioned-off carthorses and rescued donkeys, all grazing together.

"Horses, ponies and foals. Oh my!" she breathed.

And, not tomorrow but the next day, they would all start to come true.

CHAPTER TWO

The removal men banged on the door at seven the next morning, and in less than two hours, all the furniture was packed into the van, leaving bare boards – and wallpaper surprisingly bright where wardrobes and bedheads had kept it from fading.

It wasn't home any longer.

"Oh, come on, come on," Jinny muttered under her breath, as everyone gathered in the kitchen for a last cup of tea before setting off. Jinny couldn't bear to stay. She hated this terrible, lost time when she belonged nowhere – was left floating with nothing to hold on to. "If the wind of God came now," Jinny thought, "we would all be blown away like dust. I'm not the Jinny Manders who lived here, but who I'm going to be I don't know."

"Oh, come on, come on," Jinny muttered more loudly, making her father scowl at her and Petra drink her tea more slowly.

At last the boss removal man stood up. "Better be off," he said. "Got a tidy way to go."

Mr. Manders was going with the removal van, waiting while the furniture was unloaded at Finmory, then coming back to Inverburgh where, hopefully, Mrs. Manders and the children would be installed at the Gordon Hotel. They were all spending the night there, then driving on to Fin-mory the next morning.

Mike and Jinny waved goodbye to the van, then ran back upstairs to where Petra and their mother were packing last-minute things into carrier bags.

"I can smell those kittens already," moaned Petra.

Mike suggested a clothes peg for Petra's nose, but removed the basket of kittens and rushed them down to the back seat of the Rover. Mrs. Manders had not been overjoyed when she had found them the night before, and Mike wasn't risking a return visit to the pet shop on their way north.

"Now, do you think we've remembered everything?" Mrs. Manders said as they all stood at the front door.

"Everything. Absolutely everything," Jinny assured her.

"Don't rush me," said her mother. "This is our final exit."

Mike did a jet tour, running from empty room to empty room.

"Not even a Manders' flea left," he reported.

"Right, then. This is it." And Mrs. Manders closed the door with a bang.

They packed bags into the already overflowing boot and climbed in the car. Petra in front, Mike and Jinny with the kittens in the back.

As Mrs. Manders started up the engine, Jinny looked back at the blank, curtainless windows. For a moment, she thought she saw someone move, but it was only a shadow. "It might have been myself," she thought wildly. "Myself watching me go." And she twisted round, staring out through the windscreen, staring towards Scotland and the North.

They drove through the centre of the city that they all knew so well, on between rows and rows of crumbling, brick terrace houses and then through the lush Stopton suburbs, until Mrs Manders turned on to the boredom of the motorway. She drove steadily on the inside lane. On and on they went. Drugged by the flash of passing cars and the glimmering, whale's back ribbon of road, Jinny's eyes closed. She woke gritty and cross. Next to her, Mike was still asleep, and Petra was telling her mother some

19

long, involved story about Pamela Cook being so rude to Miss Berry.

"Are we nearly there?" asked Jinny, but no one bothered to answer her.

When they stopped for lunch, the hillsides were furred with forestry pine trees, and, far ahead of them, Jinny could see the faint, half-imagined bulk of mountains, pale grey and dusk purple, rearing up into the sky. She breathed in gulps of clear, sharp air.

"Can't you feel it?" she demanded. "It smells quite different to Stopton."

"What?" said Petra.

"Scotland, of course," said Jinny scornfully.

"Don't talk nonsense," said Petra. "We're still in England."

"But I can feel it blowing down to meet us. Eagles and pine trees and lochs."

"Never mind being blown down on," said her mother impatiently. "Eat up those sandwiches or it's going to be the middle of the night before we reach Inverburgh."

But it wasn't. They got there just before six, and after two misdirections found their way to the Gordon Hotel. Inside it was dark, with stags' heads on the walls and tartan carpets on the stairs.

"All the way from Stopton!" said the girl at the reception desk, as if they had come from the other end of the earth.

By the time Mr. Manders arrived, they had all washed, eaten every scrap of food that had been left in the picnic basket, and were slowly starving to death in the lounge.

"How did it go?" asked Mrs. Manders. "What's it like?"

Only Mr. Manders had seen Finmory before, and that had been three years ago.

He spread out his hands and rolled his eyes ceilingwards. Without speaking, he sank on to the settee next to his wife.

"Did the van break down?" demanded Petra.

"The doors opened and you've lost all the furniture?" guessed Mike.

"No," said their father. "We got there O.K."

20

"What's it like?" repeated Mrs. Manders suspiciously.

"Vast. Vaster than vast. I've phoned the Post Office to fix up an internal phone system."

"Oh no!" cried Mrs. Manders.

"Joy!" cried Jinny.

"We'll need to wear identification discs," Mr. Manders said seriously. "It's quite on the cards that we won't meet each other for months once we move in."

"It's not really as bad as that," said Petra.

"Nothing within miles. Only a farmhouse. Total isolation."

"I don't believe you," stated Mrs. Manders. "And I don't intend to believe you until I see it for myself."

Mr. Manders laughed. "Well, it is larger than I remembered," he said, and led the way into the dining room.

Mike was finishing his second helping of trifle when Mr. Manders looked at his watch.

"Pity you're all so worn out after your journey," he said.

"I'm not," said Mike instantly.

"Nor me," said Jinny.

"If you weren't all longing to get to bed I did happen to notice that there's a circus on just outside Inverburgh."

"Oh yes," cried Jinny and Mike. "Yes, let's."

Mrs. Manders and Petra settled down in the lounge to watch the colour television, while Jinny, Mike and their father drove to the outskirts of Inverburgh, where a big top was pitched on a stretch of waste ground.

The air was filled with grinding fairground music and the shouting voices of the crowds jostling around the stalls and amusements.

"Bumper cars?" pleaded Mike. "Oh, please, Dad?"

"Not if you want to see the circus," said Mr. Manders. "It starts in five minutes."

"The circus, the circus," insisted Jinny, jumping up and down on the muddy, crushed grass.

They went across to where a clown banging a drum was wearily urging people to hurry along to the greatest show on earth. Mr. Manders bought three tickets, and followed his children through the opening in the flapping canvas. A woman in a spangled costume showed them to their seats in the second row.

"You don't want popcorn. You've just finished a big meal," exclaimed Mr. Manders, but already Jinny had pushed her way out into the passage and was buying three bags.

"You need it for a circus, for crunching when they're on the high wire and catching each other on the trapezes," she explained, when she brought the popcorn back.

"Well, sit at the end," her father told her. "Don't come squeezing past us again."

He was beginning to wonder if the circus had been the brightest of ideas. The last circus the Manders had attended had been Billy Smart's, but already it was obvious that this one wasn't going to be quite the same. Under the clown's make-up, Mr. Manders had been able to see all too clearly the tired face of an old man, and beneath the woman's spangles her costume had been a soiled grey.

Jinny crunched her popcorn and the band crashed to a crescendo. The ringmaster strutted in, cracked his whip, announced the first act and the Jet Setters came into the ring.

Mr. Manders watched in embarrassment as they missed easy catches, fumbled simple routines and failed to balance even one plate on the end of a spinning pole. The applause that followed them out of the ring was a weak wash of sound that died almost before it had begun. The dogs, clowns and acrobats who followed them were all equally poor. Jinny clapped her hands almost raw in an effort to make more noise. At the interval she bought more popcorn. "Not for excitement," she explained, handing out second helpings. "Just to stop it being so awful."

"Want to go?"

"No," said Mike. "There might be lions."

Fervently, Mr. Manders prayed that there would not be lions.

"There's bound to be horses," said Jinny hopefully. "Perhaps they'll be better."

The horses were the last act, and, to Mr. Mander's relief, there hadn't been lions.

Two aged white rosinbacks cantered heavily around the ring while the ringmaster flicked their sunken quarters with the lash of his whip. The spangled lady who had shown them to their seats stood insecurely with one foot on each broad back. Now and again she clapped her hands and cried, "Hoop la!" in a shrill voice.

Jinny gritted her teeth. She wished that the circus was over and they could go back to the hotel. She was sitting close enough to the ring to be able to see every detail of the horses – their patient, watery eyes, the harsh bits pulling back their lips, their scarred legs and sunken necks. One of them was broken-winded, and the harsh sound of its breathing tightened Jinny's throat. She hated the ringmaster, hated his pleated lips and beady, watching eyes. She flinched under the crack of his whip as if it stung against her own skin.

"And now, ladies and gentlemen," the ringmaster announced, as the two horses went out of the ring, "a final, special attraction. For the first time under canvas we present to you – Yasmin, the Killer Horse. Death lurks in her flying hooves. Tonight, at great personal risk, I have decided to allow her to make her first public appearance."

Jinny heard her father groan and stir irritably in his seat.

"All the way from Arabia – Yasmin, the Killer Horse."

Drum beats drowned his voice, and into the ring galloped a rich-chestnut mare with a white blaze and four white stockings. Jinny gasped with a sharp intake of breath, felt her scalp creep and a sudden coldness clamp down her spine.

The horse was a pure-bred Arab. She came, bright and dancing, flaunting into the ring, her tail held high over her quarters, her silken mane flowing over the crest of her neck. Her head was fine-boned and delicate, with the concave line of the true Arab horse. Her dark, lustrous eyes were fringed with long lashes and the nostrils wrinkling her velvet muzzle were huge black pits. She moved around the ring like a bright flame, her pricked ears delicate as flower petals. Her legs were clean and unblemished and her small hooves were polished ivory. After the dull ache of the rosinbacks, she was all light and fire.

Jinny sat entranced, hardly breathing, and then her breath burst out of her in a throbbing gasp. She loved the chestnut mare. As if all their long day's travelling had only been for this. As if she had come all the way from Stopton only for this, to see this sudden gift of perfection.

Mr. Manders glanced at his daughter and felt his heart tighten with fear at what the future must hold for her, for she would always allow herself to love too deeply, and always suffer for it.

Suddenly, the ringmaster's whip cracked down on the chestnut's shoulders. Not the flickering sting he had used on the white horses, but a lash with the full force of his body behind it.

"No!" cried Jinny. "No!"

The chestnut reared. Her forefeet slashed the air like razors. Then she turned on the man, her neck low and snaking. Again he lashed her, and again she reared up.

"No!" screamed Jinny. "Stop it!"

Before her father realised what was happening, Jinny had jumped up from her seat, flung herself over the low barrier, dashed across the ring and thrown herself at the ringmaster.

"Don't you dare whip her! Don't you dare!" Jinny cried, grappling with the man, struggling to pull the whip out of his hand, kicking against his booted legs with her sandshoes.

For a second, the ringmaster was taken completely by surprise. Just long enough for the chestnut to gallop past them and out of the ring. The audience, thinking it was all part of the act, clapped with more enthusiasm than they had shown during the rest of the night.

The ringmaster gripped Jinny by the scruff of her anorak and shook her furiously. The band began to play the National Anthem, and the tiered rows of people pulsed slowly into the passages and began to make their way out of the tent.

Mr. Manders went to claim his daughter.

"That's enough," he said abruptly when the ringmaster, his face puce with fury, began to swear at him. "I don't know what the R.S.P.C.A. would have to say about your whole set-up, but it strikes me that they might be interested." And he turned, putting his arm round Jinny's shoulder, and steered her out of the ring.

"But couldn't you buy her instead of a Highland pony?" Jinny pleaded from the back of the car. "Oh, Daddy, please. She can't stay in that terrible circus. She can't."

"The Highlands are to take you to school. You couldn't ride that wild horse. You know that perfectly well. So don't, Jinny. Stop it now," said Mr. Manders.

"She's only young. I don't suppose anyone has tried to break her in gently. She's not wild. She shouldn't be in a circus. That brute of a man whipping her."

"You can't do anything about it, Jinny. There's nothing you can do." And Mr. Manders shut his ears against his daughter's pleading.

"Nothing you can do about it," he thought bitterly. But as he drove back to the Gordon, he wasn't thinking about horses that shouldn't be in circuses, but about the families he had worked with in Stopton. People who lived in decaying, overcrowded, rat-infested rooms and the kids who roamed the streets because there was nowhere for them to go – neither in the evenings, nor in life.

"She what?" exclaimed Petra. "She ran into the ring and kicked the ringmaster! Oh, you didn't!"

Jinny scowled at her sister.

"Long past 'time for bed'," said Mrs. Manders.

Jinny lay on her back in the narrow hotel bed. Tears drained into her throat. She saw in her mind's eye the chestnut mare flowing round the dingy circus ring, bright and burning, and she thought how the Arab should be free to gallop over the open land at Finmory. What was the point of there being open moors and hillsides if she had always to think of the chestnut being whipped round the circus ring, boxed from one stopping place to another until she became soured and vicious, or, even worse, broken and hopeless like the white rosinbacks?

CHAPTER THREE

"Finmory is over there," said Mr. Manders, pointing through the car window to where green hillsides, scarred with grey outcrops of rock, sheered up from the road.

"You mean we stop the car and climb?" asked his wife incredulously.

"Could do. Probably get there quicker. We stick to the main road for another four miles, then strike off to the left along a road that eventually brings you back to the other side of these hills."

Jinny put her head down on her knees. She could just manage to catch a glimpse of blue sky above the hills.

"Should Mike and I get out and walk over?" Jinny asked hopefully, imagining Mike and herself standing silhouetted on the very top of the hillside, staring down on Finmory, being the first to see their new home.

"No," refused her mother automatically. "Most certainly not."

Packed in the back of the car, the three children were tense with anticipation. They seemed to have been waiting for so long to see Finmory, and now they were nearly there.

"Couldn't you drive just a little bit faster?" suggested Mike. "You're going like a funeral."

"We'd *be* a funeral if I put on any speed. This is a filthy bit of road. Bad enough, I should have thought, when there was only local people using it – but now there's all these blasted tankers and lorries on it, it's nothing but a death trap. I'll stick to thirty, thank you very much."

They turned off on the road that led to Finmory. It went through Glenbost village, which was only six or seven whitewashed crofts scattered about the roadside, one sell-everything shop, two petrol pumps almost submerged under the rusted wrecks of old cars, and two churches – one painted green, with its corrugated iron roof tied on with rope.

"That's your new school," Mr. Manders said to Mike and Jinny, pointing out a stone building.

"Cor!" exclaimed Mike. "It's only one room!"

"And the schoolmaster's house attached," said Mr. Manders. "Probably only be about a dozen pupils."

"You mean we'll be in the same class?" demanded Jinny. School in Stopton had been a modern building made of plate glass and concrete. "I'll be in the same room as Mike?"

"Doesn't look up to much," said Petra smugly. She was too old for Glenbost School and would be going to Dunin-

26

ver Grammar School, staying in the school hostel during the week.

"In the same class as my brother," said Jinny in disgust as she stared uncertainly through the back window. Although she was very grateful not to have to stay in a hostel, she had never thought of a school with only one room in it. A tall, hook-nosed man with a red face and bald head had come to the schoolhouse door and was watching their car. Instantly, Jinny disliked him.

"D'you think that's the teacher?" she asked Mike, but by the time Mike had looked round the man had gone inside again.

They rattled over a cattle grid and followed the track over bleak moorland.

"But there's nothing," said Mrs. Manders. "Not a thing."

"Sheep," said Mike.

At the far edge of the moorland, mountains shouldered up against the sky. Cloud shadows raced over them so that their colours seemed to flow and change as you watched – deep purple turned to blue that faded into bleached pinks and mauves. Waterfalls streaked black gorges with threads of brilliant white as they crashed down the mountains' sides, and patches of dried moss were a vivid saffron gold. Ravens croaked, disturbed by the car, and two buzzards flew up from the telephone wires that followed the road.

"Oh, honestly, Tom," said Mrs. Manders. "Really!"

The track turned and dropped down to a farm, half-hidden in a clump of pine trees.

"We'll come back later for milk and eggs," said Mr. Manders. "That's the farmer, Mr. Mackenzie," he added, as a man driving a tractor in one of the fields by the farm waved to them. "Nearly there now."

The car crawled slowly along a muddy, rutted track, twisted through a broken-down gateway, and followed the overgrown drive that pushed its way between top-heavy, fungussy trees to Finmory House.

Mr. Manders stopped the car and flung himself back in his seat with a gesture of triumph. "We've made it," he shouted, pushing his splayed fingers through his beard. "Finmory, here we come."

27

They all burst out of the car to stand staring at the four-square, solid, stone house.

"It's smashing," breathed Mike.

"Sea at the bottom of the garden!" exclaimed Jinny. "And mountains peering down the chimneys."

"Looks terribly damp," said Mrs. Manders, laughing as her husband swung her round and kissed her.

"Huge," said Petra. "I'll be able to have Susan to stay."

"Why not?" agreed Mr. Manders, taking an enormous key from his pocket and setting it in the lock of the massive, iron-studded door. The lock turned with a groan worthy of a fairy-tale castle. Mr. Manders set his shoulder to the door and pushed it open.

Jinny dashed past him into a high, echoing hall. She stared into rooms full of dust and cobwebs, with windows that rattled in their frames when she opened the doors. The ceilings were decorated with crumbling plaster-work – so far above Jinny's head that she had to crane her neck back to see them properly. In two of the rooms their Stopton furniture huddled nervously together in the middle of the floor.

"But curtains," her mother said despairingly, as Jinny ran up the wide flight of stairs. "And carpets! Where will we ever find carpets?"

A corridor ran the length of the second floor. Its windows looked out towards the sea, and the doors of the bedrooms opened off it.

"Two bathrooms with absolutely antiquated loos," Mike yelled from further down the corridor.

Each bedroom opened on to a room decorated in a different colour.

"The yellow bedroom, the blue bedroom, the pink room, red room," Jinny shouted as she ran from one to the next.

At the end of the corridor, Jinny discovered an almost vertical ladder of stairs. She climbed up, opened the door at the top and found herself in a room divided into two parts by an archway. The window of the room on the left looked out to the sea.

"Mine," thought Jinny. "Mine."

Through to the other part of the room she ran, her feet leaving dark prints on the dusty floor. On one of the walls was a mural of a chestnut horse. It was a red horse with yellow eyes that charged towards her through a growth of blue and green branches drooping under the weight of fleshy, white flowers.

Jinny heard steps coming up the stairs. She flew to the door.

"They're mine," she cried. "I've bagged them. These are my rooms."

Mrs. Manders and Petra stared at her in surprise.

"Don't panic," said Petra. "We're only coming to look."

"But these are attics, probably the servants' rooms at one time," said Mrs. Manders, looking at the low, sloping ceiling and seeing Jinny's mural as scribbling on the wall that would have to be painted over. "Are you sure this is the room you want for your bedroom?"

"Quite, quite, utterly positive," stated Jinny. "Quite, quite, utterly sure."

They had coffee, cheese sandwiches and apples, sitting in the kitchen with the kittens pouncing on their feet. The previous owners had left a long, oak table behind them.

"Shouldn't think they'd ever find another kitchen big enough for it," said Petra, looking around the room, which seemed almost as big as the whole of their Stopton flat put together.

"Right," said Mr. Manders, pushing back his chair, when they had all finished eating. "Working party fall in."

"I'm going up the hill," said Mike.

"Oh no you're not," said his father. "We'll all work until four. Then we'll all go out."

"But I'm . . ."

"No buts."

Petra and Jinny did their best to clean out the kitchen. They scraped a growth of grease off the Aga, roused hairy Methusela spiders and black beetles from the corners under the sinks, tried to sweep the rush matting – making the kittens sneeze – and unpacked dishes and pans into their own kitchen dresser, which looked like something from a dolls' house in Finmory's kitchen.

Mr. Manders and Mike fixed up beds. "Not permanent, only somewhere to be going on with." Mrs. Manders tackled a bathroom and the room with the bay window that looked over the garden to the sea.

"Stop. Everybody out," boomed Mr. Manders, just when Petra and Jinny were beginning to think that he had forgotten about knocking off at four.

"Not until I have a cup of tea," said Mrs. Manders, pushing her hair out of her eyes and leaving streaks of grime over her forehead. "What a place. We'll all die of some dreaded dirt disease."

"Our lungs choked with dust like vacuum cleaner bags," agreed Jinny. "We'll need to empty them out."

They walked together down to the sea. On one side, the hills dropped steeply to the path, and on the other were two fields belonging to Mr. MacKenzie. To reach the beach, they had to climb a rampart of sea-smooth boulders, then slither and slide down an avalanche of pebbles to the small sandy bay, enclosed on both sides by pincer jaws of black, jagged rock. The sea pounded up the beach in thunderous, foam-crested breakers, and the air was loud with screaming gulls.

"Pinch me," commanded Jinny. "Wake me up. I'm dreaming."

Mike obliged and pinched her hard.

"Pig!" she screamed, and chased him madly over the sands until they fell in a struggling heap.

"Behave yourselves," said Petra. "What will people think?"

But there were no people, only the domed head of a seal watching them curiously from the safety of the water.

Jinny lay flat on her back staring up at the gulls as they soared and swung in mazy patterns with effortless sweeps of their powerful wings. And suddenly she was back in the circus ring. The memory of the chestnut horse drowned her in a wave of blackness. Where was the horse now? What right had she to be here with so much freedom and space, when the chestnut was probably standing in a dark horse-box, waiting for the evening performance when she would again be goaded into attacking the ringmaster.

Jinny sprang to her feet.

"I'm going back to the house," she shouted to the others, who were exploring rock pools.

"What's wrong?" she heard her mother call – and her father's voice telling them to leave her alone.

Jinny's feet slapped down on the uneven ground as she ran faster and faster, stumbling and tripping, the wind drying her tears. If she could only run hard enough and fast enough she would escape from the crack of the ringmaster's whip and the fear-filled eyes of the Arab.

Reaching their garden, Jimmy slowed down, rubbed her arm across her eyes and walked towards the house. In sight of the heavy front door, she stopped and stared. There was someone sitting on the step. A thin young man, his bent knees sharp under his faded jeans, his black sweater hanging loosely about him, his strawy hair long on his shoulders. He seemed to be asleep, with his head resting on his folded arms. At his side was a bulging pack and a shaggy mongrel held by a length of rope. The dog saw Jinny, pricked his ears and barked. The young man woke and looked up.

It couldn't possibly be. But it was.

"Ken!" Jinny yelled, "Ken!" and went full tilt, tearing up the path towards him.

"How you doin' then?" Ken asked, as he uncoiled himself from the step and stood up slowly, laughing at Jinny's delight.

"How did you find us?" Jinny demanded. "How did you know we were here?"

"Dropped in," said Ken. "Thought you might be needing a hand with the garden. Could do a little digging. Heard Tom was a potter now. Could give him a hand with that, too. Know a bit about it."

"You mean you're going to stay?"

"If you'll have me."

Jinny flung her arms wide, shook the weight of her long hair for brimming happiness.

"Of course we'll have you," she exclaimed.

Ken smiled down at her from his lanky height, his green eyes laughing with her. Jinny could never remember what Ken's face looked like. It was always changing. Other people wore masks that you could remember, but Ken's face was different.

"And this is Kelly," Ken said, indicating the dog. "He

31

came along. I was hitching a lift and he appeared beside me. Got into the cab with me and now he's here."

Kelly's yellow eyes looked straight at Jinny. Under his thatch of grey and brown hair he considered her distantly.

"Of course you can both stay," said Jinny. "You know you can."

Even Petra was pleased to see Ken.

"Exactly what we're needing," welcomed Mr. Manders. "A bit of brawn to help us reclaim this wilderness. Do your folks know you're here?"

For a second, the light went out of Ken's face. His eyes hardened to a cold watchfulness.

Mr. Manders waited. "I've got to ask. You know that, Ken. You're not eighteen yet."

Ken had been put on probation for breaking into a warehouse with four other boys. He had said nothing to defend himself, but on the last day of his probation he had said to Mr. Manders, "I'd nothing to do with it." "I never thought you had," Mr. Manders had replied.

"Seventeen this time round," said Ken. "I was over ninety not so long ago, but I don't expect you to consider that. Yes, my parents know. You can phone them to check up. They're even going to send me a cheque every month, they're so pleased to be rid of me."

What could it be like, Jinny thought, terrified, to belong to a family who didn't want you. She knew Ken's family weren't like most of the people her father had worked with. They were rich. A detached bungalow, a low slung car and a country cottage.

"Well, we want you," Jinny said loudly.

"I'll phone tomorrow," said Mr. Manders.

"Settled?" said Ken. "O.K.? I can unload, then." He opened his pack, laid a sleeping bag on the floor, and set out bags of brown rice, wholemeal flour and soya flour on the kitchen table. "Arranged with the shop in Stopton to send regular supplies, so I'll not cost much to keep."

"Come and see my mural," Jinny said, remembering it as they finished washing up the supper dishes.

Her father, Mike and Ken went with her. In the grey evening light, the red horse seemed to glow in the dark room.

"Wonder who painted it," said Mike, while Ken crouched down on his heels, examining it in silence.

"We went to a circus last night," began Jinny, "and there was a chestnut Arab . . ."

"Oh no," Mike groaned, "not again." And he and Mr. Manders went back downstairs while Ken stayed, silently listening to Jinny's heartbreak.

"And I can't do anything about her," Jinny said at last, reaching the end of her story.

"You shouldn't have gone," Ken said, his voice harsh. "Have nothing to do with people who put anything in cages."

"But that's zoos."

"Don't give it us," said Ken. "You know quite well what I'm saying."

He stretched upright, balancing on his toes, his eyes still on the painting of the red horse.

"But what can I do?" cried Jinny. "What can I do to save her?"

"We don't know what we can do," Ken told her. "We none of us know. You didn't know I'd be here tonight did you? Yet here I am."

He turned on silent, cat feet and left Jinny alone.

Not knowing why, Jinny went to find a sheet of paper and the box of pastels. Kneeling on the floor under the watching eyes of the red horse, Jinny drew a picture of the chestnut mare. Not as she had been at the circus, but galloping free over the Finmory hills, her mane and tail fanned out by the sea wind, her whole body alert and vivid with the smells, sights and sounds of the wild country.

When it was finished, Jinny stood looking down on the picture as if it had been drawn by someone else, or as if she had looked through the window to discover the horse galloping there.

Jinny stood for a long time just looking, and then she found a roll of sellotape and stuck the drawing of the Arab on the wall opposite the red horse.

CHAPTER FOUR

On their fourth morning at Finmory, Jinny woke early. For a second, she couldn't think where she was. The window was in the wrong place and her bed should have been the other way round. Then she remembered. Finmory!

Jinny jumped out of bed, and, picking her way through the assault course of books, boxes and clothes that covered her bedroom floor, she ran to the window. Beyond the tangled garden was the quicksilver line of the sea. Gulls soared above the stillness and the sky was blue and distant, without a cloud. It was going to be a blue day. Jinny felt it shiver through her. Too special a day for them all to go on scrubbing and disinfecting and arranging furniture. If they were going to spend their time slaving away in the house, they might as well have stayed in Stopton. No one, absolutely no one, not even her family, and certainly not Ken, could possibly want to work on a day like this, Jinny thought.

She went under the archway and looked out of her other window. The sun was still a luminous disc, neat as a new two-pence piece. The early morning light made the moors and hills more mysterious than usual. In the dark valleys of shadow anything might be lurking.

"That's where we'll go," Jinny said aloud to the red horse. "We'll go to the very top of the hills, so that we can see right down the other side. If you were real, we would go together."

Jinny stood staring resolutely at the red horse, but it was too late. She didn't want to ride over the mountains on the painted horse who could never be real, but on the chestnut Arab.

"It's no use. I've thought about her," Jinny admitted to herself as she turned round to face her drawing of the Arab. Where was she now? Still at Inverburgh, or already miles away? "I'll never see her again," murmured Jinny. "Never."

Other people were always telling her not to go on wanting things that she could never have. Forget about them, they told her. But how could she forget when she hadn't forgotten? She could only pretend she'd forgotten, and that was no use.

By breakfast time, the blue day had established itself – golden and green and blue. Even Mrs. Manders, who was keenest on carpets and curtains and washed windows, couldn't ignore the weather.

"Stay shut up in the house today, and, when you die, God will demand to know what you did with His great glorious gift. And you will say, 'I scrubbed my floors'," teased Mr. Manders. " 'Godliness is before cleanliness', He will roar, and down you will go to hell."

"No way," said Ken. "He will explain and give you another day to enjoy."

"Never mind that rubbish," said Petra. "Where shall we go? I think we should take a picnic down to the beach and sunbathe."

"Oh no!" exclaimed Jinny. "We're going up the mountains. To the very top. I knew when I woke up that that was what we'd all do today."

"Is that a fact?" said Petra.

"We'd be able to see for miles," said Mike.

"Oh yes," said Jinny. "I know. Come on."

Ken carried the haversack with sandwiches, flasks, fruit and lemonade.

"Let me know when it gets too heavy and I'll take a turn," said Mr. Manders.

"It won't," said Ken. "I let it carry itself."

They climbed over the rocky ground behind the house, stopping to push open the creaking door of the croft and peer into the cobwebbed, dust-filled space.

"My studio and pottery," said Mr. Manders.

"You'll have spiders' footprints all over your pots," said Mike. "And mice. They'll probably nibble the edges."

Mr. Manders trod warily over the rotting floorboards and turned on a tap at the sink. Pipes groaned and creaked, and thick peat-brown water burst out of the tap, choked to nothing, then spluttered out again.

"For goodness' sake turn it off, Tom," shouted Mrs.

35

Manders above the noise. "The whole building is going to fall down on top of you."

Mr. Manders turned off the tap and the shuddering stopped. He looked around at the decay and damp. "You are completely mad," he told himself. "You should be pulling this ruin down, not kidding yourself that it will ever be a pottery." For a moment he remembered his office in Stopton, with its modern furniture and fitted carpets.

"Very nice," said Ken's voice behind him. "Very nice indeed. We'll get it together in no time."

Mr. Manders jumped, not realising that Ken had come into the croft. The boy was looking around him, his eyes bright with enthusiasm.

"When I think of the times I've sat in that ticky-tacky bungalow bedroom, thinking of all I could do if I only had a place like this . . ."

"And now you've got it," said Mr. Manders.

Ken looked straight at Mr. Manders. "Thanks," he said.

Outside, Jinny turned cartwheels of impatience, entangling herself with Kelly, who had come up to inspect this unusual human behaviour.

They climbed over the rusty wire that separated the grounds of Finmory from the moors.

"There's a path," pointed Mike.

"Sheep track," said his father.

Jinny ran ahead of her family, sitting on boulders to watch as they came towards her, then running on ahead again. As she climbed upwards, the world unrolled beneath her. Every time she stopped to look back, new headlands, black as jet against the aquamarine sea, had sprung into sight. As she struggled up over each peak of hillside, moorland sprang up around her – marsh and rock, glimmering lochans, the calm reaches of Loch Varrich, and oceans of bracken rolled away from her. Finmory House and Mr. MacKenzie's farm were tiny Monopoly pieces set in the pattern of cultivated fields.

The hill grew steeper, and sometimes Jinny had to climb on hands and knees. Below her, her family stopped to examine Petra's heel. "A blister," Jinny thought, knowing from a lifetime's experience the tender state of her sister's feet. "They can't be going to stop now. Not when we're

36

almost at the top. Well, I'm going on," she decided, and began the final scramble.

It took Jinny another ten minutes to reach the crest of the hill.

"Keep going. Don't give up," she muttered to herself, and then, with a final effort, she made it. She stood up to see the land stretching down on the other side in one, green, rolling sweep, to the grey, snail-trail of the road from Inverburgh. Cars and lorries were matchbox models. Jinny stood waving her arms and shouting for joy.

" 'Behold a giant am I'," she yelled, filled with the exhilaration of standing on top of the world.

Ken was the first to reach her. He stood beside her, laughing.

"Can they see us from their cars?" Jinny asked him.

"They wouldn't think to look," said Ken, swinging the haversack from his shoulders.

"I'm going to make a kite," said Mike, joining them, "and bring it up here to fly."

"Great," agreed Ken.

"What are those animals down there?" Jinny asked suddenly. "They're not cows, are they?"

"Well, they're not sheep," said Mike, looking at the seven or eight shapes that were grazing half-way down the hillside.

"Elephants?" suggested Ken. "Unicorns?"

Jinny stared, shading her eyes against the sun. They couldn't possibly be . . . But they were!

"Ponies," she screamed. "They're ponies!"

"Trust Jinny," said Mr. Manders, as the others reached the top of the hill. "Take her anywhere and all she finds is horses."

"I'm going down to see them," called Jinny, already running towards the ponies.

Her feet went faster and faster over the rough sloping ground. Ponies on the Finmory hills!

She ran full tilt until she was close to the little herd and then fell into a clump of heather to stop herself.

The ponies had seen her coming, and were standing watching her suspiciously, ears pricked through overgrown forelocks, forefeet planted primly together, ready to

37

whirl and gallop away from the intruder in an instant.

"It's all right," Jinny reassured them. "There's the good ponies. Steady now."

There were eight Shetland mares and five woolly-coated foals. Jinny plucked a handful of grass and held it out to a skewbald. The mare snorted warily, taking care to keep herself between Jinny and her foal.

"It doesn't look very special grass," Jinny agreed, "but I'll scratch you behind the ears and you'll like that. Bet you're itchy as anything under all that mane. I know what it's like having long hair in the summer."

As she spoke, Jinny eased herself closer to the Shetlands. Reluctantly, she supposed that she was too heavy to ride them, but maybe she could train one of them to pull a cart. Jinny was driving two of the ponies along the road to Inverburgh when her foot slipped on a tussock of reeds – she lost her balance and fell sprawling to the ground. She sat up to see rumps and tails vanishing over the hillside.

A man's voice laughed. Jinny jumped to her feet, and saw Mr. MacKenzie sitting on a boulder, grinning at her.

"Aye," he remarked, as if they were meeting in Inverburgh High Street, "it's a grand day."

"I never saw you. Were you there all the time?"

"Up taking a look over the ponies. Now and again I take a bit walk to myself and see how they're doing. On a fine day, you understand."

"Are they yours?"

"Aye."

"I was going to speak to them."

"I saw that. I was just about to stop you. That skewbald's a right bad one. Kick your head off as soon as look at you."

"Oh, she wouldn't. Not my head."

"As wild as tinks, the whole bunch of them."

"But doesn't anyone ride them?" demanded Jinny.

"Ride them?" Mr. Mackenzie spat derisively out of the corner of his mouth. "They haven't had a rope on them since they were foaled. I keep them for breeding, that's the thing for the cash these days. Off to America with them."

"Oh," said Jinny. She stared down at the road, watching

38

traffic that had grown into recognisable cars and lorries now that she was further down the hill. "I wasn't actually so much thinking of riding them," she admitted to the farmer. "More driving them?"

"Then think again, lass," suggested Mr. Mackenzie.

"Oh," said Jinny, wondering if he would really notice if one of his mares was missing, since he didn't seem to have much interest in them as individuals.

"And how's the family? Getting settled in?"

"We're up on the hill having a picnic . . ." began Jinny, her eyes still on the road, her mind half on the thought of a foal tied to the back of the cart as they trotted into Inverburgh. She saw four gaudily painted vans and trailers appear round the corner of the road from Inverburgh and thought, "What's that?" Then she thought, "Circus" and "Arab" at the same time, and felt the sun go out, the grey earth cold and made of metal. On the road beneath her, the chestnut Arab, shut in one of the horse-boxes, was being driven away from her for ever.

"Look at that stupid idiot," said Mr. MacKenzie, pointing with the stem of his pipe in the opposite direction from the circus vans.

Jinny saw a bright yellow oil tanker booming down the road, straight towards the circus vans.

"No bloomin' wonder folk are killed on that road."

The driver of the tanker could not see round the corner to the lumbering circus vans and the swaying sideshows stacked on the trailers. The driver of the first circus van could not see the bulk of the oil tanker speeding towards him. Only Jinny and Mr. MacKenzie could see the road on both sides of the blind corner.

The oil tanker was in the centre of the road as it took the bend.

"He'll hit them!" Jinny cried, her voice a helpless scream, for there was nothing she could possibly do to stop the accident happening.

Her nails dug into the ground as the oil tanker rounded the corner in the middle of the road, saw the circus vans, and swerved violently.

Jinny let out her breath. He had missed them. They were safe. The terrifying picture of the Arab's horse-box,

39

crushed into shattered wood – and screaming, wounded horses – vivid as colour telly, began to flicker out. Then the tanker's rear wheels seemed to skid, and the yellow, uncontrolled bulk swung across the road and rammed into one of the circus vans.

The sound of grinding metal reached them a fraction after they saw it happen, but already Jinny was tearing madly down the hillside.

"No place for a lass," shouted Mr. MacKenzie as he caught up with her. "May be people hurt. Get back with you."

Jinny hardly glanced at him. What did people matter when the Arab might need her? She could feel her lungs as pain in her back, the muscles in her legs burning, and her heart trying to jump through her throat, but she kept on running.

The driver of the oil tanker was slumped over the wheel. Men were struggling to open the truck door.

"The horses? Where are the horses?" shouted Jinny, but none of the circus people seemed to hear her. The van that had been hit was lying on its side with the trailer that it had been pulling concertina'd into it. From inside the trailer, Jinny could hear the crash of hooves and the screaming whinnying of terrified horses. Three men, one of whom Jinny recognised as the ringmaster, were trying to open the ramp at the back of the trailer.

"Here it comes, Joe," one of them yelled, as the ramp yawned open.

"Be ready to catch them in case they're loose," the ringmaster warned.

"Is the Arab in there?" Jinny demanded, but again no one seemed to hear her.

When the ramp was down, they led out the two rosinbacks – one with a bleeding gash on its shoulder.

"Get out of the way," the ringmaster swore at Jinny as she pushed past him, trying to see into the box. He swung his arm at her and she dodged back out of his reach, but she had had enough time to see that the horse still in the box was the Arab.

"Look out for this brute," the ringmaster shouted, as one of his men went into the box to move the parti-

40

tion that had separated the Arab from the other two horses.

Jinny craned forward to watch the man unhook the slatted barrier. She caught a glimpse of the Arab's head – sweated dark with fear, a frenzied eye rolling in a white socket, and ears clipped back – before the horse reared up, knocking the man aside, and came plunging desperately out of the box and down the ramp. From the end of the rope halter swung the metal bar to which the horse had been tied.

"She'll break her leg if she gets it caught in that," Jinny yelled. "Catch her. You've got to catch her."

For a split second the Arab stood, dazzled by the light, then reared again. The ringmaster snatched at the halter rope but dodged aside to miss the swinging metal bar.

Jinny saw the man miss the rope and the other people jump out of the way.

"Her legs," Jinny thought – and where the others jumped away, she threw herself against the Arab's shoulder, smelling the acid stench of the horse against her face, as her hands gripped the cheek pieces of the halter and dragged it down over the Arab's ears. The horse swerved and bucked, tossing her head violently. Jinny lost her balance and fell, but her hands were still knotted around the halter. The Arab was free.

With a piercing neigh, the horse surged up the hillside, rearing and bucking, standing for a moment of stillness like a heraldic beast, her head high and tail plumed. She screamed from the pits of her nostrils – and far up the hill- side one of the Shetlands whickered shrilly in reply. The Arab gave one last tremendous buck, her hind hooves high in the air, crashing the gold cymbal of the sun, and then she was away – thundering, drumming – her gallop- ing hooves beating their tattoo of freedom as she raced over the hillside.

Tears poured down Jinny's face, her whole body shook with sobbing. Behind her, the ringmaster swore in useless anger, and a police car swung in to the scene of the accid- ent.

The policemen forced open the cab door and, twenty minutes later, the driver was on his way to hospital. The crashed vehicles had been pushed off the road and the two rosinbacks loaded into another trailer.

"You'll not get near your horse," Mr. MacKenzie told the ringmaster. "I'd need to round the Shetlands up and bring them all down to the farm. And I'll not be thinking of that for a month or two yet."

The ringmaster glared at the empty hillside. Jinny thought he was like a brimstone, pantomime devil.

"If I'd a gun, I'd shoot the useless brute," he muttered. "No saying when we'll be back this way again."

"I'll charge you a pound a week for grazing, or I'll give you twenty pounds for her," offered Mr. MacKenzie.

"Forty," said the ringmaster.

"Thirty," said Mr. MacKenzie, as he turned to walk away.

The ringmaster had to call him back to accept his offer. The farmer put his hand in his hip pocket, brought out a wad of dirty paper, and peeled off three ten-pound notes.

"Lucky for you Murdo took away the scrap this morning. I'll have a receipt, if you don't mind."

In the early evening, the Manders and Ken made their way back to Finmory. Jinny walked silently beside her father.

"I don't know how you manage it," he said.

"Neither do I," said Jinny.

"You're not bounding very much," said Petra nastily, because her blister was hurting and she needed a quarrel to take her mind off it. "Usually, when something like this happens to you, you're all over the place."

"Not this," said Jinny, patiently explaining. "You don't bound when the most wonderful thing in the world has just happened to you. You feel empty somehow."

And she walked on, seeing the stone walls of Finmory, the hills sleeked smooth after the day's sun and the far, mirror glint of the sea. Yet, more clearly than any of these, Jinny saw the reaching neck of the Arab, her winnowing fringe of mane and her ears alive to the sound of her rider's voice as Jinny rode her home to Finmory.

CHAPTER FIVE

It was a week before Jinny even glimpsed the Arab again.

"They smell me coming," she declared.

"I'm not surprised," said Petra.

"You're meant to keep down below the skyline," advised Mike.

Jinny tried crawling through the bracken, and her arms came out in a rash.

"I think I'm allergic to bracken," she sighed, " – and it was working. I got quite close to them."

"How close?" asked Petra.

"Well . . ."

"Close enough to see them without a telescope?"

"Sort of," admitted Jinny.

Ken went with her, one afternoon, to see if he could help.

"The problem," said Jinny, "is that they've got miles and miles and miles of moorland to graze over, and the Shetlands know it and I don't. There I am, crawling along, all flies and itch, while they are standing on the next hilltop, laughing at me. And even when I do see them, they gallop off and I can't find them again."

"Difficult," agreed Ken.

"She's the worst," said Jinny. "Standing there like a giraffe, ready to warn the Shetlands if a bird as much as moves on the horizon."

"We won't find them if you can't stop talking," said Ken.

"I'm usually by myself," said Jinny indignantly, "so it can't be that." But she stopped talking, and followed in Ken's silent footsteps.

After about two hours' tracking, they caught a glimpse of the ponies grazing on the shoulder of the next hill. Most of the mares had their heads down, stuffing themselves industriously, while their foals were paper cut-outs pasted in the pools of shadow beneath rocky outcrops. Only the

Arab standing apart, snatching a mouthful of grass, then looking warily about her while she ate it.

Ken had hardly put his finger to his lips to tell Jinny that the horses were in sight, when the Arab's warning neigh bannered the silence. Hardly pausing to check, the mares wheeled and were away. The foals bumbled into sudden life and cantered, stiff-legged, at their mothers' sides. At their head the Arab floated, swift as a bright, wind-blown cloud shadow.

Jinny held her breath as she watched them gallop out of sight. For a split, pico second the air was disturbed by their furious stampede and then it settled again into stillness.

"She is beautiful," murmured Jinny longingly, her breath escaping with the words, as she flung herself down on the ground. "And you needn't think that if we go on we'll find them on the other side of the hill because we won't. They just vanish. Today's been a good day. At least we've seen her."

"True," said Ken.

"But that's no use," exclaimed Jinny, springing to her feet – spreading her hands wide to emphasize her words. "It's no use. How am I ever going to ride her when I can't get near her?"

"She doesn't intend to let you. And I don't blame her. If I'd escaped from a circus you wouldn't get near me, either. Give her time."

"But she's got to get to know me," said Jinny despairingly.

"You'll never get near her this way," said Ken. "Discover a place they're fond of, where they go a lot. To them, this moor's like Stopton was to us. Places where you go when it's hot; places for night time, best place to be in the early morning. It doesn't look to them the way it does to us. Find one of their favourite places and hide there until they come."

Jinny nodded. It was the best suggestion anyone had made yet.

"And call her Shantih."

"What?" said Jinny.

"You haven't found a name for her, have you?"

44

"No," Jinny admitted. "She was Yasmin in that circus; but I'm not calling her that."

"Then call her Shantih. It means peace. Makes a difference what you call people. Names alter things."

Jinny didn't see that they did, but she liked the sound of the word. "Shan-tih," she said slowly. "O.K. Shantih. That's her name."

But being rechristened Shantih instead of Yasmin didn't seem to have much effect on the Arab. She still fled like a red-gold ghost whenever she sensed Jinny's presence. Jinny tried picking one place and waiting there, hopefully hidden in the bracken, but Shantih seemed to know where she was and kept the Shetlands well away from her.

"Sometimes I despair," Jinny moaned to her sister a fortnight later.

"Sometimes we despair," Petra said, "of you ever helping us to get this house in order."

"My rooms are done," said Jinny, feeling slightly guilty.

"Your rooms!" said Petra. "Now that is really decent of you. Really big of you to go to all the trouble of taking your clothes out of your case and putting them into your wardrobe."

"I've done more than that," said Jinny. "I've pinned my posters on the wall and . . ." She paused, trying desperately to think of something else that would equal the kitchen garden Ken had started; the seemingly endless scrubbing, cleaning and decorating that everyone except herself had been doing, and her father's and Ken's transformation of the broken-down croft into a reasonable pottery. She couldn't think of anything. Glancing at Petra, Jinny didn't feel that her sister would be impressed by her drawings of spiders, beetles and flies that Jinny had made while she lay hidden, waiting for a glimpse of Shantih. Jinny herself thought they were quite good. She thought about them now to take her mind off Petra's expectant, smug face. She had made herself really look at the insects so that they stopped being "Yeugh" creepies and became fascinating creations, a whole underbracken world that had nothing to do with the giant crash of humans.

"See," exclaimed Petra triumphantly, "you can't think of one other thing you've done to help."

"Well, you can't say I've been lying in bed," Jinny protested.

"Next best thing," said Petra.

Jinny decided to retire gracefully. She went to look for her mother. In the Stopton flat you had always known where people were by just listening, but at Finmory you had to safari round before you found anyone. Jinny stopped at the kitchen to stock up with biscuits, in case she should miss her mother the first time round and have to circle the house twice. Glancing back at the trail of biscuit crumbs, Jinny wondered if it might be possible to lure Shantih with a trail of oats, but she decided that the sheep would probably eat them, and went on looking until she found her mother painting a bathroom.

"Can I help you?" she asked.

Mrs. Manders looked at her doubtfully. "Don't get it in your hair," she warned, handing Jinny a brush.

"'Course not," said Jinny, sloshing the brush into the white emulsion and attacking what seemed a suitable wall. "I'm helping because Petra says I haven't."

"True," agreed her mother. "But it's all right. I'd rather see you outside. Won't be long until you're back at school."

"Oh, weeks yet," said Jinny.

"Not here. Scottish schools start at the beginning of September. You start next Thursday, and Petra goes off the day before. It will be strange not having her at home all the time."

"No!" Jinny cried, swinging the brush in the air and cascading herself and her mother with paint.

"Look at the mess, Jinny. Do be careful."

"I thought we'd weeks yet. Weeks and weeks. I'll never catch Shantih before next Thursday. Never."

"The horse won't vanish because you go to school."

"But don't you see," cried Jinny, waving her brush wildly in the air, "I've got to be able to ride her before I go to school."

"Stop waving that brush around. You'll have the place covered in paint."

"I must be able to ride her before we go to school, because you're going to buy us ponies to ride to school and it MUST be Shantih for me."

46

"So this is what you've been imagining. But there's not a chance. We are going to get you a pony, but never Shantih. Even if she were half tame, she wouldn't be suitable."

"She would," said Jinny, scrubbing paint into the wall. "Oh, yes she would."

When Mr. Manders heard Jinny's idea, he only said, "Bring her down to the house and I'll have a look at her."

"You know I can't get near her," said Jinny, spacing every word slowly and deliberately.

"Yes, I know," said Mr. Manders, "and that's why we're going to see Miss Tuke tomorrow. She runs a pony trekking centre, and she's agreed to let us have two of her trekking ponies until next June."

Jinny went to bed still black and sulky.

"You're being silly, Jinny Manders," she told herself severely. "Tomorrow you're going to get a pony and that's what you've always wanted, isn't it? So what?" replied the bit of Jinny that always seemed more real than all the common sense in the world. "So what? That's not what I want now." And Jinny pulled the bedclothes over her head, screwed up her eyes and curled herself up into a tight, defiant knot.

Mr. Manders, Mike and Jinny drove to the trekking centre the next afternoon. Miss Tuke was pleased to see them.

"I can't tell you how glad I am when someone reliable offers to take over any of my ponies for the winter. That's where my profits go. And I'm sure I can trust you. I've heard all about you from Mrs. MacKenzie. So nice for them having a family at Finmory again, especially after that last lot. Utterly impossible, they were. Now, have you ridden a little?"

Jinny said she had. Mike said he hadn't but he felt as if he knew how to, like knowing how to swim even before you could.

"Good show," said Miss Tuke without conviction. "You'd better have Punch, then. He's certain he knows how to look after humans. And Bramble for you, my dear."

Jinny scowled up at her, still trying to pretend that she wasn't feeling excited.

"Really it's an Arab I want, not a Highland," she informed Miss Tuke.

"But how unsuitable," stated Miss Tuke, and led them down to a paddock where two Highland ponies were standing nose to tail, keeping the flies off each other.

Miss Tuke gave the children a halter each. "Punch is the grey and Bramble the black. Now let me see you catch them."

Jinny dragged the halter rope behind her and walked slowly up to the black pony, who was dozing peacefully. She slipped the rope over his neck, and the pony opened his eyes and regarded Jinny with a cynical gaze. He pushed at her anorak pocket, nudging hopefully, and, despite all her determination, Jinny's mouth stretched into a grin. She fitted the halter on to the pony's head, pulling his furry ears through the head piece and straightening his bushy forelock, then she clapped his thick-set neck, already woolly with his winter coat. He was to be her pony. Not Shantih, but, all the same, her pony.

She led him back to the gate, where Miss Tuke was telling their father about feeding and shoeing. "Hay and pony nuts," she was saying. "As long as they have adequate shelter, they're better outside."

"Well done, dear," she said to Jinny and went to help Mike, who was in danger of hobbling Punch with the halter.

Under Miss Tuke's watchful eye, they took a dandy brush over the ponies and saddled them up.

"Now we'll see how you get on with them," Miss Tuke said, as Jinny and Mike struggled on to the ponies' backs.

"Trek forward," shouted Miss Tuke in a loud voice, and the ponies moved sedately forward in first gear. "If they're ever having you on, remember those magic words – 'Trek forward'. Never fails. Now take them down to the paddock and ride them round."

Even when she was falling off them, Jinny had always thought that the ponies at the Stopton Riding School were on the slow side, but compared to Bramble and Punch they had been atomic. Obeying Miss Tuke's instructions, they walked the ponies round, halted them, mounted and dismounted, and walked them round again.

Jinny glanced back at Mike. He was sitting comfortably astride the Highland, looking completely at ease. "Trust Mike," Jinny thought. Riding was going to be another of the things that Mike did naturally and couldn't care less about. Jinny groaned, and turned back to concentrate on keeping her heels down, her knees against the saddle and her legs in what she hoped was the correct position.

"Try a trot," suggested Miss Tuke.

Jinny shortened her reins and applied the correct aids as taught by Major Young's assistant. Bramble plodded on, head down. Jinny pressed her legs tighter against the hairy bulk of horse.

"Trot," she said. "Trot on." Bramble flicked an ear.

"You'll need to wake him up," said Miss Tuke. "Kick him on. They don't do much trotting out on the treks, but once you have them to yourselves they'll soon start to put a little more effort into life. Now Bramble, move. Get on with you."

Encouraged by Miss Tuke, Jinny kicked hard. She felt Bramble's plod turn into a walk.

"That's the way," encouraged Miss Tuke, and Jinny kicked harder, stirrups and heels banging the pony's sides.

"There, you've done it. He's away," cheered Miss Tuke.

For a second, Jinny felt the pony change into a trot. She banged her heels hard into his sides. Bramble stopped dead, twitched his quarters in a token buck and Jinny went flying into the air. Before she had time to realise what had happened she was sitting on the ground, while Bramble looked down at her, ears pricked, nostrils wiffling, an expression of innocent amazement on his face.

Jinny sprang to her feet, fumbled the reins over the pony's neck and clambered back into the saddle.

"Now," she told the pony, "you needn't think you're getting away with that. I'm in charge here and when I say trot, we trot." As she spoke, Jinny urged Bramble forward, her elbows flapping, heels kicking and her seat bumping up and down in the saddle as she forced Bramble to trot. "Get on with you. Get on."

Bramble tried another half-hearted buck, but this time

Jinny was ready for him. She pulled up his head and sent him on.

"He'll canter for you," shouted Miss Tuke.

Jinny sat down and Bramble was cantering. She felt as if she was going faster than a Derby winner. Sky and hills, Miss Tuke and her father were blurred with speed. The clasp fell out of Jinny's hair, which streamed out behind her as they cantered round. She forgot everything except the hairy pony and this new-found delight of speed.

"Enough," called Miss Tuke. "Slow down."

Jinny heard her as if she were hailing them from outer space. She wanted to go on forever, never to stop.

"That'll do, Jinny," called her father's voice, and reluctantly Jinny steadied Bramble to a trot, then to a walk. She clapped the pony's neck and shoulder. "Bet you enjoyed that as much as I did," she whispered.

"That was super," said Mike, and for the first time since she had been bucked off Jinny remembered her brother.

"Were you cantering?" she asked him. "Are you O.K.?"

"'Course I'm O.K. Punch did the cantering. I just sat here."

"Oh," said Jinny, realising as they rode back towards Miss Tuke that Mike had been able to trot and canter without any trouble. She snorted in disgust, remembering the painful hours she had spent in Major Young's paddock learning to post.

"Well, I can see you'll manage them," Miss Tuke said, laughing at Jinny. "Don't suppose he'll try it on again. If he does, just sort him out the way you did just now."

"Did I?" said Jinny.

"You did," said Miss Tuke.

They rode the ponies back to Finmory, Miss Tuke promising that she would be over before the end of the week to see that they were settling down.

The ride home was mainly plod – sometimes plod that gradually became standstill until Jinny and Mike roused the ponies with cries of "Trek forward".

When they reached home, they turned out Punch and Bramble into the field between their garden and the sea.

"I can watch them from my bedroom window," thought Jinny, as the ponies rolled luxuriantly, and her family made

50

aren't-they-hairy type remarks. But it wasn't only two shaggy Highlands that Jinny saw. Almost as clearly as if she had been there, Jinny could see Shantih, her chestnut coat dazzling in the setting sun, her lifted head and her dark liquid eyes drinking in the magic and wonder that humans could only dream about.

"But of course!" Jinny exclaimed aloud.

"What?" demanded Ken.

"Oh, nothing," said Jinny hurriedly, for no one must know, not even Ken, in case they tried to stop her. The idea was so obvious that Jinny couldn't understand why she hadn't thought of it before. She would ride Bramble over the moors to find the Shetlands, and when she found them, Shantih would think it was only another horse. She wouldn't be afraid. She wouldn't run away. "I'll go tonight," Jinny promised herself, and shivered, goose-over-her-grave, with excitement.

Jinny sat on her bedroom floor between the mural of the red horse and her own picture of Shantih. She was drawing Highland ponies, trying to capture the expression on Bramble's face when he had bucked her off; trying to draw the way they stood, resting a hind hoof, muzzles almost touching the ground as if they had been there without moving for centuries. She was drawing because it was the best way to fill in the waiting until her family were all in bed.

Her mother knocked on the door, telling Jinny to stop reading, put her light out and go to sleep. Jinny switched her light off and sat in the patch of white, moon-cold beams that streamed through the window. Cisterns gurgled and chugged, bedroom doors banged shut. Jinny listened to the silence – her ears creeping. She stared through the windows at the hills that shouldered dark against the moon-bright sky. Tiptoeing to the other window, she could see the huge globe of the moon – so low and heavy that Jinny could have touched it if she had wanted. The sea between the jet-black cliffs was luminous, quicksilver, and the two ponies were dark, rounded shapes against silvered grass.

Jinny swallowed dryly. She was afraid, afraid to go out alone into this bleak, two-dimensional world. There might

51

be anything out on the mountains on a night like this. Perhaps she should go tomorrow . . .

"Jinny Manders, you are a coward," she said under her breath, and stood on her head the way Ken had taught her to do. He said it calmed your nerves. Then she put on her anorak and made her way through the sleeping house, out into the moonlit garden.

She found Bramble's bridle in the outhouse that was to be the ponies' stable, and, wading through deep pools of shadow, she went down to the field. Bramble allowed himself to be caught without any trouble. Jinny squeezed him through the gate, only just managing to shut it before Punch got through as well. She sprang up on to Bramble and urged him forward.

The black pony, sensing Jinny's determination, walked out steadily, while Punch screamed his desertion, trotting madly up and down the hedge, lungeing against the gate. Jinny watched the house, dreading to see a light come on in one of the bedrooms. But the black gap windows remained dark, and Jinny rode on up the hillside.

She was fairly certain where the Shetlands and Shantih would be. She knew that in the evening they usually made their way to a ring of standing stones, and Jinny thought that they must spend the night there. She knew the way — first, a fairly clear track through the bracken, which took you to a burn; you followed the burn up over the hillside, and from there you could see the jagged shards of rock silhouetted against the skyline. That was where she would find Shantih.

Sure-footed and willing, Bramble picked his way over the rough ground. "I expect you're glad to get out on your own instead of being stuck in a line with all those others," Jinny chatted. The pony flickered his muffed ears to the sound of her voice.

It was bitterly cold. So cold that Jinny's feet in their sandshoes changed from cold to pain and then into nothing. Her legs stopped above her ankles. She buried her hands in Bramble's mane for warmth, and was glad she was riding bareback, feeling the living, comforting bulk of the pony as part of herself.

A bird screeched, ripping the silence, making the skin

52

tighten on Jinny's neck. The mountains seemed to shrug in closer as she rode, and the moon was a single eye staring straight down on her. "Shantih, Shantih, Shantih," Jinny whispered under her breath, using the name as a charm to control her imagination and stop it stampeding into werewolves and unstoned dead who wandered by night. Bramble's hooves clattered on loose stones, and crushed through bracken and heather as he walked steadily on.

When they left the stream to go up the hillside towards the standing stones, Bramble's pace quickened, his neck arched and he whickered softly. Jinny had to hold him back from breaking into a trot.

"Steady," she whispered. "Easy now. It's too rough to trot." But she felt her stomach turn over with the same excitement. She was right. The herd must be at the standing stones. Jinny crouched close to Bramble. She pressed her cheek against his neck, riding with her arms low.

They heard the Arab's challenging whinny, and then saw her – black against the skyline. She came towards them at a racking trot, circled them suspiciously, her tail high over her quarters, the moon shadows accentuating the dark pits of her eyes and nostrils and carven head. Bramble stood stock still, squealing when Shantih came too close. Jinny lay on Bramble's neck without a movement, only following Shantih with her eyes. The Arab came closer. She stretched out her neck, blowing over the strange pony. Jinny felt the warm breath on her hand. Bramble squealed, but didn't move. They stood poised, nostril to nostril, the thick-set, stolid black Highland and the Arab, all fleet and fire, flame frozen under the moon.

Jinny stretched out her arm and ran her hand down Shantih's sleek neck.

There was a moment when Jinny thought the Arab was going to stay; a moment when she was gentle under Jinny's caress. But it was only a moment, over before Jinny could allow herself to believe that it was happening. Then, with a wild whirl of mane and tail, a bunching, clattering panic, Shantih had charged through the watching Shetlands and they had all vanished into the night. Bramble plunged to

53

follow them, but Jinny managed to control him and turn him back to Finmory.

Ken and Kelly were at the field gate when Jinny got back.

"I reckoned that was where you'd be," said Ken, when Jinny told him. "I came out to shut this idiot up. Thought he'd wake your whole family and then there would have been trouble."

Ken held open the field gate, and Jinny rode Bramble through and returned him to Punch.

"How did it go?" asked Ken.

Jinny hung herself over the gate, waiting for her feet and legs to return to life.

"Did you get near her?"

"Yes," Jinny said. "Yes. I touched her. She let me touch her."

CHAPTER SIX

Jinny rang the schoolhouse bell and waited. She hadn't wanted to come, but her father had insisted that she and Mike should ride to Glenbost, introduce themselves to Mr. Gorman, the schoolmaster, and make sure that there was a field and shelter for the ponies while they were at school.

"Seeing it's the last day of the holidays only makes it all the more necessary," Mr. Manders had insisted impatiently, his mind on driving Petra to her school hostel that afternoon. "What are you going to do tomorrow if there isn't a field? Hold their reins through the classroom window?"

"There's nothing but fields," said Jinny, stating the obvious.

"You need a field with a fence round it," said Mr. Manders. "I agree with you there is nothing but grass, but wild grass is quite different to a tame field."

"Perhaps Mr. Gorman would like to see you before the term starts," suggested Mrs. Manders. "I know they did at Stopton."

"This is not Stopton," snapped Jinny. She had been

planning to have a last ride over the moors in the hope of seeing Shantih again, before the prison gates of education closed her in, leaving her only weekends of freedom. "I feel it in my bones that Jinny Manders and Glenbost School are not going to compatabalize."

"Wherever did you get that word from?" asked her father in disgust.

"Made it up," said Jinny, "or my bones did. They feel incompatabilization towards that school."

Before she rang the schoolhouse bell, Jinny had peered through the high classroom window. About eight, old fashioned, double desks were arranged in rows. In one corner of the room was a low table and four small chairs. There were two blackboards. On one were arithmetic problems about taps filling baths, trains arriving at stations and shopping bills. The other was covered with cramped handwriting that Jinny couldn't read, and the instruction to parse and analyse. The only touch of colour in the whole room was an ABC pinned on the wall beside the low table.

"Bones," thought Jinny, "as usual you were right." And she walked like a prisoner to the scaffold and rang the schoolhouse bell.

"Ring it again," shouted Mike, when no one came. Jinny gave the bell another ring and told Mike to stop letting the ponies eat the hedge.

She stood fidgeting on the doorstep. "Our last day," she thought, "and we're stuck here. Oh, come on, come on." And being pretty sure that there was no one in the schoolhouse, Jinny kept her finger hard down on the bell button.

A man's footsteps came clattering downstairs. Jinny hardly had time to take her finger off the bell before the door was thrown open. The tall man whom Jinny had glimpsed from their car on their first day at Finmory stood there. Mr. Gorman, Jinny presumed. He had obviously been asleep. The ruff of grey hair that fringed his bald, domed head was flattened on one side of his head and fluffy on the other, the neck of his shirt was open and his eyes had the shocked state of someone who has been woken up suddenly.

"Good afternoon," said Jinny, hoping that Mr. Gorman

55

would hear it as polite, which it was meant to be, and not cheeky, which she was afraid it sounded.

"Did you ring that bell, girl?" demanded Mr. Gorman.

"Yes," said Jinny. "I think my father arranged . . ."

"Never dare to come to this door again and ring my bell in that manner."

As Mr. Gorman shouted, his face became bright red. Jinny stared, fascinated, as the scarlet flush spread over his bald head and down below the neck of his shirt.

"Do I make myself clear?" Mr. Gorman's nose curved over his wet baby lips, his bullet eyes orbited their sockets like mad molecules. "Do I make myself quite clear?"

Jinny gulped.

"What do you want?"

"I want Shantih," thought Jinny. "I want nothing else in my whole life except to ride Shantih and paint pictures. That's what I want."

She stared up at Mr. Gorman, who was beginning to fade into a pink glow, and couldn't think what she was doing there.

"Don't stare at me with that insolent look on your face."

"The ponies," gasped Jinny. "Is there a field for them while we're at school?"

"So that's who you are. From Finmory, eh? Well, we've had the likes of you before. We've seen your type come and we've seen you go. But listen to this, my girl, while you're here you come to school every day. Do you understand?"

"Of course. We always do."

"Don't you dare answer me back," shouted Mr. Gorman, going scarlet again. "Now get off my doorstep and out of my garden. Pupils use the other gate."

"Sorry," said Jinny, and retreated to Mike.

"But didn't you ask about the field?" said Mike.

"Couldn't. He's mad."

They went into the shop and asked Mrs. Simpson. She came to the door and pointed out the field.

"Now, it'll be that wee field there, where you'll leave the beasties. The lot from Finmory used to leave their ponies there, that's when they bothered themselves to attend at all. A crowd of hippies if you ask me. With the long hair and the beads and the beards. Chanting to some heathen idol. We were fair relieved to see the last of them."

Mike and Jinny checked the field fences and made sure there was water and shelter, then rode home.

"Long hair and beads and beards," imitated Mike. "What terrible people. We'll need to cover Dad and Ken up before we allow them out."

"We'll send Petra for all the shopping," giggled Jinny, but the thought of shopping had reminded her of the problems on the blackboard. Perhaps they hadn't been left over from last term. Perhaps they would be waiting for her tomorrow morning.

"It's taken us nearly an hour," said Mike. "We'd better leave before eight tomorrow morning, just to be sure we're not late on our first day."

Reluctantly, Jinny agreed. To hear Mike say before eight tomorrow filled her with the cold, hollowness of knowing that it was really going to happen.

But it was after half-past eight when they left Finmory the next morning. Mrs. Manders had felt that plaits would be more suitable for school. As usual, Jinny had disagreed, and it had taken them nearly a quarter of an hour to arrive at their usual compromise of tying Jinny's hair back. The ponies had been difficult to catch, and at the last minute Mrs. Manders had come running after them, waving Jinny's navy school skirt.

"I can't ride in a skirt."

"Take it with you. There's bound to be somewhere you can change. The teacher didn't sound to me as if he would welcome you in jeans."

"Well, give it to me," said Jinny crossly, and she stuffed the skirt into her schoolbag. "Now come on, or we're going to be late for lunch."

"It's all your fault," snapped Mike – so that Jinny knew he was feeling as uptight as she was. "I wouldn't have been late by myself."

"We'll gallop," commanded Jinny. "Kick them. Kick them hard."

But a trot was the most they managed. Speed in the morning was not acceptable to the trekking ponies' union.

"Aye, you two are for it," said Mr. Simpson, standing in his shop doorway. "Here, I'll see to them for you."

Gratefully, Jinny and Mike dismounted and gave their reins to Mr. Simpson.

"Are we very late?" asked Jinny.

"Half an hour. It'll be the belt for you both."

"What did he mean – the belt?" Mike asked, as they ran across the road to the school.

"Probably hang us from the ceiling with a belt," said Jinny. "He's crazy enough for anything."

They stopped in front of the school door to catch their breath.

"Look at our hands," said Mike.

Jinny looked. Her hands weren't just dirty, they were caked with mud and grease from Bramble. She gave them a useless rub on the seat of her jeans. "It's too late to do anything about them now," she said. "Come on. This is it." And she lifted the latch and pushed the door open.

Mr. Gorman was sitting at a high desk. The children, seated in rows, glanced up quickly then back down again. One of the smaller boys sitting at the low table was crying into his plasticine.

"Come in. Come right in. We're very pleased to have visitors. Aren't we?"

The class looked up again.

"Well, aren't we? Answer."

"Yes, sir," they answered with one voice, and having been given permission to play a part, they put down their pencils and stared at the strangers.

"We're sorry we're late," began Jinny, and to her dismay her voice came out high and shaky, "but . . ."

Mr. Gorman banged his clenched fist on the desk. He stood up, his black gown vulture-winged about him and the scarlet spread over his face.

"We don't have 'buts' in this school. We come to school on time."

"The ponies," squeaked Jinny.

"Ah yes, proper little Harvey Smiths, aren't you. Taxi's not good enough for you? I dare say your father will be one of these do-gooders, looking after the world that's done

58

very well without him for the past million or so years. Is that right? Is that right?"

"Yes," said Jinny, "it is. That's why we're here. Dad didn't want to live in the city any longer. He says cities are destroying us, that we've got to find a simpler way to live. Move to the country and grow our own food . . ."

Mr. Gorman's thunderous silence made Jinny's voice fade away. Perhaps he didn't want an answer to his question.

"Is that so now? An environmentalist? Isn't that the word you'd use? Well, I'll tell you the word I use. The word all decent, hard-working people use."

Jinny stood mesmerised, staring up at Mr. Gorman, who seemed to have swollen into a scarlet-faced monster, beak-nosed, ready to swoop down on her.

"Layabouts, that's the word we use. Isn't it?" he demanded from his captive class.

"Yes, sir," their voices responded.

Jinny wanted to shout back at him, to shout the words she would use to describe *him*, but to her disgust she felt tears brimming in her eyes. She bit hard into her bottom lip to stop it trembling.

"Our father was a probation officer," said Mike clearly. "And if you think probation officers are layabouts, I don't think you know much about them."

For a second, Jinny thought Mr. Gorman was going to explode.

"Sit down," he roared. "Sit down."

Blindly, Jinny turned towards the rows of desks.

"There at the back, girl. Next to Dolina. And you, boy, there."

Jinny found herself sharing a double desk with a large, black-haired girl. Mr. Gorman threw an exercise book, a reading book, a spelling book and a pencil on to the desk and told Jinny to get on with the work on the blackboard. Surreptitiously, Jinny wiped her eyes and started on the only problem she knew how to do. When she had copied it out, she sat hunched over her desk, staring in silence at the pencilled numbers.

At lunchtime, Dolina showed her where they sat on the cloakroom pipes to eat their sandwiches.

"Do you think you'll be liking it here?" Dolina asked.

"No," said Jinny.

"Well, my mother says that it's a good grounding we get with Mr. Gorman. None of that nonsense but we can all read and write."

"I can read and write," said Jinny, "and we did lots of other things Music and Movement, and making things, and painting and poetry and plays."

Dolina turned pale cod eyes on Jinny's enthusiasm. "Och, we wouldn't be wasting our time with such rubbish."

"It wasn't rubbish. We did great things. We made a monster once, nearly as high as the ceiling, out of wire and papier maché. I painted the head and we gave her bicycle lamps for eyes, and we all went back one night to see her lit up in the dark."

Dolina stared into the middle distance.

"Why does your father make you ride those cart-horses?"

"Make us ride them?" Jinny echoed incredulously. "Having a pony to ride is one of the best things about Finmory."

"But you'll not have hot water?" Dolina demanded. "My mother says she wouldn't be living there, not for the pension."

In the afternoon, they sat with their reading books open on their desks, and one by one Mr. Gorman called them out to the front of the class to read.

"Where are you up to?" Jinny whispered to Dolina.

"Page 23," Dolina whispered back. "But you'll have to start at the beginning."

"Come out the child who spoke," roared Mr. Gorman.

Jinny started guiltily.

"Was it you, Jennifer Manders? Stand up. I'm talking to you. Did you speak?"

"Dolina was telling me," stuttered Jinny.

"So it was you, Dolina Thompson. The first day back and you can't keep your mouth shut. Well, it will be no change. Come out here."

Jinny's mouth opened and shut but she made no sound.

She wanted to say that she'd spoken first, that she'd only been asking Dolina about the reading.

"I was only . . ." Dolina began.

Mr. Gorman gripped her by the shoulder and dragged her close to his desk.

"Did you or did you not speak?"

"Yes," said Dolina.

"Then let's get it over with."

"It was me," Jinny tried again, but no one seemed to hear her protesting squeak.

Mr. Gorman took something out of his desk. He stood up in front of Dolina. "Hold out your hand," he said.

Dolina stood, stupidly holding out her hand, palm upwards. There was no sound in the room. All the children stared at Mr. Gorman and the fat lump of Dolina, standing there holding out her hand. Jinny watched as if it were television. She knew she was frightened, but she didn't know why. She tried again to tell Mr. Gorman that she had spoken first, but her throat was nightmare tight and she couldn't say anything.

The thing Mr. Gorman had taken from his desk unrolled into a strip of leather, two-tongued. He raised his arm, let the leather strap hang down his back and with his other hand he straightened out Dolina's fingers.

Suddenly the bubble burst and Jinny knew what was going to happen. This was the belt that Mr. Simpson had been talking about. Mr. Gorman was going to hit Dolina and she had to stand there and let him; and really it should have been herself, Jinny Manders, standing there. She stared in horror. In her whole life, Jinny had never seen a child punished like this.

"And it's all my fault," Jinny thought. "I spoke first. But I didn't know. Miss Dickson didn't mind us talking." Jinny saw for an instant the bright Stopton classroom — flowers and paintings, the Book Corner, the Music Corner and the Discovery Corner, the tea chest overflowing with old cloths for Drama, and the smell of the white mice.

The belt cut through the air and cracked into Dolina's hand. Jinny was sick before she could get out of the room.

"I'm never going back there," Jinny told Mike as they rode home. "Never."

Punch could only be persuaded to trek forward with his nose almost touching Bramble's rump. It made conversation difficult, but meant that Mike couldn't see that she was crying.

"You heard what they called me. 'Clipe'. It means telltale. But I didn't mean to. I tried to tell him it was my fault."

"Ian MacKenzie says he belts all the time. He says it doesn't hurt. They're all used to it. Dolina is always being belted for talking."

"I'm never going back."

"You've got to."

"I'd die if he tried to hit me. I'd fight him."

"You must go to school."

"Daddy won't let us go there when he knows what it's like."

"If you make enough fuss," warned Mike, "you'll have us back in Stopton."

"I don't care," said Jinny. "I'm not going near that man ever again."

"If you get back home tonight and start on, the way you can, you'll have us all back in Stopton. And I don't want that. I love it here."

"I don't care."

"But you care about Shantih. You can't expect another circus van to bring her down to Stopton and crash outside the front door."

Jinny didn't reply. She swallowed hard, scrubbed at her eyes with her knuckles and straightened her shoulders. If Mr. Gorman belted her every day, if she had to spend the next two years doing nothing but problems and parsing, she could never leave Finmory, not while Shantih was there.

"Come on, let's canter," Jinny shouted, and she startled Bramble into a sudden gallop.

CHAPTER SEVEN

By the end of October, Jinny's schooldays had settled into a pattern of numb endurance. None of the other children spoke to her. If she tried to speak to them, they shouted, "Tell tale tit, your tongue shall split, and all the little doggies shall have a little bit." So Jinny stopped trying to explain, and spent her lunchtimes with Bramble and Punch. She shared their lean-to shed if it was raining, and if it was dry she took Bramble for a ride, escaping for half an hour into a pretend world of being a hunted outlaw with a price on her head.

With a bit of help in the evenings from her mother, Jinny learnt how to do the arithmetic problems and the knack of parsing and analysis, which made up the day in Glenbost School. If Mr. Gorman was feeling pleased with himself, he allowed the children who had finished the set work on the blackboards to look at a volume of Chamber's Encyclopaedia. If he was in a bad mood, the class had to sit upright, still and silent, with their reading books open in front of them. Mike had been belted twice. Jinny had shut her eyes so that she wouldn't see it happening. But she had heard it.

"It didn't hurt," said Mike afterwards.

"I would die," said Jinny. "It's not whether it hurts or not. It's letting him hit me. I couldn't."

Jinny missed Petra.

"But you were always fighting," said Mrs. Manders.

"That's what I miss," moaned Jinny. "She made me surer of me. When I saw her fidgeting about with her cold cream and her rollers, and practising the same bit over and over again on the piano, that let me know I'd never be that sort of person."

"I miss her too," agreed Mrs. Manders. "At least she likes her school. I worry about you."

"I worry about Shantih," countered Jinny.

"Are you sure that you wouldn't like us to have a word with Mr. Gorman?"

"That would be THE END," refused Jinny.

On the Friday evening before the Monday half term, Mr. MacKenzie was waiting for them when they rode past his farm.

"Now you'll be having a holiday on Monday," he called to them.

"Half term," answered Mike.

"Three whole days before I have to go back," said Jinny, grinning at the thought. She was going to spend all her time with the ponies. The Shetlands had come to accept Bramble, and hardly bothered to stop grazing when Jinny rode up to them. Only Shantih still moved away, to stand alert and watching – nervous at being separated from the herd, yet too cautious to allow herself to be approached by a human. She would stand whickering to the Shetlands, urging them to follow her out of danger. Jinny hadn't managed to touch her again. If she did ride Bramble closer, Shantih would wheel away and gallop in a wide circle before she stopped at a safe distance – to stand sentinel, ready to be off again should Bramble take another step towards her.

"So you'll be free on Monday?" Mr. MacKenzie inquired.

"Free?" said Mike. "Well, I'm going into Inverburgh with Alec Clark."

"Why?" Jinny asked Mr. MacKenzie.

"I was thinking I might be bringing down the ponies into the wee paddock. I'll be taking a foal or two up to the sale on Wednesday, and I was thinking you might help me with the round-up."

"And Shantih?" cried Jinny.

"Och now, it wouldn't surprise me if she came down too."

"I can't," said Mike.

"I'll ask Ken," said Jinny. "He'll come."

On Monday morning, Jinny and Ken rode over to the farm. The air was sharp with early frost, the mountains charcoal shadows, and the smoke from Finmory rested on the chimney in a vertical plume, like the smoke in a child's drawing.

Jinny sang as she rode. In an hour or two, Shantih

64

would be in Mr. MacKenzie's paddock. Surely she would stop being so afraid, would let Jinny feed her and groom her. Surely she would realise that she wasn't going to be taken back to the circus. "Maybe," Jinny thought, "when the Shetlands go back to the moors, Shantih will stay with me."

"Don't," said Ken. "Stop it."

"Stop what?" said Jinny, turning to scowl at Ken, warning him not to spoil her morning.

"Embroidering your dreams," said Ken. "You'll only be hurt."

Jinny didn't reply. She felt Shantih's warm breath on the palm of her hand as they stood together, watching the Shetlands return to the moor.

In the farmyard, Mr. MacKenzie and Ewan, one of his married sons, were waiting, mounted on two heavy dun Highlands.

"Aye, it's yourselves," greeted Mr. MacKenzie. "Come away now, and we'll have them down in no time. Ewan saw them over by the back of Finmory Beag. We'll circle round and they'll not be knowing what's happening to them till we have them tucked into the paddock."

Mr. MacKenzie led the way out of the yard, shouting to his wife to be ready to shut the yard gate once the ponies were inside. Jinny rode with Ewan, making him laugh as she told him about her attempts to reach Shantih. Ken rode behind the others. He was only there because Jinny had persuaded him to come. He didn't like chasing animals around. He hated to see them panicking from human beings. Ken thought it was one of the basic things that made everything go wrong.

Sheep, grazing stiffly after the night's cold, moved slowly away from them; disturbed crows shuffled their wings and creaked into flight as the riders approached.

They had ridden for about an hour when Mr. Mac-Kenzie reined in his pony, and said that, if Ewan was right, the Shetlands should be over the brow of the next hill.

"We'll come around behind them and just keep them going, easy like. No rushing them. Keep them walking. Once we have them moving in front of us, they'll be no bother. The old yins know there's a touch of oats for them when they come down to the farm."

"What about Shantih?" demanded Jinny. "She'll not know."

"Now don't you be upsetting them all for that warrior. Let her come or not as she likes."

"That's what I'm here for," said Jinny.

"Don't fret yourself," said Ewan. "She'll not be leaving her mates."

They rode over the brow of the hill – and below them was the herd.

"Spread out in a line," said Mr. MacKenzie, as Shantih neighed a warning and the ponies clustered and turned to stare suspiciously at the riders.

"Easy now, easy," warned Mr. MacKenzie, and they walked their mounts slowly down the hill.

Shantih waited, poised for flight, neighing her fear to the Shetlands. But the older mares were used to being rounded up, and continued to graze, only walking slowly forward as the riders approached.

They rode towards the farm, the Shetlands trickling in front of them, while Shantih tore this way and that. Her neck was stretched like a stallion's as she tried to turn the herd; then with a screaming whinny, she would thunder out of sight – only to swing round and come cantering past the Shetlands, nipping and pushing, trying to make them gallop away with her.

"She's like me," Ken thought. "Desperate to be free, yet afraid to leave her friends."

Jinny's face was drawn inwards, her eyes strained as she watched Shantih's wild display.

As they came closer to the farm, Shantih left the herd and galloped away over the hills. Jinny rode looking back over the moor, searching the barren ground for the red gold of the Arab. "Come back. Oh, come back," she willed.

They reached the broad, rutted track that led to the farm. On one side was a stone wall, while the other was open to the moor.

"Watch them here. Don't let them turn. Keep them moving," shouted Mr. MacKenzie.

Ewan rode closer, and the mares broke into a ragged, shuffling trot. Foals shrilled and their mothers answered. The unshod hoofs tapped the earth. Jinny could see Mrs. MacKenzie holding open the yard gate, ready to close it when the ponies were through – but there was still no sign of Shantih.

"Keep them going on. Keep them moving," instructed Mr. MacKenzie.

All the Shetlands were trotting now. The slope down to the farm and the strange horses pressing close behind them fired them with urgency. Jinny rode at the side of the herd, chivvying them on. A mare swerved out from the shaggy mass and Jinny rode at her, swinging her arms, and turned her back.

"Well done!"

Suddenly Shantih came, cantering furiously down from the moor. She circled the herd and was trotting at their head.

Mr. Mackenzie swore. "Watch the horse, she's going to turn them."

As Mr. MacKenzie shouted, Jinny, too, saw what Shantih was trying to do. She urged Bramble forward past the musty sweat of the Shetlands until she was riding close beside Shantih. The Arab snaked her head at Bramble, lips peeled from her teeth, eyes rolling, then she turned and lashed out with both hind hoofs, missing Bramble's shoulder by a hair's breadth.

Jinny stood up in her saddle, shouting at the pitch of her voice, waving her arms – driving Bramble close in to the Arab, forcing her to keep going forward, preventing her from turning and leading the Shetlands back to the moor.

At the yard gate, Shantih saw Mrs. MacKenzie. She stopped dead, tried to rear her way back to freedom, but the press of Shetlands carried her through the gateway and into the yard. The gate clanged shut on the last of the Shetlands. They were all safely inside.

Jinny flopped over Bramble's neck.

"You haven't the red hair for nothing," laughed Mr. MacKenzie.

Ken turned Punch and rode away, sick with himself for

67

having been part of it. It had been the way he had known it would be – humans hunting terrified animals. He jumped off Punch and, walking at his head, took an apple out of his pocket and shared it with the pony.

Jinny didn't even notice that Ken had gone. She waited impatiently until all the ponies had been driven out of the yard into the paddock. The Shetlands who had been down before went straight to the feeding troughs, while Shantih careered round the paddock.

"She won't jump out, will she?" asked Jinny.

"Not over that fence," said Ewan. "No horse will jump wire as high as that."

Jinny came back to the farm after lunch. All the other ponies had settled down, but Shantih was still raking around. Jinny climbed between the strands of wire and, speaking softly, held out the carrots she had brought for Shantih. The Shetlands clustered round her, nipping and kicking, Jinny pushed through them, chasing them away.

"Shantih," she murmured. "Shantih. Gently now. Gently. I only want to speak to you. There now. There now. Easy now. No one's going to hurt you."

But the Arab hardly seemed to notice that Jinny was there. She was wild and terrified, a caged creature hurtling herself from one end of the paddock to the other. When Jinny did manage to corner her, she stood for a second, trembling, pressing herself against the fence, and then plunged past Jinny and went back to her furious, driven speed.

After about an hour, Mr. MacKenzie came out from the farm and told Jinny to stop upsetting his animals.

"There's no advantage to be chasing her round like that. And it's not myself will be coming to drag you out when one of them gives you the kicking you're asking for."

Reluctantly, Jinny climbed out of the paddock.

"Couldn't you help me catch her? Once I got a halter on her I could groom her."

"Are you completely daft, lass? Give over with your nonsense. You haven't the time or the strength to be tackling that yin. It's a man she'll need after her. Now give over with you. Take a telling and don't be going in there again."

Jinny stood by the paddock gate, watching Shantih's useless raging.

"I'm not going to make you go back to a circus. You belong to me now. You've got to trust me. You don't have to trust everyone, but you've got to trust me. Oh, stop being so wild. I've saved you twice. I won't hurt you now."

But the Arab's eyes were fixed on the mountains and freedom.

Jinny came back for the milk later and tried again. Shantih seemed calmer now, and Jinny tried pretending that she wasn't interested in her. She scratched dense-haired Shetland necks, and fed them bits of carrot that were meant for Shantih, never so much as glancing at the chestnut, but no matter how cunning Jinny was, Shantih was always at the other end of the paddock.

Early the next morning, Jinny went back to the farm. Most of the Shetlands were still lying down, or standing more than half asleep. Only Shantih was still on guard. Jinny tried to feed her over the gate, but whenever the Shetlands smelt food they came pushing and shoving, chasing Shantih away from the gate. Jinny climbed into the paddock and trailed pointlessly up and down after the Arab.

After school it was still the same. Ewan was in the yard with his father, deciding on the foals for tomorrow's sale.

"Would I be putting a rope round her for you?" Ewan offered. "Och, I could have her on the ground in a minute. She's needing learnt a lesson. Take the temper out of her."

"Don't you dare," threatened Jinny.

"And how will I sell her with the two broken legs?" asked Mr. MacKenzie.

"You wouldn't sell her. You can't. She's mine."

"Would that be a fact? Well, steady yourself, for I'll not be selling her until the Spring. That's when the toffs will be paying the fancy price for herself."

Jinny waited until it was too dark to see Shantih any longer, then she rode slowly home. Bramble was annoyed at being kept out so late. When Jinny turned him out after his feed, he didn't wait for a carrot the way he usually did, but went off into the night, shouting for Punch.

A lump choked in Jinny's throat. She went back to the

house, saw the light on in the pottery, and, leaving her school bag at the back door, she went to see who was there.

Ken was sitting at the wheel, doodling with a lump of clay. The grey hearth rug of Kelly opened unsuspected eyelids to examine Jinny through amber eyes.

"Not on?" asked Ken.

Jinny couldn't speak. She sat down on the ledge beside Ken.

"Nobody love you?"

"Well, they don't," said Jinny. "Even Bramble didn't want a carrot. It's all right for you. Look at all this . . ." And Jinny gestured at the shelves already beginning to fill up with pots – some glazed and decorated, some still grey and dead, waiting to be fired. "You've done all this. Put new windows in . . ." Jinny went on pointing, to the large window which now made up one side of the pottery. "And the roof and all the gardening. Daddy's got his book. Petra loves her beastly school . . ."

"Poor Jinny."

"Well, it's true. I can't get near Shantih. She's there in the paddock and I still can't catch her. What am I going to do?"

"People are so impatient. Not only want, but want everything NOW."

Ken treadled the wheel, and the clay slimed into life under his long, bony fingers. In his hip pocket was the cheque from his parents. It had come direct from his father's bank. "This way they know that I'm not starving to death and they don't even have to write to me," Ken had said.

Seeing the cheque, Jinny felt a swell of conscience – for that would be worse, so much worse. But she pushed the thought away from her – she couldn't allow herself to think about it at the moment.

"What am I going to do?" she demanded again. Nothing in the world mattered, except finding a way to tame Shantih. It was worse seeing her so close and still not being able to reach her. "How can I make her trust me?"

"Make?" echoed Ken. "*Make* her trust you? It's the making she doesn't trust, and why should she? You'd need

70

years to recover if someone had treated you the way she's been treated."

"Mr. MacKenzie will turn her loose again tomorrow," said Jinny. "I haven't got years."

Ken treadled the wheel into a blur of speed. Jinny had to wait until he stopped it revolving, sliced off the pot and lifted it delicately on to a bat.

"There was a book," he said. "I remember the photographs. A woman who had trained wild horses in the Argentine. Going up to them with her hands behind her back, breathing love and trust into their nostrils. Tremendous."

"Yes," said Jinny. "That's what I want to know. How to tell her I love her. That she doesn't need to be afraid."

"Get the book if you like. It would give you the patter. But you know it all yourself, if you'd only give yourself the chance. Stop grabbing."

Jinny looked up the number of the County Library and phoned. A girl's voice answered, and Jinny did her best to explain what she wanted.

"I know the one," said the girl. "It's a fairly old one. Might just be in reserve stock. Hold on, and I'll see if I can find it."

Jinny held on, fingers crossed, until the girl came back. "Hullo?"

"Have you got it?"

"You're in luck. I've got a copy and it's the right one. It's got the photographs in it."

"Oh, thank you," cried Jinny.

"Will you come into Inverburgh for it?"

"I must have it tomorrow," said Jinny. "But I can't get to Inverburgh. I'll be at Glenbost."

"The Mobile Library goes through Ardtallon tomorrow," suggested the girl. "I could give it to Thomas and you could collect it there. He'll be at Ardtallon round about two."

"Where's Ardtallon?"

"Oh, only about four miles from Glenbost. The far side from Inverburgh. What's your name?"

Jinny told her, and put the phone down slowly. She had to have the book. If the author had been able to tame wild

71

horses, surely it would tell her how to tame Shantih. If she was going to Ardtallon tomorrow afternoon, she would need to play truant. Jinny stood with her hand still on the smooth comforting shape of the receiver. Her father was going to see the owner of a craft shop, who was interested in buying some of the pottery, so there was no chance of him driving to Ardtallon. She couldn't ask Ken to walk there. She would need to go herself.

Jinny thought about Mr. Gorman's rage. She thought about the belt. But it didn't matter. It was for Shantih. Once she had the book it would tell her what to do.

CHAPTER EIGHT

Straight, solid torrents of rain blotted out the mountains, joining the low clouds to the grey-green land. The village of Glenbost was closed in a paperweight of rain. Through the schoolroom windows, Jinny could see nothing but rain – the first stage of another Flood. She finished the day's problems, ruled a neat line under them, and took her exercise book out to Mr. Gorman's desk. He was doing a crossword puzzle and didn't look up.

She went back to her desk, noticing little things that normally she would have missed – knots in the scrubbed wooden floor that suddenly looked like Shantih, the wooden grain flowing like her mane; a mummified wasp that had lain in a windowsill corner since the summer, and a gust of peat reek from the clothes of a boy who dropped his pencil and bent to pick it up.

Jinny sat down next to Dolina's rejecting back. Just by glancing at Dolina's back, Jinny could tell the mood she was in. She pretended to herself that she didn't care if nobody spoke to her, but really she did. All the time she had to be on her guard against the other children in case she should forget – and try to speak to them, giving them the chance to stare at her, then turn away giggling, leaving Jinny with awkward hands and feet, not knowing what to do with herself while they laughed at her.

The rain drummed on the roof, overflowed from a broken rone, and cascaded over the window. Jinny ruled the cage of lines that would dissect Mr. Gorman's chalky scribble into clauses. In another hour it would be half-past twelve, and they would stop for lunch. That was when Jinny had to escape. She swallowed hard, not allowing herself to pick at the thought. She was going to do it and that was that.

She had seen Mr. MacKenzie loading the ponies for the sale that morning, as they rode past on their way to school.

"You'll have said goodbye to your fancy horse?" he had shouted through the downpour.

"What?" yelled back Jinny, lifting the flap of her sou'-wester.

"I'll be putting them back on the hill when I've got these aboard."

"Oh no!" cried Jinny. "No! You can't. You mustn't! I didn't know. Please don't let them go until I see her tonight. Oh, Mr. MacKenzie, promise. Please."

"They'll have my good ground churned into a midden, penned in on a day like this."

"Well, just Shantih. Keep Shantih?"

"Give over plaguing me with your nonsense."

"Please," demanded Jinny.

"Until this evening, then. And that's final."

"That'll be enough. I'm going to get . . ." Jinny had stopped herself just in time, remembering that if she told nobody, nobody would know. "Thank you, Mr. MacKenzie," she had shouted as she trotted after Mike.

Because it was so wet, there were more children than usual sitting on the cloakroom pipes, eating their sandwiches. They munched silently, staring at Jinny as she buttoned herself into her oilskins, pulled on her wellingtons and collected Bramble's tack from its corner.

"Are you riding in this?" Mike asked.

"I've got a headache," Jinny told him, loudly enough for the others to hear. "I'm going for a ride to see if it will help. If it doesn't, I'm going home."

Mike looked dubiously at his sister, knowing she was lying, and guessing it was something to do with Shantih. "Have you told Mr. Gorman?"

73

But Jinny, clutching saddle and bridle, was sploshing her way down the path.

Both ponies were standing inside their lean-to shed. Jinny squeezed between them and had Bramble's bridle on before he realised what was happening. A few minutes later she was riding him back up the road to Finmory. Eyes watched her from the cloakroom window. Mrs. Simpson called from her shop doorway to ask what was wrong.

"I'm not feeling well," Jinny shouted back. "I'm going home."

Bramble trotted briskly forward, his ears pricked, willing and bright, despite the weather. He thought he was being ridden home to the feed that was always waiting for him when he got back to Finmory.

"There's a good pony," encouraged Jinny, clapping his neck, her hand sinking into the wet sponge of his winter coat. "On you go," and she hurried him out of sight of Glenbost.

Once she was absolutely certain that the last croft was safely hidden behind a hill, Jinny halted Bramble and took out of her pocket the diagram she had copied from her father's Ordnance Survey map. She studied it, then carefully returned the sodden piece of paper to her pocket. She was planning to cut across the moor behind Glenbost. Marked on the Ordnance Survey was a dotted line that ran across the moor and joined the road about a mile from Ardtallon. A dotted line meant a footpath. It had been perfectly clear on the map. Bramble tugged at his bit, turning his head against the rain, fretting irritably at the pointless delay. The moors were desolate under the downpour, the familiar landmarks of the hills were hidden by the mist. In the flat, grey landscape, there was no sign of the confident dotted line that would lead them to Ardtallon.

"We'll need to go across country," Jinny told Bramble. "Cross country," she said again loudly. It made her think of explorers striking out into the unknown, of intrepid horses and riders tackling the house-sized obstacles at Badminton. "And all we've got to do is ride across a bit of moor." She gathered up the slimy reins, kicked her

74

wellington heels hard against Bramble's sides, and tried to turn him off the road.

Bramble remained a solid, immovable bulk. Jinny's heels bounced ineffectively against his wooden sides. She pulled at the reins, trying to upset his foursquare balance. Bramble went into reverse. Jinny kicked and shouted, terrified that a car would come past and find them there, and in some way organize them back to school. Bramble suddenly flung himself sideways. Jinny lost a stirrup and clutched at a handful of mane as the pony bucked, and, head down, charged for home.

For a second, Jinny clung to the pony, kippered over his neck, certain that she was coming off. But the friction of her oilskin trousers against the wet saddle leather gave her a moment of purchase. Somehow, she pushed herself back into the saddle, struggled to recapture her dangling stirrups and hauled in the slippery reins. She had stopped feeling cold or wet; stopped thinking about what would happen if Mr. Gorman found out; she had only one thought in her head – to get Bramble to Ardtallon in time to meet the library van.

Despite Jinny's efforts to slow him down, Bramble charged on.

"Right," Jinny thought. She found her second stirrup, dug her knees against the saddle and swung Bramble round off the road and across the moor. He tried to stop, to fight his way back to the road, but Jinny had caught him by surprise and forced him to keep on galloping. "Go on, go on," she urged. "Get on with you." Ardtallon was somewhere to the left of Glenbost, and that was where they were going. They hadn't time to worry about dotted lines on maps. She forced Bramble on into the grey nothingness.

One minute they were cantering over firm ground. The next, Jinny felt Bramble's quarters sink, and his neck and shoulders rear above her. Too late to do anything to stop herself, she fell backwards. She rolled clear of the pony and scrabbled on to hands and knees, to see Bramble with his forelegs dug into firm ground, struggling to free himself from a bog. Jinny screamed, and stumbled to grab his reins.

She pulled frantically at the pony's bridle, shouting at

him, urging him to free himself. Bramble's eyes stared from his head as he clutched the solid ground with hooked fore-legs, struggling violently. There was a squelching explosion as he burst free. He stood with his head down, fighting for breath, like a point-to-point horse in the winner's enclo-sure.

Jinny waited until he had recovered, then remounted. Covered in mud herself, she hardly noticed the state of the saddle or the pony. She knew that she had been mad to gallop a pony over treacherous moorland on a day like this. Bright behind her eyes was the frozen frame of Bramble fighting to free himself.

"If he hadn't known what to do himself, there was noth-ing you could have done to save him," chided Jinny's con-science. "You would have killed him."

"If you don't get a move on, you'll be too late. The library van won't wait. You won't get your book. Mr. MacKenzie will turn Shantih out on to the moors again. You won't have another chance," warned another voice in Jinny's head.

With a filthy hand, Jinny pushed back dripping rats' tails of hair from her face. She knew which voice she always listened to in the end. She gritted her teeth and forced Bramble to gallop, watching for the fluorescent warning of the green scum that marked the bogs.

It was Bramble who found the path that was the dotted line on the map. Jinny had been completely lost. Even when they reached its safety, Jinny wasn't certain which way led to Ardtallon. She let the reins fall on Bramble's neck. He turned instantly towards Finmory. Jinny swung him round and, ignoring his protests, pushed him into a trot and then a canter. She had no idea what time it was. She only knew that it seemed much longer than an hour since she had left school.

"Please, please let the library van still be there," she prayed, as Bramble's hooves clattered along the road to Ardtallon.

When they reached the first of the Ardtallon crofts, crouched under the rain, Jinny looked around anxiously for any sign of the van, haunted by the dread that she would be too late, that the library driver would have been and gone. Then she saw it, a bulky, dark green van parked in front of the village shop.

As Jinny approached, a woman clutching books under an umbrella came out of the van and a man began to fold up the steps that led up to the door of the vehicle.

"Wait!" Jinny yelled. "Wait for me."

The man and the woman stared as Jinny, oilskins flapping, rode down on them. She floundered off Bramble's back and caught a glimpse of their reflection in the shop window. Jinny was covered in streaks and rivulets of mud, and Bramble was clotted with lumps of black peat and plastered with slime.

"I am glad you're still here," Jinny exclaimed, smiling, expecting the man to smile back at her, but he only stood in the doorway of his library van, staring down at her, waiting. The woman tutted under her umbrella. Jinny tried smiling at her, but Dolina's expressionless cod eyes looked blankly back at her. Jinny's stomach rolled. She must be Dolina's mother.

"You've got a book for me," Jinny said, turning back to the man. "I phoned up the Central Library last night and the girl there said she'd put it on the library van for me today."

"I'll not be knowing you?" said the man, as the woman tutted off into the rain.

Jinny didn't see that it mattered – most of the assistants in the Stopton library hadn't known her.

"You'll not be a member of the library?"

"No, we've just come to live here. I'll join now."

"What's your name and address?" asked the man, taking a form out of a drawer.

"Jinny Manders," Jinny told him, peering into the van at the tempting shelves of brightly-jacketed books. The man was leaning on a counter that separated the cabin of the van from the library shelves. At one end of the counter was a pile of books. The top book had a slip of paper sticking out of it. In scrawled capitals Jinny read, 'MANDERS. PHONE CALL. ARDTALLON STOP'.

"That's it," Jinny cried in delight. "That's it. You've got it. That's my book – the one on top there."

Jinny's grin spread from ear to ear. Even if she got the

77

belt tomorrow it had been worth it. The book would tell her how to breathe trust and gentleness into Shantih; how to let her know that she would never hurt her, never let anyone else terrify her, never ever again.

"Address?" demanded the man, his features solid as a carved figurehead.

"Finmory House," said Jinny.

The man put down his pen, tore the form into two pieces and dropped them into a waste paper basket.

"In that case," he said, "you're taking no books from my van. I might have known from the sight of you. Twenty pounds worth of books the last lot of hippies from Finmory stole from the County Library. Books that they were on at me to get specially for them, and never a one of them returned."

"But they had nothing to do with us!" exclaimed Jinny. "Nothing at all. We never even met them. Finmory was empty when Daddy bought it."

"Not another of my books goes out to anyone coming from Finmory."

"They're not *your* books," retorted Jinny. "They're for everyone to borrow. You MUST give it to me."

"For everyone to borrow that brings them back. And if you were from Buckingham Palace I wouldn't be handing over one of my books to a tink like yourself, standing in the road shouting at me."

Jinny listened in blank astonishment, slowly realising that he really wasn't going to let her have the book. She dropped Bramble's reins, sprang into the van and made a grab at the book. Her hand closed on it a fraction before the man gripped her wrist and forced her to drop it.

"Don't you dare be pushing your way into my van. Get out with you and back to school where you belong."

With his hand on the scruff of Jinny's oilskin, he propelled her back into the road. The van door was banged shut, and in seconds the van was swaying down the road, taking Jinny's book with it.

"You suppurating slug, you ponging pig – you liverwort!" Jinny did a war dance of hate in the deserted road.

As she rode home, following the track over the moors,

78

she could still hardly believe that anyone could have been as mean as the driver of the library van.

Jinny reached home without being seen. She left Bramble in his stable munching down his feed, then, taking off her oilskins, which were pointless now since her clothes seemed to be soaking, she ran back to the farm. She knew Shantih was still there, for she had heard the mare's screeching whinny as they had ridden past.

The Arab was standing alone in the middle of the paddock. Mr. MacKenzie had kept his word.

"Shantih," Jinny called. "Shantih." And the mare came plunging to the gate. The bright gold of her coat was darkened by the rain to a liverish purple, her legs were sleeked into bony skeletons, her mane was laid flat against her neck and the wisp of her forelock was plastered down her face. She pushed at the gate, thrusting her weight against it, clattering it with frantic forehooves, a crazy mare for the storm witch to ride.

Jinny paused, knowing that on a day like this it would be more impossible than usual to get near Shantih. She thought she heard the farm door being opened, and knew that if it was Mr. MacKenzie he would want to turn Shantih back on to the moor.

Trying to remember everything that Ken had told her about the methods the woman had used to tame wild horses, Jinny ran up the side of the paddock and climbed through the fence.

"Shantih," she called again.

The Arab turned towards her but stood still, unwilling to leave the gate.

"Hands behind my back," Jinny told herself. "So she knows I'm not trying to catch her. Breathe slowly and gently, hold my face out towards her."

Jinny moved slowly, placing each foot carefully in the mud. Usually, by this time, Shantih would have galloped off to the other end of the paddock.

Jinny stood still, murmuring soft, comforting reassurance. She took another step forward – and another. Stood still again, blowing through her nose, speaking to the horse with her breath. She had stopped trying to remember the things that Ken had told her from the book. He had been

79

right, she didn't need anyone to tell her what to do; she knew, had always known. Breathing was the way to calm horses. It was the way they spoke to each other. Spoken words were only breath chopped into little pieces, and animals didn't need to do that. They breathed.

Shantih stretched out her neck, reaching her head out towards Jinny. Her rain-carved head was delicate and precise as a wild flower. She took a hesitant step towards Jinny.

Slowly, lovingly, Jinny breathed. She didn't let her excitement come up to the surface of her mind. All her attention had to stay on her breathing, as it created a gossamer thread that drew Shantih towards her.

Hesitant, flinching, her every nerve tensed to spring back, Shantih took another step towards Jinny.

"What's up with you now? Would you look at you, standing there like a dooley in the pouring rain."

The disharmony of Mr. MacKenzie's roar broke the spell of breath. Shantih flipped into the opposite, terrified and wild again, she reared.

"No. Oh no!" shouted Jinny, but she yelled at the farmer for spoiling everything, not at the horse rearing menacingly above her. Shantih's foreleg moved more swiftly than Jinny could see. She only felt the blow on her shoulder that sent her sprawling into the mud, heard Mr. MacKenzie's yells as he came dashing to the gate, pelting Shantih with gravel he had grabbed from the yard.

"Are you still with us?" he demanded.

Jinny slithered to her feet. "Of course," she said crossly.

"The brute could have had you dead." And Mr. MacKenzie fired another round of stones to where Shantih tore up and down at the far fence. "Now get that gate open and let's be seeing the last of her."

"No . . ." said Jinny, but Mr. MacKenzie was already dragging the gate wide.

"Come on then. Let's be shut of you," he shouted at the horse.

Jinny stood watching helplessly as Shantih charged into the yard, spooked and shied at the outbuildings, then saw the open gateway that led on to the moors. She went high stepping through it, electric with fear, then stretched into speed, low to the ground, desperate to find the Shetlands again, to get as far away as possible from everything to do with humans.

"Oh, why did you have to come just then?" cried Jinny. "Why just at that moment?"

"That's a fine way to be thanking me for saving your life," said Mr. MacKenzie.

"But why?" cried Jinny. "Why? Just when she was getting to know me."

CHAPTER NINE

"My mother saw her at the library van yesterday afternoon," Dolina announced the next morning.

Jinny wasn't in the least surprised. She had been expecting it. There had been a lot of trouble at home last night. First of all over the state of Jinny's clothes, and, when they had found out where she had been, about the undesirability of such behaviour.

"But I'd done all my work for the day," Jinny had defended herself. "All I would have been doing would have been sitting up straight with that reading book open in front of me. And I've read it fifty thousand times already."

"When Mr. Gorman asks where you were, you've to tell him the truth," said Jinny's father.

"He might not ask," Jinny had replied hopefully.

Now, sitting next to Dolina's back, Jinny didn't feel so optimistic. She hadn't slept much last night because of the pain in her shoulder where Shantih had kicked her. Her parents hadn't found out about that yet. Jinny had examined her shoulder in her dressing-table mirror. When she prodded it experimentally, the pain had stabbed down her arm, making the bedroom walls swing about her, so that Jinny had decided that it was better to leave it alone. This morning it hurt if she even moved her arm.

"Good morning, boys and girls."

"Good morning, Mr. Gorman," responded the class as their teacher walked in.

The boys saluted and the girls curtsied. Jinny stretched

out her left arm to balance herself and the pain ripped through her, draining the blood from her face and leaving her panting for breath as she sat down again. If her shoulder didn't get any better she would need to tell her mother and risk hospitals and injections.

When Mr. Gorman reached Jinny's name in the register, he stopped and stared at her.

"So you've returned to the fold, Jennifer Manders." The class waited expectantly. "Have you brought a note?"

"No," said Jinny.

"Stand up, girl, when you're speaking to me."

Jinny stood up, keeping her arm close to her side, taking care not to move it.

"And may I enquire why not?" asked Mr. Gorman. "Come out here."

Jinny went out. She was thinking hard about Shantih, about the moment when the Arab had been so close to her – not tricked, but coming towards her of her own free will.

"And where were you yesterday afternoon?"

Jinny thought about Saturday, when she would go up the moors and find Shantih again, when there would be no Mr. MacKenzie to spoil everything.

"I'm waiting."

"I went to Ardtallon to get a book from the library van."

"A book for yourself?"

Jinny nodded. "I had to go."

"Indeed," said Mr. Gorman. "Indeed. You had to go? You had to play truant? You had to tell lies? Because that's what you did, that's exactly what you did."

The scarlet temper flooded over his high-bridged nose, flushed around his peering eyes and bloomed over the bald dome of his head.

Jinny looked straight at him. She knew he was going to belt her, and now that it was actually happening she only wanted to get it over; to be back at her desk away from the staring children.

Mr. Gorman took the strap out of his desk and laid it on the lid in front of him.

"Hold out your hand and let this be a lesson to you. No more jaunting off whenever the notion takes you."

Jinny held out her right hand.

"The other hand, girl," ordered Mr. Gorman. "You'll be telling me next that you can't hold a pencil."

Jinny lifted her left hand about six inches from her side and gasped aloud with pain.

"I can't. I've hurt my shoulder."

"Indeed, indeed," syruped Mr. Gorman. "Now don't tell me any more of your lies. Hold out your hand."

"I can't . . ."

Mr. Gorman made a grab at her hand. Jinny heard the scream that rang around the classroom, but didn't connect it with herself. In the far distance, she heard Mike shouting at Mr. Gorman to leave his sister alone, and then she was falling down and down, the classroom walls flowing outward like a science fiction nightmare.

Jinny came to sitting at a desk, with her head between her knees. She struggled to sit up. "It wasn't because he was going to hit me. It wasn't. I've hurt my shoulder but I'm all right now. I'm quite all right."

When Mr. Manders got Jinny to Inverburgh General Hospital, the doctor there didn't agree. He was very annoyed that Jinny hadn't been brought in the night before.

"The muscle is badly torn, and I dare say the bone is cracked. We'll know after the X-ray."

But the bone wasn't damaged, so they strapped Jinny up with rolls of elastoplast and let her go home.

"It would have to be my left shoulder. If it had been my right arm, I could have stayed off school."

"Why didn't you tell me?" said her mother.

"You were cross enough with me as it was."

"But only because you do such irresponsible things. I'm only cross because I love you."

"I know," said Jinny. "But I can't remember it all the time. When you're cross I just think you're cross. And when Shantih is all wild and mad and won't let me near her, I know it's because of the way she's been treated. She didn't mean to kick me. We have to remember that."

"I'll say this for you," laughed Mrs. Manders. "You are

83

gifted at turning a conversation round to suit your own ends."

"A few more inches and she'd have kicked your face," said Petra, when she came home on Friday night to be impressed by Jinny's strapped shoulder.

"All I've done is twist my shoulder a bit," Jinny said to Ken. "It's stopped hurting. Couldn't have been serious when all they did was put sticking plaster on it."

"You make it sound as if they stuck on a Band Aid," said Ken.

"The fuss everyone's made. Even Mr. Gorman asked if it was O.K. But no one wants to hear about Shantih. No one wants to know about her. And I'm all smashed up about her. As if I'd been put into a blender and turned on at Hi Speed. I don't know what to do next."

November was grey and wet. A wind moaned in from the sea, driving the rain. Day after day, Mike and Jinny fought their way through pouring rain to and from Glenbost.

"My feet are webbing over," complained Mike. "Wish I were old enough to go with Petra. It's O.K. for her. Special minibus on a Monday morning, and brought home to the door on a Friday night."

"I couldn't be away all week," said Jinny. "I couldn't leave Shantih."

"Wouldn't make much difference if you were on the moon."

"Would," said Jinny. "She might need me."

But the words sounded hollow, even in Jinny's ears. The first Saturday after Shantih had been in Mr. MacKenzie's paddock, Jinny had got up at seven and set off up the hills to find the ponies. She didn't ride because she couldn't think what she would do with Bramble while she was breathing to Shantih. It was after dark before Jinny got back home.

"And about time too," said her father. "Another quarter of an hour and Ken and I would have been up those mountains searching for you. How can I be expected to write when I'm wondering where you are all the time?"

"I didn't realise it was so late until it started getting dark. Then I went the wrong way."

84

"You do know, don't you, that Mr. MacKenzie, who was born here, would think twice before he went wandering over those hills alone at night?"

Jinny knew. She had been scared, wandering around, trying to find her way back; had felt panic breathing on the back of her neck, forcing her to run. Jumping down from a rock, she had landed on a soft patch, and for seconds she hadn't been able to wrench her feet free – had felt the sucking mouth of the bog trying to pull her down.

Standing in the safety of Finmory kitchen, Jinny shuddered. One of Mr. MacKenzie's favourite stories was about a Shetland that had been sucked down into a bog and died of starvation. When Mr. MacKenzie found her body, only her head was left above the emerald slime.

"Double pneumonia, that's what you'll have next," predicted Mrs. Manders. "On you go, and have a really hot bath while I'm getting you some supper."

Jinny obeyed her mother gladly, shutting the door on Petra's questions about whether or not she had managed to get near Shantih – for in her whole day's wanderings, Jinny had only glimpsed the Arab once.

After three more weekends – all equally fruitless – Jinny was on the edge of despair.

"But what else can I do?" she asked Ken one evening, when they were sitting together in the pottery – Jinny half-heartedly making a coil pot which she knew she would never finish. Making pots was too slow for her. She liked decorating other people's, but Ken said that was cheating.

"November is the hopeless month," said Ken, who was examining dishes that had come out of the kiln that afternoon. "Everything is hopeless in November."

"You're telling me," said Jinny. "How can you love someone the way I love Shantih and not be able to reach her? She could be in the stable. I've got it all ready for her."

Years ago, when Finmory had been a farm, one of the outbuildings had been a feed house and stables. Now the Manders kept their bins of oats and nuts, and bales of hay, and the ponies' tack in it. Joined on to the feed house were two stalls, in fairly good order, where Punch and Bramble were fed and groomed. Opposite the stalls was a large loose box. It had been filled with rubble and rotting planks of wood. Helped by Mike, Jinny had cleared it out and put down a thick bed of straw.

"Thought that was for Punch and Bramble."

"They don't need to be inside. The Shetlands are O.K. as well. But not an Arab. An Arab can't survive out on the moors all winter. They all hate wind and rain, like this, but it's much worse for Shantih. She hasn't got a thick winter coat to protect her the way the others have."

"Maybe when it's colder she'll come down for hay," suggested Ken.

"She won't," prophesied Jinny. "Not Shantih. She'll die up there on the moors rather than come near humans." And she squashed the beginnings of her pot back into a lump of clay.

"Like the rest of us," agreed Ken. "Wants her own way."

He was moving the pots about on the shelves, trying to find space for the newly-fired ones. He lifted each dish with consideration and care, without any hurry or sense of irritation. It was as if, under his hands, the mugs and coffee pots, bowls and vases agreed to move closer together and accept the newcomers.

The wind flattened the rain against the window, whistled through cracks and crevices, fingered at the roof, searching for weaknesses – driving rain between the old slates and the new ones that Ken and Mr. Manders had added in the summer.

"Perhaps if you'd left her alone," suggested Ken, "she would have settled by now. But you can't leave her alone, can you?"

"No," said Jinny. "I can't."

She threw the lump of clay into a bin and left Ken to himself, surrounded by the curved shapes of the pots, winking and gleaming in the light of the bare electric bulb. They were already sold. At the end of the month they were to be packed up and taken to a craft shop in Inverburgh.

The wind grabbed the door, slamming it shut behind Jinny. She paused for a moment, then launched herself out into the dark. As she struggled back to the house, the wind buffeted her from side to side. She leant against it, felt it packed solid – almost like water into which she could have plunged and flown. The furious crests of the waves flashed whitely on the horizon, and behind Jinny the mountains tightened their roots against the force of the gale.

The kitchen door was bolted. Jinny banged with both fists against it until her mother opened it and she blundered into the warmth and light.

"We had to bolt it to keep it shut," explained Mrs. Manders. "What a night! It's the worst we've had yet."

They went through to the front room.

"We ought to be out with lanterns," said Mike, looking up from his homework. "Luring ships to their doom on the rocks."

"Feel free," said Jinny.

"Ken still out in the pottery?" asked Mr. Manders.

"Think he's just coming in," said Jinny, crouched over the fire which swirled and gusted. The wind howled under the door, lifting the carpet. The heavy curtains swayed and the house was full of creaks and groans. If you listened carefully under all the other noises, you could hear the thunderous, grating boom of the sea crashing up Finmory Bay.

"If it's like this tomorrow, we'll not be able to go to school," said Mike.

Normally such ideas were squashed at once, but tonight neither their father nor mother bothered to disagree.

"Wish he'd come back in," said Mr. Manders, lifting the curtain to stare out into the glistening blackness. "Think I'll go and get him. Not a night for man nor beast."

"But Shantih is out in it," Jinny said, and she was glad that the Arab had the Shetlands for company. Probably they had survived much worse storms than this one.

When Mr. Manders and Ken came back in, they all sat around the fire, roasting potatoes in the ashes. Mike caught Jinny's eye and grinned, drawing her attention to the clock on the mantelpiece. It was almost eleven o'clock. Jinny grinned back, but underneath she felt uneasy. No matter how hard she tried not to, all she was doing was listening to the storm gathering strength outside.

It was after midnight when Mrs. Manders, at last, suggested that they might as well all go to bed and try to sleep.

Jinny lay curled in bed, her ears straining and her neck tense. Usually she loved being in bed, warm and cosy, while the wind raged outside, but tonight the wind was trying to get inside. It struck against the house as if it were a solid force, a sledgehammer of air. Every time it struck the window, Jinny's heart seemed to hesitate, waiting for the glass to splinter and let the monster into her room. The darkness was full of bangs and thuds, as loose objects, or anything which the wind could tear from its foundations, went batting through the night.

"It must stop soon," Jinny thought. "It can't get any worse. It's a hurricane. A typhoon." And she saw Finmory sucked up and spiralled into space. To pick up a house and fling it away would be nothing to a wind like this. It rode in from the ocean, raged up the flat fields in front of Finmory, thudded against the stone walls and broke into waves of fury to swell, moaning and screaming, over the moors.

Jinny heard her father go downstairs again. She got up too, dressed, and followed him down. Soon they were all standing around the Aga, drinking coffee.

"Keep back from the windows," cautioned Mr. Manders.

"Should we go out to see Bramble and Punch?" Jinny asked, hoping that no one would suggest she go alone.

"They'll be fine," said her mother. "Tucked in under the hedge, I expect."

"You couldn't stand in this," said Mr. Manders. "No, I mean it. I can remember . . ."

They never heard what he could remember, for, as he spoke, a terrifying surge of wind burst over the house. Mrs. Manders swore afterwards that she had seen the walls tremble. Pictures fell to the floor, ornaments leapt from shelves, and the light swung in crazy circles. Somewhere outside there was a thunderous explosion.

"The pottery!" yelled Ken. He sprang to the door, wrenched it open and, with Mr. Manders at his side, ran into the night.

"You're not to go with them," Mrs. Manders shouted, but Jinny was already through the door. Ken grabbed her hand, and they raced together through a world without gravity, where solid objects zoomed and soared, where invisible talons ripped the earth.

"But what's happened to it?" shouted Jinny, standing oblivious of the tumult around her, staring at the unbelievable mound of rubble that only a few hours ago had been the pottery.

"But I'd sold the pots," groaned Mr. Manders, "and I've spent the money."

It was as if the destruction of the pottery had satisfied the wind, for only an hour or so afterwards the gale had blown itself out, and the wind that snuffled over the scattered debris was tamed and guilty.

Mike and Jinny were allowed to have the day off school. "Seeing you were up all night," said Mrs. Manders. "Now that doesn't mean that any of us who might be thinking of going up the moors to look for a certain horse will be allowed to do that."

"But . . ."

"No. Tomorrow's Friday. You can wait till Saturday."

Jinny was helping Ken to drag branches out of the drive when she saw the postman's red van.

"Letter for K. Dawson, addressed here."

Jinny ran to take it from him. It wasn't Ken's typewritten envelope containing his monthly cheque, but a cheap brown one, fingermarked, and addressed in smudged biro. Jinny didn't like the look of it. It reminded her that Ken had been on probation. The thought made her glance away from Ken when she gave the letter to him.

Ken put it in his pocket without opening it, but Jinny knew by his silence at lunchtime that he had read it. He ate his fruit and raw vegetables – then sprang abruptly from the table.

"I'm going down the beach by myself," he announced abrasively, and was gone.

"Something wrong?" Mr. Manders asked.

His wife said she didn't know what it could be, and Jinny said nothing.

"Thought we might have had a proper look at the pottery. See what sort of state the kiln is in," grumbled Mr. Manders. "The roof beams must have been riddled with dry rot to come down like that. A ghost of a chance that some of our stuff in the bottom shelves might have survived. But I'd need Ken to help me lift the roof off."

"He might not be long," soothed Mrs. Manders.

"Don't see what he had to go marching off like that for. Not today. You'd think he'd care. Lots of the pots were his. Some nice stuff. Better than some of my pathetics."

Ken didn't come back until after seven. He came into the front room where the Manders were sitting around the fire.

"You look frozen," welcomed Mrs. Manders. "Come and warm yourself."

Ken's lean face was pinched and tense, his nose sharp with the cold, his green eyes, opaque pebbles, looked around scornfully at the firelit room.

"I'm O.K. here," he said, and sat down in an armchair in the far corner of the room. He folded his legs to sit cross-legged, and held up a sliver of sea-bleached wood, concentrating on the grain of the wood, cutting himself off from them.

Jinny, kneeling in front of the fire, tried to go on with the pony book she was reading, but suddenly it didn't seem to matter whether Kirsty won the show-jumping or not. She knew something was wrong with Ken. "It's to do with that letter," she thought, and wished she could say something that would let Ken know that they all wanted him here, that living at Finmory was better because he was with them, that, if they could, they wanted to help him.

"Wouldn't you like some supper?" asked Mrs. Manders, which was her way of saying what Jinny wanted to say.

Ken didn't answer.

"Thought you might have given me a hand to try and lift the pottery roof," said Mr. Manders.

"Oh, don't go on at him," Jinny thought, groping desperately for words to cover over Ken's silence.

"So that's what you thought," said Ken, staring straight at Mr. Manders. "You're pretty good at the thinking. Yes, I'll give you that. You've got it together here, haven't you? All safe and blanket-stitched round the edges. You've forgotten Stopton even exists."

90

"Ken!" protested Mrs. Manders, while Jinny sat frozen, her eyes fixed on the meaningless black print of her book.

"Oh, you're writing about it O.K. And you'll make money out of it because you're pretty quick with your thinking. But what about the ones that are still living in it? What about them? Existing in rotten, stinking derries or back ends. Doesn't matter much, does it? They're not good enough to think, or, if they do start thinking for themselves, the police soon interfere."

"You know I see it that way too," said Mr. Manders. "But I could do nothing, Ken. I had to get out. What I'm trying to say in my book is what you're shouting now. I'm shouting in my book. And if it's published, more people will hear me. Some of them may even open their eyes and see."

"Is that a fact?" said Ken. "Big deal."

Jinny starfished her fingers through the pile of the rug and heard Mike swallow gulpingly.

"If I'd stayed on in Stopton any longer I'd have gone mad or deaf. Started using labels – yobs, vandals, muggers."

"Well, that's how you see us, isn't it?" challenged Ken.

"You think that?" asked Mr. Manders.

"Think?" said Ken. "No, I don't think. I'm one of them. I know."

"Don't," pleaded Jinny. "Don't. You don't mean it."

"And I'll tell you what I know," continued Ken, ignoring Jinny. "You're the same as my parents, and you make me sick."

Ken leapt up and dashed out of the room.

The next afternoon, when Jinny and Mike came out of school, Ken was waiting for them at the gate of the ponies' field. His pack was at his feet and he was holding Kelly by a length of string.

"What's wrong?" cried Jinny, running towards him. "What's the matter?" she asked again, although she had known from the moment she had seen him standing there that he was leaving.

"I'm splitting," said Ken. "Keep an eye on Kelly for a

91

day or two in case he tries to follow me." And he gave Kelly's string to Jinny.

"But why? Why? Have you told Dad?"

"Take joy," said Ken, lifting his open hand to Jinny, and before Mike had reached the gate, Ken was walking down the road without a backward glance.

CHAPTER TEN

Mr. and Mrs. Wright and their two daughters, Susan and Belinda, friends of the Manders from Stopton, came to stay for Christmas.

Petra, who had been very friendly with Susan Wright, was dashing round the house making last-minute adjustments to paper chains and holly before the Wrights arrived, and wishing aloud that Mr. MacKenzie hadn't given them their Christmas tree and then they could have bought a silver one from Boots.

"They don't make all this mess and they look really nice. Nobody has real trees nowadays."

"The Wrights had a real one last year," Jinny reminded her.

"And Susan loathed it."

"She would," thought Jinny. "And Belinda would hate it, too."

Belinda Wright had been in Jinny's class. Like Susan, she was pink marshmallow plump, with flaxen hair and wide blue eyes that leaked glycerine tears when Belinda wanted her own way. At Stopton, Jinny had done her best to avoid her. "And now she's coming all this way to plague me," Jinny thought sourly.

"Aren't you going to change out of those filthy jeans?" Petra asked. "They'll be here any minute."

"They won't," said Jinny. "It'll be hours before they arrive."

"You can't be sure," said Petra. "And what would you feel like if they caught you looking like that?"

Jinny groaned.

"Don't just stand there. Go on and get changed."

Jinny gazed hopelessly at her sister. She couldn't be bothered replying. As if it mattered what she was wearing, when the Wrights had seen her hundreds of times in her usual jeans and sweaters. As if it mattered what the paper chains looked like, or how the parcels were arranged around the tree, or how the Christmas cake was decorated. As if any of it mattered when Shantih was starving.

Jinny slammed the door behind her and went through to the kitchen.

"You're not going out?" said her mother.

"I am," said Jinny, and went.

Kelly, who had been lying by the back door, followed at her heels. Jinny had explained to him that he was to stay with her until Ken came back. Kelly had stared at her unblinking, until Jinny had admitted that Ken hadn't mentioned coming back to her, either.

Jinny went down to the ponies' field. "How about a ride?" she suggested, as Bramble came trotting across to her. She caught him by the forelock, manoeuvred him through the gate and led him up to the stables to put his bridle on.

"Now, quietly," she warned, as she sprang on to his back. "If they hear us, they'll stop us."

Cautiously, Jinny circled the ruin of the pottery and turned Bramble towards the moors. He was fresh, not having been ridden since they had broken up four days ago. Jinny let him canter on. "If they call me back now, I can pretend I don't hear them," she thought.

The hills, scoured by the November gales, were bleak under the lead sky. Bramble's hoofs crunched through coral remains of heather. Bracken crackled as they cantered over it, and when Bramble clipped a hidden rock, it rang with a sharper note than the porous summer stone. Kelly loped at their side, a low slung, grey shape.

Since the beginning of December, the Shetlands had been easier to find. The cold weather was drawing them down closer to the farm.

"They'll need hay soon, won't they?" Jinny had said to Mr. MacKenzie, hoping that this would be a sufficiently roundabout approach. What she really wanted to tell him was that he must feed the ponies, for that was the only way Shantih could be fed. Jinny had tried taking a bucket of nuts and oats up to her on the moors, but it had caused such a stramash of biting and kicking that Jinny wasn't keen to try again.

"They wouldn't be looking to it. I've seen the deep snow and they'd rather go scratching for a bite of grass than touch the hay I'd put out for them."

"But Shantih won't be able to do that."

"Then she'd best be learning," Mr. MacKenzie had said.

Jinny found the Shetlands sheltering, rumps to the wind, in the lee of a hill. They watched Bramble's approach, but didn't move. Only the Arab started away in a few panic-swift strides, then turned to watch.

Jinny halted Bramble. She knew if she went any closer, Shantih would gallop off and the whole herd would be disturbed. Looking at the Shetlands, Jinny couldn't tell what condition they were in. Their dense coats and haystack manes and tails made them appear rounded and fat. But Shantih had no camouflage. Jinny could see only too clearly her bones angling through the harsh, staring coat, her sunken quarters and concave neck; even her face seemed chiselled and hollowed where the skin clung tightly to her bones.

"And if she would only come with me," Jinny grieved, "there's a stable and a bed and food, all waiting for her. If she would only trust me."

"Shantih, come with me," she said aloud. "Come on the horse. Come with me." But the icy wind whipped the words from her lips and dried the tears in her eyes.

Jinny waited with Bramble until he had finished his pony nuts, then she put him back out in the field. She had seen the Wrights' car in the drive, so she knew that they had arrived. As she walked towards the house, Jinny could see into the lighted rooms. Mrs. Wright and her mother were in the kitchen, her father and Mr. Wright were drinking beer, while Petra and Susan sat next to each other on the settee, still being stiff and polite. Belinda, in frilled, pink-checked denim, was sitting in the chair that Ken had occupied the night before he left.

"Oh no, no," thought Jinny, "I can't go in there. I can't bear sitting listening to her." And for a moment she almost turned and fled back over the moors to Shantih. But it was only for a moment. Dragged by hooks, like the men in the Old Testament, Jinny went on up the path and into the house.

After dinner, Petra, Mike, Susan and Belinda played Scrabble. Jinny, relieved that only four could play, said that she didn't want a turn.

"She can't spell anyway, can you?" said Belinda.

"She can now," said Mike. "Mr. Gorman makes you be able to spell."

Surprised, Jinny supposed it was true, but the thought of school only made her feel blacker than ever. She sat leafing though a magazine that the Wrights had brought with them, reading about a children's art competition and half listening in to the adults' chat as they talked about Stopton.

"Saw that boy the other day," said Mr. Wright. He was a social worker and knew many of the people that Mr. Manders had worked with. "The boy you had staying down here with you. What was his name again?"

Jinny froze into attention, her eyes still on the magazine in case any of the adults should notice that she was listening.

"Ken," said Mr. Manders. "Ken Dawson."

"That's the one. He's back with his old crowd. Tried to speak to him, but he just looked straight through me. It's when you find a boy like that – good background, everything going for him – who deliberately chooses that kind of company, you wonder sometimes whether it's worth it."

"He left us on an impulse. Up and off," said Mr. Manders. "No explanation."

"Only a matter of time until he's back in the courts. I don't understand that type of boy. I do not understand him."

"If you don't understand him," Jinny thought, "how can you help him?" She hadn't told anyone about Ken's letter, but it looked as if her guess had been correct. Ken was back in Stopton.

Once, Jinny had seen Ken with some of his friends. She knew the way he could look through you. He had been with three other boys and two girls. Their hair, their

95

clothes, and the way they moved, let you know straight away what they thought of the Saturday afternoon shoppers who prowled the streets, grabbing with greedy eyes through shop windows. In Jinny's world, she could be more or less certain about people using handkerchiefs, not crying or shouting in public, not suddenly kissing or attacking each other, but Ken's friends had looked as if they knew nothing about such limitations. They would do what they wanted to do.

"Yet if I had to choose, I'd rather be with them than here with Susan and Belinda," Jinny thought. But it wasn't true. Not deep down true. For one of the boys had looked at Jinny with empty, glittering eyes. She had felt her flesh creep tighter on her bones and had scurried after her mother and Petra, glad to stay close beside them while they shopped, and afterwards, when she had been out in Stopton by herself, she had glanced quickly over her shoulder just in case the boy should be watching her.

"When there's bad in them, it seems as if it has to come out regardless of anything you do for them." But Jinny had lost interest in Mr. Wright's self-satisfaction.

She went up to her room, threw the magazine on a chair and stared out over the moors, into the cold and dark to where Shantih was, wondering what could have been in the letter to make Ken leave them all. Kelly came padding upstairs, pushed open Jinny's door, and lay down at her feet.

"I'm not like Mr. Wright," Jinny told him. "I understand how there are some things that you have to do, no matter what. But what was it, Kelly? Did he tell you?"

"Are you coming down for a cup of coffee?" called Mrs. Manders.

Jinny came back to herself with a start. "No," she shouted, feeling her body stiff with standing for so long at the window.

"We're having hot mince pies."

"Oh," said Jinny and went downstairs.

Christmas was presents – and Belinda crying because her father had bought her the wrong kind of watch; so much food that they all felt sick and cross; and making sure that Belinda wasn't bored.

"She's your guest," her mother kept telling Jinny.

"And I am trying," Jinny kept telling her mother. "Everything I can think of I've tried. I'm not interested in Stopton and she's not interested in here. So what can I do?"

"You know she's scared of horses. Why you had to sit her on Punch and take her over the hills to stare at that wretched Arab, I can't imagine. No wonder she was sick," said Petra.

"We only walked. I have to go and see Shantih," retorted Jinny. "You keep telling me to look after her, so I took her with me," she added, ducking away from their criticisms.

The thought of Shantih was like toothache – toothache at the North Pole where there were no dentists. Every day, Shantih seemed to be poorer than she had been the day before. Jinny had tried to get food to her again, but the Arab had refused to come near her, and the Shetlands, in a kicking, squealing mob, had knocked the bucket out of Jinny's hand and gobbled down the oats.

"We're all going for a drive, taking a picnic with us," Mrs. Manders announced brightly after breakfast.

"I'm not," said Jinny.

"Nor me," said Mike.

"You are disgusting children," despaired their mother. "Why can't you come with us?"

"There's only three days left before we go back to school," said Mike, "and I promised Alec that I'd go and see him one day in the holidays."

"You know I hate sitting in a car when I don't need to," said Jinny.

When they had gone, Jinny went to see Shantih. She found her easily, but it was too cold to wait for long and Jinny was glad to ride back down, out of the icy, searing wind. Glad in a way to escape from Shantih, for it wasn't her imagination, as Petra insisted – the flesh really was melting away from Shantih's bones. Jinny could make out each separate rib, and the horse's spine was like a knotted rope linking her flat shoulders to her angular quarters. Jinny could do nothing to help her. Her family didn't believe her – they all said that Mr. MacKenzie knew more about looking after horses than Jinny did, and that she was exaggerating when she said Shantih was starving.

Finmory House was hollow with only Jinny in it, full of sudden creaks and groans that you only noticed when you were alone. Jinny made herself a mug of coffee and cut herself a proper piece of Christmas cake – not a little finger slice that you couldn't taste. She carried them up to her bedroom. The Wrights' magazine was still lying on the chair, and Jinny remembered the art competition. She read about it as she ate her cake.

Sixty pounds was the first prize. It might be enough to pay someone who knew how to train horses to come to Finmory and help her to catch Shantih. Jinny munched marzipan and walked down the hillside towards Finmory. Walking beside her was the man who knew all about horses. He was leading Shantih. "Yes, I expect you'll be able to ride her in a week or two," he said.

The competition was for any kind of picture to represent Wildlife Awareness Year; any medium you liked – collage, watercolour, pastel, oils, anything. Jinny's eyes darted over the rules and regulations.

"I'll paint Shantih," she thought. "Sixty pounds."

She filled a jam jar with water, laid out paper and her box of watercolours on the bedroom floor and sat back on her heels, staring at the white, empty sheet, waiting until her picture grew inside her head, behind her eyes, waiting until she saw it in colour. Then she stretched out her hand, feeling almost blindly for the brush, and began to paint.

When the picture was finished Jinny stood up, hardly glancing at it. She went down to the kitchen, cut another large chunk of cake, and took Kelly for a quick run down to the beach. When she got back, she went slowly upstairs to see if she had managed it.

It was good. She had mirrored the magic, enchanted quality of the Arab, the moment before she turned and fled. Her chestnut coat echoed the russet tones of the bracken that reached away to the mountains and the luminous clarity of the autumn sky.

But it wasn't enough, it needed something more.

"The insects! The drawings I did in the summer."

Jinny felt like a blown-up balloon as she scrabbled

through her drawings to find them. She knew exactly how she was going to do it. With a fine, black, felt-tipped pen, she began to copy the insects on to the foreground of her watercolour.

The black line flowed sure and precise, as all the creeping, crawling things that Jinny had drawn in the summer came to life again on her painting. When she had drawn the insects she didn't stop. She went on to draw sheep, rabbits, foxes, crows, gulls and kestrels, seeing them all as clearly as if she were crouching on the moors, watching them. High above Shantih she drew a golden eagle with its wings outspread. Her drawings made a web of textured living with Shantih burning at the centre. It was the best thing she had ever done.

Jinny found cardboard and paper, wrapped her drawing up and bound it in sellotape. Her hands fumbled as she hurried to get it done before her family returned. Her handwriting sprawled over the label. When she had finished she lay flat on the floor, poured out.

The next day, Jinny rode into Glenbost and posted her entry. The day after that, the Wrights went home.

"Two more days and I'll be back in Mr. Gorman's clutches," Jinny thought, as she watched the Wrights settling themselves into their car. "Not tomorrow but the next day I'll be back at school."

"Don't forget to let me know what you decide," Mr. Wright called from the car.

"Will do," answered Mr. Manders.

"What have you to decide?" Jinny asked, when the Wrights had driven away.

"What's the matter?" said Petra. "Are you going to get a divorce?" It made Jinny wonder what it would be like to be part of a family who couldn't make that sort of joke in case it was true.

"Well, it's like this," began Mr. Manders when they were all inside again, "they still haven't filled my post in Stopton. They've had one bloke in it, but he only lasted a couple of months. They've shuffled things around a bit and they've offered me a promotion. Bill Wright was genned up to persuade me."

"Leave here?" gasped Jinny.

"You mean go back to Stopton?" said Mike.

"But we live here now. This is where we live," said Jinny. "Of course we can't go back. Finmory is home."

"Listen for a minute," insisted Mr. Manders. "It's not as simple as that. There's the cash to consider. I had to pay back all the pot money and that's pretty well all I've made since we've been here. The money from Mum's house won't last for ever. And this chance won't come again."

"What about your book?" asked Petra.

"When, and *if*, it is ever published, I might make two or three hundred pounds – which might feed us for a week or two."

"Once it's spring we can all live on vegetables, like Ken. All you need to buy are the seeds."

"It'll help," said Mr. Manders. "But it's the whole thing of staying here or going back to Stopton. It's now or never. We've got to decide."

Jinny tried to think what it would be like to live in a city again, to walk out of the house on to pavements, to have thousands of people pressing down on you, to go to the pictures and museums again – but she couldn't remember it properly. It had been before Shantih.

"Well, I'm not going back to Stopton," she announced. "I'm for never."

"And you don't need to tell us why," said Petra.

"Mike?" asked Mr. Manders.

"Not likely."

They waited for Petra to give her considered opinion.

"I don't want to change schools again," she said. "I'd feel a bit silly going back when I only left a few months ago."

"There you are. I told you so," said Mrs. Manders to her husband. "Nobody wants to leave. So stop going on at yourself. WE ALL LIKE IT HERE. Ken's done marvels with the garden, and you'll soon get the pottery going again."

"Pity Ken got itchy feet. We need him. Still, that's it settled? No one for Stopton?"

"Of course not," said Jinny.

By the afternoon, when Jinny rode over the moors to

pay her usual visit to Shantih, the sky was heavy with black clouds that had come sweeping in from the sea, greedily engulfing the whole sky. Jinny shuddered and hurried Bramble on. She had never felt the moors so menacing before – even when she had ridden over them at night there hadn't been this sense of waiting, this threat of forces about to be unleashed.

She rode for an hour, searching all the places where the ponies were usually to be found, but there was no sign of them. A wind whistled through the dead bracken and honed the edges of rocks. It seemed to Jinny that there was nothing alive in the whole stretching moorland except herself and Bramble. No birds or rabbits, only a solitary gull that sheered inland, white against the black sky, and cried a warning to her.

Suddenly Jinny turned for home. One second she was searching for the ponies, the next she was cantering back to the safety of Finmory. Nothing was so important as to get off the moors before it was too late.

Lying in bed that night, Jinny counted the bad things – Mr. Gorman and going back to school, the fact that her father had thought about returning to Stopton – and although no one had wanted to go, Jinny knew only too well that once a thing had been talked about that made it possible. Ken being back in Stopton, back with that boy who had looked at Jinny as if he could kill her and hardly notice it, and, worst of all, she had run away from Shantih, had fled home when Shantih might have been needing her. Everyone was predicting snow, and Jinny couldn't imagine how Shantih would manage out on the moors if it came. "There's only me to love her, and I didn't go on looking for her," Jinny thought, and turned away from herself into sleep.

Next morning the clouds hung sulphur and purple, the moors, hills and sea, etched in shades of grey, waited, holding their breath.

Despite the weather, Mrs. Manders organized her three children into Inverburgh for hair cutting and school clothes. Although her shoulder was perfectly better and she had taken the strapping off weeks ago, Jinny had to go into the hospital to let them have a look at it. It was after three when they left Inverburgh, and already the street lights were on. When they branched off for Glenbost, they drove into an opaque, grey darkness.

"Nip out for the milk, someone," Mrs. Manders said, stopping the car at the MacKenzie's farm.

Jinny nipped. "Don't wait for me. I'll walk," she said, glad to escape from the prison of the car.

"Well, take the torch," said her mother, handing out the flashlight that was kept in the glove compartment.

Jinny walked across the yard, feeling that there was something different, and realised that it was the sound of sheep. She could smell them, too, cloying and warm.

"Where have the sheep come from?" Jinny asked Mr. MacKenzie, as he ladled milk into her can.

"Brought them down from the hills," he said. "It's the day we've had of it, but that's them all safe. Not often the weather's for giving us a warning like this."

"You really think it is going to snow?"

"Last time it held off for a day or two, like this, the snow was so deep you couldn't see a wall for it, just flat white snow."

"What about the ponies? Did you bring them down, too?"

"Didn't need bringing. They're all down at the wall behind the barn. Know better than we do what the weather's going to be."

Jinny left the full milk can at the farmhouse door. She ran round to the back of the barn, her feet following the beam of torchlight.

"Shantih," she called. "Shantih."

The torch beam shone through the dense gloom, and she saw the Shetlands crowded together by the wall. The light glinted on eyeballs and showed bushy manes and hairy bodies.

"Shantih," Jinny called again, as she swung the torch beam back and forward, searching the darkness for the Arab. But there was only the Shetlands.

She climbed over the wall and stumbled through the mud, her torch beam cutting wildly through the dark. But there was no panic of startled hoofs, no chestnut shape standing apart from the others. Shantih wasn't there.

102

Jinny ran back and banged on the farmhouse door.

"Shantih's not with them," she cried, when Mr. Mac-Kenzie, his boots in his hand, a horny toenail sticking through a hole in his sock, opened the door. "She's not there."

"Now that'll be right," he said. "I didn't see her myself."

"Then we'll need to go and find her."

"You take the milk and be off home with you. If she's fool enough to stay out on those hills tonight it's not myself will be bothering with her."

And Mr. MacKenzie slammed the door shut in Jinny's face.

CHAPTER ELEVEN

Jinny's bedroom door creaked as she turned the handle, shattering the silence of the sleeping house. She froze, cradling the door still, hardly breathing as she waited, dreading to hear the sound of someone getting up to investigate the noise. But there was no movement. No one had heard her.

Jinny eased the door open, inch by inch, and slipped out. Cautiously she crept downstairs, testing each step before she put her weight on it. She stood in the hall, waiting for her heart to stop banging so loudly, before she opened the kitchen door. She saw her oilskins hanging from the hallstand, thought that if it did start to snow while she was on the moors they would keep her dry, and reached up for them. A walking stick clattered to the floor. The crash reverberated through the house.

"Run for it. Get out now or they'll stop you," screamed a voice in Jinny's head, but she couldn't make her legs move. No matter how hard she tried, they wouldn't move.

"What are you doing now?" demanded her father from the top of the stairs. He came down two at a time, pulling on his dressing-gown. "Well?"

"I'm going to find Shantih."

"You most certainly are not."

"But I *must* go. Why isn't she with the Shetlands? She must have hurt herself. I've got to find her before it starts snowing. She'll die if I don't find her."

"Now listen to me, Jinny. You know perfectly well that it is quite out of the question for anyone to think of going out there tonight. You know how dangerous it is."

"But Shantih's . . ."

"If you got caught in a blizzard you wouldn't stand a chance, and you know that as well as I do, don't you?"

"Yes, but if I go now I'll be back before the snow. I must go. Anyway, it may not snow."

"You are to do no such thing. I wouldn't let you go this evening and I certainly won't let you go now."

"I've got to . . ."

"Oh, for goodness' sake have some sense. She's probably with the Shetlands by now."

"Then let's go and see," said Jinny. "Please."

"You are going straight back to bed, but before you go, I want your promise that you won't try to go out again tonight."

"I can't . . ."

"Then I'll wake Petra and put up the camp bed in your room for her."

"You wouldn't!"

"I would. Now no more of this nonsense. Promise."

Jinny stared down at the floor. She had to find Shantih. She had to.

"Then I'll wake Petra."

"Oh, all right then. I promise. But when we find Shantih's skeleton on the moors it will be all your fault." And Jinny pushed past her father and ran back to her room. She buried her face in her pillow and cried herself to sleep.

Jinny woke from suffocating nightmares – sharply awake into a moment of not knowing who or what, where or when, only aware of an atmosphere of terror that was everywhere. Then she remembered – Shantih. Jinny sat up. Her alarm clock said half-past six. It was morning.

"Promise you won't try to go out there again tonight," demanded her father's voice.

"But it's morning now," Jinny thought. "I only promised that I wouldn't go out at night."

She got up and dressed. Hesitated in front of her bedroom door. If they caught her again she wouldn't have another chance. She gritted her teeth, knowing what she had to do. "Just do it. Don't think. Do it."

She walked across her bedroom to the window that looked out on to the hills and opened it. The darkness was a solid wall, the cold swept in at her, but it still wasn't snowing.

"If I don't go, Shantih will die. If I don't go, Shantih will die." Jinny repeated the words under her breath until they made a stronger pattern than her fear. "If I don't go, Shantih will die."

She sat astride the windowsill, reached to her left and felt the rusty drainpipe. Before their mother had caught him, Mike had climbed up and down the drainpipe. Up once to rescue a kitten and down once for a dare. Jinny had watched him with the scared fascination of someone who has no head for heights.

"If I don't go, Shantih will die."

Jinny stretched out with both hands and brought her other leg over the windowsill. She crouched there for a second, then squirmed her weight on to the pipe. For a terrifying moment she felt it move away from the wall, and thought she was going to be too heavy for it. She clung tightly – knees, feet, and hands, her cheek pressed against the stone. "If I don't go, Shantih will die." The icy metal gnawed at her hands, froze her body as she slithered down. Halfway down, the pipe branched out, and she was able to rest her feet before she went on. "If I don't go, Shantih will die." But her arms and legs were limp, and buckled under her weight. She couldn't make them hold on, knew that she must fall, but in the blackness she had no idea how far away the ground was. Her feet slipped away from the pipe. She hung for a moment by her hands, but they wouldn't hold her and she fell.

A rhododendron bush caught her. She struggled out of it, tested her arms and legs to make sure they were still attached to her, then realised that she had made it. "Pretty good, pretty good," she praised herself.

Jinny walked through the dark to the stable and felt along the inside of the door until she found a halter. She stumbled her way to a bin, then filled her anorak pockets with oats. Her foot kicked something that had been standing on the floor. It fell over, and Jinny crouched down to find out what it was. Her fingers closed on the torch. She must have left it there last night after she had fed the ponies. "That's a sign," she thought, switching it on gratefully. "Now I'm bound to find her."

An old pair of Petra's wellingtons were standing in a corner. They were a bit big, but had heavy socks rolled up inside them. "Better than my sandshoes," Jinny decided, and put them on. She found an ancient sweater of oiled wool that belonged to her father and pulled it on over her anorak, tying it round the waist with a handy piece of binder twine. She shone the torch through to the other half of the stable. The thick bed of straw, which Jinny had kept fresh for weeks, waited for Shantih.

"I'll find her, and this time I'll bring her home," Jinny swore as she left the shelter of the stable and set out into the dark.

First she checked the farm, just in case Shantih had joined the others, but there were still only the uneasy flock of sheep and the Shetlands.

"All right for you," Jinny told them. "Why didn't you wait for Shantih? Little hairy pigs to come running down here and leave her up there alone."

Jinny followed the farm track that led out on to the moors. She stomped her feet down into the rutted mud, clapped her hands, pulled the polo neck of the sweater over her head and shouted the Arab's name into the blanket dark. A burn crossed the track and Jinny turned to follow it up over the moors. She knew it would take her close to where they had picnicked the day the circus van crashed. She hoped from that vantage point she would be able to spot Shantih. Jinny felt sure that something must have happened to her, that she needed help.

Jinny tried to keep the stream on her right, but often the marshy ground made her take wide detours. If she tried to hurry, it only made her stumble and fall more than ever. Her feet caught on clumps of reeds and heather roots.

Once she dropped the torch. It went out as it hit the ground and the blackness sighed in. Jinny dropped to her knees, felt around herself in a wide circle. "Don't move your feet or you'll never find it," she thought as she searched over the ground. There was a clatter as the torch rolled over – its light came back on, and Jinny clutched it to her. Tripping and falling, she trudged on, always listening for any sound that might be Shantih. Her torch beam swathed through the dark. "Shantih!"

Gradually the darkness grew less dense, a long luminous streak shone in the east, and a grey light moved across the sky, revealing waves of petrified moorland lifeless as a moonscape. Jinny peered into the greyness, searching everywhere for the chestnut glint of Shantih, but she could see no sign of her. Jinny meant to climb to the top of the hillside, then quarter back towards Finmory. She tried to run, swinging the halter rope, shouting songs at the top of her voice, hoping that the disturbance might rouse Shantih, but in the vast reaches of the moor Jinny's voice was no more than a shrill squeaking. The mountains and the moors were indrawn and fortified. Any life that was still abroad was no concern of theirs as they meditated on the coming snow.

The first flake splodged down on to Jinny's arm and lay on the black sweater like a soft fifty-pence piece. Another fell on her face, hot against her numb cheek. Jinny looked up and saw the snow coming hurtling down, not floating filigree, but a silent bombardment that beat down faster and faster – came pelting, hurtling straight at her. Jinny bent her head and ploughed on.

In no time, the hillside was patchworked grey and white. When Jinny stopped and looked round again, the white was a smooth covering, only broken here and there by dark patches sheltered from the snowfall by overhanging rocks.

"I must go on," Jinny hold herself. "When I reach the top, I'll easily spot Shantih against the white."

Yet when she stopped again and looked back, she realised with a shock that she could hardly see for any distance. The falling snow was thicker than fog. The sound of her own breathing was loud in its silence.

"I'll need to go back or I'll be lost. If I go on now, I won't be able to find my way home. But I can't go back without Shantih."

Jinny switched on the torch again. Its beam bounced back from the falling snow as if it were a solid wall. "Dark as night," Jinny thought, and suddenly, as if it had been whispered in her ear, she knew where Shantih would be. If she had hurt herself, and Jinny was sure she had, she would have gone to where she felt safest, where she always went at night, to the standing stones. For a moment Jinny hesitated – to reach the standing stones she would need to strike across the moors. "I should go home," she thought. "I should." Then she spun round, waded through the burn, and set off in the direction of the standing stones, fighting her way through the thick suffocation of the blizzard.

"You are mad," said one voice.

"If I don't find her, she'll die."

"You'll die if you're lost in this," the voice assured her, but Jinny plunged on.

Now that it was snowing, it wasn't so cold. The moors were no longer indrawn and menacing, but almost like spring, making Jinny laugh aloud as she ran, leaping into hollows already smoothed flat with drifting snow. She threw snowballs through the steady curtain of flakes, caught snow on her outstretched tongue and thought about sledging.

"I'm O.K.," she grinned, recognising a twisted rowan tree. "I know that tree. It's not far now. And Shantih will be there at the standing stones waiting for me."

Jinny laughed aloud as she galloped through the snow. In the magic of this world there was nothing to hold on to – no time, no place – so that when she met the rowan tree for a second time, she had to stand and stare suspiciously at it, wondering if she had been away from it or if she had been standing there all the time.

"You've been following me," she shouted at the rowan, but her accusation was muffled by the closeness of the snow. Jinny took two strides away from the tree and it had vanished.

"Well, that's that tree sorted out," Jinny chuntered to herself as she went on lifting her feet slowly up and down.

108

up and down. "I'd have been better in my sandshoes. I might have known that Petra's boots would hold me back."

She sat down in the snow to take off the wellingtons.

"I'll skim over the top of the snow in my bare feet," she thought, but she couldn't manage to pull off the boots. "Need to rest my hands. It's all the parsing that Mr. Gorman makes me do. They're worn out." She spread out her hands, watching the snow bury them in a blanket of white. It was surprisingly warm sitting in the snow. Jinny lay down. She closed her eyes, but the white blizzard was inside her head as well, it raged behind her eyes, furious as the storm-tossed crests of the waves. It became a white horse, wild and untameable.

"Shantih!!" screamed Jinny, and leapt to her feet. She stood shaking her head, swinging her arms against her body, stamping her feet.

Another second and she would have been asleep. They would never have found her. She would have been dead. No more Jinny Manders.

"You've got to keep moving," Jinny told herself. "Keep your mind on real things. You've got to get to the standing stones."

Jinny moved like a robot through the deepening snow. Every six steps she stopped to touch her toes, stretch her arms out to the sides and then above her head. She thought of Shantih, beginning at their visit to the circus, and went over every single time she had seen the Arab. Then she went on into the future, thinking of when she would be able to school her and ride her – then she repeated all she had ever read about schooling horses.

Something sitting on the high crags whistled for a wind. Jinny heard it coming, moaning over the moor, roaring over the hills until it reached her, engulfing her in white spirals as it plucked up the newly fallen flakes to dance them in mad whirlwinds that mingled with the falling snow.

The voice of the wind whispered and called, making Jinny shout to it, thinking that someone was there. She began to see figures in the blown eddies. She ran to them, thinking it was Shantih, but before she could reach them the wind sucked them away, and there was only the steady, endless fall of snow.

109

Jinny was crying now. She was cold again. Her teeth wouldn't stop chattering. And she was afraid. Sometimes the wind-blown shapes were monstrous and evil, sometimes tiny darting things that came chittering, whispering, pecking at Jinny with iron teeth, but were gone before she could catch them.

Jinny still called the Arab as she staggered blindly on, but now she was calling to Shantih to come and save her, to plunge through the terrors, scattering them to nothing with her real presence.

Jinny stopped suddenly, stood perfectly still, every sense skinned. She was sure she had heard a voice calling her name. It had been quite different to the moaning chatter of the wind, as real as her mother's voice waking her from a nightmare. She heard it again.

"I'm here. I'm here," she yelled. "Here I am!"

A snow shape loomed towards her. Was real. Was Ken.

"How you doin' then?" he asked.

"Ken!" screamed Jinny, and fell through the snow into his arms.

"Go easy now," he said, comforting her. "What you doing up here?"

"I'm looking for Shantih."

"That's what we reckoned. Saw a sheltered bit in the rocks back there. Come on."

Jinny and Ken went back and crawled into an overhang between two rocks. It stank of sheep, but was dark and gentle after the glaring whiteness.

"Call me Bernard," said Ken, taking a bottle filled with brandy from an inside pocket of his parka. He handed it to Jinny. "Two gulps, that's all. Don't want to have to carry you home."

Jinny gulped and spluttered, then felt the heat of the brandy flow through her. She couldn't stop shaking. "When did you come back?"

"This morning."

"Are you going to stay?"

Ken grinned. "Typical woman. Yes, I'm staying. It was too much. They don't want to hear what I could tell them. So. Here, have some food." And Ken produced chocolate, nuts and raisins from the depths of his pockets.

110

"Now," he said, when Jinny had eaten, "let's get back. The others are out looking for you."

"Back? Oh no. I'm going to the standing stones. That's where Shantih is."

Ken looked straight at her, considering.

"She'll die if we don't find her. How would you like it if people stopped looking for you? Just went home and left you to die?"

"How do you know she's there?"

"I know," said Jinny.

"Well, have another slug of brandy before we go."

When they squeezed back out on to the moor, the snow had almost stopped. The flakes hung in the air, drifted gently down from a clear sky. A miraculous white world stretched about them, rolling, curved, deceptively gentle.

"Whee!" exulted Ken.

"Come on," said Jinny, as she turned towards the shards of stone, dark against the sky, and began to plod doggedly towards them.

"Go lightly," said Ken. "Let your breath take you. Unhook your mind and we're there already."

As they reached the final climb to the standing stones, Ken slowed down, letting Jinny battle on ahead. He understood that she had to be the first to reach Shantih, or have time to hold on to herself if her intuition was wrong and the Arab wasn't there.

Snow rose like a smoke screen in front of Jinny as she floundered through it. Her eyes were fixed on the upright slabs of stone, their gaunt outlines softened by the snow – but she could see no sign of Shantih. The snow around the stones was as undisturbed, as pristine, as the rest of the moor.

Jinny had stopped calling the Arab. If she wasn't at the standing stones, Jinny didn't know what she would do next. Ken might make her go home. Both her father and Mr. MacKenzie were out on the hills searching for her. It would be bad enough listening to what they would have to say to her if she found Shantih, but much, much worse if she had to go back without finding her.

A few yards away from the stones, Jinny stopped.

"But she must be here. She must . . . Shantih," Jinny yelled as she dashed forward. "Shantih!"

In the circle of the stones Jinny stood desolate, staring hopelessly about her. Shantih wasn't there.

"Please God. Please."

She ran desperately through the circle to the far side, where the snow had drifted smooth and high – a white, lifeless emptiness.

But there was something different about one of the drifts. It was somehow the wrong shape.

Jinny fell on her knees and dug into the snow with her hands and arms, scattering it furiously about, shouting to Ken to come and help as she cleared the snow away from the outstretched body of the Arab.

CHAPTER TWELVE

"She's dead, isn't she," Jinny said, not really asking, because she didn't need Ken to tell her what she could see for herself.

"Looks like," agreed Ken.

"I'm too late. If I'd gone straight from the farm last night . . ."

"No good saying 'if'. Does no good."

Suddenly Shantih kicked back with a hind leg, a violent reflex action.

"She's not!" screamed Jinny. "She's alive!"

The mare's eye opened slowly, stared vacantly, then focussed. Seeing humans, she swung her head up, trying to escape from them. She struggled to stand, but her legs slipped away from her in the snow and she fell back, her tongue hanging loosely from the side of her mouth.

"We've got to make her stand up," said Jinny. She knelt beside the Arab, talking love to her as she slipped the halter around her head and knotted it securely. "Come on Shantih. Up, get up. You can't stay here. You're safe now. We've found you but you mustn't give in. You've got to try. We must get you back home."

Jinny ran her hands over the thin neck and shoulder and

112

pulled Shantih's ears between her hands, remembering from somewhere that this was the way to warm a cold horse.

"I'm touching her," Jinny thought. "I'm really with her for the first time," and joy, stronger than any brandy flowed through her, warming her, giving her strength to go on fighting.

Again Shantih stretched out her neck and head and struggled to lift herself with her forelegs.

"Don't let her stop," warned Ken. He was at her shoulder, pushing with all his strength to stop the mare sliding back down. Jinny stood at Shantih's head, pulling on the halter.

"Get up! Get up!" she yelled, but Shantih's hoofs splayed out and she collapsed again.

"Let her rest a minute," said Ken. He took off his parka and spread it under Shantih's forelegs. "Give her some grip. Right, now try her. We've got to get her moving before the snow starts again."

Jinny glanced at the sky. The bright clearness was clouding over – burgeoning, purple-black clouds jostled and swelled.

"O.K.," Jinny tugged at the halter rope. "Get up," she yelled. "Get up with you."

Shantih half lifted her head. She looked as old and worn as the most weary of Stopton's cart ponies. Her eyes were dull and glazed, and her long, scraggy neck gave her a weird, haunting look. Despite Jinny's efforts, she sank back into the snow.

"Here, give me the rope," said Ken. "Now, when I get her head up, don't give her the chance to pack it in."

"Don't hurt her," said Jinny. "She isn't strong enough to stand."

"If we can't get her up, we'll have to leave her. Tom's out searching for you, and Mr. MacKenzie. If we all get caught on these hills tonight it won't do any of us much good."

"But you wouldn't leave her here?"

"Yes I would. Rather one animal than four humans. Now."

Ken jerked savagely at the rope, jerked life into Shantih.

113

He raged and lashed at her with his voice, forced her to keep on struggling. Jinny rattled her fists on the mare's bony sides, kicked against the deadness of her quarters, ran back and launched herself against the stubborn bulk.

Shantih dug her forehooves against Ken's parka. For a terrifying moment she stayed balanced between standing and falling back. Then, with a whinny of pain, she was upright.

"Very good," praised Ken. "Well done."

"Look at her leg," cried Jinny. "That's why she was stranded up here."

Shantih's near hind leg was swollen from the fetlock to above the hock. It stuck out stiffly behind her, looking as if someone had stuffed a feather cushion beneath the skin. Jinny ran her hand over the swelling and felt it burning hot. Shantih flinched away from her and nearly fell.

"Get her home first," said Ken, and Jinny saw him glance quickly at the sky. The clouds leaned over the hills and the remaining patch of clear sky shrank as they watched it.

"Right," agreed Jinny, taking the halter from Ken. "See the burn down there? We go down to it and then follow it along. There's a track through the bracken after that, but we'll just need to guess. Perhaps we'll be able to see Finmory by then."

They made slow progress, black specks crawling over a white wilderness. At every step they had to stop and wait, while Shantih balanced herself on her three sound legs and dragged her swollen leg behind her.

"Keep her moving," ordered Ken.

"She wants to rest," pleaded Jinny.

"She can't. Don't let her stop."

Ken walked ahead of them, checking their way for unsuspected drifts, sudden pits, treacherous boulders hidden in the snow, or bogs, their warning green lost under the white.

They reached the foot of the slope and started to follow the burn. All the sky was black cloud now, and the hills had slipped out of sight into grey gloom. Every now and again a solitary snowflake floated down, making them look up anxiously, expecting to see the sky falling about them.

114

Jinny, stumbling at Shantih's side, hardly knew where she was. Sometimes she thought she was alone again, that she had found Shantih by herself, then Ken, shouting a warning, would bring her back to reality and she would answer him, saying nothing – only wanting to make sure that he was really there.

"We haven't far to go now. There's a warm bed, and hay, and a feed," Jinny told the mare, trying not to look at the bony face, not to hear Shantih's harsh breathing, not to see the grossly swollen leg. "When we get back we'll phone for the vet. He'll come at once. You'll be all right then."

"It's about here that we leave the burn," Jinny called. "Finmory is over that way."

"Certain?"

"Think so."

"Right. Don't let her stop."

Now they had left the stream behind them, the white landscape was all the same. They couldn't pick out any familiar features. Everything was transformed by the snow.

"We should be further down," Ken said, stopping to peer about him. "We're wrong. We want to go further this way."

Jinny followed, with Shantih dragging and stumbling at her side.

When the snow began to fall they stopped again.

"Watch out," Ken warned – but it was too late. Shantih was down. Jinny looked helplessly at her, watching the snow flakes settle on her chestnut coat. She hadn't the energy left to force her up again.

Suddenly they heard voices. Listened for a second.

"Tom!" yelled Ken. "Tom! Over here!"

"Dad," cried Jinny, as she plunged towards the sound. "I've found Shantih. I've found her."

Mr. MacKenzie and Mr. Manders strode towards them.

"Thank God," said Mr. Manders. "You blasted idiot of a child."

"I'd tan the hide off you if you were mine," added Mr. MacKenzie. "What were you after having us all out on the hill on a day like this?"

"It's her leg," said Jinny. "I think it's poisoned."

"That wastrel of a mare," muttered Mr. MacKenzie, as Jinny hurried him over to look at Shantih's leg.

"Man, am I glad to see you. We're spaced out," said Ken.

Mr. MacKenzie took Shantih's halter rope and swung it at the mare, hitting her about the head and neck.

"Don't hurt her," cried Jinny, but Shantih had already splattered to her feet.

"She's no lap dog. It's a horse you're dealing with. Aye, it's the poisoned leg, and a real bad one at that," Mr. MacKenzie said, examining Shantih. "Poor brute. Well, let's be getting her back. Finmory's nearest. Have you the stall for her?"

"It's been ready for weeks," said Jinny.

"Then we'll be getting her there as fast as you like." And the farmer set off confidently into the gloom.

"How can you tell where we are?" demanded Mr. Manders.

"I'll be sixty-seven next July, if the Lord allows, and I've been on these hills since I could walk. It would be the sorry day if the wee touch of snow were to make me lose my way."

As they followed Mr. MacKenzie, the snow grew heavier. Jinny was longing to be home, to be warm and safe again, to be inside, out of the snow.

"You'll need to phone the vet at once," she said to her father.

He brushed snow out of his beard and looked down at her sternly.

"Will do, whenever we get home. I'll say no more just now, but when this is over you and I are going to have a very serious talk."

Jinny nodded, a lump choking in her throat at her father's words. "How can you do it?" she thought. "How can you balance not hurting people, not worrying people and doing the things you have to do?" – but it was too impossible to think about now.

When they reached Finmory, Jinny led Shantih into the box she had prepared for her and took off her halter. The mare fell heavily into the straw, her injured leg uppermost. She stretched out with a groan, her head sank down, and

116

she lay still. Tears poured down Jinny's face. She had imagined this moment so often, bringing Shantih home to Finmory, but never had she pictured it like this.

"Can't get through," said Mr. Manders, coming back from the phone.

"Aye," said Mr. MacKenzie. "The Ardtallon line'll be down, but I doubt if Jim would be coming out on a night like this. Even if he'd the mind to it he wouldn't be getting here. A pity for the mare. It's a wonder the new drugs they have these days. Might have pulled her through."

Jinny scrubbed her face against the sleeve of her sweater, pushed her hair back from her face and straightened her shoulders. A moment ago she had been longing to be in the house, drinking hot soup, telling the others about her adventure before she went to bed. The thought of sleep, of being able to let her eyes close, had filled her mind, but now she pushed the temptation away. She hadn't fought all day to bring Shantih home just to let her die now.

"Well, what shall we do?" Jinny demanded. "If the vet can't come we'll need to look after her ourselves."

"Aye, but you don't give up easy," said Mr. MacKenzie. "You'll not be having a horse rug?"

"No, but there's plenty on my bed."

"No need, I'll go and get you one. Take a wisp over her and try to warm her up a bit."

Jinny twisted a wisp out of straw and knelt beside Shantih, rubbing her over with strong sweeps of her arm. The mare was nothing but bone under her tight skin. Jinny straightened her forelock and ran her hands tenderly over Shantih's face.

"You're all right now," she murmured. "You're safe now. I'll stay with you until you're better."

Mr. MacKenzie came back with a heavy horse blanket, bandages and a tin of kaolin paste. He threw the blanket over Shantih and packed straw underneath it.

"Now then, let's be seeing to her leg." His gnarled hands felt Shantih's leg. "Aye, it's nasty. Would you look at that. There's the puncture that's caused the damage."

The swelling was hard and tight and burning hot. Jinny could hardly believe that it could be caused by the tiny wound.

117

"It's got the dirt in it, but we'll put the poultice on and hope for the best, though I'm doubting she's too far gone. The poison's right through her."

Mr. MacKenzie showed Jinny how to heat up the tin of kaolin paste on top of the Aga, carry it out to the stable, spread some on a pad, slap the hot poultice on to Shantih's leg where it was punctured, then bandage it into place.

"You'll need to change it yourself in the morning."

Jinny nodded.

"I'll be away then, and get you to your bed."

"I'm staying up with Shantih."

"Your mother'll be putting the hems on that notion."

"I am."

"Then I dare say you'll be getting your own way as usual. Try her with a drop of water – be taking the chill off it now. I'll come over tomorrow and we'll make a mash if she's still with us. Don't be upsetting yourself now if she dies. She's no but an animal."

"She isn't going to die," stated Jinny.

Her mother insisted that Jinny changed into dry clothes and had a proper meal, but she didn't argue when Jinny said she was going to stay with Shantih.

"She's unconscious," said Petra. "What difference does it make whether you're there or not?"

"I think she knows," said Jinny. "Knows that she's not been abandoned, not just left with no one caring. That there's someone fighting on her side."

It was after midnight when Mr. Manders went out for a last look at Jinny. He expected to find her asleep, and was ready to carry her into the house and up to her bed. He heard the painful rasp of Shantih's breathing as he approached the stable. An oil lamp cast flickering shadows over the cobwebbed walls. Jinny was kneeling by Shantih's head. The soft murmur of her voice stopped as she realised that her father was there.

"How is she?" her father asked.

"She's O.K.," said Jinny fiercely.

Her father waited for a minute or two.

"Sure you won't come to bed?"

"Sure."

118

There was nothing he could do to help her. He shut the stable door and walked slowly back through the snow. "Even your own children," he thought. "You can't live for them. They all have to live for themselves. Go through it all for themselves."

Ken brought flasks of coffee and sandwiches at about four in the morning. He stayed, sitting cross-legged in a corner of the box, until it was light outside, a silent, luminous, white light.

Jinny changed the poultice on Shantih's leg. The swelling was still hard and tight. Several times during the night she had offered the mare water, but she couldn't even get her to lift her head. Jinny had sponged her muzzle and bathed away the matter from her closed eyes, but Shantih had shown no sign of knowing that Jinny was there.

Mr. MacKenzie came over after lunch.

"No dead yet?" he said. "She's no giving in easy. I've brought the bran, but from the look of her she'll not be interested."

"Is there no way we can get the vet to come?" pleaded Jinny.

"You'll not be getting through to Jim until the men have been out to fix the wires, and from the sound of it the forecast is no much good."

"Where does the vet live?" Ken asked.

"A house the other side of Ardtallon. You'd know it by the wee men in the garden, though I'm thinking they'd be under the snow this weather, with their wee red caps pulled down over their ears."

It was after eight when Ken returned from Ardtallon. Although he hadn't said anything, Jinny had guessed that he was going to try and reach the vet. She didn't hear him coming into the stable, but looked up to see him standing there watching her, and she knew from the blankness in his eyes that he'd been unsuccessful.

"He wasn't there," Ken told her. "He was out at a farm when the snow started. Stranded. I told his wife how it is here, so he'll come if he can. She didn't think there was much hope until the snow lifted."

"Thanks for trying," said Jinny, her voice shaky with disappointment. At the back of her mind had been the

119

hope that the vet would come back with Ken. "Thanks for going back out into the snow." Jinny shuddered, remembering the terror of being lost in the white wilderness. It seemed a long time ago. Something she had read about or dreamt. Now the only real thing in her life was to stay with Shantih, to fight with her for the next breath and the next. Not to let her give in. To be there with her.

Ken crouched down beside the Arab. She had been poor before, but now the fever that gripped her had wasted away all the flesh and muscle. Her bones seemed jumbled together, her legs were like the legs of a discarded marionette, chucked down carelessly on the straw.

"She's much worse," said Jinny in a flat, expressionless voice. "And there's nothing I can do to help her. If the vet doesn't get here, she'll die."

"We should know what to do ourselves," Ken said. "Once we would have known what herbs and plants to use to cure a fever, and clean her leg, but now all we can do is wait for someone else." And he thought that he would find out about plants, how they could be used to cure, then the next time something like this happened he would be able to help.

"What's the weather like?"

"In Ardtallon they're all expecting more snow."

Jinny said nothing. More snow would mean there was no hope of the vet getting through tonight.

"How about some kip?"

"No."

Ken left her alone with Shantih, and Jinny settled down again at the Arab's head. She was better alone. Although she had to admit that Shantih didn't show any sign of noticing them, Jinny felt that her family dropping in and chatting disturbed her. And she had to answer them, taking away her concentration from Shantih.

"I couldn't sleep," Jinny told her mother when she came down before midnight to try and persuade Jinny to come in to bed.

"This is the last night, then. Tomorrow morning you must get some sleep. Ken will stay with her."

Jinny thought that she could argue about it tomorrow. Now she only wanted to be left alone.

"You're going to live," Jinny murmured to Shantih. "Soon it will be spring again, and you'll be well and fit. I'll ride you everywhere. We'll go away together for weeks and weeks, riding on every day. I'll pitch my tent somewhere different each night. Sometimes by the sea, and we'll gallop over the sands and swim out into the waves. We'll go to gymkhanas, and you'll win the showing and the jumping. They'll all have heard about you, and when they see us riding into the show field they'll think that I'm only a scruffy trekker, then someone will recognise you. 'That's Shantih,' they'll say. 'Haven't you heard about her?' . . ."

Jinny's voice, whispering into Shantih's ear, made less sound that the mare's irregular breathing; less sound than the scuttering of mice in the rafters; made no disturbance at all beyond the lamp lit globe which contained the girl and the Arab. But Jinny's voice persisted. It went on and on into the night. Defying her sleeping family, defying the remote withdrawal of the white silent world – defying all the common sense that picked at the back of her mind, urging her to sleep, insisting that anything she did could make no difference, telling her not to be so silly. Jinny's voice whispered on.

At first, Jinny didn't notice the pattering, then thought it was only mice. But it was brisk and steady, tapping, drumming, beating – growing stronger each moment. She dashed to the stable door and stared out. It was pouring with rain. Not more snow, but rain. Rain that would clear the roads.

By two in the morning, when Jinny changed Shantih's poultice, it was still pouring. Trees were bare again, their snow blossom vanished. Slabs of snow overhung the eaves of the house, leaving black gaps in the white thatch. The snow on the ground was gnawed and pitted by the steady downpour.

Jim Rae, the vet, reached Finmory shortly after four. Jinny heard his Land-Rover and ran out of the stable to meet him.

"Thank you, oh, thank you for coming," she cried.

"Thank the lad who had my wife so churned up she was turning me on the doorstep to get me here. Well, let's have a look at the horse."

121

The vet knelt and examined Shantih. Jinny waited, her teeth clenched, afraid to hear what he would have to say. Before he spoke, Jim Rae opened his bag, fitted phials to his syringe, and injected Shantih three times.

"She's still with us," he said, standing up, "and if she'd been for packing it in, she wouldn't be here now. The jabs I've given her should kill the infection, but she's had a long fight of it."

"But she will get better?" demanded Jinny.

"She's very weak," said the vet, "but her heart's strong, and she's fighting. If she can hold out until the drugs take effect, she'll make it. Now how about a cup of tea? Is there only yourself up?"

"I shouldn't leave her."

"Och, come away with you. You'll not be refusing me a cup of tea."

"Oh no, of course not. It's just . . ."

The vet steered Jinny out of the stables. "You've done fine," he told her. "My wife says the place is full of the gossip about yourself setting off in the snow to save her. She'll manage a few minutes by herself. There's no more you can do for her now."

Jim Rae sat down at the kitchen table and lit his pipe, while Jinny struggled to fill the kettle and put it on the Aga. She put the biscuit tin on the table, and it seemed very important that she should get it in exactly the correct spot. Not too close to the vet or he would think that she was trying to make him eat them, not too close to herself or he would think she was being greedy. Jinny stood, stupidly moving the tin backwards and forwards. Then she collapsed into a chair. She laid her head on the table. Her eyes closed.

"When I've made your tea, I must get back to Shantih," she said, but her eyelids wouldn't open. She was asleep.

Ken came downstairs to see if Jinny needed any help, thinking she was heating up the kaolin.

Jim Rae introduced himself. "I'm brewing up. The official brewer has passed out. Would you like a cup?"

"She's bushed," said Ken. "Days since she's had any kip."

"Let her sleep. There's nothing more she can do."

"I'll carry her up to bed. Shantih?"

The vet shook his head. "Not good," he said. "But plenty of spirit. I don't often see a horse as far gone as that one and still breathing. She may pull through. It's thanks to the lass, if she does."

CHAPTER THIRTEEN

When Jinny woke up, it was broad daylight. She couldn't think what she was doing in bed when she should have been with Shantih. Pulling on jeans and struggling into her sweater, she pushed her feet into her shoes, and, still half asleep, fumbled her way downstairs. There was no one about.

She ran through the kitchen and out into the yard. It had stopped raining, but the ground was porous and dank. Everywhere there was the sound of water – dripping from trees, swollen burns gushing and frothing down from the moors, the remaining islands of snow shrinking and flowing away. Only the tops of the mountains were still white. Low in the west, the sun made a glistening thumb print through the pearl grey clouds. Jinny realised that it must be late in the afternoon.

She dashed across the yard. At the door of the stable she stopped, afraid to go in. She wrapped her arms round her body, and stood shivering, digging her fingers into her shoulders. If Shantih was worse . . .If she was dead – only a lifeless bulk lying covered in the straw . . . But Jinny had to find out. She had to go on and discover what had happened while she had been asleep.

Jinny took a deep breath. She opened the stable door, waited for a second, surrounded by the familiar bins and sacks and the towering bales of hay. Then she turned her head slowly, not wanting to look, but knowing there was nothing else she could do.

The Arab was standing with her head over the half door of the box, watching her.

For a moment, Jinny could only stand and stare, could hardly allow herself to believe what she saw. Shantih gave a small whinny, flurrying her nostrils, welcoming Jinny.

"You're better!" Jinny cried. "You're better! Oh horse, horse, horse!" And Jinny was opening the box door and flinging her arms around Shantih's neck, pressing her face against the thin neck, clapping the bony shoulder and rubbing her hands over the mare's harsh coat. Shantih turned her head, nuzzling Jinny's shoulder. Her face was still gaunt and wasted, but her dark eyes were calm and bright, her ears pricked and alert.

"And you're not afraid of me any longer. You know me now, know that I'd never hurt you. Oh, Shantih."

Jinny heard a sound at the stable door, she looked up and saw her family and Ken.

"She's better," Jinny shouted to them. "She's not going to die."

"We know," said her father, as they all came crowding round Shantih. "We wanted you to find out for yourself. The vet was here again yesterday. He was pleased with her then and she's come on a bit today."

"Yesterday?" queried Jinny.

"You've been asleep for a day and a night and most of today," said Mike.

"I haven't!" exclaimed Jinny. Maybe she was still asleep. So often had she dreamed of standing like this, Shantih lipping at her outstretched palm, her breath warm and trusting. Jinny pinched herself hard, but she didn't wake up. It was all real, was truly happening.

"Here's the vet now," said Mr. Manders, as they heard the Land-Rover churning its way up the drive. "He said he'd try to come back today."

Jim Rae slammed the Land-Rover door shut and came into the stable with a long, striding walk.

"Well, how's the miracle horse?" he asked. "And her rescuer conscious again. Things are looking up. Unbelievable, really. Some stamina there to pull her through."

When the vet had left and her family had gone back into the house, Jinny filled Shantih's water bucket, mucked out and put down a fresh bed of deep straw. Every few minutes she would stop what she was doing and just stand watching Shantih pull at her hay net. She would go up to the Arab and rub her neck, run Shantih's ears through her

124

hands and talk to her. Jinny's mouth stretched from ear to ear with sheer happiness.

The swelling in Shantih's leg had gone down a lot, and the vet had said that now the poison had been cleared out of her system it was only a question of time, good feeding and care until she was perfectly fit again.

"Soon you'll be quite, quite better," Jinny told Shantih before she left her for the night. "You're really mine now, to stay with me for ever. Soon I'll be able to ride you."

Happiness overflowed in Jinny. She went back to say goodnight to Shantih for one last time, to straighten her silk-fine forelock and make certain that her rug was on correctly. She could hardly bear to leave her.

"And that's not all," said Mike. "School . . ."

"Thought you were keeping it a surprise?" interrupted Mrs. Manders.

"Oh, so I am," remembered Mike.

But Jinny hadn't been paying any attention to him. She was galloping Shantih over the flat sand of Finmory Bay, the sea wind blowing out the mare's mane and tail as her flying hoofs crescented the sand.

"You've missed two days," said Mike, as they rode into Glenbost the next morning.

Jinny had hardly given it a thought. Even now, with Mr. Gorman's power coming closer and closer, she wasn't really thinking about him. She was hoping that Ken would look after Shantih properly.

"I hope he remembers to shake out the hay before he fills her net," Jinny said.

"Who?" said Mike. "Mr. Gorman? More likely to shake you out."

"He won't," said Jinny. "I've got a note." And she couldn't think why Mike was laughing.

They left Bramble and Punch in their field and went across to school.

"Who stuck the snowmen on the windows?" Jinny asked in surprise, looking at the cotton wool figures glued to the glass. It was absolutely the last thing she could imagine Mr. Gorman allowing.

But before Mike had time to answer, the other children, who had been standing in a group in the school doorway,

125

came out to meet them. Dolina was first. Jinny stood still. She felt the familiar clutch of fear tighten her stomach as she remembered the misery of sitting next to Dolina's silent back.

Dolina marched straight up to Jinny. Her cod eyes looked over Jinny's shoulder.

"I'm sorry about last term," she said. "Not speaking. It wasn't your fault that Mr. Gorman wouldn't be listening to you. We'll not be keeping it going this term?"

Jinny's mouth fell open in total amazement, but before she could think of what to say to Dolina, the other children were pushing round her.

"Weren't you afraid to be going up the mountains by yourself and in the storm?"

"How were you knowing that the horse would be at the Stones?"

"My father says there was a man went up there in the snow one winter and they never found him again. Not ever a trace even."

Jinny listened in astonishment. She had been expecting that if they had heard about her adventure on the moor they would only make fun of her.

"Right, children. In you come," called a woman's voice. Standing in the school doorway was a young woman with hair almost as long as Jinny's.

"She's Miss Broughton. The new teacher," explained Dolina. "It's the weird things she has us at."

"Where's Mr. Gorman?"

"He'd the wee heart turn just after the New Year. He's not too serious, but they say he won't be coming back to the teaching."

The classroom was transformed – walls bright with pictures, in one corner a bookcase full of paperbacks, along one wall a table labelled FIND OUT FOR YOURSELF and covered with instruction packs. There was a nature table and a table with piles of paper, crayons, paint jars and sticky, coloured squares.

"Now, you'll be Jinny," welcomed Miss Broughton. "I've heard all about you. What would you like to do this morning? Write the story about your adventure on the moors?"

126

"What I'd really like to do," said Jinny, her voice squeaky with disbelief, "is to paint a picture of Shantih on the moors and the snow monsters."

"Fine," agreed Miss Broughton, "and after you've finished it, you can make up a sci-fi story with your monsters in it. Or a play?"

"I *must* be dreaming," Jinny said to Mike as they rode home. "There's no other explanation."

But if Jinny was dreaming, it went on through January and February and into March, as Shantih grew sleek and well again. Her chestnut coat was gleaming and supple and her silken mane and tail as fine as Jinny's own hair. By March, she was out during the day, sharing the same field as Punch and Bramble. When Jinny came home from school, Shantih was always waiting at the field gate, whinnying a welcome. If Jinny called from her bedroom window, the mare would look up from her grazing, searching for Jinny, then, seeing her at the window, would walk to the corner of the field nearest to the house and wait, watching her mistress. She had all the pure-bred Arab's magic, that note of brittle vulnerability mixed with the enchantment of a dream horse.

Jinny didn't want to start riding her until she was quite certain that Shantih was really fit again. She led her about in a halter – down to the farm, along the road to Glenbost, over the moors and along the shore. All her fear of humans had vanished. It was only if she got a fright that she would rear away, as sudden and wild as she had been on the moors.

Then, once evening at the end of March, Jinny was walking back with the milk. The air was gentle and warm. Buds furred the etched branches of the trees, a flush of green grass tinted the moors, and suddenly Jinny knew that it was the right time to start riding Shantih.

The next evening she adjusted Bramble's bridle and went down to the field. Shantih came trotting to the gate.

"Going to ride you tonight," said Jinny. "How will that be?"

The mare pushed her soft velvet muzzle into the crook of Jinny's arm. Jinny scratched her behind the ears, flipped stray locks of mane over to the right side of her neck, and very gently lowered the reins over her head. Then she slipped the thick snaffle into Shantih's mouth and lifted the bridle over her ears. When she had buckled the throat lash and noseband, Jinny gathered up her reins and gently, talking all the time to the mare, she lay over her withers.

Shantih stood quite still, hardly paying any attention to Jinny, relaxed and easy. Jinny slid her arms round Shantih's neck.

"Whoa, the lass. The good horse. Steady now, easy the girl." Slowly and carefully, Jinny lifted her leg over Shantih's back and sat astride her.

Shantih turned an enquiring head, nibbled at the toe of Jinny's sandshoe, asking what all the fuss was about.

Jinny touched her legs against Shantih's sides and flexed her fingers on the reins, then Shantih was walking out with a gay willingness, her neck arched and proud, her dark, lustrous eyes looking around her as Jinny walked her in wide circles.

"You've got chestnut hairs all over the seat of your trousers," said her mother.

"I was riding Shantih," said Jinny. "She was perfect. Absolutely perfect."

Jinny hurried Bramble home from school the next afternoon. She was planning to ride Shantih along the road to Glenbost. As Bramble passed the farm gate, he stopped suddenly and gave one of his trumpetting whinnies. A chorus of shrill neighs replied, and Jinny realised that the Shetlands must be in the paddock. She rode Bramble across the farmyard to have a look at them. She hadn't really seen them since the blizzard.

"Aye," said Mr. MacKenzie, who was leaning on the gate, ruminating over his ponies. "It's yourself."

"They're looking well," said Jinny.

"No bad," agreed Mr. MacKenzie. "The yearlings will be off tomorrow. A wee touch pocket money that'll be."

"I was riding Shantih last night," Jinny said. "I'm going to ride her along the road to Glenbost tonight."

"That's obliging now," said Mr. MacKenzie. "Save me the trouble of coming to fetch her."

"What?"

"She'll be for the sale tomorrow," said Mr. MacKenzie, staring out over the shaggy mass of Shetlands.

"What do you mean – sale?"

"I told you long ago that I'd be taking her ladyship to the spring sale."

"But she's mine!" cried Jinny. "She's mine! I rescued her. I've looked after her. I've fed her. Shantih's MINE."

"Och now, enough of that nonsense. You know fine that I bought her from the circus man, and I've thrown in enough free hay and oats with the stuff your father's bought from me to keep two beasts, leave alone one scarecrow like her."

"You don't mean it?" demanded Jinny. "You can't mean it."

"That I do, lass. You can buy her from me for a hundred – and that's giving her away dirt cheap, seeing you've had so much going on with her."

"I haven't got a hundred pounds. Of course I haven't got a hundred pounds."

"In that case we'll say no more about it. Just you be bringing her over here tonight."

"Oh, please, please, Mr. MacKenzie, don't sell her. You can't sell her tomorrow. I'll find some way to make the money. Please."

The farmer turned away from Jinny. "Get off with you," he said gruffly, and stomped away into the farm.

Somehow Jinny rode Bramble back to Finmory. She couldn't cry. It was too bad for crying. She knew without asking that there was no chance of anyone giving her a hundred pounds. Not a chance in the world. Ken and Mr. Manders had re-established the pottery in one of Finmory's spare rooms and the shelves were filling up again, but they still hadn't made up for the pots they had lost in the gale. A publisher was interested in Mr. Manders' book, but he hadn't made a definite offer. There was nothing Jinny could do before tomorrow. Nothing. It was no use. All her struggling had been for nothing.

Clenched and desperate, Jinny turned Bramble out into the field. Shantih was at the gate but, after a quick glance, Jinny couldn't bear to look at her. She turned away and walked up to Finmory House. Its grey stone walls were enduring and strong. For so many years they had sheltered humans, all loving and hating, all powerless not to go on struggling. And in the end, it was no use. There was nothing you could do about anything. No matter how hard she tried not to, Jinny couldn't help seeing the red-gold shape of the Arab dancing in her mind's eye.

"Thought you were going to ride Shantih again tonight," her mother said, as Jinny walked into the kitchen.

Jinny shook her head.

"Mr. MacKenzie is going to sell her. Tomorrow at the sale. He wants a hundred pounds for her."

"Oh no! Did he tell you this just now?"

Jinny nodded, the lump in her throat choking her.

"I am sorry, pet, but we couldn't possibly."

"It's O.K.," gulped Jinny. "Didn't think you could." She fled out of the kitchen straight into Ken.

"Letter for you," he said.

Jinny took the letter. It was a large brown envelope with her name and address typed on it. She sat down on the bottom step of the stairs to open it, and pulled out a magazine.

"Who could have sent that to me?" Then she saw the letter. Her eyes pounced on it, devouring words – "*pleased to inform*" . . . "*judges*" . . . "*page* 16" . . . "*first prize*" . . . "£60". She scrabbled the magazine open to page sixteen, and there was her competition painting, glossy and changed in its reproduction, and beside it was her name and address – winner of the first prize.

"Sixty pounds!" Jinny screamed, jumping to her feet. "I've won sixty pounds!"

She tore through to the kitchen, waving the magazine. "Look – my picture!" she yelled. "I've won sixty pounds."

"You've what?" said her mother, but Jinny was already tearing across the yard, running faster than she had ever run in her life before, her feet battering down the track to the farm.

Mr. MacKenzie was standing by the milking shed when Jinny arrived, too out of breath to speak. She could only hold the magazine open in front of him and point to her name.

"It's no a hundred," said Mr. MacKenzie, when he had

130

at last realised what Jinny was telling him, but she knew from his voice that he didn't mean it. "What about the other forty? Have you thought of that?"

"H.P.?" suggested Jinny.

"You painted this yourself now? Just you did it?"

"Yes."

"Well, you be doing me two of the farm and we'll call it a deal."

Jinny threw her arms around his neck and kissed him.

She went back to Finmory, walking slowly, joy singing and bursting out of her.

"You're mine now. Truly mine," she told Shantih as she put her bridle on. She led the Arab out of the field, sprang lightly on to her back and rode her down the path to the bay.

"It's all beginning," Jinny said aloud. "An Arab of my own to ride, to train and to love."

The freedom of the craggy moors and the open sea stretched around Jinny. She ran her hand down Shantih's strong, sleek neck as the mare walked out with an even, reaching stride, her ears flickering to the sound of Jinny's voice. Long summer days lay ahead of them both, when they would ride together far into the hills, discovering hidden lochs and secret beaches, but always the strong, grey walls of Finmory House would be there – waiting to welcome them home again.

"I do love you," Jinny said, meaning not only Shantih but Finmory and her family and Ken; the hills and the sea; not only the soaring delight of the eagles but the insects as well. "I love you all so much."

And she sat astride Shantih, laughing for sheer joy. It was all possible now.

A Devil to Ride

CHAPTER ONE

The chestnut Arab bucked suddenly, heels high, her head tucked between her front legs, her body twisting as she bucked again and again. Jinny Manders clutched the front of the saddle with both hands, tightened the hold of her bony knees and clung on desperately. She didn't know what else she could do.

"Whoa, Shantih, whoa the horse. Steady, Steady."

The words were jolted out of Jinny's mouth and scattered into the silence of the April evening. Bramble and Punch, the two Highland ponies who were grazing in a far corner of the field, didn't even flicker their ears at the sound of Jinny's voice. The waves lapped up the deserted sands of Finmory Bay, the moors and mountains that surrounded Finmory House were wrapt in their own mysteries. For hundreds of years they had seen humans come and go while they stood still. The skinny girl and the violent Arab horse were no concern of theirs.

"Whoa. Steady. Stop it. Stop it. Steady now."

After the fourth buck the Arab paused. Jinny relaxed her hold and patted the sweated neck. Shantih bucked again: heels flung skywards, head and neck disappearing from in front of Jinny as she went soaring through the air, her long, straight, red-gold hair flying out behind her.

Jinny landed on her feet as neatly as a cat, Shantih's reins still clasped tightly in her hand. It had happened so often to her in the past few weeks that Jinny was beginning to wonder if she couldn't work in a somersault before she landed. But she only wondered that to stop herself from thinking too much about what would happen if her mother or father or Petra, her elder sister, were to see one of Shantih's explosions. Mike, her younger brother, had seen Shantih rearing with Jinny one night.

"She is pretty wild, isn't she?" he'd said.

" 'Course not," said Jinny sharply. "If you knew anything about horses you'd know that she's just fresh."

"That's not what your book says," replied Mike. "It says rearing is a dangerous vice. They can fall over backwards and *churumphch*. Strawberry jam!"

"She doesn't always rear. Sometimes she only bucks. And anyway I'd jump off before she came down."

"Rather you than me, but you'd better be a bit careful hadn't you?"

"You may not have noticed, but it is a horse I'm riding —not a knitted donkey. No one expects a pure bred Arab to behave like an ancient pony."

"Well, be careful you don't let Mum see you," Mike had replied, and Jinny had been doing her best to exercise Shantih in the early mornings or late evenings when her family were less likely to be about. It was so unlike her brother to tell anyone to be careful that Jinny knew he must have been impressed by Shantih's rodeo.

"Why are you so silly?" Jinny asked her horse.

Shantih sighed gustily and rested her head against Jinny's arm. She was calm and gentle now, all her temper vanished. Her huge Arab eyes with their long lashes looked mildly around her, her muzzle, pushing hopefully against Jinny's hand, was as soft as plush velvet.

"Don't think it," Jinny told her, doing her best to make her voice sound severe. "You are getting nothing from me. Not a thing. Pig of a horse. I hate you."

But Jinny didn't. She loved her. Loved her so much that there was nothing else in her life that really mattered, only her drawing and Shantih. There were the other things that Jinny really took for granted—her family and her home. Even living in the Scottish Highlands surrounded by sea and sky and open country was beginning to be the way things always were, although it was only last summer that Mr. Manders had stopped being a probation officer in Stopton and had brought his family away from the city streets and the continual traffic to make a new life in the Highlands. They had come to live in Finmory House, a large, grey, stone house standing by itself between the hills and the sea. Mike and Jinny rode two trekking ponies to school in Glenbost village, and Mr. MacKenzie's farm was the only other house near Finmory.

Standing scratching Shantih's neck, Jinny remembered how she had first seen the Arab in a circus, billed as 'Yasmin, the Killer Horse'. So many things had happened between the night when Jinny had fallen in love with Shantih and last month when at last the Arab had belonged to her.

"And now you're mine," Jinny told Shantih, "so why do you have to start all this nonsense? You are a nit."

Jinny put the reins back over Shantih's head and re-mounted. She knew from the light that it was getting late, too late to start another fight to try and make Shantih trot in a circle. Jinny walked her on a loose rein round the field. Once Shantih realised that there were to be no more attempts at schooling she pricked her ears and walked out willingly, whinnying to the Highlands as she passed them but not trying to join them.

"I'll ride you round once," Jinny told her. "That's the right thing to do. 'Always finish your schooling on a happy note so that both rider and mount feel satisfied with what they have achieved'," Jinny quoted from her book. "So that's what we'll do. Not that we've achieved much," she added, knowing that if she tried to take Shantih round the field twice there wouldn't be a happy note.

Jinny's book also said that if your horse was misbehaving you were to use your legs strongly, backed up by your stick. When Jinny had backed up her strongly used legs—which she took to mean kicking—with a stick from the hedge, Shantih had gone mad. Her first furious buck had sent Jinny smashing into the ground; then, rearing and bucking, she had galloped round and round the field. When Jinny had at last managed to grab her reins and hold on to them, Shantih had stood wide-eyed and shaking with fear. Her chestnut coat had been curded with sweat and she had flinched away from Jinny's touch.

It was the first and only time that Jinny had tried to use a stick on her. "She thought she was back in that circus. She thought I was the ringmaster that whipped her," Jinny

137

had accused herself as she broke the stick into pieces and threw it away.

After this, the only solution that Jinny could think of was to hold on while Shantih reared or bucked. "If only I could get better at staying on then she would get fed up with trying to get me off and start to behave herself," Jinny reasoned. But somehow Jinny nearly always ended up on the ground.

"Jinny," called a voice from the field gate.

Jinny dismounted quickly, just in case, and led Shantih towards the gate.

It was Ken. He was standing by the hedge, almost invisible in the gathering spring dusk. His black sweater and faded jeans blended into the shadows of the hedge; his bony face was calm and still and his fair hair grew long past his shoulders. The Manders had first got to know Ken when he had been on probation for being with other boys who had broken into a Stopton warehouse. When his probation was over Ken had said to Mr. Manders, "I'd nothing to do with it." "I know," Mr. Manders had acknowledged.

Ken had arrived at Finmory on the Manders' first day there, bringing Kelly, a grey-thatched, yellow-eyed dog, with him. Ken was seventeen. His parents had washed their hands of him except to send a monthly cheque to him through their bank. "I'll stay, if you'll have me," Ken had said, and they had all gladly accepted his offer. He worked with Mr. Manders in the room that they had converted into a pottery, knowing far more about it than Mr. Manders did, and he had dug a kitchen garden out of Finmory's overgrown wilderness. "Feed us all," Ken said. "What do you want to go on eating animals for when the earth's bursting itself to feed us?" Jinny had never known Ken to eat anything that came from an animal.

It was Ken who had helped Jinny to save Shantih. Ken who had saved Jinny's life.

"How's she doing then?" asked Ken, reaching out his long-fingered hand to gentle Shantih's head.

"I've just finished riding her," Jinny said hurriedly. "She's looking better, isn't she?"

138

"Beautiful," agreed Ken. "Rather see her without all that gear strapped on to her though."

"I've got to ride her," exclaimed Jinny. "No one has a horse and doesn't ride it."

"There was some old bloke somewhere used to read from the Bible and his horse came to listen."

"I expect he was a saint," said Jinny, knowing Ken's old blokes. "And I'm me. I'm going to ride everywhere on Shantih, trekking and cross country and dressage . . ."

Jinny saw clearly the flat dressage arena, the white test markers, the crowds round the corded barrier. She felt Shantih stop correctly in front of the judges as she lifted her stick and touched the brim of her bowler, remembering to smile.

"Mike seemed to think you were using her as a means of suicide, and your Mum sent me to say what about the milk?"

The dressage arena vanished. Jinny began to say, "What did Mike tell you . . ." then clapped her hand to her mouth. "I forgot again!"

"I'll go."

" 'S O.K. Mr. MacKenzie will have left it for me in the milking shed."

"You going to ride over?"

"She's done enough for tonight," Jinny said, not looking at Ken. "I'll give her some nuts and then I'll get the milk."

Jinny led Shantih up to her loose box. Years ago when Finmory had been a farm this outhouse had been stables. The Manders used part of it as a feed house and tack room. There were two stalls for Bramble and Punch, the ponies they had borrowed during the off season from Miss Tuke's trekking centre, and opposite the stalls was a loose box that was now Shantih's.

The Arab barged through the doorway, knowing that she was going to be fed. Jinny took her tack off and gave her some nuts.

"I shouldn't be giving you anything," Jinny told her, tipping the scoop of pony nuts into the trough. Shantih paid no attention to her, but crunched her way steadily through them while Jinny took a dandy over her.

139

When she had turned Shantih out with the black Bramble and the white Punch, Jinny hung over the field gate watching her roll then trot across to the other ponies. The heavy bulk of the two Highlands made Shantih seem more like a fairy-tale horse than ever, Jinny thought. She was all lightness and air as she danced her way across the field.

"Haven't you gone for the milk yet?" accused Mike. "There isn't a drop left and Dad's wanting coffee. He sent me to hurry you up."

"I'm just going," said Jinny, and she set off along the track to Mr. MacKenzie's farm. Petra, who was nearly fifteen, went to Duniver Grammar and stayed at the school hostel during the week, but Mike, who was nine, and Jinny, who was eleven, both went to the school in Glenbost and took it in turns to fetch the milk from the farm. When it was Mike's week it was like being back in Stopton with regular deliveries, but when it was Jinny's her family realised that they were living in the remote Highlands.

"But I do try to remember," Jinny explained. "I've drawn a picture of Buttercup VII. Mr. MacKenzie says he knows it's her because of her leer. And I pin it on my bedroom door when it's my week. But when I've forgotten I can't remember and it's only when I see Buttercup VII leering at me that I remember I've forgotten."

Mrs. Manders listened to Jinny's excuses.

"Couldn't you always go at the same time every day?"

"I wish I could," agreed Jinny. "I do wish I could. But it's a waste of time making timetables for myself. I never ever manage to stick to them."

As Jinny wandered her way to the farm she wondered if timetabling Shantih might help to calm her down a little. She didn't want to calm her down too much—only enough for Jinny to stay on her.

"Every morning an hour's hacking," Jinny thought. "Or maybe two hours. Then when she's settled I could try lungeing her again." She had tried lungeing Shantih three times already but each time had been disastrous, with Jinny on the end of the clothes line being dragged round the field by a mad, dervish horse. "But perhaps if I did it regularly, every single day of the Easter holidays, it might improve her," thought Jinny. "I'll make a timetable and I'll stick to it." She saw the timetable in her mind's eye. She would draw pictures round its edges, pictures of Shantih doing turns on the forehand, collected canters, and half passes.

But the bubble burst. A thousand timetables would make no difference. They would only mean that Shantih would be able to throw Jinny off at more regular intervals.

"I don't know enough," Jinny thought desperately. "I don't know the right things to do. My riding just isn't good enough. I've never had any proper lessons and sitting on Bramble isn't really riding. Not like riding Shantih. Books are no good. Reading them it all sounds so easy but they're no use when I'm flying through the air," and Jinny groaned aloud. She knew only too well that each time Shantih played up and got away with it she was learning that she could do exactly as she liked with her.

"What I need is someone to help me. Someone who knows the right way to do things. If only I had a different family," longed Jinny, and saw herself as a Pony Club child walking beside her mother as they went down to the field together to lunge Shantih. "Don't worry, dear, I'll soon take the tickle out of her feet, then you can get up and I'll lunge you both for a bit. Soon tighten up your seat," breezed Jinny's Pony Club mother.

"Would you look where you're going?" warned Mr. Mac-Kenzie, as Jinny nearly walked straight into him. "Your head's wasted, lass."

"Sorry," gulped Jinny, suddenly realizing that she had reached the farm.

"I'll be giving you a penny for them."

"Not worth it," said Jinny. "Sorry I'm late for the milk."

"Now that would be nothing unusual. It's got the chilblains waiting for you in the milk shed."

Jinny fetched the full cans of milk.

"I hear you've been having a wee bit of trouble with your horse?"

Jinny scowled suspiciously at the old farmer. Sometimes she thought he knew everything that happened at Finmory, though how he found out she could never understand.

"A rare battle you're having with her and her winning

141

every time. You'll be for working on the circus act I'm thinking, her being a circus horse?"

"Is that so?" said Jinny.

"Aye, it might be. I told you well it's a man that one's needing."

"If you mean one of your sons knocking her about that is the last thing she needs, no matter how often you tell me."

Mr. MacKenzie stared out over the hills, sucking his pipe.

"Is it more a wee touch of class you have in mind for her?"

"What?"

"Then I've the very news for you. You'll be knowing Craigvaar House?"

"Yes," said Jinny. Craigvaar was a modern, snow-cemmed house with a housekeeper to keep it smooth and cared for while the family who had built it lived in Sussex. Since the Manders had been at Finmory there had never been anyone except the housekeeper staying at Craigvaar. It stood alone on a part of the moor that Jinny didn't know very well, but she had ridden past it once or twice when she had been out on Bramble. She had looked curiously at the clipped hedges, neat flowerbeds and reaches of smooth lawns. Standing up in her stirrups, Jinny had thought that she could make out several loose boxes almost hidden from view by rhododendron bushes, but she had never seen any sign of horses.

"Well, it's like this, you'll be having the new friends for the holidays. There's word in the village today that the Burnleys are coming for Easter."

"Are there any children?"

"A wee bit more than children. Clare will be thinking herself a young lady now and Spencer's away to Oxford, so I hear, so that'll be him out of the short trousers."

"More Petra," said Jinny. "Not much good to me."

Mr. MacKenzie regarded her disapprovingly. "It's the terrible speed you have on you," he said. "Would you be waiting a minute until I get the words out of my mouth. I haven't reached the horses yet."

"Horses!"

"If you were in the know with the horsey set the way

142

you're not," teased Mr. MacKenzie, "whenever you were hearing the name Clare Burnley you would be saying, 'Not *the* Clare Burnley,' and I'd be telling you, 'The very one'."

"I've never heard of her," said Jinny. "Is she a show jumper?"

"Indeed she is, and winning the big cups at all the shows in the South. She'll be one of these superstars, I'm thinking. Always with the winners."

Jinny narrowed her eyes and considered the farmer. She knew him well enough by now to suspect that he was pulling her leg.

"Now don't be looking at me like that. It's the truth I'm telling you. Clare Burnley herself stood where you're standing now, telling me all about the rosettes and cups she was always winning at the big shows."

Jinny grinned.

"Now don't you be laughing. Clare can stay on a horse, not like some I could mention."

"Are they bringing their horses with them?"

"Two. She'll be for the Inverburgh Show, winning all the cups there with her grand horses."

Jinny could tell from the tone of the farmer's voice that he wasn't too keen on Clare, but she thought that if Clare won cups for show jumping she must know quite a bit about horses.

"Do you think she'd help me with Shantih?"

"Well, I wouldn't like to say that. Don't you forget it's the toffs you're talking about when you're talking about the Burnleys."

As Jinny walked home she pictured Clare Burnley as dark and dashing, confidently riding a bay thoroughbred and wearing a black jacket, cream breeches and gleaming black boots.

"Camel's milk?" asked her father, who was going bald on top but had a thick beard the same colour as Jinny's hair. "Been to the Sahara for it?"

"No," said Jinny, "just to the farm BUT . . ." and she launched into a technicolor description of Clare Burnley and her horses.

"This going to be your Easter thing?" asked Ken, but not

really asking, more as if he knew before anything happened how it would all be in the end.

"Oh yes," Jinny assured him. "It's a smashing chance. She's bound to know all about schooling green horses."

"Bad enough sending kids to school, never mind horses," said Ken.

"How are you going to get to know her?" asked Mrs. Manders.

"Oh, I'll ride over. I expect she'll have heard about Shantih and be pleased to meet me," replied Jinny as casually as she could, trying not to think too much about her own jeans and sand shoes compared with Clare's breeches and boots—and not looking at Ken.

CHAPTER TWO

Jinny decided to ride to Craigvaar the next Saturday afternoon. She asked Mike to come with her. He said he would and went to catch Bramble and Punch.

"Where are you going?" Petra asked. Jinny told her. "I'll come too," said Petra.

"But you never ever ride," Jinny said, staring in dismay at her sister. "I mean you never do. So why should you want to today?"

"All the more reason why I should have a turn," replied Petra.

"Mike's coming," said Jinny. "And we're only going to look at the house. Mr. MacKenzie doesn't think the Burnleys have arrived yet. So you needn't think you'll meet them. And if you come there aren't enough horses."

"You can ride Shantih," said Petra.

"But there aren't enough saddles," stated Jinny desperately. The last thing she wanted was for Petra to see her being bucked off Shantih and go and tell their mother about it.

"Mike can ride bareback," organized Petra. "He often does."

"But we're going now," said Jinny, "and you haven't

144

done your practising." Petra was going to be a piano teacher when she left school and she practised faithfully every day. "Surely you don't want to come when you haven't done your practising. You'll fail your exam."

"Don't worry, I'll do it when I get back."

"Oh don't be so mean," said Jinny. "What do you want to come for? I'm telling you the Burnleys haven't arrived yet. You just think they're upper class and posh, the kind of people you want to get to know so that you can talk about them at school. But you needn't bother coming today because they won't be there."

"What's the matter?" asked Petra, giving her sister a hard stare. "Are you afraid to ride Shantih?"

"Don't be so silly! Of course I'm not afraid. I just don't see why you want to come with us today," and Jinny marched down the garden to the stables. She could see it was going to be one of those days when everything went wrong. "Well, you can groom Bramble yourself," she shouted back over her shoulder.

Mike had caught the ponies and brought them in to their stalls.

"I've got them," he said when he saw Jinny taking down a halter.

"Petra's coming," said Jinny darkly.

"Petra!" exclaimed Mike in amazement. "But she never does."

"It's the Burnleys," said Jinny. "She wants to get to know them so they can all be frightfully frightful together. Well, I shouldn't think they'll be a bit like that. Horsey people aren't. And they may not even be at Craigvaar."

"You're not going to ride Shantih?"

"Yes I am," said Jinny defiantly. "Of course I am."

"Then we'll never reach Craigvaar. All we'll do is watch her throwing you off."

"That's only when I'm schooling her," snapped Jinny. "She's quite different when we're going for a ride."

"Now let's get a move on," said Petra, coming into the stable. "We want to get there while it's still dry. What shall I do?"

145

Mike handed her a dandy and reluctantly Jinny went off to catch Shantih.

Shantih, waiting at the field gate, whinnied when she saw her. She pushed her head into the halter and crushed through the gateway before Jinny could get the gate open properly.

"Steady, steady," muttered Jinny, shutting the gate while Shantih pranced at the end of the rope in her eagerness to follow the Highlands. "Now behave yourself," said Jinny sharply. "Petra's coming with us and we don't want to let her see you carrying on."

Shantih broke into a trot, dragging Jinny towards the stable. Her head was high in the air, her hoofs tittuping on the ground as Jinny dug her elbow hard into her shoulder to stop her cantering.

"Oh stop it, Shantih," Jinny muttered between clenched teeth. "Behave yourself. Stop being such an idiot."

Shantih took no notice of her. She charged through the low stable doorway and, with a clatter of hooves on the stone floor, stormed her way into her box. Jinny just managed to avoid being crushed against the door.

"Gosh," said Petra. "She is fresh. Is she always like that?"

"Like what?" said Jinny. "If you mean alive, yes she is always alive and that's the way I want her to be."

Shantih stood alert and tense while Jinny groomed her. She stuck her head into the air, refusing to let Jinny put her bridle on.

"Can't you manage?" asked Petra.

"Of course I can," said Jinny, standing with the bridle in one hand while Shantih's giraffe neck stretched out of reach above her.

"Here," said Petra, bossing her way into the box, and because she was taller than Jinny she was able to put her hand over Shantih's nose and hold her head down while Jinny slipped her bridle on.

"Thanks," said Jinny ungratefully.

"That's all right," said Petra. "Miss Benson was only saying the other day that even when I don't know much about a thing she could always rely on me to be sensible."

Jinny groaned aloud. There was no doubt about it, her sister was sensible.

Jinny slid the saddle on to Shantih's hard, high back and buckled up the girth. Mike and Petra had taken their ponies out into the yard and Shantih pushed against the box door, clattering it with her forehoofs, trying to follow them.

"Oh, wait a minute," shouted Jinny, her voice muffled under the saddle flap as she struggled to tighten the girth. "Now get back and wait a moment." Jinny yanked at Shantih's bit and she skittered back in a wild flurry of mane and tail.

"Right," said Jinny and led her out to where the other two were already mounted.

"Which way are we going?" asked Mike.

"Along the road to Glenbost and then up the track to Craigvaar," said Jinny, pulling down her stirrups. The other way was to go straight on to the moors and to ride over the hills to Craigvaar, and Jinny didn't fancy taking Shantih straight on to the moors. She needed the trot along the road to settle her.

Jinny swung herself into the saddle and felt Shantih sink back on her quarters. Then the chestnut neck arched above her as Shantih reared. Automatically Jinny leaned forward. She found her other stirrup and as Shantih touched down she closed her legs against Shantih's sides and urged her on.

"Ready?" asked Mike.

" 'Course," said Jinny. "She'll jump over the top of you if you don't get a move on."

Punch laid back his ears and kicked out peevishly as Shantih came plunging into him.

"Oh for goodness' sake get a move on," said Jinny, tugging at Shantih's reins to keep her behind the ponies. She knew that once they were trotting Petra would need to concentrate on her posting and wouldn't be able to look behind to see what was happening and Jinny thought that would be for the best.

They rode past Mr. Mackenzie's farm and out on to the road to Glenbost.

"O.K. to trot?" asked Mike, and without waiting for an answer he roused Punch into a trot.

Jinny sat down hard in the saddle and kept Shantih behind the rounded rumps of the Highlands. "You're not going in front," she told her horse. "I know what you'd do if you got in front, next thing we'd be galloping over the horizon. This is quite fast enough."

A gusting wind blew shreds of black cloud over a scoured sky. The mountains were leaden and rooted, four-square, into the moorland. Moors, sky and mountains were etched shades of grey.

As Jinny rode, the tight knot in her stomach unclenched a little. She felt Shantih relax, her trot become more even, her shies at blown strands of dead bracken or sudden birds were less violent. She was beginning to accept the bit and move less rigidly. Jinny clapped her sleek neck and laid her hand on the rounded bulk of the mare close behind her saddle. Perhaps it was a good thing that Petra had wanted to come with them. Riding with both ponies was giving Shantih more confidence. Jinny knew that if she had been by herself Shantih would have been bucking and rearing long before this.

The scarlet Post Office van came rattling towards them. The Highlands trotted sedately on. Shantih stared, pop-eyed. She cantered on the spot, her tail kinked over her back, snorting through wide nostrils as the van passed her, then she plunged after the ponies, shrieking to them not to leave her behind.

"She hardly looked at it," Mike called back.

Jinny grinned. "There's a brave horse," she praised. "Well done the clever old horse."

But Jinny knew that if she had been by herself she could never have got Shantih past the van. They would have been galloping flat out back to Finmory by now. Knowing this made the day seem more grey than ever. The mountains squatted like monster toads against the skyline, their heavy gloom weighing down on Jinny as she rode. There was just a chance that the Burnleys might have arrived at Craigvaar. Should they be there, this wasn't the way Jinny wanted to meet them, all cluttered round with her family. If they met Clare Burnley now, Jinny knew who she would talk to and it wouldn't be herself; it would be Petra.

Jinny scowled at her sister's back. The triangle of Petra's headscarf flipped neatly over Petra's dark curls, her anorak and corduroy trousers looked smart and sharp-edged the way clothes always did on Petra. Jinny's long tails of red hair snarled in the wind, her anorak was crumpled and clinging and the tears in her jeans were cobbled together with Jinny's giant stitches.

"But I'm the one who needs to get to know Clare. She's going to help me to school Shantih," Jinny thought. "She must know I'm the one who's mad about horses. She must. She'll see Shantih and know that she's an Arab."

"I say, that's a stunning Arab you've got there." Jinny could hear Clare's voice quite clearly. She saw her walking towards Shantih, taking firm strides in her gleaming black boots. She held out her hand to clap Shantih, shook her long dark hair and looked at Jinny with a friendly, level gaze. "Where did you find this one?" she asked.

A sheep unfolded suddenly at the roadside. Shantih flung herself sideways, Jinny lost a stirrup, banged her nose on Shantih's neck and saw stars.

"Dreaming again?" said Petra scornfully.

"I was not," denied Jinny. "You weren't even looking at me so how could you know what I was doing?"

"I don't need to look," said Petra. "I know too well."

"Turn up here?" asked Mike, and they all slowed their horses to a walk as they followed the rutted track over the hillside.

In spite of Jinny's efforts to keep Shantih back, by the time they had reached the turn in the track that brought Craigvaar into sight she was well ahead of the Highlands. Looking down at the detached house with its snow-cemmed walls, immaculately painted woodwork and landscaped grounds, Jinny realised that asking Clare Burnley for help wasn't going to be as simple as it had seemed standing in the kitchen at home. Everything about Craigvaar was smoothed with money. The tennis court, the clipped hedges, weedless gravel paths, formal flowerbeds and modern outbuildings. It all looked as if it were wrapped in an invisible plastic balloon that protected it from the gales and winter snows. As if, Jinny thought, it had been pre-packed in Sussex and dropped down here from a helicopter.

Shantih fretted irritably as Jinny tried to make her stand

and wait for the others. The open moorland stretched out around them; space and freedom blew down from the hills where Shantih had once roamed wild with Mr. MacKenzie's herd of Shetlands. She stood gazing round through her huge Arab eyes with their fringing of long lashes, drinking in the wild moorland. Jinny knew that if she eased her fingers the least fraction on the reins or tightened her legs on Shantih's sides they would be away, galloping like fire over the moors.

A bit of Jinny longed to urge Shantih forward. She had often galloped the Highlands over the moors but they were native ponies, sure-footed and canny. Shantih would blaze over the bracken and heather, light and swift as fire, and yet Jinny was afraid that she might come down, breaking a leg, which was the same as killing yourself when you were a horse, or flounder into one of the emerald green bogs that could suck a horse down to its death no matter how hard it struggled to escape.

At the back of Craigvaar a large paddock was fenced off from the moorland by white-painted railings that sparkled in the grey light. Jinny looked at it longingly.

"And what a car," she thought. Jinny didn't know much about cars, but she did know that the one which crouched opulently in front of the house wasn't a Mini.

"But if the car's here," Jinny thought suddenly, "that means *they* must be here too."

Although the track to Craigvaar was open to anyone, Jinny felt that she was trespassing. She looked quickly round for Petra and Mike.

"Hurry up," Jinny shouted, but they didn't hear her. Mike had dismounted and was examining something by the side of the track.

Jinny glanced back at Craigvaar—and started with delight. A girl with curly blonde hair had brought a steel grey horse into the paddock. As Jinny watched she uncoiled the lunge rein from her hand and, flicking a long-lashed driving whip, sent the grey horse round at a walk.

For a second Jinny hesitated, torn between a sudden shyness and the realisation that this was her chance to speak to Clare, for surely the girl must be Clare Burnley. Mike was still crouching down by the side of the track. Petra was leaning over, watching what he was doing. And really Jinny didn't want them with her when she was talking to Clare. Mike didn't matter but Petra would make her say all the wrong things and laugh at her afterwards.

"They can catch me up," Jinny decided. "It's their own fault for being so slow," and she let Shantih trot forward.

Jinny turned off the track to ride down to the paddock and Shantih's trot became a canter, no faster than a slow trot but coiled like a spring ready to burst out into furious speed.

When Jinny reached the paddock the girl paid no attention to her. Jinny's heart sank. If this was Clare Burnley she wasn't in the least like Jinny's imaginings. She was quite fat, maybe not so much fat as solid. Her face was large and round, and her curly blonde hair was stylishly cut and set. Her hand on the lunge rein was firm and unyielding and she grasped the whip tightly in her other hand.

"Hello," said Jinny, but the girl didn't even look up.

Jinny tried again.

"Hello," she repeated in a louder voice. "I do like your horse." The horse was a sixteen two hunter with a hogged mane and clipped out heels. He had the same solidity as the girl, as if they were both building up their weight to be weighed in gold, thought Jinny.

Still the girl didn't reply. "Perhaps I shouldn't interrupt when she's lungeing," Jinny thought and watched silently as the horse walked round obediently. It was obvious that the girl knew what she was doing. The grey horse moved like a lumbering, clockwork toy. Used to the grace and lightness of Shantih, Jinny could only see him as a heavy, half dead thing.

"Trot," commanded the girl, and instantly the horse was trotting, his spiky neck arched, his Roman nose tucked in and his hoofs' drumbeat steady.

Petra and Mike came into sight and Shantih whinnied to the Highlands through wide nostrils. Still the girl didn't take her eyes off her horse. Jinny swallowed uncomfortably, realising that Clare Burnley was ignoring her on purpose.

"Perhaps it isn't that I'm disturbing her, perhaps she just doesn't want to speak to me," thought Jinny, as Clare

151

brought the horse into the centre of the circle. "Well, I'll not be disturbing her if I speak to her now," she decided and urged Shantih closer to the paddock fence.

"He lunges very well," Jinny said, making sure that her voice was loud enough for Clare to hear. "I wish I could lunge Shantih like that."

Without looking up, slowly and decisively Clare Burnley turned her back on Jinny. She gave the grey a piece of carrot then with a crack of her whip sent him round in the opposite direction.

"Well . . ." thought Jinny, but she didn't have time to put into words what else she thought. As the whip cracked Shantih reared straight up. Again Clare flicked her whip over the grey horse's back and Shantih touched down, wheeled round and was tearing over the moor in a panic-driven frenzy. Clinging to her back, Jinny hardly realised what had happened. She had felt Shantih rear suddenly and with a reflex action had dropped her reins and grabbed a handful of mane and then there was nothing but blinding speed. A blur of speed that flashed the moorland unfocused past Jinny's eyes. There was nothing she could do but sit tight, as, plunging and terrified, Shantih burst through the grey silence.

Sometimes Shantih stumbled on a loose rock or caught her hoof on a heather root or rabbit burrow; once Jinny felt her quarters sink in the boggy ground and for a fear-bright moment felt her struggling to release herself; but the impetus of her flight threw Shantih forward over all obstacles. Whether she was racing uphill or careering down sheer rocky slopes, Shantih never slackened her breakneck pace. To Jinny they almost seemed to be skimming above the rough ground, like a form of flying.

Gradually Jinny began to get her breath back. She sat up and tried to pull on Shantih's reins, but Shantih's head was stretched low in front of her and Jinny might as well have been riding in a halter for all the difference the snaffle bit made. She looked around, not recognising the part of the moor they were on. Then to her right Jinny saw the silver glint of Loch Varrich. They must have galloped for miles to have reached it. Loch Varrich was beyond the standing

152

stones and not a place Jinny visited very often. There was a deserted eeriness about the sheet of water so alone and so high in the hills. Then Jinny remembered how flat the ground was at the sides of the loch. If she could guide Shantih towards it she would be able to gallop her in a circle until she came to her senses and slowed down.

To Jinny's relief Shantih plunged on towards the loch. Pulling on one rein with both hands Jinny managed to turn her, and force her to gallop in a wide circle when they reached the shore.

After Jinny had galloped her round several times she felt Shantih's frenzied speed slow down a little. "Whoa, steady, steady, steady. Whoa Shantih," cried Jinny, and for the first time since she had started galloping Jinny felt that Shantih had heard her, remembered that there was someone on her back. Gradually she slowed down to a canter, then to a jagged trot and at last to a walk.

Jinny threw herself to the ground and collapsed. Her legs, worn out with holding on, stretched uselessly in front of her, but her grasp on the reins brought Shantih to a halt. She stood with her muzzle brushing the ground, legs splayed, blood red nostrils gasping at the air. Her face was dark and dripping with sweat and her chestnut coat curded white between her legs and round her belly.

"Oh horse, horse," said Jinny despairingly. "What did you have to go and do that for? And with Petra there to see you. She'll tell them all about it. Make it sound worse than it really was. And Mummy'll start to worry. Oh Shantih, why did you have to be so silly?"

Jinny knew that it had been Clare's whip that had scared Shantih, that she had been given a fright, but she also knew that if her parents got it into their heads that Shantih was dangerous they would stop her riding the Arab.

"You could have broken your legs galloping like that."

Jinny knelt beside Shantih and examined her legs. There were a few scratches, and a cut on her off fore was bleeding a little. Jinny looked back over the hillside, the way they had come. She couldn't imagine how Shantih had galloped over such rocky ground without falling.

Jinny dipped her handkerchief into the loch and bathed

Shantih's leg. To her relief she saw that the cut was little more than a scratch. "Your lucky day," she told the mare. She loosened Shantih's girths, and, walking beside her, led her towards the dark shapes of the standing stones. Once she reached the stones Jinny knew her way back to Finmory.

At the head of the loch there was a clump of pine trees. Not forestry battery trees, but gnarled and real. A hawk was roosting on the dead topmost branch of one of them. It launched itself into the air as Jinny and Shantih approached, sailing over their heads on huge wings—wings that flared across the entire sky, turning upwards at the tips as the bird sailed and swung, riding the air currents. It twisted its head, watching them with a bright yellow eye.

"Not an eagle," Jinny thought. "Too much white on it, and yet it's too big to be anything else."

The hawk tilted a wing and sailed into a distant speck.

"I'll tell them about it," Jinny said to Shantih, "when they start going on about you."

Jinny's family started to go on about Shantih as soon as it saw Jinny. First it was Petra, who had got home before Jinny and given a breath by breath account of Jinny's vanishing out of sight over the moor.

"Well, once she'd started galloping I was enjoying it so much I thought we might as well have a really good gallop," lied Jinny.

"You did not," said Petra. "You should have seen your face. You were scared stiff."

"I was not."

"Well, I would have been scared stiff for you if I'd been there," said Mrs. Manders. "It does look as if you'll need to find someone to help you with Shantih. She's too much for you by yourself."

"Don't think that that Clare Burnley will be much good," said Mike. "There was Jinny going like the wind and Petra screaming and d'you know she never even let on that we were there. Just kept on playing at circuses with that old horse."

"That's what did it," said Jinny. "Shantih thought she was a ringmaster, cracking that whip."

Mr. Manders and Ken had been in Inverburgh buying

154

clay and glazes for their pottery so that they didn't hear about the runaway until the evening.

"Well?" said Jinny's father when he got home. "Let's hear your version. Mr. MacKenzie has given me his."

He glanced quickly at the sideboard in case there was a letter for him. Since he had been at Finmory, Mr. Manders had written a book about the appalling social conditions in Stopton and the hopeless dead end lives of the young people who were trapped there. Now he was waiting to hear from the publisher, watching for every post in case there should be a letter accepting his manuscript. To her dismay Jinny saw that the only letter for her father looked very like a telephone account.

"Mr. MacKenzie seemed to think you galloped from Craigvaar to Loch Varrich?"

Jinny supposed that she had.

"And what would have happened if you'd come off and hurt yourself?"

"But I didn't. That's a hypo-thingy question and Enoch Powell would refuse to answer it. And anyway I wouldn't have been riding Shantih on the moors if Petra hadn't wanted to meet the Burnleys."

"Don't pass the buck," said her father in his we-are-not-amused voice. "One thing for a horse to get a bit of a fright and gallop off. Quite another for it to go mad."

Jinny felt it was time to remember the strange hawk.

Mike brought down his bird book but Jinny couldn't find a picture that looked like her bird. She spread her arms out, curling up her fingers, and soared round the room.

"It's wings bent back at the elbows," she said.

"Must have been an eagle," said Mike. "That book's got all the British birds in it."

"No way," said Jinny, "unless someone had been dis-tempering it. And it was huge."

"A roc?" suggested Ken.

"Maybe," agreed Jinny. "And Shantih was Sinbad's flying horse."

Jinny shivered, reliving the thrill and exultation of her gallop. But really she knew that Shantih had been danger-

155

ously out of control, that it had only been good luck that had prevented them from falling. Clare Burnley would never have allowed a horse to behave like that with her. Jinny remembered the girl's control of the heavyweight horse she had been lungeing. If that had been me standing in the centre the horse would have been doing exactly as he liked, Jinny admitted to herself.

"Flying horse or not," said Mr. Manders, "there is to be no more of this dangerous galloping about. You must find some way of controlling Shantih."

Jinny knew from the tone of her father's voice that he meant what he said, and she knew that her mother was right —she needed help to school Shantih.

"Are you sure that Clare Burnley saw us?" Jinny asked hopefully. "Maybe she just didn't notice us?"

"Blimey," said Mike, "we were like a tornado in her back garden."

"I am sure, sure, sure she saw us," said Petra.

Jinny fiddled with her hair. Getting Clare to help her wasn't going to be as easy as she had hoped, but it still seemed the only way.

CHAPTER THREE

It was a week before Jinny saw Clare Burnley again. Twice she had ridden Bramble over the moors by Craigvaar but there had been no sign of Clare or her horses. Once when they were riding home from school the Burnleys' car had roared past Mike and herself, almost pushing Bramble into the ditch. The man driving it had been so like Clare that Jinny was certain he must be her father. She had caught a glimpse of his fleshy hands gripping the wheel and his stolid, lardy face staring straight ahead.

"Road hog," Mike had yelled after him.

"He won't hear you," Jinny said as she soothed Bramble's ruffled dignity. In Glenbost, people on wheels usually made way for people on legs and that was the way Bramble liked it.

"If I were shouting down his ear he wouldn't hear me," said Mike.

Jinny agreed, but as the ponies plodded on she couldn't help wondering what it would be like to be sitting at the wheel of a powerful, humming monster, driving straight on, so secure and safe that you didn't even notice that other people existed, never mind worrying about what they might be feeling.

On Friday, Jinny and Mike broke up for the Easter holidays. The last afternoon had been an Open Afternoon when the parents had come to school to see their children's work. When the Manders had first come to Finmory Mr. Gorman had been the schoolmaster and the children had spent all their time struggling with endless arithmetic problems, parsing and analysing, reading and spelling,.and being belted if they spoke. But now Mr. Gorman had retired and Miss Broughton was their teacher, and Glenbost's one classroom wasn't like a schoolroom at all. In some ways it was better than being at home. There was always something new and interesting to do.

Before the parents arrived Jinny had looked round the classroom with a warm satisfaction, like taking bread out of the oven. They'd all done well and their work was there to prove it. George MacKenzie's project on Scottish oil—neat and full of facts; Dolina's project that had started off with taking exact notes of everything her family ate for a week and had allowed Dolina to cook traditional Scottish food for them all, then had led on to the problems of food supply in an Indian village; Ian Cuthbertson had found out about fish farming, and Mike's project on astronomy meant that his stars and planets were pasted over the classroom windows and ceiling.

Jinny had created a world of horses—which hadn't sounded as if it would have much arithmetic in it. "Can they count?" Miss Broughton had asked. "Of course," Jinny had replied indignantly. "Not in tens then," Miss Broughton had said. "They haven't got ten fingers." "No," Jinny had agreed, "but in fives—four hoofs and a head."

So Jinny had had to work everything out for her horses in the scale of five. It also meant that she had been able to paint and draw Shantih whenever she had wanted to.

"What did you like best?" Jinny nagged her parents as they came out of the school together.

"Dolina's shortbread," teased her father.

"Oh, I mean best of *my* bit," said Jinny.

"Your pencil drawings of Shantih lying in the straw," said her mother.

Jinny stood still in delight. "Fancy you knowing! Just fancy you knowing," she cried. "They are my absolutely best thing." In a few delicate lines Jinny had managed to capture the essence of the Arab; the stored energy packed in her muscles; the vibrant life of her mane and the almost brittle appearance of her fine-boned legs. "Oh, I am glad you liked them."

"I need some things from the shop," said Mrs. Manders, and they all walked across the road to Glenbost's one and only shop, Jinny still glowing from her mother's appreciation.

Just before they reached the door the Burnleys' car came zooming down the street and stopped in front of the shop. The car doors were flung open and suddenly the village street seemed overflowing with Burnleys. They flooded, loud voiced, up the steps into Mrs. Simpson's.

"My dear Mrs. Simpson," cried the slim, black-haired lady as she angled her jaw, leaned forward over the counter, closed her eyes and pressed her cheek against Mrs. Simpson's. "How wonderful to see you again. And how are you? Not a thing has changed. We are all so delighted to be back. I've just been telling Pogo how naughty he has been not coming in to see you before this. When Clare told me that she and Daddy had been at Craigvaar for a whole week and hadn't been in to stock up at your dear little shop I could hardly believe it. I am just not interested in free offers from a supermarket when Mrs. Simpson can supply us with anything we'll want."

"Oh Ma, do try to understand," Clare Burnley's voice bellowed from her gum boots. "Mrs. Simpson, don't listen to her. Pa had to go into Inverburgh and I was with him

158

so I just popped into the super and bought a very few essentials. I knew Ma would be straight in here the minute she was off the train, I really knew she would."

"Pogo, do come and say hello again to Mrs. Simpson. Coming back to Glenbost would not be the same if you weren't here. I'm forever telling our grocer at home about the wonderful service you give us in Scotland."

"Gosh, yes," echoed Clare.

Jinny was standing in the shop doorway, watching in amazement as Mr. Burnley, swelling out of his check tweed suit and bulging under his deerstalker, came obediently striding into the shop. A tall boy followed him in.

"Spencer, darling, come and say hello to Mrs. Simpson," Mrs. Burnley commanded after her husband had shaken the shopkeeper's hand.

The boy slanted his jaw against Mrs. Simpson and held out a limp hand. He regarded her distantly under his lowered eyelids.

"Poor Spencer," said his mother. "It is just too too boring for him. He's only here for one day. Sunday he's off again, aren't you, darling?"

"But Miss Clare will be staying?" asked Mrs. Simpson.

"Gosh yes," said Clare. "I've got the nags with me. I wouldn't dream of missing the Inverburgh Show. It is my favourite show. I mean to say, even when I'm at Windsor or the White City I'm just wishing like mad all the time that I was at Inverburgh. There is nowhere else like it."

"Well, I'm sure they'd all be missing yourself if you were not to be going and that's a fact I'm telling you," said Mrs. Simpson, her mouth smiling at Clare.

"Might give them the chance to win their own cups for a change, eh?" chortled Mr. Burnley.

"Have you a nice big box?" asked Mrs. Burnley, "and then we can take everything home together. Now Spencer, you shall choose supper tonight."

Spencer's lizard eyes flickered over the crowded shelves. His black pencil-line moustache crawled down the corners of his mouth. The expressionless oval of his face was bland as a reflector disc.

159

"But is there anything here one would want to eat," he drawled. "I can't see a single thing."

"Now don't be so tiresome, darling. I shall choose for you. Can you remember last summer you had those wonderful cans of pheasant?"

Mrs. Simpson remembered. She had bought in half a dozen tins knowing that eventually the Burnleys would buy them all.

Mr. Manders and Mike went for petrol and Mrs. Manders went back into the school to ask Miss Broughton if there was any more news about the new comprehensive that was being built in Inverburgh.

Jinny just stood and stared while Mrs. Burnley filled two boxes with supplies. So could hardly believe that the Burnleys were real.

"What a shower," said Mr. Manders when at last they were driving home. "They must have spent a fortune."

"Rather loud," laughed Mrs. Manders.

"Loud," agreed her husband.

"Good job Ken wasn't there to see them," said Mrs. Manders. "He would have been telling them what possessions do to you."

"Too much even for Petra," grinned Mike.

Jinny was silent. She was staring through the car window, seeing nothing, hearing nothing. Inside her head the Burnleys moved in a golden haze, strong and powerful. They weren't like ordinary people, not people Jinny knew.

"Darling, you shall choose supper."

"But would one want to eat anything that's here?" said Jinny, moving in her golden dream.

She sat beside Clare as they drove up from the Burnleys' Sussex estate, bringing up Shantih and Clare's horses to win all the cups at the Inverburgh Show.

Astride Shantih, Jinny circled the Burnleys' paddock at a collected canter. Clare stood in the centre, sun glinting on her bright face.

"Gosh," she enthused. "That really is the most terrific horse you've got there. Don't mind telling you I'm boringly jealous."

Mike poked Jinny in the ribs. "Wake up," he said. "We're home."

Jinny was jolted back to reality, blinking in amazement as she realised her father was stopping the car in front of Finmory.

"D'you think," Jinny asked her mother, "you could alter that pair of Petra's cavalry twill trousers for me?"

Arms full of shopping, half in, half out of the car, Mrs. Manders turned in astonishment. "I've been trying to get you to try them on for months!" she exclaimed. "Whatever made you think of them just now?"

"Dunno," said Jinny, but she did. Clare had been wearing cavalry twills.

After a mug of coffee, a cheese sandwich and two tomatoes, Jinny went to catch Shantih.

"I'm going to lunge you," she told her horse. Shantih regarded her with a mild gaze. "Here you are now, looking as if butter wouldn't melt, but the second I get you out in the field you'll be all over the place like a kite. It's an anchor you need."

Jinny considered the idea as she groomed. Some kind of hook attached by a rope to the saddle that you could throw into the ground when your horse bolted. The Manders' patent safety horse anchor. But she decided that most people wouldn't be very keen to be seen with it hanging from their horses. She gave Shantih's quarters a final thwack with the duster then went in search of the clothes line and someone to help.

"No," said Ken. He was in the pottery trying out a new glaze. "And don't ask me again. If you feel you must make that horse dizzy," Ken shrugged his bony shoulders, "then that's up to you. But don't keep asking me to help you."

"It's to improve her," pleaded Jinny. "All the books say you must lunge a horse to improve it."

"Did you ever," asked Ken, "see a horse, left alone to be a horse, going round and round in circles by itself?"

Jinny didn't answer. She banged the pottery door and went to look for Mike.

A quarter of an hour later she was knotting the clothes line on to Shantih's bit ring by herself.

"Clare Burnley didn't need her family to help her," Jinny told Shantih, "so I don't see why I should need mine. Her grey didn't need anyone to lead him round so I don't see why you should."

Jinny led Shantih down to the field. Punch and Bramble, who hadn't been fed that day since they hadn't done any work, came over hopefully.

"Get out of the way," Jinny warned them, her voice as close to a Burnley boom as she could manage.

The Highlands ignored her. She flicked the end of the clothes line at Punch, remembering too late that that was the one thing that was certain to upset Shantih. Punch only looked surprised but Shantih flung herself away from the rope, almost pulling it out of Jinny's hands.

"Oh, get away with you!" she screamed at the ponies. "Go on. Go and eat grass."

Bramble twitched his ears. He had smelt the sugar in Jinny's pocket and was more interested in it than in grass. Jinny picked up a handful of earth and threw it at the ponies. They looked offended. Shantih plunged backwards and this time Jinny dropped the clothes line and Shantih cantered to the far corner of the field.

"Dehydrated dogfish," swore Jinny, which was what her father said when she was there and he couldn't say what he was thinking. Bramble wuffled at her jeans' pocket and Jinny slapped him hard on the nose. "Didn't you notice," she demanded, "I've just thrown stones at you to scare you off."

Bramble's feelings were hurt but he knew now that Jinny definitely had sugar. "Get away," Jinny yelled. The Highlands ignored her. She ran at them, shaking her arms and drumming her fists against Bramble's shoulder. The ponies took a few reluctant steps away from her but by the time she had picked up the end of the clothes line and wound Shantih in they were close beside her again.

Jinny stood breathing slowly and deeply, then she dropped the clothes line, caught the ponies by their forelocks and led them out of the field and into their stalls.

"You can stay there and rot," she told them and, fastening their head-collars securely, she marched back to the field.

"Right," she told Shantih, "let's get lungeing."

Jinny picked up the clothes line and led Shantih into the centre of the field. She straightened her shoulders, set her feet firmly on the ground and looked sternly at her horse.

"Round you go," Jinny said, still trying to sound like Clare. She swung her arm out to send Shantih round in a circle but the chestnut shied away from her, turned her head in towards Jinny and stuck her quarters out of the circle. "That's all wrong," said Jinny. "You're not meant to do that. I stand still and you walk round."

Jinny made a dash to try to get behind Shantih and chase her round but no matter how quickly Jinny moved Shantih was quicker. Jinny could not get behind her. This way and that the Arab and the girl careered about the field.

At last Jinny gave up. She sat down on the grass, her face scarlet, tears of frustration burning her eyes. This was the kind of thing that would never happen to Clare Burnley. At the end of the rope Shantih watched suspiciously, ready to spring away should Jinny show any sign of standing up again. She rolled her eyes nervously, snatched up a mouthful of grass and stood not swallowing it, tense and quivering.

"Oh horse," said Jinny. She got up slowly and with a lump of sugar in her open palm walked towards the chestnut. Shantih dropped her head to Jinny's hand, lipped up the sugar and stood crunching it. Jinny fed her more sugar and ran her hand lovingly down her neck, straightening her tangled mane.

"It's no good going on like this, tormenting each other," Jinny told Shantih bitterly.

"Then come for a ride," said Ken's voice.

Jinny jumped and looked round. Ken was leaning over the field gate.

"I'd like to try and see your hawk," he said.

"I can't ride Shantih," said Jinny, telling the truth because it was Ken. "She might get a fright and go mad again."

"I'll ride her," offered Ken.

Jinny looked at him, wondering if he meant it. Now and again he would take one of the Highlands and go for a ride

163

over the moors by himself, but most of the time he thought
horses should be horses not human transport.

Ken sprang over the gate. "You take Bramble," he said
and took the clothes line from Jinny and began untying it
from Shantih's bridle. "Watch you don't let Kelly out. I've
shut him in the kitchen. He'd want to come with us if
he knew."

By the time Jinny had turned Punch out and got Bramble
ready Ken was mounted on Shantih and waiting in front of
the stable for her.

"Your stirrups are far too long," said Jinny, because it
was the only criticism she could think of. Shantih was standing quite still, relaxed and easy.

"She would have been mucking about all over the place
with me," Jinny thought, settling herself astride Bramble's
broad back.

"Loch Varrich?" Ken asked.

"The clump of pines at this end."

"Know them," said Ken and he led the way on to the
moors.

"Up to the standing stones?" asked Jinny.

"Quicker way," said Ken, and instead of going up to the
stones he followed a sheep track round to their right.

Ken let Shantih walk on a loose rein, and when she shied
or broke into a canter, he sat there seeming to pay no attention to her. Plodding along behind him, Jinny could just
make out the comforting whisper of his voice as he soothed
Shantih, gentled her, assured her of the rightness of the
world when he was with her. Jinny smiled to herself, feeling
her own distress flow out of her into the calm silence of the
hills. She let go of her jealousy—jealousy that Ken could
ride her horse better than she could. It didn't seem worth
bothering about. There was nothing in Ken that said, "Look
at me. See how clever I am." He only showed you how easy
it all was, how simple, if you would only learn to let it be.

The low light from the sun buttered the moors, spreading
gold and shadow. The rocks, starved throughout the winter,
sucked in the last of the daylight, and the mountains, a hazy
mauve, drifted between the sky and the earth.

Ken rode along the flat moorland until they were past the

hill crowned by the standing stones, then he turned and followed a sheep track that led over the hills.

"Want to change?" he asked, turning to Jinny.

"Oh, yes please."

They changed horses.

"Be easy now," said Ken, taking Bramble on in front. Jinny nodded, left the reins loose on Shantih's neck and sat balanced in the saddle. The Arab walked with a deft, delicate stride, her neck arched, her ears sensitive, the evening light glinting in her luminous eyes, her nostrils wrinkling— yet she was calm and gentle. For the first time Jinny felt there was no fear in her. They rode through pink and golden light, through washes of primrose and ice green; over land so still that Jinny could smell and taste the silence.

"Ken's way is quicker," Jinny thought as they came over the rise above Loch Varrich. Far behind them the sea glinted aquamarine against its jet black cliffs but the expanse of the loch had no colour in it. It lay, magic, remote, withdrawn, a stretch of white light in the glowing evening.

They rode slowly down towards the loch. Suddenly Ken stopped, looked back at Jinny, and, hardly moving his arm, pointed down to the water.

The hawk Jinny had seen the day before was flying low over the water. It paused, trembling on outstretched wings, hovering kestrel-like above its own reflection, almost motionless. Then, in a fury of speed, it plunged into the loch with talons outstretched, wings sabred back. Water exploded about it as it crashed the surface. It rose with a fish gripped in its feet, gave two beats of its powerful wings then seemed to shimmer into a crystal, rainbowed jewel as it shook the drops of water from its feathers.

The horses had seen the hawk. They stood as transfixed as their riders.

The hawk, still gripping the fish, flew to the group of pine trees. It stooped low over them, then it seemed to Jinny that for sheer and utter joy it rose up into the air, up through the glowing evening, rising with rapid wing beats until it was a pinned silhouette far above them, its wings spread wide. It hung there motionless, then came hurtling down, riding the air in wide sweeping spirals, calling all the time with a repeated high-pitched note; lord of the sun's rays; supreme and independent. It swept low over the pines above a mass of branches and twigs, landed on a topmost branch, looked fiercely around, then began to tear at the fish with its hooked beak.

Ken and Jinny waited, watching it. Then, without speaking, they both turned their horses at the same moment and began to ride back to Finmory.

Words were dried up in Jinny. She didn't have any for what she'd seen. Only a brightness that linked the great bird with the way she felt about Shantih; linked the hawk's flight and the Arab's speed. They were almost back at Finmory before she found anything to say.

"It's not an eagle, is it?" she asked, as Finmory's grey, substantial walls, the plume of smoke drifting from the chimney and her mother taking in the washing brought Jinny back into herself.

"An osprey," said Ken. " 'As is the Osprey to the fish, who takes it by sovereignty of nature'."

Jinny picked on the one bit she had understood. "But you hardly ever see them in Scotland," she said. "Only on that bird reserve place at Loch Garten."

"But we did," gloried Ken. "We did by sovereignty of nature."

Jinny stood watching Shantih rolling after she had turned her out. Somehow she didn't want to go in and hear her family talking about the osprey. Not just yet. She realised suddenly that she had forgotten all about Shantih being too wild to ride on the moors. She had ridden home as relaxed as if she had been on Bramble.

"Wish Clare had been there to see her," Jinny thought as she turned to wander contentedly back through the garden. Then she stopped stock still.

"I'll bet even the Burnleys would want to know about an osprey," Jinny said aloud into the darkening evening.

CHAPTER FOUR

Mr. and Mrs. Manders, Ken and Mike walked to Loch Varrich the next morning, taking Mr. Manders' binoculars with them. The potatoes Jinny had boiled for their lunch and the sausages she had fried were all cold by the time they got back and Petra's fresh fruit salad was tingeing into a rusty brown.

"You've been ages," Petra said as they came bursting into the kitchen. "Did you see it?"

"But really you didn't need to ask," Jinny thought. One glance at their faces told you that they had seen the osprey. They were all bright with having seen such a hidden thing.

"Two," said Mr. Manders. "His mate has arrived."

"They were super," said Mike.

"I can't believe they've come to Finmory," said Mrs. Manders. "They can't be the same pair as the ones on the nature reserve at Loch Garten, can they?"

"No," said Mr. Manders, pinching a cold sausage out of the frying pan. "I read up about them. There are several pairs nesting in Scotland but hardly anyone knows where. The Royal Society for the Protection of Birds publicized the Loch Garten ones so that everyone could have a chance to see them and realize for themselves how important it is to encourage them to start nesting here again. They used to nest all over Scotland but they were wiped out by egg-collectors taking their eggs and so-called naturalists shooting them so they could stuff them."

"They're giving us a second chance," said Ken. "To see if we know any better yet."

"What I know," said Jinny, "is that Petra and I have been slaving over a hot stove all morning and you're all so late your dinners are stone cold solid."

"I thought you'd been slaving over Shantih," said Petra.

Jinny didn't reply. She had spent most of the morning grooming Shantih, who was in her box looking like a show

167

horse, waiting for Jinny to ride her hopefully in the direction of Craigvaar.

"The most important thing," Mr. Manders said as they sat down to lunch, "is to keep everything about the ospreys absolutely secret. Not to talk about them at all. Say nothing."

"Shouldn't we tell the R.S.P.B.?" asked Mrs. Manders.

"I think we should wait until we're certain they're staying," said Mr. Manders.

"They were adding sticks to their nest this morning," said Mike. "I think they'll stay."

"If they're still around on Monday we'll phone the R.S.P.B., find out who their nearest official is and let him know," decided Mr. Manders. "Until then not a breath to anyone. Understand?"

" 'Course I wouldn't say anything," Mike assured his father.

"Some of the teachers at school would be really interested," said Petra. "I shouldn't think they'd tell anyone who would want to harm them."

"No," stated Mr. Manders firmly. "Absolutely no one. Tell one other person and they know someone they're certain they can trust so they tell them and in no time we'll have the moors full of birdwatchers. No one meaning to do any harm but nevertheless scaring off the ospreys, stopping them nesting or chasing them off their nest long enough for the hoodie crows to get at their eggs. And there are still some egg-collectors who'd take their eggs if they knew they were there."

Jinny had got up from the table and was filling bowls with Petra's fruit salad.

"Shall we go and see them this afternoon?" Petra asked her.

"Ken and I are going back to put up a hide," said Mr. Manders. "You can come and help. We've found a cave that should do if we rig up a screen in front of it. Far enough away not to risk disturbing them but near enough to see them with the glasses."

"You go with them," Jinny said to her sister. "I'm going to ride."

Jinny gave Shantih a final polish before she put her tack

168

on. In the dark box the chestnut's coat rippled with white light when she moved. Her mane and tail flowed silken, almost liquid, and her hoofs were gleaming with Mr. Manders' lubricating oil. She had been in her box for most of the morning and wanted to get out. She pushed restlessly against the half door, whinnying to Punch and Bramble, her neck arched and ears straining to hear their reply before she swung away to clatter round the box again.

"What I should do is school you for a bit first," Jinny told her. "That's supposed to settle you down. Only it wouldn't. You'd buck me off."

A bit of Jinny longed to be going with the others to see the ospreys. With her father's binoculars she would have been able to see the details of their feathers, the cold yellow eyes and the black curve of their beaks. But they weren't as important as the chance of seeing Clare.

"Did you know there are ospreys on the hills?" Jinny would say to her, and even the Burnleys would have to be interested in that.

Jinny ran her duster down Shantih's neck for a last time and went out to the tack room to get her saddle and bridle. Ken was standing in the doorway.

"Thought you were all going back to the ospreys," Jinny said. She wasn't pleased to see him. She knew from the way Shantih had been dashing round her box that she wasn't going to stand calmly in the yard waiting for Jinny to mount the way she had done last night for Ken, and Jinny would rather not have Ken watching the performance.

"We're waiting until it's dusk," said Ken. He stretched out his arms above his head, spreading his fingers wide. "How your family does manage to complicate things," he said. "There's old Tom dashing around organizing us all. Talking about phoning a society, building a hide. *One could not say, watching a hawk: I ought perhaps to do this for him*," quoted Ken, "but blimey, Tom can. We can't leave anything alone."

"You don't want the wrong people finding the nest," said Jinny scraping dried grass off Shantih's bit.

"Then leave them alone," despaired Ken. "Oh forget it. I'm only raving on." He spun round and Jinny thought he

169

was going, but he turned back. "Where are you off to?" he asked.

"Thought I'd ride towards Glenbost."

"Craigvaar?"

"Well, why not?" Jinny kept her eyes on the snaffle.

"Don't go sounding off about the ospreys," warned Ken. "Don't go looking for Clare Burnley so you can tell her."

"Wouldn't matter if the Burnleys knew," said Jinny, still not looking at Ken. "They wouldn't harm them. They're not the sort of people who'd go bird nesting."

"Why? Because they're rich?"

Jinny didn't answer.

"Phew! As if that made any difference. Tell no one. Understand?"

Jinny scrubbed at the green joints of the snaffle. She didn't want to hear what Ken was telling her.

"You can't know what people will do," Ken insisted. "So keep your mouth shut, understand?"

"I never said I was going to tell her," said Jinny.

"Then don't do it," said Ken, and to Jinny's relief he turned and left her.

When she had put Shantih's tack on she went inside to brush her hair, put on a clean sweater and change her usual messing-about-in anorak for her school one. She rubbed her black lacing school shoes on the sweater she had just taken off and put them on. Then she opened a drawer in her dressing table and took out a pair of yellow string gloves. She looked at them warily. Two years ago they had been a birthday present from an aunt who had heard that Jinny was keen on horses. They were not the sort of thing that Jinny ever thought of wearing. She put them in her pocket. Examining herself in the mirror, Jinny decided that she looked almost respectable. Only her faded, patched jeans looked like herself and since her mother hadn't had time yet to alter Petra's they were all she had, so that was that.

Jinny led Shantih out into the yard and swung herself into the saddle as the Arab plunged up the garden. Checking that no faces were watching from behind the windows, Jinny steered her horse back towards the track to the farm.

170

Shantih raked against the bit, fighting to get her head down and start bucking. Jinny clung tightly on to the saddle. The gentleness of last night was totally forgotten. Like a rubber ball, Shantih bounced and propped from one side of the track to the other.

"Oh stop it," beseeched Jinny. "Behave yourself, you idiot."

But Shantih was wild and uncontrollable. There was no understanding between herself and her rider.

They passed the farm at a flaunting trot, Shantih's hooves clattering faster and faster on the road to Glenbost. Her neck was stretched hard and rigid, her mouth at the end of the reins was an unyielding block of metal. Jinny braced her feet against the stirrups, and tugged with all her strength at the reins, but it only seemed to make Shantih's trot faster and more unbalanced.

"What would Ken do?" Jinny thought frantically. She knew that she was out of control, that she had no way of slowing Shantih down. A car rattled past them and Shantih panicked forward into a gallop. Jinny felt the same power surging through her horse as had carried them over the moors in a madness of uncontrollable speed.

Fear lent Jinny strength. She yanked furiously on the reins, jabbing Shantih in the mouth, no thought in her head except to bring Shantih back to a walk. Shantih changed to a trot but her speed scarcely slackened. Her head was almost vertical. Jinny could see the rolling whites of her eyes, her flaring nostrils and her foam-spattered lips.

"And I'm doing it to her," Jinny thought. "It's me that's making her like this. She wasn't like this with Ken. Everything I do with her is wrong but I don't know what else to do." Jinny blinked away tears. Her back and arms ached with pulling against Shantih and her legs had gone slack against the saddle. She was jolted helplessly up and down as Shantih battered on.

"I'll need to turn her back home," Jinny thought, knowing that once they reached Glenbost there might be more cars and certainly people to see her and report back to her mother.

Jinny shortened one rein, her hand only inches from

171

Shantih's bit. She kicked with her opposite leg but her heel bounced off the hard wooden surface of Shantih's side. With her head twisted sideways, Shantih continued to trot madly forward.

Jinny saw the track leading to Craigvaar ahead of her. "I'd need to tell Clare there were dinosaurs on the moors to make her speak to me if she saw me now," Jinny thought.

No sooner had the thought come into Jinny's head than she heard the sound of hooves coming from the direction of Craigvaar. Shantih heard them too. She stopped dead, then whinnied with a blast of noise that seemed to reverberate over the moors and hills and bounce back off the mountains.

Jinny felt her stomach freeze and her throat go dry. She knew it must be Clare. In desperation she sawed the reins, drumming her heels against the solid, tense block of Shantih. If she could have turned her she would have galloped her across the moors to escape from Clare. With terrifying certainty, Jinny knew that once Shantih saw Clare's horse she wouldn't be able to control her. Anything might happen. Jinny clenched her fist and battered it against Shantih's shoulder, shouting at her, kicking her, trying everything she could think of to bring Shantih's attention back to her rider. But it had no effect.

Round the bend in the track came Clare and Spencer Burnley. Clare astride the heavy grey and Spencer on a black thoroughbred. Shantih thundered out a welcome to them. The black horse squealed in reply and Jinny heard the crack of Spencer's stick down the horse's ribs.

The Burnleys trotted down the track, their horses schooled and obedient. They were talking to each other in loud voices, their faces turned away from Jinny.

"She had this most fantastic little flat," Clare was saying. "*The* thing for London." She appeared to be paying no attention to Shantih and Jinny but her hands were strong on the reins and her legs pushed the grey forward. They rode towards Jinny as if she were invisible.

"Well, ask the old man," said Spencer. "Got to ask, don't you know." His black horse tittuped beside the grey, stretching his long breedy head against the tight standing martingale. "Could use somewhere like that myself."

172

Jinny felt a tremor of excitement go through Shantih as she plunged towards the horses.

"Whoa, whoa, steady, steady, steady," shouted Jinny, trying to keep her back.

Snorting like a mustang, tail kinked over her back, Shantih pranced beside the Burnleys' horses. Jinny's stirrups crashed against Spencer's. His black horse kicked out peevishly and snaked his head at Shantih. Jinny's mind had gone blank with shame.

"I say, do you mind getting out of my way?" demanded Spencer.

Jinny didn't know how to. If she shortened her reins any more she would be holding the bit. She gulped, trying to explain, but only succeeded in making a dry croaking noise.

"That's the same kid that was staring at me the other day," boomed Clare. "Would you mind buzzing off? We are trying to go for a ride and we don't particularly want company."

Jinny went scarlet. Somehow she managed to fight Shantih back two or three strides behind the Burnleys but she could only hold her there for a second. Shantih sank her weight down on to her quarters and reared straight up, then, with a leap like a *capriol*, she had soared through the air and was barging her way between Clare and her brother.

Clare swore, adding something about the value of her horse. Plastered over Shantih's neck, stirrups clattering loosely by Shantih's sides, Jinny couldn't quite hear what it was.

"Oh, enough of this," said Spencer. "It really is too much," and he urged his horse into a canter.

Jinny heard Clare's deep laugh mingling with her brother's high-pitched, "Yawh, yawh, yawh," as their horses cantered down the road. She felt herself slipping helplessly to one side and tried to knot her fingers into Shantih's mane but knew that she couldn't stop herself from coming off.

There was a moment when a million hoofs seemed to be crashing down dangerously close to Jinny's head, moments when she was still holding on to Shantih's reins and the tarmac was skimming past under her eyes. Then she was

173

lying in the road watching Clare and her brother galloping along the verge, closely followed by Shantih in a blur of dangling reins, orbiting stirrups and flying hoofs.

Jinny lay for a minute or two before she could pull herself together enough to get up and walk stiffly to the side of the road. The sleeve of her good school anorak was badly torn. Her mother would not be happy about that, she thought. The side of her face was smarting and when Jinny put her hand up to it she discovered it was bleeding. She dipped one of her string gloves into the ditch and wiped her face on it.

The horses were all out of sight, and, terrified that they might meet a car or one of the occasional farm tractors, Jinny staggered after them. Her mind had gone numb. She couldn't bear to think about what had happened, but ran head down, her eyes fixed on the road and the school shoes that swung in and out of her vision; shoes that she recognised with surprise as her own each time they appeared.

"Hi," said Ken.

Jinny stopped running, stood swaying, then managed to lift her head high enough to be able to focus on Ken. He was leading Shantih.

"How did you . . ." began Jinny.

"Here," said Ken, grasping her by the elbow and guiding her to a rock at the roadside. "Sit down and get your head between your knees."

Minutes later Jinny looked up and was relieved to find that things were standing still again. "Is Shantih all right?" she asked.

"Fine," said Ken. "Slightly soiled by the company she was keeping when I caught her. I was walking into Glenbost when they all came storming down the road."

"Where are the Burnleys now?" Jinny asked.

"Over the moors and far away," said Ken. "Did you go up to Craigvaar?"

"No," said Jinny, telling the truth but knowing it was a lie. "They passed me on the road and Shantih would go with them."

"And they galloped away after you'd fallen off?"

Jinny's mind flipped lightly through the events of the last half hour.

174

"Don't think they like me much," she admitted." Can't say I blame them. I was making a fool of myself."

"That's why they galloped off leaving you on the ground? Cool, man, cool. Real nice folks to know. Introduce me sometime."

"Stop it," said Jinny, and getting to her feet she took Shantih's reins from Ken and began to lead her home.

It had been foul of the Burnleys to treat her like that, but Jinny knew how mad she got when stupid people kept trailing after her. She saw the Burnleys in her mind's eye riding bright and strong on their well-schooled horses. She didn't blame them for galloping off. She blamed herself for being so feeble.

"Didn't get a chance to tell them about the ospreys then?"

"Sometimes," said Jinny, "you are my least favourite person. I wasn't going to tell them."

"Well don't," said Ken. "Just don't."

CHAPTER FIVE

Mr. Manders phoned up the Royal Society for the Protection of Birds on Monday morning. He had been at Loch Varrich with Petra and Mike and they all felt sure that the ospreys were nesting.

"They were cracking off branches, big bits some of them, and carrying them in their feet to the nest. Took them ages to get them tucked in where they wanted them to go," said Mike.

Jinny had spent the morning ironing. She was helping her mother to make up for the ruin of her good-school-anorak.

"But why ever did you have your school one on?" her mother had demanded, gazing in dismay at the ragged sleeve. "It was new at Christmas."

"When Petra wears her good clothes everything's all right. She's being smart. But when I wear them it's shout, shout, shout. When you've completely spoiled my life I'll need to go to a psychiatrist and he'll understand me."

"Jinny," warned her father.

"Let me know when you're going and I'll come too," said her mother.

"Ride there on Shantih," suggested Mike. "Get cheap rates for parties of three."

"Ha, ha," said Jinny. "I'm glad you all find it so funny. I don't find it a bit funny to think that now Shantih belongs to me I don't know enough to school her *and* there's not one of you knows enough to help me."

"I thought," said her mother, "that we were talking about your anorak."

"I'm *thinking* about Shantih," Jinny said, and, slamming the door behind her, she had gone upstairs to her bedroom. She had stood at the window, looking down the garden to where Shantih was grazing peacefully with the ponies.

"If you think about it you'll be crying," Jinny had told herself, and she had found some paper and tried to draw the ospreys. She gave up after two or three unsuccessful attempts and went back, elbows on the windowsill, chin propped on her hands, to stare almost blindly across the garden to the sea, dreaming of how it might have been if only Shantih had behaved herself.

"Two men from the R.S.P.B. will be here this afternoon," Mr. Manders now told them, coming off the phone. "They were thrilled by the news. Osprey sightings have been reported in this area before but this is the first year anyone's reported a nest."

"Did you tell them that I was first to see it?" Jinny demanded.

"You can tell them yourself," said Mr. Manders.

"Bet Mr. MacKenzie knows," said Mike.

"Mr. MacKenzie knows everything," lamented Jinny. "When I go for the milk today he'll know everything about me falling off Shantih in front of the Burnleys, he'll know about the ospreys and he'll know that the R.S.P.B. men are coming here."

"How could he possibly?" asked Mrs. Manders.

"Well," said Jinny, "you'll see."

The two men from the R.S.P.B. arrived at about four o'clock. The one driving their battered Ford van was middle-aged, bearded, and peered like a caddis fly from the shell of his duffle hood. Sitting beside him was a young man with a fresh complexion and glasses. He introduced himself as Peter Stevens and his companion as Major Dobbington-Smith— "known to one and all as Dobbin." They shook hands with everyone, refused Mrs. Manders' offer of tea and, accompanied by Mr. Manders, they set off immediately for Loch Varrich.

Jinny went for the milk. She had a bet with herself about which subject Mr. MacKenzie would mention first—her violent separation from Shantih or the two strangers with powerful binoculars round their necks. Jinny decided on Shantih and lost.

"You'll be wanting extra milk for the visitors?" Mr. MacKenzie asked her.

"Please," said Jinny, thinking that no matter what she did these days she was never right. "Two more pints. I've brought an extra can."

"They'll be friends of your father's?"

"Yes," said Jinny.

"Keen on the bird watching?"

"Yes," said Jinny.

"I was thinking so, seeing them all away up the hill before they'd properly had time to get their feet through the door."

"Were you?" said Jinny.

Mr. MacKenzie spat thoughtfully. "I was just saying only the other day that you'd all taken a powerful notion to be tramping up to Loch Varrich, and before this you haven't even been saying as much as good morning to the wee loch."

Jinny said nothing.

"You'll have chiselled out the sea eagle I'm thinking," said Mr. MacKenzie, pouring out Jinny's milk.

"I knew you'd know," exclaimed Jinny.

"Aye," agreed Mr. MacKenzie. "There's not much moves on the hill but I have my eye to it."

"Well, one of your Shetlands had a great lump of wire caught up in her tail about three weeks ago, and Mike and I caught her and pulled it out. She nearly kicked Mike's face in."

177

"Och, I knew it fine. I don't trust them an inch myself. I was hoping you would notice it. I knew if you spotted it you wouldn't be resting until you'd the whole business sorted out. I dare say it was yourself that spotted the sea eagle?"

"If you must know," said Jinny, "yes it was. And the two men are from the R.S.P.B."

"Is that a fact you're telling me? I'd never have guessed it, and them looking like American tourists with their cameras and their fancy glasses."

"Do the ospreys always nest there?"

"In the old days, yes. Then it was the gentry like yourselves were for shooting them for taking the trout out of the loch. But the past year or two now they've made a go at the nesting again, and not a soul but myself knowing. Last year did they not manage it with the one wee one? So I'm hoping all your nonsense will not drive them away this year."

" 'Course not," said Jinny. "We're trying to protect them."

"Leave well alone," suggested Mr. MacKenzie.

"That's more or less what Ken said."

"Aye, he's not such a dooley as he looks, that one." Mr. MacKenzie lowered his head and looked at Jinny out of the corner of one pink-rimmed eye socket. "He's more fit for that mare than yourself, that's for sure."

"I suppose you know all about that too?"

"Straight from Clare Burnley's own mouth. Asking me who this girl was with the fancy horse and not able to stay on its back for two seconds together."

"I dare say you told her," said Jinny, picking up the milk cans.

"Indeed yes. I said we were acquainted. I'm thinking she'll be a bit lonely with her brother going off with his friends and leaving her here alone. Looking for a friend herself, I shouldn't wonder."

"Won't be me," Jinny told him and set off back to Finmory.

It was nearly dark by the time Dobbin, Peter and Mr. Manders got back.

"Not a doubt. They're nesting all right," said Dobbin,

178

standing in front of the drawing room fire. "What a piece of luck. What an afternoon. And you're the young lady who saw them first?"

Jinny said she was.

"Good. Good. Now the thing is to keep it secret. Not a word. Not a word from any of us," and he looked round them all, his glare resting slightly longer on Ken's long hair than it did on the others. "Clear on that? Good. Good. Pity you used the phone this morning. Never know who might overhear. In the early days at Loch Garten they sent telegrams to each other by code. Military operation. That's how we look at it. Trust no one. Even a duke may have an egg-collector lurking under his skin. Can't judge from the outside. Now, let's get down to brass tacks, get the details worked out."

Mrs. Manders suggested that before the details were planned they should all have supper.

When they had eaten, they all sat round the kitchen table and worked out a plan of campaign, as Dobbin called it.

Jinny told them that Mr. MacKenzie knew about the nest and that the ospreys had reared one chick last year.

"Good. Good," said Dobbin. "That means the locals aren't in the habit of popping up to the loch for a picnic, or someone would have spotted them last year and we'd have heard about them."

"You hardly ever see anyone on the moors," said Jinny.

"Good. Good," said Dobbin, and Peter said it only took one person to ruin the birds' chances and that the sooner they got a guard rota worked out the sooner he'd be pleased.

"Right away," said Dobbin. "She'll probably start laying tomorrow or the next day. Usually lay three eggs. Hatch out in about five weeks. Once the first egg is laid, until they hatch—that's the danger time. Got to man a watch day and night. Mrs. Manders, ma'am, do you think you could put up with two of our fellows bunking down here for the next month or so?"

Mrs. Manders said that as long as they had their own sleeping bags they would be most welcome.

"Good. Good," said Dobbin, and began to draw a grid on a large sheet of paper. "Guard duties," he announced.

179

"Know you young people will be bursting at the seams, longing to help."

Jinny regarded the mesh of lines with suspicion. It looked dangerously like a timetable to her.

"I have my horse to ride," she said, glaring round at her family, challenging them to make any remarks about her riding.

"Fit that in," Dobbin assured her, ruling his lines. "Two chaps on at night. One during the day. How about you kids taking over some of the daytime watches? Fit you up with a walkie-talkie. See any signs of a stranger, contact base and reinforcements will be over at the double."

"Doubt if any egg-collector would risk it during the day," said Peter. "Not now it's illegal."

"One good thing," said Mrs. Manders, "is the openness of the site. You can spot anyone approaching for miles around."

"True," said Peter. "Definite advantage."

When the duty roster, as Dobbin called his timetable, was filled in, Jinny's first spell of duty was in two days' time.

"I'll need to exercise Shantih tomorrow," Jinny thought. Coiled at the back of her mind was the knowledge that she hadn't ridden her today.

"I didn't have time," Jinny thought, but she knew that if she had really wanted to ride she could have made time in the afternoon. "It's just that I don't want to go on making her more disobedient. And that's all I'm doing. Worse and worst and worstest. Why can't I just explain to her that once she stops being so silly then we can both start to enjoy ourselves? Maybe she thinks it's me that's silly. Maybe she wants me to understand and let her run wild with the Shetlands again."

But Jinny didn't believe that. When she called from her bedroom window, Shantih would look up from her grazing and whinny, knowing her; or she would come trotting gladly to the field gate. It was only when Jinny was riding her that things went wrong.

Dobbin and Peter, who were both staying for the night and going out to the hide at dawn, went to bed early. Dobbin had to be back at business the next day, but Peter, who worked for the R.S.P.B. was to stay and be joined by another helper.

Going to bed, Jinny thought about the ospreys, out in the night at that very minute, exposed and vulnerable. She thought of the egg-collectors who had overheard her father's phone call speeding through the darkness in powerful Dick Dastardly cars, all converging on Finmory, waiting to pounce the minute the eggs were laid. What had Ken said? Something about not thinking, when you saw a hawk, that you ought to do things for it. But protecting it was different, protecting it while it hatched out its eggs, so that soon there would be ospreys again in Scotland and lots of other people would be able to see what she and Ken had seen —the sudden crystal bloom when the osprey shook its feathers dry, and its soaring, effortless mastery of space.

The next morning when Jinny brought Shantih in she could feel at once that her horse was in a good mood. She stood still while Jinny groomed her, lowered her head for the bit and hardly blew herself out at all when Jinny was tightening her girth. Jinny led her out of the stable and quickly sprang up into the saddle. Shantih turned her head, mild-eyed, looking round at Jinny.

"Don't you look like that," Jinny told her. "You know as well as I do that you're not always like this."

Shantih nibbled at the toe of Jinny's shoe, then waited quietly for her rider to tell her where to go. Jinny wondered whether she should go to the field and try once more to make Shantih walk and trot in a circle. For a moment she was undecided.

"Oh, fiddle it," Jinny said aloud. "It's too nice a day to start fighting with you. We'll go down to the beach," and Jinny lightly touched Shantih forward.

She walked out with a neat step. When Shantih was in a mood like this everything about her was sharp and exact, even her mane, spiked out by the sea breeze, seemed to form a rhythmical pattern with the swing of her shoulders and the arch of her neck.

" 'Morning has broken like the first morning. Morning has broken like the first day'," sang Jinny tunelessly.

The tide was out and the sand firm and printless. Jinny let Shantih trot the length of the bay, then cantered her back. Shantih only bucked once, and then it was more kicking her heels in the air for fun, rather than bucking. Jinny walked her about and then trotted. The calm sea glinted kaleidoscope lozenges of light, gulls screamed through the blue spring air and Jinny felt floating with happiness that Shantih was going so well.

"I say, you jolly well ought not to trot them on wet sand. Terribly bad for their tendons."

Clare Burnley on her black horse was coming towards them. With Clare riding him, the horse looked weedier than he had done with Spencer. Clare's solid bulk pressed the lightness out of him, took away the sparkle.

Jinny's mouth dropped open with sheer surprise. Amazing enough that Clare Burnley should appear at Finmory Bay, but even more incredible that she should be standing there chatting.

"I came over to see if you were still in one piece after yesterday's disaster. We were just going to bring your horse back to you when this boy appeared from nowhere and grabbed her."

Jinny's mouth cracked down another notch at such an obvious lie. She didn't think Clare or Spencer had shown the least sign of caring what happened to Shantih or herself.

"I've been talking to old MacKenzie about you, and he told me about your horse. Pretty tremendous—rescuing her from a circus and saving her life. I expect you are jolly proud of it all."

Jinny had never thought of it like that. It had been love, not pride, that had made her fight on and on to save Shantih.

"And he showed me the paintings you did for him. They're absolutely something. I could hardly believe you could have done them. I mean to say you'd think a real artist had painted them. It would be super if you could come over to Craigvaar some day and draw my nags for me. Mr. MacKenzie says you're crazy about horses, so I expect you'd enjoy having a look round the tack room and seeing some of my rosettes and things. Of course, they are only the

182

ones I've picked up in Scotland. All my cups are kept at home. Wouldn't be safe leaving them up here when we're in Sussex. As Pa says, no point in inviting the locals to break into Craigvaar."

Words thundered out of Clare like a waterfall.

"I mean, imagine what it would be like if we had word in the middle of winter that Craigvaar had been broken into. The bore of having to come buzzing up here. I couldn't abide being up here in the winter. Ma says it's only families like the MacKenzies who have never known anything else who could put up with it. I mean think of the parties one would miss. Let's face it, winter is the time when everything happens in town. You're stuck up here all the year, aren't you? But then I don't suppose you're old enough to bother much about parties and shows and things."

Jinny had managed to get her mouth shut again. She sat on Shantih mesmerised by Clare's presence. She could not believe that Clare was spending time talking to her, that she actually seemed to have come looking for her.

Clare's short blonde hair curled round the edges of her hard hat. It was a new hat—still dense, velvety black. Her blue tweed jacket and fawn jodhpurs were made of thick, expensive material and her black jodhpur boots were highly polished. Her thoroughbred twitched his silk-fine hide as he waited motionless. His tack was dark and mellowed, better than new. Clare sat solidly in the saddle. She rode with long stirrups, her feet pushed well home. Her hands were moulded round the reins like lumps of Mr. Manders' clay.

"Your mare's a bit on the skinny side," said Clare. "How old is she?"

"I'm not sure," said Jinny. "About six, we think."

'We' meant herself and Mike and Jinny's pony book with the diagram of horses' teeth in it. Had anyone else suggested that Shantih was skinny Jinny would have exploded in their face, but somehow Clare Burnley was different. She knew about horses. She was allowed to criticise.

"Just a youngster then. That's why she's so green. Do her good to be ridden with other horses."

183

"I ride her with our Highlands," Jinny said, making it sound as if Bramble and Punch were their own ponies and not borrowed trekkers.

"Oh, I mean other *horses*," said Clare. "Goodness, I'd think it would bore the pants off her having those two mini cart horses keeping her back all the time."

Jinny was very fond of Bramble—his tough independence, his native sureness on the moors, but at Clare's words Jinny's idea of Bramble seemed to change. Somehow he became something to be ashamed of. Not the sort of animal Clare would have in her stable.

"Gosh, would you look at the time! I'll need to dash. Ma and I are going over to see our little man this afternoon. Does the most wonderful weaving. Really pretty. The sort of thing you could not buy in London."

Clare turned the black thoroughbred with confident dominance. He looked almost seventeen hands, hardmuscled and fit, but Clare made him seem like a child's pony.

"And you will come over, won't you? Ma would adore to meet you. I'll come and pick you up in the car if you like."

The sea wind fanned Clare's words out into space so that when she had ridden out of sight Jinny couldn't be certain that she had really said them. Perhaps she had said something quite different. If it hadn't been for the hoofprints in the sand, Jinny would have been willing to believe that she had dreamed it all.

Jinny walked Shantih along the crimpling edge of the waves. She was too happy to go home yet. She wanted to keep the warm, fizzy happiness bottled up inside her for a bit longer. Riding back to Finmory she was still sealed inside the golden bubble. She hardly saw the mountains or the sky. Clare Burnley had really and truly stood talking to her. "Just as if I was her friend," Jinny said aloud to Shantih.

"Don't be too disappointed if you don't hear any more from her," Mrs. Manders said after Jinny had told her about their meeting. "She is a good bit older than you."

184

"Oh, Ma!" exclaimed Jinny. "Don't be such a bore. She's coming for me in their car. She said."

"Shouldn't it be, 'calling for me in the Bentley?' " asked Ken.

CHAPTER SIX

Brian Craven, the other man from the R.S.P.B., arrived that evening with his sleeping bag wrapped in polythene and strapped to the back of his scooter. He was small and wiry and worried a lot about pollution.

"You feel that no matter how much you do, it can't be enough. What can I do against all the factories that are churning out their muck, all the nice, kind, ignorant idiots pressing their filthy aerosol cans, the murderers spreading their chemical poisons everywhere?" he demanded, and sank his head into his hands, narrowly missing the plate of broth that Mrs. Manders had just put down on the table for him. "Still, the ospreys haven't given up, so why should I? When am I going to see them?" and he began to gulp down his soup.

"We do the night watch," Peter told him. "Dobbin worked it all out before he left. Then Ken comes up early morning and one of the kids changes with him at about eleven."

"Two of us," corrected Mike. "Dobbin thought that since it was our first time at the hide, Jinny and I should go together."

"Don't see why it needs you both," said Petra. "I was there by myself." Petra had acquired a notebook and was keeping a careful record of every move the ospreys made while she was on watch.

"Mike can go by himself if he wants to," offered Jinny quickly. She was haunted by the fear that while she was in the hide Clare might arrive to take her to Craigvaar.

"Don't spoil it," said Mike. "It's all arranged. We're going together."

185

"I'll die," thought Jinny. "I will, I'll die if Clare come for me and I'm stuck up on the moors."

"Couldn't you phone her?" Mrs. Manders had suggested. "Let her know you can't go tomorrow."

"No, of course I can't. She may have meant next week or she may have forgotten all about me by now," Jinny had snapped. She hugged the terrible fear to herself that if Clare did come and Jinny was watching the nest she wouldn't bother to come again. Jinny would have missed her chance of getting to know someone who could help her school Shantih.

At breakfast, Brian and Peter were full of enthusiasm for their night's watching.

"She's probably laid her first egg," said Peter. "We think she's beginning to brood."

"Nearly certain," agreed Brian. "For the next five weeks it's Red Alert."

Through the window Jinny could see white scuds of cloud racing over blue sky, their moving shadows patching the sunlight on the kitchen floor.

"I don't care about the ospreys," she thought rebelliously, but she did really. She wanted to do all she could to make sure that the great birds should be allowed to rear their young without being disturbed. It was just that she cared more about Shantih, about finding someone who could tell her what she was doing wrong. She had been up early that morning, riding Shantih in the field and had been bucked off twice.

"Come on, Jinny," Mike yelled from the bottom of the stairs. "It's a quarter to eleven and we're meant to be at the hide to let Ken away at eleven."

"There's no chance of that," thought Jinny sullenly. She had been waiting as long as she dared, praying for the sound of the Burnleys' car coming up the drive.

"The rota will be all mucked up if you don't come now," shouted Mike. Jinny made a face at herself in the mirror and stomped reluctantly downstairs.

"Fiddle his stupid old timetable," she said. "Thought we were meant to be on holiday."

"You wouldn't say that if you were Ken waiting for us

186

to arrive at eleven and we're not even going to be there for half past."

Mike was already mounted on Punch. They would share the pony on their way to the hide and Ken would ride him back. Jinny took a last hopeful look down the drive, a last listen for the least sound that might be the Burnleys' car, but there was nothing. She turned and ran to catch up with Punch and Mike.

She pushed the thought of Clare out of her mind. "Maybe she didn't mean it," Jinny thought as she walked beside Punch.

"Can you believe that we ever lived in Stopton?" Mike asked.

Jinny shook her head.

"That this is us going to guard ospreys?"

"Can't," said Jinny. "Can't."

She swung her arms wide through the open space, spinning round, blinding herself with her hair. They were so lucky to be themselves. So much had happened since they'd come to Finmory.

Jinny stopped and looked back at the house. Parked at the front door was the Burnleys' car.

"She's come," Jinny screamed. She saw Clare get out of the car, her curls bright in the sun. "Clare's come for me and I'm not there!"

"Dad'll tell her to come back tomorrow. It doesn't matter."

"Of course it does," raged Jinny. "She may never come back. Never. Shantih won't have a chance to be properly schooled." Clear in her mind's eye Jinny saw Clare standing in the centre of the schooling circle, correcting Jinny's faults as she rode round on Shantih. "I've got to go with her!"

"You can't," said Mike. Mrs. Manders had come out of the house and was talking to Clare. "She'll have gone long before you could get back down."

"Let me have Punch," demanded Jinny and for a moment she thought of trying to drag Mike off the pony.

"Don't be daft," Mike said, kicking Punch on up the moor. "Ken's waiting for us."

187

Jinny made no move to follow him. She stood staring down to where her mother and Clare were still standing talking. She knew it was true that she could never reach Finmory in time. Jinny glared round furiously. There must be some way. The roof of Mr. MacKenzie's farm caught her eye and instantly she was tearing full speed over the moor towards it. Clare might stop there on her way home.

Jinny sprang and leapt from tussocks of reeds to rock face to heather. She hurtled down to the farm, throwing herself on faster and faster, never glancing down to see where her feet would go next. She gasped for breath, sucking in air that burned like drinking cold water after curry. Her heart shook her body with its jumping but she forced herself on until at last she staggered into the farmyard and saw the Burnleys' car with Clare leaning out of the window talking to Mr. MacKenzie.

"Well hello!" cried Clare. "However did you get here? Anything wrong?"

"Saw . . . your . . . car." Between words Jinny stopped and gulped for breath. "Was running . . . to catch . . . you."

"Your Ma said you'd gone for a ride in the hills and there wasn't the remotest chance of your being back before the evening. She made it quite clear that there was absolutely no point in my hanging around."

"Changed . . . my mind."

"It's the hard time that mother of yours has trying to keep tabs on you," said Mr. MacKenzie.

"She knew," said Jinny, still too breathless to even begin to argue. "I just changed my mind."

"Jolly glad you did," boomed Clare. "Ma wants you to come over for lunch. Actually she's expecting you. I mean to say I knew you were keen to see the horses so I really more or less said you would be coming. She'll be frightfully put out if you don't."

"Oh, yes please," said Jinny.

"Do you want to tell them at home? Go back and change or anything like that?"

"It's O.K. They'll know where I've gone."

"Just as you like," said Clare.

It wasn't really as Jinny liked. She knew from the expression on Clare's face that she didn't think much of her appearance. Jinny glanced down at her splashed jeans and muddy wellingtons. Under her old anorak she was wearing a heavy sweater that had once belonged to Petra. It reached to her knees but had been meant to keep her warm in the hide. Jinny quite understood that she wasn't at all the kind of guest Mrs. Burnley would be expecting to arrive for lunch but she was afraid that if she went back home to clean herself up she would be re-routed back to Mike.

"At least be having the decency to take the moor off your boots before you get into the posh car," said Mr. MacKenzie.

Jinny sluiced water from the trough over her wellingtons.

"But what a bore for you," said Clare. "Don't be too particular. We'll be out in the stables most of the time and I can easily lend you a pair of slippers to wear when we go in for lunch."

Mr. MacKenzie fixed Jinny with his gimlet eye. "Be minding your manners and keep a good hold on your tongue. Don't be shaming me now in front of my friends."

"Phooey," said Jinny, and dived into the car next to Clare.

"We all think he's a perfectly sweet old man," said Clare as they drove to Craigvaar. "Perfectly sweet."

It was not the word Jinny would have picked to describe Mr. MacKenzie.

Clare drove up the drive and parked in front of Craigvaar.

"Now I'll tell Ma we've arrived and then should we go down to the stables? Would that be the thing?"

Jinny was left standing uncertainly beside the car. She looked round cautiously at the bowling green lawns and their controlled flowerbeds; the gravelled drive marching between ankle-high posts and chains and the two stone lions guarding the doorway.

"Ma is jolly pleased you've come," said Clare, emerging, "but she says will you excuse her if she doesn't come out to say hello just now? We do have Pat and Heather to help us, but Ma's so fussy about the cooking she just has to be there to see to it herself. So I thought if it was all right with you we'd trot down now to see the nags and maybe ride this afternoon? How would that be?"

"Oh, yes," said Jinny, just managing to stop herself blurting out her utter surprise that Clare should even think of letting her ride one of her horses.

They went round the side of the house, over lawns bounded on one side by a tennis court and through a shrubbery until they came to the stables. There were four loose boxes. The horses, hearing them coming, were looking out expectantly over their half doors.

"Gee back," Clare shouted at the grey, swinging her arm at him and making him plunge and swing back into his box. She opened the door and Jinny followed her in.

Inside, the grey seemed even more massive than he had outside. His shoulders and quarters bulged with muscle from his round, deep-ribbed body. He carried his broad, Roman-nosed face on a thick-set neck. He was a horse made to pack into a cube or as if he were not quite free of the stone block from which he had been carved.

"Meet Huston," said Clare. "I've only had him for a year. Pa bought him for me to get me going in the open jumping. He was absolutely wonderful for that. I won dozens of comps on him last summer but he is rather slow so one hardly knows what to do about keeping him. Of course, what I would really like is a top class event horse, but they cost thousands these days."

Jinny clapped Huston's neck and the flat, impersonal expanse of cheek bone but he paid no attention to her.

"He looks as if he'd be a good hunter," Jinny said because she thought it would sound the right thing.

"Oh goodness no, far too slow."

They left the mountain of Huston standing carved in the middle of his box and went to see the black horse.

"We'll not go in," said Clare. "Jasper is rather spooky. Quiet as a lamb with me but he is inclined to have a go at a stranger. Mind you, he is a super horse. I should say he's won more cups for showing than almost any other horse one could name. Of course, I do take him around a bit and now I can drive the horse box myself it does make a tremendous difference."

Jasper made a grab at Clare's arm, ears pinned down on his blue-black reptilian head.

"Don't you dare," roared Clare. "Or I'll be in there with my big stick."

The black horse gloomed away from Clare's voice. He stood in the far corner of his box, kicking boredly with a hind leg. His coat shimmered like black ice.

"You must spend hours grooming him," said Jinny knowing how long it took her to polish up Shantih.

"Gosh no," laughed Clare. "I plug in my brushes. Electric groomers. Don't tell me you haven't heard of them?"

Jinny decided not to say that she enjoyed grooming Shantih. Standing beside Clare it did seem stupid to enjoy work when a machine could do it for you.

"Now the tack room," said Clare, marching down the row of boxes and opening another door at the end of them.

They stayed in the tack room until lunchtime, Clare pointing out different rosettes that were pinned round the walls and telling Jinny how she had won them.

Lunch was fish pie, eaten by Jinny with a knife and fork but by the Burnleys with a fork only, and a dessert of fruit, which was a bowl of apples and pears. Jinny picked an apple and took a bite out of it. The Burnleys laid theirs on their plates and cut them into small pieces, but to Jinny's relief they didn't seem to notice her. In fact they hardly seemed to notice that she was there at all. After Mrs. Burnley had shaken hands and said what wonderfully pretty hair Jinny had and Mr. Burnley had said, "Manders? Manders? Don't think I know your father," no one said another word to Jinny. They sat and talked to each other about people they knew who all seemed to have been doing wonderful, fascinating things.

"Now, darlings, what have you planned for this afternoon?" Mrs. Burnley asked when Pat had cleared the table.

"We're riding," said Clare.

Mrs. Burnley said that if they were going to ride she did think that perhaps they should go now because she had promised Dinkie Clifton that they would all be over for drinks before supper.

"Can you tack up Huston?" Clare asked.

Jinny thought she could and Clare handed her his tack.

The huge grey stood perfectly still, only his ears twitching as Clare bawled at Jasper. Jinny felt as if she was saddling up a house—he was so huge compared to Shantih. His legs were like pillars, his back like a table top and Jinny had to march round him to get from one side to the other.

"Jolly well done," said Clare, crashing her hand down on the saddle to make sure it was sitting correctly on Huston's back, and checking the tightness of his throat lash. "Now will you ride this fellow and I'll take Jasper?"

Jinny nodded. She was too excited to trust her voice.

"Wellingtons are not the thing for riding but I'm afraid my boots would drown you. But I can lend you a hat. One always feels it is so important to get into the habit of never riding without a hard hat. It was Ma's idea to keep one or two old ones up here so I can usually kit out my friends. Come along and we'll find one for you."

The third hat Jinny tried on fitted her.

"Keep it well down," said Clare, banging it more firmly on to Jinny's head. "And here's a stick. One should never ride without a stick. Don't you agree? Must say that squib of yours could have done with one across her ribs the way she was carrying on when we met you."

Jinny said nothing. She didn't feel it was the right time to start explaining why she never used a stick on Shantih.

Clare gave Jinny a leg up on to the grey, chucking her high above the saddle, so that she nearly went flying over the other side.

"Thought we'd go for a hack first and then back to the paddock," Clare said when she was sitting astride Jasper, and she led the way out of Craigvaar.

Once on the road the horses settled into a steady jog. In minutes they seemed to be through Glenbost and trotting along the road to Ardtallon. The most Jinny could do was to keep her mouth shut. She couldn't stop it grinning. She had never known riding like this before, so controlled and effortless. Huston seemed to be so powerful and yet was obedient to the least tightening of Jinny's fingers on the reins, the least touch of her leg against his side.

"How do you like him?" asked Clare.

"He's super," said Jinny.

"He's pretty well schooled, I'll say that for him, and he is fit. Barbara, our girl at home, is an absolute wonder at feeding horses. I expect you notice the difference after your beast. Really, I'd be rather ashamed to be seen out on her."

"She's too fresh as she is. I can't give her any more oats."

"Oh, feeding isn't just a question of shovelling in oats. You have to know what you're doing."

And Jinny thought as they rode on that it all came back to the same thing: she didn't know anything. "If only my family were like Clare's," she thought. "If only I knew as much as she does."

"I'll tuck this fellow away in his box," Clare said when they were back in the stable yard, "and then we'll take Huston into the paddock and give him a jump."

In one corner of the paddock were five jumps built out of smart red and white poles, all standing at about three feet.

"D'you want a jolly round them?"

Jinny swallowed hard. She couldn't bring herself to tell Clare that she had never jumped before.

"O.K.," she said.

"Canter him round a few times, then over you go when you're ready. He's got a big leap in him, so watch out for it, but I'll guarantee he won't stop."

Jinny cantered Huston round the field. He had a slow, comfortable, rocking horse canter and Jinny was able to sit down tight in the saddle. She shortened her reins and rode at the first jump, trying to remember all she had ever read about jumping. "Lean forward when he takes off, keep your knees tight and your heels down and don't catch his mouth," she told herself. But all she was actually thinking about was that she was riding one of Clare Burnley's horses, that she was learning to jump in Clare Burnley's paddock.

Huston cantered steadily at the first jump, cleared it

effortlessly, landed heavily on the far side and they were cantering towards the second almost before Jinny realised that they had left the ground.

With the same easy confidence Huston cleared the first four jumps. Jinny turned him up the middle and felt him gather speed for the last one. Yards in front of the poles he shot into the air, sailed high above them and stretched himself to land far out over the other side. Just in time Jinny jack-knifed over his shoulder, dug her knees tightly into the rolls of the saddle and let the reins slip through her fingers. In a stride or two Huston had come back to a walk.

"He went well for you," boomed Clare, striding towards them. "Glad to see you'd enough sense not to interfere with him. When a horse knows about jumping the way he knows about it, one is best to leave him alone. I mean to say that when Pa picked him he picked a horse that was going to teach me to sit on over decent-sized fences."

"That was wonderful," enthused Jinny. "It was super. He just flew over them. Oh, if only Shantih could jump like that," and Jinny was sailing over Clare Burnley's jumps on Shantih, her horse as confident as Huston but twice as fast.

"Bring her down and give her a school over them," offered Clare, as if she was suggesting that Jinny should have another piece of cake.

"Oh, but I couldn't. I can't even lunge her properly. I could never start jumping her."

"Nothing to lungeing. Let them know who's the boss, that's all. I've been lungeing my own ponies since I was about seven, I suppose."

"Clare," called Mrs. Burnley's voice. "Phone."

"Wonder who?" said Clare. "Hang on here a tick."

She ran into the house, leaving Jinny to walk Huston round the paddock. She looked longingly at the jumps, aching to go round them again but she was too afraid that Clare might return and order her home.

"I say, I'm frightfully sorry dashing off like that," said Clare, when she came back a few minutes later. "That was Tim Foster, terribly nice chap, didn't realise we were here.

He's coming over in an hour or so. Would it be a bore if I were to drive you home now? I know what Tim's like once he starts talking and we are going out for drinks this evening. Would you be awfully offended?"

"No. That's O.K.," Jinny said, and in no time Huston was packed back in his box and Jinny was sitting next to Clare being driven back to Finmory.

"I'll drop you here," said Clare, stopping at Finmory's gates. "It has been wonderful getting to know you like this."

"I've had a smashing day," said Jinny, getting out of the car. "Thank you very, very much."

"I say, you didn't really mean it, about not being able to lunge your nag?"

"I did. She just plays about with me."

"Well, the thing is," said Clare, "why don't you bring her over to Craigvaar and I could sort you out a bit?"

"Oh, but ... would you? Would you really?"

"I'll bring the box over for her. Tomorrow's no use. Bobs and Bunty are with us for the day. How about Friday? Well, that's it definitely arranged. No point in me slaving away looking after two horses by myself when we could cope with them together."

Clare turned the car and drove away. Jinny vaulted over the gate, went leaping and running up the drive, burst into the house and through the hall to the kitchen. Her mother, Mike and Peter were sitting round the table drinking tea.

"I'm going to Craigvaar," she shouted. "Clare's bringing her horse box for Shantih and she's going to teach me how to lunge her. And I rode one of her horses. And I jumped!"

Jinny flung herself round the kitchen, stamping her wellingtons, shaking her hair and waving her arms.

"Big deal," said Mike, and Jinny remembered about the ospreys.

CHAPTER SEVEN

Jinny's alarm clock woke her into the cold grey light of very early morning. She stretched out one arm to switch off its hideous disturbance then remembered that last night she had left it on the other side of her room so that she couldn't switch it off and go back to sleep. Jinny muffled the noise by curling under the bedclothes, but by the time it had exhausted itself she was wide enough awake to know that she had to get up. To make up for yesterday's desertion Jinny had agreed to take the early morning watch at the osprey's nest.

After her first mug of coffee she felt a little better.

"It's a drug," said Ken, coming into the kitchen with Kelly shadowing his heels.

"Don't care," said Jinny making herself a second mugful. "Why are you up so early?"

"Thought I'd walk up the moor a bit with you," said Ken. "I'm looking for some plants for my compost. My book says they should be picked before the sun has been on them."

"Not much danger of that," said Jinny, looking out at the grey gloom.

Ken walked, Jinny rode Bramble. She was pretending that Ken wasn't there. Last night when they had all been telling her what they thought about her for spending the day at Craigvaar, Ken hadn't said anything. Jinny felt that this was why he was with her now.

"You're not really taking Shantih over to the Burnleys'?" asked Ken, so that Jinny knew she'd been right.

"Am," she said.

"Forget it," said Ken. "She doesn't want you."

"Clare does. She asked me to come."

"Only because her brother's away and she's bored hairless."

"She's going to teach me how to lunge."

196

"Is that what she was doing when she rode off and left you lying on the road?"

"She didn't mean to."

"Didn't notice you'd fallen off?"

Jinny ignored his sarcasm. "Clare's sending her horse box for Shantih tomorrow and I'm going over to Craigvaar as well. And if you'd like to know, I might be going with them to Inverburgh Show."

"Don't do it," said Ken. He clicked his bony fingers together, a sharp sound in the pearly silence. "Stop now," he commanded. "Don't go on with it. Great what you've got here. Enjoy it. Live this and don't go complicating it all."

Jinny blocked herself off from him. She thought hard about Huston, the excitement of jumping, the luxury of Clare's tack room. She didn't care what Ken said—she was taking Shantih to Craigvaar. She glanced down at him and he looked straight at her, his eyes flint hard.

"You don't need to go on," Ken said. "I'm giving you the chance to get off. Tell Clare Burnley you're not playing her game."

"Honestly," said Jinny, "one wonders what all the fuss is about."

"Well if you must, you must," said Ken, and Jinny knew he had totally abandoned herself, Shantih, and everything to do with Craigvaar. It was as if he had been shining a torch directly at her face but now he had switched it off.

"I'd better get a move on," Jinny said, to break the silence. "They'll be expecting me."

Ken nodded and Jinny pushed Bramble into a trot.

Peter and Brian were stiff and cold after their night of watching.

"All's well," Brian said. "She's been brooding all night and he's off fishing at the moment. May have gone down to the sea."

He gave Jinny the binoculars. She looked through them and exclaimed with surprise. Although the hide was in a cave on the hillside and Loch Varrich lay in the hollow a good distance from the hills, Jinny could see every blade of grass by the lochside and each smooth tiny pebble. The glasses were far more powerful than her father's. Jinny found the mass of branches and twigs, high in the pine tree, that was the osprey's nest. The hen osprey seemed so close that Jinny could see every detail of her black, hooked beak, the crest of feathers lying flat on her head and her great yellow eye that seemed to be staring straight at the hide.

"You got her?" Peter asked, breaking the spell.

"Cor!" breathed Jinny, taking the glasses away from her eyes and seeing the nest as a hardly visible shape. "They are terrific glasses. Oh, I should love to have a pair like these all the time!"

"They're Dobbin's," said Brian. "Don't think we could afford them."

Before they went, Brian and Peter showed Jinny how to operate the walkie-talkie. As well as watching for any disturbance at the nest, she was to scan the hills sloping down to the loch, and contact Finmory should she see anyone at all.

"Petra's coming to relieve you about eleven," said Brian. "Now no dozing off. You have to concentrate all the time you're on duty up here."

"And no nipping off to see your friends," warned Peter.

Jinny scowled at him. It was bad enough having her own family telling her what to do without a complete stranger bossing her about as well.

Left alone, Jinny settled herself down. She arranged the cushion on top of the wooden box as comfortably as she could. Then she sat with her elbows on her knees, the glasses to her eyes.

Daylight stretched over the sky, colours dyeing the grey hillside to life. Jinny's arm ached and her legs were cramped but she stayed still, her glasses trained on the hen osprey who never moved either, seeming almost a part of the nest.

The cock osprey came flying towards the pines, carrying a fish in his talons. For a second, the balance of the hills and the loch changed. Everything drew in its breath to a moment of stillness, the focus held in the wings of the hawk.

The hen stood up in the nest, chuckling to her mate, took

the fish from him and flew with it to the topmost branch of a neighbouring pine where she began to eat it. The male stood for a minute, glaring around him, then he settled down over the eggs.

Hardly daring to blink, Jinny stared, magnetized by the wonder of it. Yet she felt cold and squirmy at the same time. She was an intruder prying into the private lives of the ospreys. She had no right to be staring at them so rudely. Shivering, Jinny wondered if God might be staring down at her without her knowing anything about it.

When the hen had eaten the fish she came back to the nest and the cock flapped to a high branch where he sat motionless.

Jinny took a pad of drawing paper and a pencil out of her pocket. Quickly, almost guiltily, she sketched the osprey. Her pencil sweeping in the line of the hawk's flight, the strength of its talons and the reflector scan of its fierce yellow eyes. She had drawn several pictures of the ospreys —the male flying, sitting on the edge of the nest and brooding, motionless, almost like a branch of the pine, and two of the female tucked into the nest—and was just beginning to draw the osprey diving on the fish when she suddenly remembered that she was meant to be on guard.

Quickly Jinny looked round the hillside, but as usual there were only sheep to be seen.

"Thank goodness for that," she thought. "After yesterday, if I'd let anything happen to the eggs I think they'd have murdered me."

Petra arrived riding Punch and said she was sorry she was late. Jinny said it was O.K. because she didn't know the time, and Petra said how could she take accurate notes about the ospreys' behaviour if she didn't know the time. Jinny said it did make things difficult, and escaped on Punch.

She got back to Finmory as her father was loading crates of pottery into the car to take in to Inverburgh to the gift shop that bought it from him.

"Take Jinny with you, seeing Ken's not going," suggested Mrs. Manders. "There's a sale on at Smythe & Binns. Girls' anoraks for three pounds. If they're worth having you could buy one for her. She'll need to get a new one for school."

"But I'm going to ride Shantih," protested Jinny. "Couldn't Daddy just buy one that's my size?"

"No," said Mrs. Manders, "he could not."

Jinny decided not to argue. She could do with a new anorak, then if she went to the Inverburgh Show with Clare she would be able to wear it.

Mr. Manders parked in a side street close to the gift shop and Jinny helped him to carry in the crates of pottery.

"Joy, joy, joy!" cried Nell Storr, who owned the shop. "Delight to see you, to see you—delight! Sold out of your last lot, and I've got a special order for you. Eight of those huge jars for growing herbs and things in. Customer bought two and back the next week to order eight more."

"Grand," said Mr. Manders, writing down the order while Jinny wandered round the shop. It wasn't a tartan trash gift shop, but full of things that you didn't see anywhere else. Nell Storr bought nearly all her stock directly from the craftsmen who made it.

Jinny was looking longingly at some wood carvings when her father called her over.

"This is Jinny," he said, and Nell held out her hand, purple nail-varnished and heavy with rings.

"Nell was saying that she might be interested in selling some of your drawings," said Mr. Manders. "Pity we didn't think—you could have brought some of them with you."

"Have you a sketch book on you?" asked Nell. "I know I never move without mine."

Jinny knew that she still had her sketch pad in her pocket. She hesitated. Normally she would never have shown her drawings to anyone, but if Nell bought some, and paid her for them, Jinny would have money of her own: perhaps enough money to buy a saddle for Shantih, for when the ponies went back to their trekking they would be taking their tack with them. Jinny studied Nell. She liked the bright kaftan she was wearing, the painted eyes, the fuzz of black hair and the face that was ugly but interesting. Jinny decided to risk it. She took the pad out of her pocket, laid

200

it on the counter, and began slowly to turn over the pages.

The first drawings were of Shantih galloping, done in Indian ink with water colour washes. Then there were some of Kelly, two or three of Mr. MacKenzie and his sheep, one of Bramble's head, and a few of an enormous spider she had met in Bramble's stall. Then there were the drawings she had done that morning of the ospreys.

"So you've been to Loch Garten?" asked Nell.

"Oh, no," said Jinny, "I drew them on the moor this morning."

"But surely that's an osprey?" Nell took the sketch pad from Jinny and turned it to her last drawing of the hawk taking a fish from the loch. "Yes. There it is, an osprey."

Jinny felt her face flood crimson. She looked helplessly at her father and at the tall, bald man who was standing next to him and had been looking at Jinny's drawings while he waited to be served.

" 'Fraid we've never made Loch Garten. Not on the money you pay me. Jinny copied them from Mike's bird book."

Nell looked intently at the drawings and Jinny knew that she didn't believe her father.

"Mike's bird book or not," said Nell. "I like them. I'll give you a fiver for four of the horse sketches. I'll mount them on coloured card, mark them up at two pounds each and if they sell we can discuss terms."

"Oh, thank you. Yes. Thank you very much indeed."

Nell chose the four drawings she wanted and gave Jinny a five pound note.

"Excuse me," said the man, who had been listening. "I would like to purchase one of your drawings of the osprey. They are beautifully done. You have a great gift and it pleases me to see proof that the human hand is still superior to the machine—that the camera is still inferior to the work of an artist. You see not with but through the eye."

Jinny snatched her pad and stuffed it into her pocket.

"They're not for sale," she stated. "My brother wants them. He only lent me his book so that I'd draw them for him."

201

"If that is so perhaps you could tell me your address, and later I will write to you to see if you have been making any more bird drawings."

"You needn't bother," said Jinny, "because I shan't be. I only draw horses."

The man had a face creased like the skin on sour milk, pebble glasses that magnified his eyes, and a morticed mouth.

"My apologies," he said to Mr. Manders. "I did not mean to offend."

An assistant came bustling up and the man walked away with her.

"Stranger to me," said Nell. "Liked your work though. Be sure to let me see some more of it the next time Tom's coming in."

Back in the car Jinny looked despairingly at her father.

"I forgot they were in it," she said.

"Can't be helped now. Didn't like the way that man was so interested in them."

"Well, he doesn't know where I saw it. I didn't give him our address."

"He saw me bringing in the pots. They're all marked Finmory. Or he's only to ask Nell. Still, spilt milk. Now let's go and see about buying you some respectable clothes."

Buying the anorak was quite painless. The first one Jinny tried on fitted her. Walking back through the store they passed a rail with a notice above it saying 'Sale Garments. Uncollected orders made to measure.' Jinny looked at them as she walked past. There were skirts and trousers and at the end of the rail a pair of jodphurs. Jinny grabbed her father's hand. "Look," she cried, and lifted the jodphurs off the rail. She held them against herself. "They'd fit me," she said.

"Eight pounds fifty," said the assistant. "Very best quality reduced from twenty pounds. We've had rather a lot of trouble trying to sell them. In fact, to tell you the truth, they've been with us for a year now. Too long a leg fitting for the average size."

"If they fit, you pay three and I'll pay the rest," said Mr. Manders.

Jinny took them into a fitting room and wriggled into them. They were a bit wide at the waist, but apart from that they fitted perfectly.

"Just think," said Jinny to her father as they drove home, "all the time we've been at Finmory these jodhs have been waiting for me."

"A beautiful thought," agreed her father.

"D'you know," Jinny confided, "I think my life is caught in a whirlpool. Everything is happening to me. Everything! And tomorrow I'm taking Shantih to Craigvaar, and I'm learning to jump, and I've sold some of my drawings, and now if I got to the Inverburgh Show I've got jodphurs to wear!"

"Oh, Jinny," said her father, "slow down."

But Jinny didn't hear him. She was riding Shantih over the jumps in Clare's paddock, soaring clear and high over them all while Clare watched in admiration.

CHAPTER EIGHT

Clare drove the horse box up the drive to Finmory. The low branches of the trees rattled against its sides and it swayed from side to side as the wheels caught in ruts.

"Jinny," called her mother, "Clare's here."

Frantically Jinny stared at her reflection in her wardrobe mirror. She could not make up her mind whether to wear her new jodphurs or not. She had put them on and taken them off three times already. They certainly looked smart, but somehow Jinny felt they were too dressed up to wear when she was only going to Craigvaar.

She heard the horse box stopping and struggled out of the jodphurs. "I'll keep them new," she decided, "in case I do go to Inverburgh Show with Clare," and with relief Jinny pulled on her usual jeans. She ran downstairs and out to the stables where Shantih was waiting, groomed and shining, already suspicious that something unusual was going to happen to her.

"You can take the box round to the back," Mr. Manders told Clare. "Think Jinny's round there."

Slowly the box trundled round the side of the house and across to the stable.

"Nag ready?" Clare asked, jumping down from the cab.

"She is," said Jinny, "but Mummy wanted to know if you'd like a cup of tea?"

"Oh dear," said Clare. "Do you think she'd be frightfully upset if I didn't? Would it be rather rude? It's just that I would like to give my beasts a really decent exercise today. Poor dears didn't get out at all yesterday, and I thought if you came over now we could have lunch at home and then get them out for a good long ride. Got to keep them on the ball for the show. I don't know what Pa would say if Huston didn't win."

"It doesn't matter," said Jinny. "It was only if you wanted one."

Mr. Manders came up and Jinny introduced him to Clare.

"Jinny was telling me that you're a potter. Now I do think that's terribly clever. I'm just hopeless at anything like that."

"Only moderate myself," admitted Mr. Manders. "It's Ken that's the potter."

"Ken?"

"He's a friend who stays with us," explained Mr. Manders, and Jinny asked quickly if she should bring Shantih out. She didn't particularly want Ken to meet Clare.

"I'll get the ramp down," said Clare. "Has she been boxed before?"

"Yes," said Jinny, suddenly remembering that the last horse box that Shantih had been in had crashed. If she had remembered before she would have thought of some way of stopping Clare bringing her horse box to Finmory. Jinny was suddenly certain that Shantih would remember the accident.

She put Shantih's halter on, knotting it securely at the

204

noseband, and started to lead her out of the stable. Shantih stopped dead in the doorway, her front legs braced, eyes goggling, ears almost meeting with surprise at the sight of the horse box.

"It's all right," Jinny assured her. "It won't hurt you. Come and look at it. There's a good horse. Come on now."

"Bit spooky is she?" demanded Clare.

"The last horse box she was in was hit by a lorry," Jinny explained. "I expect she remembers it," and she scratched Shantih's neck and rubbed her shoulder, whispering encouragement to her as she took a hesitant step forward.

"There's the horse," said Jinny. "That's the way." And Shantih allowed herself to be persuaded to walk out of the stable doorway.

Jinny managed to lead her towards the box and to turn her to face the ramp but then Shantih froze and refused to move another step.

"Get her going," said Clare.

"Why have you stopped?" said Mr. Manders. "Go on, take her into the box."

"What do you think I'm trying to do?" asked Jinny, scowling at them both.

"Wake her up then," shouted Clare. "Haven't you got a stick? Here—I'll chase her for you," and Clare came striding towards Shantih, waving her arms and shouting at her.

Shantih snorted through wide nostrils and plunged away from her, almost knocking Jinny down.

"Don't," warned Jinny. "If you upset her she'll never go near the box."

"I'll upset her," threatened Clare. "She's needing someone who can straighten her out. I haven't got all day to stand around here you know."

"Just give her a minute," said Jinny, hanging on desperately to the halter rope while Shantih tugged back, half rearing, tossing her head from side to side. Jinny was afraid that it was too late already. Now that Shantih was fighting them they would never manage to force her into

205

the box. They should have coaxed her in with oats or led Punch in and out to let her see that it was safe.

"Don't be silly," pleaded Jinny. "It's only a horse box. Nothing will happen to you. Come on, Shantih, come on."

In Jinny's own ears her voice sounded anxious and impatient. If Jinny had heard that voice speaking in a foreign language she wouldn't have trusted it either.

"Oh, don't be daft. It's quite safe, Shantih. You're all right. Come on now."

The mare was electric with panic. The gaping black entrance to the horse box was filled with lurking terrors. She plunged and fought at the end of the halter. Jinny hung on, conscious of Clare's heavy-browed irritation, her father's recording presence and her own feebleness. But most of all she was thinking how beautiful Shantih was when she was like this, all bright burning energy, defying them all.

"I'm not standing here watching a horse muck around like that," announced Clare. "Don't think your daughter is fit to cope with her," she said to Mr. Manders. "Here, give me the rope. I'll get her into the box."

Reluctantly, Jinny relinquished the halter. "She won't go in now," she said.

"We'll see about that," said Clare. She yanked at the halter rope, pulling at Shantih's head, shouting at her, grim threats that were hardly more than a roar in Clare's throat. "Get up with you, you brute, garn you, you twister you."

Jinny fiddled with a strand of her hair. A hard lump choked in her throat. She hadn't wanted it to be like this. If it had been anyone else treating Shantih as roughly as Clare was doing Jinny would have been snatching her horse back, but somehow it was different with Clare. Jinny had to believe in Clare, that she knew what was best. She so longed to be part of Clare's life, to know someone who was strong and confident like Clare seemed to be, who rode at shows and hunted and knew all about horses. To believe in Clare made these things possible for Jinny as well.

"Watch yourself with her," warned Mr. Manders. "She's not used to being bossed around."

"That's her trouble," answered Clare. "Go into the

front of the box," she shouted to Jinny. "I think there's a stick in there."

"It's no use . . ." Jinny began.

"You're not going to let her get away with this, are you?" Clare's dull eyes challenged Jinny. She stood playing Shantih like a salmon on the end of a line, her heavy bulk holding her to the ground while Shantih flashed and fought not to go any closer to the box. "Go on, get it," ordered Clare.

Jinny climbed into the cabin of the box and lying on top of the dashboard was a long cutting whip. Reluctantly Jinny picked it up. Inside the cabin, Clare's shouting and the trampling of Shantih's hooves were muted. Jinny sat for a second staring through the windscreen, holding the stick. She didn't want to take it out to Clare. She knew that hitting Shantih was useless.

"Can't you find it?" demanded Clare.

Jinny jumped down from the cab and walked slowly back to Clare.

"I never hit her. It only makes her fight more."

"We'll see about that," said Clare, grabbing the stick. "Now, my lady, let's see who's boss," and Clare swung the stick at Shantih's shoulder. But before it could touch her Shantih had reared straight up as she had been trained to do in the circus. Her forehooves lashed out at Clare's head. Jinny heard Clare scream, saw the sunlight dazzle on Shantih's metal shoes before she flung herself forward and threw her arms round Shantih's neck. Mr. Manders, too, dashed forward and grabbed the rope from Clare.

Shantih's forelegs touched the ground. She tried to rear again but Jinny's weight on her neck and Mr. Manders' hold on the rope stopped her from going up again. She pulled back violently, flinging herself away from them, then she stood trembling.

"Did she get you?" Mr. Manders asked Clare.

"Well, what a temper!" exclaimed Clare. "No, she missed me, filthy brute that she is."

"She's not, she's not," protested Jinny. "She doesn't mean to behave like that," and Jinny took Shantih from her father and led her away from the horse box. "We've

207

made her so afraid that she doesn't know what she's doing."

"You're not going to give in to her?" said Clare. "If she were mine she'd go into the box or else."

"She's afraid," said Jinny again. "Lots of people are afraid to get into a car again after they've had an accident even when they know that it's not likely to happen to them again, but you can't tell a horse. They can't understand that the same thing isn't bound to happen."

"Well, what are you going to do? I can't waste any more time. I mean to say one can't stand around being made a fool of by a horse."

"I'll ride her over to Craigvaar this afternoon," suggested Jinny.

"Well, just as you like," said Clare. "I must say I'm not used to giving in to animals, but if that's your idea of how to treat a horse it's up to you, of course."

"It might be the safest thing," said Mr. Manders.

"One might say the safest thing would be to get rid of the brute before she does some real damage," said Clare scornfully. "But of course it is entirely up to yourselves. I'll see you later, if she doesn't decide that she wants to stay in her field."

Clare jarred the horse box into motion, swung it round and roared past the house, down the drive and out on to the road.

"What a carry on!" exclaimed Mr. Manders.

Jinny stared down at Shantih, who was grazing nervously. The whole atmosphere was stirred and shaken by the sudden violence. Jinny could almost feel the disturbance lapping to and fro like shattered ripples on a pond.

"Does Shantih go for you like that?" Mr. Manders asked.

"It's only when you have a stick. She's just terrified," said Jinny, stroking Shantih's damp neck and running her fingers through her mane.

"If I didn't find Clare Burnley so offensive I might almost believe that she's right. Shantih does seem to go mad. You know, she is dangerous, Jinny. Mr MacKenzie was telling us how she keeps throwing you off when you're trying to ride her."

"That's why I'm taking her to Clare's, isn't it?" said Jinny crossly. "Clare is going to help me school her."

"She wasn't very successful this morning," said Mr. Manders. "Do you really want to take her to Craigvaar? Isn't there anyone else who could help you? How about Miss Tuke?"

"She's too busy trekking," said Jinny. "And anyway I want to go. Clare's won rosettes and cups and everything. She knows about horses. Miss Tuke only knows about trekking ponies."

"Well, for goodness' sake be careful."

"I will," said Jinny. "I will. I'm never anything else."

After lunch Jinny caught Shantih and rode to Craigvaar. At least, she rode as far as the farm. Shantih wasn't keen to pass Mr. MacKenzie's tractor, which was throbbing in the yard, and, since Mr. MacKenzie was standing in the yard too, Jinny thought she had better dismount and lead Shantih past the tractor before she was bucked off.

She coaxed Shantih past the tractor, waved to Mr. MacKenzie, and walked on out of sight of the farm. She was just about to remount when she changed her mind. It was far too nice a day to go on fighting. Jinny ran up her stirrups and slackened the girth.

"Let's have a happy time," she said to Shantih. "Let's stop all this aggro."

Shantih snuffled at Jinny's neck, denying that she ever fought with anyone. Jinny laughed as the horse's long whiskers tickled her.

"It is you just as much as me," Jinny told her, but she knew this wasn't true. Shantih hadn't fought when Ken was riding her.

Walking at Shantih's head, Jinny felt suddenly happy. Wherever she looked there were signs of spring. New life stretching up to the sun, flowers and leaves uncurling, lambs with the sheep, rabbits that were too young to know any better nibbling at the side of the road until Shantih and Jinny were almost upon them. The sun was warm again, and Jinny could feel it burning the back of her neck.

"It's spring," Jinny told Shantih, skipping at her side. "The winter's had it. Wonder if I could take you for a swim in the sea?"

With Shantih walking companionably by her side, Jinny felt perfectly content. There was nothing more she could have asked for. The wild country stretching around her, the grace of Shantih and the sun's warmth were all Jinny needed. All she would ever need.

Jinny paused before she turned the bend of the track that would bring Craigvaar into view. She took a last long look over the moorland to the mountains that were close today and seemed to be almost moving as the light flowed in mauves and greys and brilliance over their hunched shoulders. In the opposite direction the sea glimmered and sparkled and dark specks of gulls soared above it, weaving land to sea, sea to sky.

"Why isn't it enough?" Jinny thought wretchedly. "Enough to live here and have Shantih with me? Why can't this feeling last?"

She didn't know why, only knew that she had to go on going on. She tightened her girths and climbed back on to Shantih.

When they reached Craigvaar, fearing that Shantih might get a fright and bolt over the perfect lawns, Jinny dismounted again and led her up the path. She rang the front door bell and waited.

"Darling," said Mrs. Burnley, opening the door. "Clare waited ages for you but she thought you weren't coming. She's taken both the boys out by herself, poor thing. They can be quite a handful for one person to cope with. Now she said if you turned up you're to put your fellow in one of the spare boxes and wait until she gets back."

Self-consciously, Jinny led Shantih down through the long garden, between the rhododendrons and on to the stable yard. The doors of Huston's and Jasper's boxes were open wide. Jinny put Shantih into one of the other boxes. She hesitated, wondering whether she should take Shantih's tack off. It seemed silly to leave it on but pushy to take it off. Jinny decided to leave it on until Clare came back. She filled a bucket and gave Shantih a drink, then leaned against the half door chatting to her, the Arab's breath sweet on her face, the sun warm.

"If only we lived here," Jinny said longingly. "Imagine if these boxes and all the tack belonged to us. I'll bet you I wouldn't come off so much if I'd a proper saddle with knee rolls instead of those old trekking saddles."

It was nearly an hour before Clare came back. Jinny heard the distant clatter of hooves on the road, then the sound of Clare's voice shouting at her horses. She came down over the moor and into the yard through the paddock gate. She was riding Huston and leading Jasper, who dragged behind at the full length of his reins.

"So you've persuaded her to come. Glad to see she's not a completely free agent. Thought you might have been over sooner. These two are pigs to take out by oneself. I'm utterly destroyed. And with a valuable beast like Jasper I mean to say one is absolutely on tenterhooks in case he even scratches himself."

Clare dismounted and handed Huston's reins to Jinny.

"We'll settle them for the night," she said. "I know it is far too early but we're out for dinner with the Cranshaws and goodness knows when we'll arrive back. Do you know them? Old Pinkie Cranshaw is an absolute old sweetie. Flatters outrageously but you know how one does enjoy it."

Jinny didn't.

"Shall I take Huston's tack off?" she asked.

"Tack off, water, quick groom, rug on, bed down and I'll bring their hay and feed."

"I've put Shantih in the box next to Huston," said Jinny, really wanting to ask if she should give Shantih some hay too.

"See to her after Huston," said Clare. "I like to get these two attended to whenever they come in from exercise. Of course, Barbara sees to all this sort of thing when we're at home, but one does feel terribly responsible when she's not here to cope."

Before she started to groom Huston, Jinny took Shantih's tack off. If Clare was going out for dinner it didn't look as if she would have time to school Shantih. Jinny didn't know whether she was disappointed or relieved.

211

When all three horses were munching their feeds, Clare and Jinny went up to the house for afternoon tea. They had it in the sun lounge with Mrs. Burnley pouring and telling Jinny how she loved her perfectly sweet hair.

"Would it be terribly rude of me not to run you back to Finmory? Daddy is just too fussy about punctuality and I absolutely must have a bath before I go out. I mean one couldn't bear to have Pinkie telling one how absolutely divine one looks when all the time one is ponging of horse."

Jinny said she could easily walk.

"I'll come over for you first thing tomorrow morning and we'll give my two a thorough good exercise before I try to lunge your brute."

"I won't be able to come until about twelve," Jinny said. It was her day to take the early watch at the ospreys' nest. Ken had taken her turn today and she didn't think she could ask him again.

"Oh lordy no! But what a bore. Why ever not? Twelve o'clock! That's half the day gone. Why can't you come earlier? I mean to say I thought that was why you were here, so we could ride together."

"I've jobs to do at home," Jinny said.

"But how quaint. Of course Heather and Pat do all that sort of thing for us. Well, if you won't I suppose you won't. One can only hope that the afternoon is fine. It seems a frightful waste to me."

Jinny said goodnight to Shantih, who was tugging at her hay net and hardly bothered to look round, then she walked home over the moors. She felt cold and empty and didn't know why. Hadn't she got what she wanted? Clare to help her school Shantih. Wasn't that what she'd wanted since she'd first heard about Clare?

As she walked, Jinny searched the sky for any sign of the ospreys, but there were only the usual crows and gulls and once the arrowed flight of a kestrel. It would be another four weeks before Peter and Brian expected the eggs to hatch. Once the young birds were out of their eggs there would be no more danger from egg-collectors. Jinny grinned to herself, thinking about watching the young

212

ospreys growing and learning to fly. "Birds out of eggs," she thought, wrinkling up her nose in amazement at the thought of an egg very much the same as the boiled one she had had for breakfast growing into an osprey.

As Jinny made her way towards Finmory she looked down at the road. There was a man walking towards Glenbost. Jinny couldn't think who he might be. In Stopton nearly everyone had been strangers but in Glenbost nobody was. The man was tall with a bald head. He was looking round as he walked and Jinny saw the sun sparkling on his glasses. She didn't know who he could be and yet there was something familiar about him. "Need to ask Mr. Mac-Kenzie," she thought, but long before she reached home she had forgotten all about him.

"We're going to lunge Shantih tomorrow," Jinny told her mother.

"In American racing stables they have a machine which they hook the horses on to and they have to go round and round until you unhook them," said Ken, talking to Kelly.

"Fancy that now," said Jinny, and she took her handful of biscuits up to her bedroom and ate them looking down over the garden to the sea.

The field looked strangely empty with only Punch and Bramble in it.

"I won't leave her at Craigvaar too long," Jinny thought. "Once Clare has shown me what I'm doing wrong I'll bring her home again." But the cold emptiness was still there, like knowing you had an appointment with the dentist. "I'm daft," thought Jinny. "I really am daft. When I get what I wanted I don't want it any more."

She found her book on schooling and read the chapter on lungeing over again, and as she read she saw herself in Clare's paddock, Shantih cantering smoothly on the lunge rein, relaxed and willing, because Clare had all the right things—a cavesson noseband and a proper lungeing rein. Clare knew the right way to school horses.

Yet there was still an emptiness in Jinny, a strange coldness.

CHAPTER NINE

It was after twelve the next morning before Jinny rode Bramble into the stable yard at Craigvaar. Shantih and Huston were looking out over their half doors. Shantih whinnied to Bramble and Jinny, wrinkling the velvet of her nose, pushing against the door to reach them. Beside Huston's huge, blank, Roman-nosed head, Shantih's delicate, dished face and wide, dark eyes looked more magical than ever. Jinny shivered with delight at her beauty, and was caught suddenly by the throat, feeling ridiculous tears springing into her eyes as she thought that Shantih was her horse. She slid down from Bramble and rubbed Shantih's neck, holding out her hand to feel Shantih lipping at it.

Clare came out of Jasper's box, a body brush in her hand.

"I'm sorry I'm so late," Jinny said. "I couldn't get away any sooner. Mummy kept finding things for me to do."

Really it had been Mike's fault. He should have relieved Jinny at eleven but he hadn't arrived at the hide until half past.

"And I told you 'to be early today," Jinny had said, snatching Bramble's reins. "You know I asked you to be early because I've to be at Clare's. You wait, you just wait until you want me to draw something for you."

"Make no difference," said Mike. "Miss Broughton always knows when you've drawn my things. Any egg-collectors?"

"Thousands," said Jinny.

All the time she had been at the hide the male osprey had sat, hardly blinking an eye, perched on the top branch of his favourite pine, while the hen was almost hidden in the nest as she brooded the eggs. Longing to be at Craigvaar, Jinny had been tempted to leave them. "There's not a chance of anyone finding them, not a chance," she thought, as she swept the hillside with the powerful glasses.

214

Sheep nibbled undisturbed, hoodie crows flapped lazily from rock to rock and a ginger cat from the farm sat petrified, waiting for rabbits. "Mike's bound to be here soon. Why shouldn't I go?"

But she couldn't bring herself to leave the hide. The thought of what the others would say if anything happened to the eggs while she should have been on guard was enough to keep her there.

"I've mucked out your mare," Clare said. "Couldn't leave her standing there. Can't do that sort of thing when one's not used to it."

"I am sorry," said Jinny again.

" 'Course, when one's had horses all one's life one rather takes it for granted. If one has a horse one jolly well looks after it and that's all there is to it."

"I won't be late again," promised Jinny, wondering how she was ever going to fit in taking her turn at the hide with being at Craigvaar. "It was just this morning."

"Far too late to exercise them now. Better have lunch first and then get them out for a really good turn this afternoon."

Jinny agreed.

"I'll give Jasper a go on the lunge. Shove that fellow in a box and you can come and watch. Pick up a few hints for your idiot."

Jinny quickly put Bramble into the last empty box. She felt that she was making a take-over bid for Clare's stables.

"He won't need any hay," she apologised to Clare. "He's fat enough." But Clare didn't seem to hear her. She had the lunge rein clipped to the cavesson and, with the driving whip in her hand, was leading Jasper down to the paddock. Jinny scuttled to open the gate for her.

"Lead him round a few times," Clare said, as she took Jasper into the centre of the paddock.

Jinny grasped the supple leather of the headcollar and led the thoroughbred in a wide circle. He was remote and cold, a metallic horse, whose mind was made up of cogs and wheels.

When Jinny let him go, Clare sent him on at a trot. Jinny stood well back and watched as the black horse flung himself forward into a gallop. She saw Clare brace herself against him. She moved in a small circle, gradually bringing the horse back from his wild outburst of speed to a collected canter, controlling him between lunge rein and whip.

Jinny watched intently. It was the first time she had ever seen a horse being lunged. Clare was doing no more than Jinny's book had told her to do, but actually seeing Clare made all the difference. As if her skill was infectious.

"What about your blood?" Clare asked, when she had finished lungeing Jasper. "D'you want me to have a go at her?"

Jinny hesitated.

"Well, if that's the way you feel! I rather got the message than you were wanting a bit of help, and let's face it, after yesterday's performance one might say you bloomin' well need some."

"Oh, I do want you to help me," cried Jinny. "Of course I do. It's just that she's so terrified of whips there's no point in trying to lunge her with a whip in your hand. She'll only go crazy when she sees it. I know she will."

"Actually," stated Clare, "I don't much fancy coping with her unless I have something in my hand. She wasn't kidding yesterday. She meant it. When she reared up she meant to get me."

"It isn't her fault," pleaded Jinny. "It was that filthy circus. They taught her to do that. It was her act."

"Tell you what, you put on her tack and I'll ride her round. I'll not use a stick but I rather think she'll find me harder to shift than she does you."

"Be good," Jinny whispered to Shantih as she put on her saddle and bridle. "Do what Clare asks. You've got to learn to behave yourself. If you don't, they'll stop me from riding you, I know they will."

High-stepping at Jinny's side, Shantih plunged down to the paddock. Her neck was crested, her tail, fanning out in the spring breeze, was kinked over her back. At the paddock gate she stuck her pint pot head into the air, screaming through the dark pits of her nostrils.

She seemed to Jinny to be a golden horse out of legend,

and for a second she admitted the truth of Ken's disgust with saddles and bridles. If Shantih were free she would rear up from the mountain tops, soar through the sky like a comet, racing to join the horses of the sun.

"I'll say this for Arabs, they are pretty little things," said Clare, taking Shantih from Jinny, "but I couldn't be bothered with one myself. Far too finicky. I've never known one that wasn't slightly potty."

Clare mounted, lengthened her stirrups and sent Shantih forward at a walk. She rode with a deep, secure seat and a short rein, her hands fixed and unyielding. With Clare riding her, Shantih seemed to shrink in front of Jinny's eyes. When she plunged forward and began to buck Clare sat solid and unmoved, kicking her on and shouting at her.

After Shantih's fourth buck Clare won. She managed to get Shantih's head up and send her on round the paddock.

"Go on," growled Clare. "Get on, you twisted vampire. Get on with you," and she pressed Shantih relentlessly into a gallop. Round and round she galloped her, and even when Shantih would have slowed down to a trot Clare forced her to go on galloping.

Jinny watched numbly. This was what Shantih needed. Clare wasn't being cruel. She hadn't used a stick. This was why Jinny had brought her horse to Craigvaar so that Clare would ride her. But was this really what she wanted? Jinny didn't know.

Clare brought Shantih back to a walk, turned her and took her round in the opposite direction. Shantih stopped. Clare roared at her and Shantih reared straight up. Clare slackened her reins, leaning forward, but she didn't move an inch in the saddle. She was as secure as if she were sitting on a rocking horse. Shantih's second rear was less defiant, and as she touched the ground again Clare was ready for her, and with seat and voice she forced her forward. In seconds, Shantih was tearing round the paddock at a flat out gallop.

Jinny tried not to look. She couldn't bear the sight of Clare galloping her horse; couldn't bear the sight of Shantih's straining body, foam-spattered chest and frantic, panic-blind eyes. Jinny clenched herself tight. "It's what

217

she needs, it's what she needs," she told herself, but really what she wanted to do was to grab Clare and drag her to the ground and never let her go near Shantih again.

"That's straightened her out a bit for you," Clare announced at last as she walked Shantih back to Jinny. "We'll get her head strapped down—stop her rearing. You're far too soft with her. That's half the trouble. One has to treat a horse as a horse or it ends up being the boss."

Jinny knew she should say something, should thank Clare and praise her riding, but she couldn't bring herself to do it.

"Don't think there's time for you to have a shot," said Clare. "We want to get lunch over and get out. Anyway, she's had enough for today. Let the lesson sink in."

Jinny led Shantih back to her box. She didn't think Clare had taught her anything, only been rough with her and proved that she was a stronger rider than Jinny. She took Shantih's tack off and rubbed her down with a straw wisp. Shantih's sides were clamped in and she stood in a corner of the box with her ears gloomed back and her tail tucked down. Clare came to the door to say that lunch was ready and Jinny followed her out, too ashamed to look back at Shantih.

In the afternoon they exercised Clare's horses. Clare, on Jasper, rode at Jinny's side, telling her stories of her horsey past.

"But really I do think my favourite was Ladybird. She was fantastic at games. The other kids just would not enter when they saw us lining up. I honestly swear that she could have won a bending race by herself."

Listening to Clare, Jinny forgot about the morning, forgot about the way Clare had ridden Shantih. She could only think how wonderful Clare was, how much Clare knew about horses and how amazing it was that she should be talking to her like this.

"My first real hunter was a big bay horse. I came home for the Christmas hols and there she was. Sixteen hands! Well, you can imagine what one felt. I'd been riding a fourteen two pony in the summer. One felt really grown up at last. And my first hunt on her! Gosh, all the gates seemed tiny. Blitz just stepped over them. And one knew how madly jealous all one's friends were. I mean to say, most of them were still grubbing about on ponies."

As they rode back to Craigvaar, Jinny saw a stranger walking down the road towards them. It was the same man she had seen yesterday, the same bald head and glasses. Jinny peered at him curiously, she still felt she should know him but couldn't place him. It wasn't until he was almost level with the horses that Jinny remembered. She caught her breath in surprise, turned quickly to Clare hiding from the man beneath her hard hat, for it was the customer from the Inverburgh gift shop and he had binoculars round his neck.

"Did you know that chap?" Clare asked. Jinny shook her head. "Seemed to know you. Odd-looking type. Birdwatcher, I expect."

Jinny told her father that she had seen the man again.

"So he's found out where we came from," said Mr. Manders. "I'll warn the others. Of course, he may be perfectly innocent, only wanting to see the ospreys."

Jinny wasn't so sure. She hadn't liked him.

"He was a grabber," she said. "Wanted to grab my drawings."

Next morning Jinny was at Craigvaar early. She had mucked out the horses before Clare appeared.

"How kind," said Clare. "Now we'll be able to get these two out at a decent hour."

"I have to be home for three o'clock," said Jinny. She had to take the afternoon watch on the nest and felt it would be better to let Clare know straightaway.

"You do lead a busy little life," said Clare. "What is it this time, down the salt mines or to the galleys?"

When they had exercised Huston and Jasper, Clare suggested they should try lungeing Shantih.

"No whip," said Jinny.

"You can ride her and I'll lunge you both," said Clare, and gave Jinny a martingale and a drop noseband to try on Shantih.

"Put your stirrups down two holes," ordered Clare, when she had Jinny and Shantih in the paddock. "You're

perched on top of her and when she starts playing up
you've no control. That's better. Now walk her round."

Jinny took Shantih round. With longer stirrups she was
able to use her legs more strongly and push Shantih on
when she tried to break out of the circle.

"Good," yelled Clare. "Now let's try her at a trot."

Shantih burst forward into a canter, then tried to buck,
but the lunge rein kept her head up.

"No you don't, you twister. Get on with you," roared
Clare.

Jinny, sitting deeper in the saddle than she normally did,
was able to push Shantih on where before she would have
been jerked out of the saddle and the horse would have
been in control.

"Nicely. Well done," shouted Clare. "Now try and
balance her. Push with your seat. Keep her there between
your hands and your seat. Good. Not too fast. Slow trot.
Good. Keep her there."

Concentrating on obeying Clare's instructions, Jinny
hardly realised that Shantih had trotted round several
times without bucking.

"Walk," shouted Clare. "Change the rein."

Jinny looked down doubtfully at her reins.

"It means walk across the circle and go round in the
opposite direction."

"Oh," said Jinny, and did so.

"This time when I say, 'prepare to trot, trot on,' that's
what I want—not a canter and then a bucking display."

Jinny nodded, all her attention on her horse.

"Prepare to trot."

Jinny shortened her reins and sat down in the saddle.

"Trot on."

Jinny, letting Shantih go forward, felt the moment when
normally Shantih would have been bucking, but now she
was able to check her, bring her back and collect her between her hands and her seat. For the very first time
Jinny felt as if she were in control of Shantih and not the
other way round.

In half an hour Clare said Shantih had had enough.

"Thank you very much," said Jinny. "She was much better, wasn't she?"

"You've got a good seat," said Clare. "I expect it's all the bashing about you've done on those Highlands. Keep your stirrups at that length and perhaps you'll be able to stay on top of her for a change."

"I think she understood what we wanted her to do," said Jinny. "I think she enjoyed it too."

"Taking her to the show on Wednesday?" asked Clare, joking.

"Oh, I couldn't," gasped Jinny, but visions of herself and Shantih trotting round a show ring lit up in neon lights behind her eyes. "But I couldn't."

"Why not? They have this thing called Handy Horse. Actually, it's only a showing class for horses who aren't good enough to show. You go round the ring all together, trot up and canter back, get on and off, and that's it. No jumping. Of course she may not win, but as long as you don't expect that, there's nothing to it. Room in the box for her."

"She wouldn't go in," said Jinny.

"I'll put Huston and Jasper in first. Might be a bit of a laugh taking an Arab to Inverburgh. Some of them won't know what she is. Nearly all cows and sheep."

"You don't really think I could?"

Clare laughed scornfully. "I'm not suggesting you take her to the White City," she said. "You're so intense about everything. She's only a horse. Have a bit of fun on her for a change."

"Do you think I could?" repeated Jinny longingly.

"Well, I jolly well would in your shoes. That's what horses are for, to get you out and about a bit. Goodness, when I was your age I was absolutely mad on Pony Club things. I would have gone anywhere."

When Jinny told her family that she was taking Shantih to Inverburgh Show, there was a moment of silent amazement.

"But . . ." began Mrs. Manders.

"But you . . ." gasped Petra.

"You'll be thrown off in front of everyone," cried Mike.

221

"If she gets the least little bit excited she bucks you off, and she'll be out of her skin at a show."

"Clare and I are schooling her," said Jinny. "Clare says I've got a good seat."

"Good and hard," said Mike, "the number of times you've landed on it."

"Isn't it too dangerous?" asked Mr. Manders. "She can't have improved so much in such a short time, and if she ran mad at the show she might hurt someone."

"Actually, that's all a thing of the past," said Jinny. "Clare says that when she was my age she would have gone anywhere, that nothing would have stopped her. So it's not going to stop me."

"Does this mean we'll need to count you out for the day of the show?" Peter asked. "Wednesday, did you say? What watch are you doing?"

"It means," said Jinny, taking a deep breath, "that I won't be free until after the show."

Jinny thought hard about riding Shantih in a show ring while everyone around her was shocked or annoyed or furious.

"I can't help it," stated Jinny. "I'll watch the ospreys as much as you like after Wednesday, but not before."

"You can do Thursday then," said Petra. "It should be me from eleven to three and I want to go to Duniver that morning."

"Anything after Wednesday," said Jinny patiently. "I don't suppose you have a hair net?" she asked her mother. "Clare says I should wear a hair net," and Mr. Manders burst out laughing.

"If Clare told you to dance a hornpipe on top of Shantih you'd do it," he said.

"Everyone with long hair wears a hair net when they're showing a horse," Jinny told him.

Jinny spent Tuesday night at Craigvaar. Before they went to bed, she and Clare went out to say goodnight to the horses.

"So quaint," said Clare. "I just cannot believe that this will be the first horse show you've ever been to."

222

"But it is," said Jinny. "My very first."

She fed Shantih the bread crusts she had brought.

"Be good tomorrow," Jinny said to her. "I don't want you to win or anything like that. Just go into the box with Huston and Jasper and stay sensible when we're at the show."

The whole of Jinny was twisted into a tight knot of excitement. Half of her was thrilled at the thought of riding Shantih in a show ring, while the other half of her was curled away from the thought; afraid that taking Shantih to a show was the stupidest thing she had ever done. Jinny knew that Shantih had improved. In the paddock that afternoon she had stayed calm and responsive, only trying to rear once; but what would she do at the show?

"This time tomorrow it will all be over," Jinny thought, "and really, the worst thing that could happen is for me to come off, and I'm quite used to that."

CHAPTER TEN

Jinny sat in the cabin of the horse box, squashed between Mr. Burnley, who was driving, and Clare. In the box behind them were the three horses. Shantih, tucked in behind Huston, had walked into the box with hardly any hesitation, which seemed to Jinny to be such a good omen that she felt anything was possible. Shantih might even win her class when the day had started so well.

"Same place as usual?" Mr. Burnley demanded.

"Gosh yes," said Clare. "Shouldn't think they'd ever change it."

Clare was wearing a black jacket, white breeches and boots. She had lent Jinny an old tweed hacking jacket, but even with this and her new jodphurs Jinny still felt a thing of rags and patches beside Clare.

"But, darling, you look really sweet. Such wonderfully

pretty hair," Mrs. Burnley had said before they left, which let Jinny know that she didn't think much of her appearance either.

"As if it matters," thought Jinny. "I don't care what I look like. The only thing that matters is for Shantih to go well."

Mr. Burnley turned the box through the gateway and on to the show field.

"We've come here some years and it's been hock deep in mud. Remember that spring when Spencer was on a little grey mare? Knew she wouldn't stand a chance in the heavy going, so he borrowed a carthorse thing from one of the farmers. Feet like sewer lids. And, by Jove, he won the jumping on it. Only animal who could stay upright. Old Spencer went round the lot. Remember that, Clare?"

Jinny stared through the cabin window as the box trundled over the field. White tents dazzled in the sun, stalls and caravans were surrounded by displays of goods for sale, and around the main ring a row of cars was already in place. There were pens of sheep and cattle as immaculate as advertisements in a butcher's shop window, and carthorses with their coats spiky with soap and their manes and stumpy tails bedecked with ribbons. Next to the carthorses were the Highland ponies and Shetlands, with long, dense manes and their tails sweeping the ground. Jinny shivered with excitement.

Mr. Burnley parked the box in a far corner of the field.

"This is where all the horsey things go on," Clare explained. "I must admit we do rather take second place to the sheep, but it is such a friendly little show. Such fun!"

Through the window at the back of the cabin Jinny could see the three horses. They were all tied up short to the sides of the box, their eyes glinting in the dim light.

"All content?" Clare asked.

"Seem to be," said Jinny.

"We'll dash across to the secretary's tent and collect our numbers before we take them out. My showing class will be first. Want to give Jasper a bit of a school before then."

Clare jumped down from the cabin and Jinny followed her.

224

"Over this way," said Clare, "unless they've changed things, which one does not even consider."

With long, springing strides Clare marched to the secretary's tent. Jinny, trotting beside her, thought that she seemed to know everyone. Permed, white-haired ladies in headscarves and sheepskins, farmers in bristling tweed suits, red-faced moustached men in bow ties and bowlers, and thin young men in sports jackets and twills all shouted greetings to Clare as she passed.

"Wonderful to see you," Clare cried to them all. "How one does absolutely love meeting everyone again."

"Clare Burnley—numbers twelve and thirty-four," said the lady at the table in the secretary's tent. "So pleased to see you here again."

"Absolutely wonderful to be here," said Clare.

"No Spencer this year?"

" 'Fraid not. Staying with friends. Chance to get out with a gun that he couldn't bear to pass up."

"Only seems like yesterday when he was in here entering for all the games," lamented the lady.

"Jinny wants to enter for the Handy Horse comp," organised Clare.

"Thirty pence entry fee."

The lady gave Jinny number fifty-seven.

"I'll keep it for ever," Jinny said as they walked back to the box.

"I should jolly well tie it on your arm just now," said Clare, "or you're bound to lose it and then there's such a fuss. I say, look, isn't that Ros? Oh, I must go and have a word with her," and Clare ran across to a girl in a scarlet trouser suit and a white fur hat.

Gradually the whole show ground was filling up. Sheep were already being judged, farmers were putting a last-minute polish on their beasts, stall owners were shouting their wares, a clutch of gas-filled balloons sailed high above the tents, children rode round on shaggy ponies and a few adults exercised their horses. The air was filled with noise and excitement. Standing waiting for Clare, Jinny shivered suddenly. She wished Clare would hurry up so that they could take Shantih out of the box and give her time to get used to the strange surroundings before it was her class.

"Oh please," thought Jinny, "please let her behave herself." Surrounded by all the noise and bustle, Jinny was beginning to realise that riding Shantih here wouldn't be the same as riding her in Clare's paddock.

"Terribly sorry," said Clare, coming back at last. "Have I been ages? Ros is such a sweet girl, so amusing, and I hadn't seen her for months."

"Been a deuce of a time," growled Mr. Burnley. "That's the first showing class in the ring just now."

"Don't panic, darling," said Clare, patting her father's arm. "We've about two hours before it's us."

In the small ring were eight or nine children's ponies.

"Gosh, I know them all so well," exclaimed Clare. "Every year the same old ponies with different kids bumping round on top."

Mr. Burnley lowered the ramp and Shantih screamed at them, rolling the whites of her eyes, tossing her head against the rope.

"Calm down," shouted Clare. "There's no need to look as if you were entering for the Derby. Lord, I hope she hasn't upset Jasper. Last thing I want is him breaking out."

"Here," she said to Jinny as she untied Shantih. "Watch out for her."

Jinny took Shantih's rope, uncertain just exactly what she was meant to be looking out for.

Feeling herself free, Shantih plunged out of the box in one enormous bound. The rope burnt through Jinny's hands and then Shantih was tearing at a flat-out gallop across the show field, the rope dangling about her legs.

"You bloomin' idiot," swore Clare, but already Jinny was running after her horse, following in the wake of her disturbance.

Shantih had gone straight towards the line of Highland ponies. Jinny could hear them squealing and their owners shouting as she ran towards them. By the time Jinny reached them, a man in blue dungarees had caught Shantih and she was standing tense and afraid.

"This your property?"

"Oh, thank you for catching her," cried Jinny. "Are the ponies all right?"

"Wouldn't hang around to find out," said the man, "or they'll be sueing you for damages."

Jinny took Shantih's rope and the Arab reared, shaking and tossing her head as she tried to escape again.

"You fit for her?" asked the man.

"She's excited," said Jinny. "Whoa, Shantih, whoa, steady. She doesn't know what she's doing when she gets a fright like this."

"Hang on to her then," said the man, keeping out of the reach of Shantih's hooves.

"Thank goodness you've got her," said Clare, running up. "Loose horse in a place like this can cause no end of damage. You were half asleep. I bloomin' warned you to look out. Honestly, Jinny, you'll need to start and look alive. I am not here to be a nursemaid to you. I expect that's her started. Don't tell me we are in for a day of her nonsense because I am just not going to stand for it!"

"I'm sorry," said Jinny. It was taking all her strength to control Shantih. She seemed to be twice her usual size. Mighty as a war horse crying ha at the sound of trumpets, Shantih plunged and fought at the end of her rope.

"Give her to me," ordered Clare. "Now get up with you. No more of this nonsense." Shantih flung up her head, wild and terrified. "Get on with you, you twisted varmit."

Back at the box, Clare put Shantih's bridle on. She gave the reins to Jinny.

"Now this time hold on to them. Take her across to that corner and let her graze for a bit. See if that will calm her down. She is a crazy squib."

Shantih snatched up mouthfuls of grass between urgent screams to the other horses. Jinny refused to let herself think that she had been a fool to bring Shantih. She had done it and that was that. Now she had to see it through. But the sight of her horse, terrified and wild, stopped Jinny being blinded by the show's glamour. Perhaps Ken was right, and it was only pride that made people bring their animals to compete against each other.

"Your class is after mine," Clare said, as she rode up mounted on Jasper. "That is if you're still taking her in for it. I must say I shouldn't blame you if you chicken out."

"I'm not going home without trying," said Jinny, and to her relief her voice sounded firm and confident, not quivering and jellified the way she was feeling.

"Pa will help you tack her up," said Clare. "I've got to school this fellow," and she trotted away, sitting tall and solid on the showy black thoroughbred.

There was no sign of Mr. Burnley at the horse box, and Jinny had to struggle by herself to try and get the saddle on Shantih. She cavorted in circles, pulling Jinny round with her, and every time she got any length of rein she tried to plunge up the ramp to rejoin Huston.

"Can I give you a bit of help?" asked a boy from school.

"If you could hold her until I get her tack on," Jinny said gratefully. "It's this fiddling martingale."

"She's a bonnie wee pony," said Archie, clinging on to Shantih's bit.

Although it wasn't exactly how Jinny saw Shantih, it was the nicest thing anyone had said about her that morning.

"She gets a bit excited at times," Jinny said, putting on her hard hat and trying to climb on to Shantih's back.

"My, but you're stiff," said Archie. "Is it the rheumatics you have?"

Jinny couldn't get her foot up to the stirrup. She hopped helplessly round, then realised that it was because of her new jodhpurs.

"Spring, girl, spring," roared Mr. Burnley. "Never thought a skinned rabbit like you would be as stiff as that. Here, I'll chuck you up."

"It's my new . . ." Jinny began, but before she could finish her explanation Mr. Burnley had grasped her knee and thrown her skywards. Luckily Shantih shied away from him so when Jinny came down she landed on top of the saddle.

When she was mounted she felt better. She rode with long stirrups the way Clare had taught her, and sat deep in the saddle. At first, Shantih refused to pay any attention

228

to her, but went on spooking and shying, barging her quarters into people, ponies and cars.

"It's all right," Jinny told her. "It's all right. Nothing's going to happen to you. I'm only going to ride you in the ring with a few other horses. Ride you up and down, that's all. We'll go back to Finmory soon, back to your own field. It's all right. Steady now. Don't get so excited, silly girl."

As Jinny walked her round, threading their way through all the life of the show, she kept her voice low and gentle, whispering to Shantih the way Ken had done when he had ridden her over the moor, and gradually she felt the mare relaxing.

When Jinny came back to the ringside, Clare and eight other horses were riding round the ring. It was obvious that Jasper would be the winner. All the other horses were only ordinary riding horses, but Jasper was a top class show horse.

"That's not fair," Jinny thought. "He's much too good to be shown against those others. They don't stand a chance. Clare couldn't have known what they were going to be like or she wouldn't have entered him."

Embarrassed, Jinny walked Shantih away and didn't take her back until the sound of applause told her that the class was over.

"Jolly good," boomed Mr. Burnley, as Clare rode out of the ring, a red rosette flapping from Jasper's bridle.

"Walkover," Clare yelled back. "Don't know why we bother to bring the cup back every year. Really, we could just keep it at home, and that would be that."

Jinny tried not to listen. She concentrated on Shantih until the Handy Horse class was announced and she could ride away from the Burnleys and the circle of friends who were congratulating Clare.

Shantih pranced round the ring like a hackney; her hooves flashed neat and precise, her face was carven and delicate-featured, and her mane lifted in a silken wave.

There were six other horses and three Highland ponies. Jinny saw Miss Tuke standing at the rails and waved, thinking that the Highlands were probably her trekkers.

The six horses were duller, heavier, and more badly put together than the ones in Clare's class.

Jinny felt sick with herself for seeing them like that. When she had lived in Stopton she would have loved to have owned any of them. They would have been beautiful to her then.

She brought Shantih to a walk behind one of the Highlands, hoping that the broad, black bottom would give her a feeling of security.

There were two judges—a weather-beaten man in a bowler, tweed jacket, breeches and gaiters who might have been made out of chewed leather, and a tall, sheepskinned lady.

When they were told to trot, Shantih tucked down her head and bucked. Jinny fought to stay on and managed it by the skin of her teeth. She gathered Shantih together and they tore round the ring at an extended trot. When they were asked to canter, Shantih galloped.

Jinny was brought in third. Two bay horses stood in front of her. A steward explained that they were to trot their horses down the ring, canter back, then dismount and remount.

The first bay gave a sober, gentlemanly performance. The second bay refused to canter.

It was Jinny's turn next. Looking straight ahead, she rode Shantih out of the line and turned her to trot down the ring. Shantih cantered, fighting for her head. At the foot of the ring she reared, swung round and galloped back to the other horses. Jinny flung herself to the ground before she reached them, which was meant to be dismounting, and then remembered about her new jodphurs. Hopping madly, she tried to get her foot into the stirrup. People round the ring began to laugh as Shantih plunged back to the other horses with Jinny, still hopping, at her side.

"Next," said the steward.

"Wooden leg?" asked the man on the bay.

"It's my new jodphurs," Jinny announced loudly, glaring up at him. "I can't bend my knee."

Her voice carried round the ring, and the laughter

230

changed to applause. Scarlet-faced, Jinny had to wait until the steward gave her a leg up. She could imagine what Clare and her friends would be saying.

"But that's it over," Jinny thought, "and I haven't come off." And she waited impatiently until the other horses had given their displays.

"Don't we go now?" she asked the man on the bay when all the horses had had their turns.

"Judge has to ride them," he said.

The chewed-leather judge came up to the first bay. The rider dismounted and the judge mounted. To Jinny's utter horror she saw that he was carrying a long cutting whip.

"He can't ride Shantih with a whip," she thought. "I can't let him on her with a whip."

Jinny couldn't think what to do, she could only sit and wait helplessly until the judge was standing in front of her.

"Now for the firecracker," he said.

"I'm sorry," said Jinny, "you can't ride her with a whip. She's afraid of whips."

"I won't use it," said the judge, "unless she needs it. I always carry a stick."

"No," said Jinny. "She's terrified of them. You can't ride her with a whip in your hand."

"Don't you say 'can't' to me, my girl. Off you get. I'll not hurt your pony."

"Oh, please understand," said Jinny.

"Either I ride your horse or you are eliminated," said the judge.

"Oh, I'll be eliminated," agreed Jinny. "That doesn't matter."

The judge beckoned a steward over and spoke to him.

"Will number fifty-seven please leave the ring. This competitor is eliminated for refusing to comply with the rules of the show," announced the steward over the loudspeaker.

Blushing scarlet and praying for an instant atom bomb to fall, Jinny tried to make Shantih leave the other horses.

"Here, what do you think you're at?" demanded the man on the bay when Shantih barged into him. "Get over with you," and he brought his stick down on Shantih's quarters.

231

Shantih bucked once, a violent, high, terrified buck. Jinny sailed over her head. The ground hit her hard, springing up to meet her, and as she lay there, stunned, she heard Shantih thundering out of the ring. Strangers crowded round Jinny asking if she was sure she hadn't hurt herself.

"I do it all the time," Jinny assured them grimly as she got to her feet.

The people round the ring not only clapped but cheered and cat-called as Jinny trudged across the vast expanse of grass to the ring exit.

"But, my dear, what an exhibition!" exclaimed Clare.

"It was you who said I should have a go," said Jinny, taking Shantih from Mr. Burnley, who had caught her.

"Whatever happened?" demanded Clare. "Why were you eliminated?"

"Wouldn't let the judge ride her. He had a stick."

"Oh honestly!" cried Clare and the blond, pink-cheeked young man standing with her yawh, yawh, yawhed at the top of his voice.

"You are the weirdest kid I have ever known," stated Clare.

"Yawh, yawh, yawh," agreed the pink young man.

The show seemed to go on forever. Jinny stood holding Shantih waiting for it to be over. People came up to make sure that she hadn't hurt herself, some to tell her that Shantih was wicked and not fit for a girl to ride, and some to ask if her new jodphurs were still too tight. Clare and her friends paid no attention to her. They talked in their loud, waffling voices, telling each other how wonderful and pretty and sweet everything was. Jinny had thought of leading Shantih home, but she was afraid of the traffic on the Inverburgh road.

She watched as Clare, on Huston, won both jumping classes. She listened to Clare's friends telling her how jolly well she had ridden to win, although it was obvious that none of the horses had stood a chance against Huston.

"It's not fair bringing such good horses to a small show like this," Jinny thought, "bringing them up from England." But she only thought it because they were

232

ignoring her. Jinny wanted to be part of the noise and bright excitement, to be the same as Clare's friends in their smart clothes, to make the same loud, empty noises, and to know the right things to say.

She wanted them to talk to her, to notice her, to tell her how sensible she had been in refusing to let the judge ride her horse. But not one of them paid any attention to Jinny or to Shantih as she pulled and fretted and whinnied.

"That's it for another year, what?" said Mr. Burnley, when at last the mounted games had dragged to a close. "Another year of triumph for you. Don't know what the locals would do if they didn't have you to give them a bit of competition?"

"Oh, I do absolutely adore Inverburgh Show," sighed Clare. "Now to get these fellows boxed. Let us hope your idiot doesn't take it into her head to play up," and Clare looked with distaste at Shantih.

To Jinny's relief, Shantih followed Huston into the box as she had done in the morning—which seemed to Jinny to be a lifetime away.

In the high cabin Clare and her father talked to each other over Jinny's head. Twice she tried to join in but they paid no attention to her.

"They think I'm a fool," Jinny decided. "And so I am. There's nothing about me that would make Clare want me for a friend, nothing about me that would interest Clare."

But there was one thing. One thing that would interest them. Jinny dug her nails into the leather seat. She thought, "I mustn't tell them. I mustn't," then she said in a voice that didn't sound like her own: "Oh, by the way, I forgot to tell you, we've got two ospreys nesting on the moors."

"You mean eagles," said Clare.

"No, I don't. I mean ospreys. The R.S.P.B. men have seen them. They're ospreys O.K."

Both Clare and Mr. Burnley were listening to her now. Jinny felt the day's disappointment and disgrace slip away as she began to tell the Burnleys all about the ospreys.

"Well, I'll eat my hat," exclaimed Mr. Burnley. "What a turn up for the book. Wait till old Spencer hears this. And right under his very nose!"

233

CHAPTER ELEVEN

Jinny didn't tell her family much about the show. She knew they would eventually hear all about her exhibition from Mr. MacKenzie, and she certainly didn't mention the fact that she had told the Burnleys about the ospreys. In fact, she tried not to think too much about that herself.

"But the Burnleys wouldn't harm them. I know they wouldn't," Jinny thought as she lay in bed. "They understand animals, they wouldn't harm them."

Jinny turned over and tried to sleep but she couldn't. She lay thinking about the ospreys. She had promised not to tell anyone about them and she had broken her promise.

"But the Burnleys are different," Jinny argued to herself. "Quite, quite different. I'm allowed to tell them."

Next morning, Jinny set off in good time for her watch over the nest. Clare had said she would see to Shantih in the morning and Jinny was to ride to Craigvaar when she was off duty at four. "It makes it all so much easier," Jinny thought as she rode Bramble up the moors. "Now Clare knows what I'm doing I don't have to make excuses all the time. That was telling lies really."

It was a bright spring day, with a blue sky and a breeze blowing through Jinny's hair and Bramble's mane, but as she rode, Jinny felt heavy and dead. She wanted to quarrel with someone, to get her temper out, but she didn't know what she was cross about, only felt it stored up inside her, sullen and black.

"I'll be glad when I'm back at school," she thought. "Glad when I've got Shantih back in her own paddock. Glad when Peter and Brian have gone away."

She looked spitefully round at the moors and the mountains and, for the first time since they had come to Finmory, Jinny thought longingly of Stopton—of a Saturday matinee at the pictures with crisps and popcorn; of walking through the busy streets; of pushing her way on to a crowded bus and of being with people, lots of people who wouldn't care who she had told about the ospreys.

"Instead of all this nothingness," thought Jinny. She kicked Bramble forward and he grunted and glowered. "Get on with you when I tell you," Jinny snarled at him. "Get on with you, you old trekking pony."

"It's all the ospreys' fault," Jinny decided. "If they hadn't come and nested here I'd never have told Clare about them. It's all their fault."

Mr. Manders knew as soon as he saw Jinny riding towards the hide that she was in a bad mood. "The sooner she brings Shantih back home and stops spending all her time with Clare Burnley the better I'll like it," he thought. But he knew his daughter too well to say anything to her. "What does she see in Clare?" he wondered, watching Jinny kicking the stubborn black bulk of Bramble up the hillside, and he was amazed yet again at how everything changed depending upon whose eyes you were looking through.

"This is *the* most stubborn beast," exclaimed Jinny. "Why one should have to ride such a creature I cannot think!"

Mr. Manders struggled to keep his face straight. "I presume you are speaking for Clare and yourself?" he asked.

"What?" said Jinny. "Oh, I am so bored. I'm so bored with everything."

"Are you?" said Mr. Manders. "Wonder why."

Jinny looked quickly at her father, but there was no way he could possibly have found out that she had given away the ospreys' secret.

"Don't know," said Jinny. "I'm just fed up."

"No more sign of your birdwatcher," said Mr. Manders. "He must have given up. Well, don't be falling asleep," and he climbed on to Bramble and rode away.

"Fed up, fed up, fed up," muttered Jinny, as she fixed the glasses on the ospreys. The male was on his favourite perch, the female deep in the nest with only her head and tail visible. "Buck up and hatch them," Jinny thought. "Hurry up and get away from here. Stupid birds."

Through the glasses Jinny saw the cock turn to stare directly at her, almost as if he could read her thoughts, then she heard the sound of hooves. For a moment Jinny thought her father must have forgotten something, but the trampling hooves sounded more like several horses and not just Bramble.

"Cooee, Jinny," called Clare's voice, and the male osprey flapped into the air.

For a second, Jinny couldn't move. She couldn't imagine what Clare was doing on the moors so close to the ospreys. What if her father had seen her? Jinny felt a cold guilty sweat prickling her skin. She stumbled out of the hide. Clare, riding Huston and leading Jasper, was only a few yards away.

"Gosh, I thought I'd never find you," cried Clare. "I'll say this for you, you've made a jolly good job of the hide."

"What do you want?" demanded Jinny. "You're disturbing the ospreys."

"Sorry. Am I being terribly naughty?"

Jinny stared uneasily at Clare. "Dad was here a few minutes ago. If he'd seen you he would have been mad with me. I told you yesterday it was a secret."

"Gosh, yes," said Clare. "Only it's a sort of emergency. I've come for you. Ma was speaking to Lady Gilbert on the phone this morning and we've been invited to visit her for lunch."

"We? I don't know Lady Gilbert."

"Of course you do. You must have heard of her Arabs. They're famous. And when she lives so close. Normally she won't let anyone near them, she's utterly possessive about them. So when she asked us over for lunch I knew you would be mad if you missed such a chance, and I grabbed the phone from Ma and told Lady G. about Shantih, and how well you are doing with her, and she is just crazy to meet you."

"But I can't come," said Jinny. She had read about Lady Gilbert's Arabs winning prizes at the Arab Horse

Show but she had never thought she would have a chance of visiting her stables. "I'm on duty here. I can't leave the nest."

"Oh, for goodness' sake grow up!" exclaimed Clare. "Here I am offering you the chance of a lifetime and all you say is 'I can't come'. Why ever not? You want to see the Arabs, don't you?"

"Of course," said Jinny crossly. "Of course I do. But I can't."

"Look, I've dragged these horses all over the moors so you can ride back with me."

"I tell you I can't come."

"You don't need to worry about your old chickens. There's never a soul on these moors. They're as safe as the Bank of England. I mean you can't, you just cannot, turn down a chance like this. To see Lady Gilbert's Arabs, to see her stallion."

"Her stallion?" echoed Jinny. "Has she got a stallion?"

"She has," said Clare and waited.

"I would have to be back before half-past three. Ken comes up at four."

"Lord, it's only eleven. Look, I give you my word you'll be back here before four. That's if you come now and stop all this boring fuss. Here, you have Huston," and Clare jumped down and handed the grey's reins to Jinny.

"I shouldn't, honestly I shouldn't," said Jinny. She hesitated, looking at the ospreys' nest. "If anything happened to them . . ."

"Oh, it won't," said Clare. "I mean to say, no one would expect you to stay here when you've the chance of seeing an Arab stud."

"We MUST be back before four," said Jinny, pulling herself up on to Huston. "My family would murder me if they ever found out I'd left them alone."

For a second Jinny hesitated, torn between going with Clare, which she knew was wrong, and staying on guard, which she knew was right. The Burnleys' car might have a puncture or anything might happen to delay them, to stop Jinny being in the hide when Ken arrived at four. But what really mattered were the ospreys' eggs. If anything happened to them while she was with Clare, it would be her fault.

Jinny leaned her weight on the pommel of Huston's saddle, ready to swing herself to the ground. "I can't come. I must stay and watch the nest." The words were in her mind. She opened her mouth to say them.

"I expect there will be one or two foals by now," said Clare.

"Foals! Arab foals!" and Jinny was trotting Huston at Jasper's side. "I've never seen an Arab foal."

Lady Gilbert's home was almost a castle—towers and turrets and slit windows set in the thickness of the walls.

Clare tugged at the heavy metal bell-pull and the noise jangled and echoed through the corridors. Lady Gilbert was stiff and elderly, and Jinny thought she didn't seem very pleased to see them. They sat in straight-backed chairs in a room that smelt of spaniels. Clare and Lady Gilbert made polite noises at each other while Jinny thought about the ospreys, wondered when they were going to see the Arabs, and tried to look as if she were interested in the conversation.

Clare and Lady Gilbert had a sherry, Lady Gilbert presumed that the child would not want one. Then they went down to a vast dining hall with a huge, polished oak table in it. At one end of the table three places were set for lunch. Lady Gilbert sat at the head of the table, Jinny and Clare on either side of her. A very old man creaked in, carrying the different courses. If Jinny had been at home she could have finished each plateful in two or three mouthfuls, but Lady Gilbert ate very slowly, putting down the heavy cutlery every time she stopped eating to talk to Clare.

A grandfather clock struck two as they got up from the table.

"Watson will serve coffee in my room," said Lady Gilbert, and began to climb the stairs back to the room they had been in earlier.

"That's two o'clock," Jinny muttered to Clare. "I told you I MUST be back at the hide by half-past three at the

238

absolute latest. I MUST, Clare. And we haven't seen the Arabs yet."

"What does the child say?" asked Lady Gilbert, stopping on the stairs and turning round to regard Jinny.

"She's hoping to see your horses," said Clare.

"Is she? Is she now?" said Lady Gilbert.

"I have an Arab," said Jinny. "I would love to see yours."

"Indeed," said Lady Gilbert and turned back to her slow ascent.

Watson brought the coffee in a silver coffee pot and Lady Gilbert poured it out into tiny cups. It was strong and bitter. Jinny sat on the edge of her chair trying to catch Clare's eye. It had taken them at least an hour to reach here and it would take them another hour to drive back to Craigvaar and then Jinny still had to get to the hide.

"Does your dear mother have difficulty in finding the right type of girl?" Lady Gilbert asked Clare. "I interview them all personally. I have never had a housemaid in service here whom I have not interviewed myself."

"Oh, come on, come on, come on," thought Jinny. "When are we going to see the Arabs? I must get back. I must."

She searched the room for clocks, found one, and saw to her horror that it was half-past two.

"It's half-past two!" she exclaimed, her voice coming out louder than she had meant it to be.

Lady Gilbert paused, looked curiously at Jinny, and went on talking to Clare.

"We've got to go," said Jinny standing up. "I'm sorry to interrupt, but I must be back home for four. Clare knows I can't stay any longer than this. I told her I had to be back."

"What is upsetting the child?" Lady Gilbert said to Clare. "Is she unwell?"

"Oh, I say, I do apologise," said Clare, "but I'm afraid that we will have to go. She has an appointment with the dentist for four o'clock."

"Sweets," said Lady Gilbert. "The ruin of children's teeth. Never allowed mine to touch them."

"What a bloomin' lie," thought Jinny, but she didn't care about anything except being back at the hide before Ken arrived. She wanted to pull Clare downstairs and into the car and make her drive at a hundred miles per hour. Anything, as long as Jinny was back at the hide for four.

"Could we go out through your stable yard?" Clare asked as they said goodbye.

"What an extraordinary request," murmured Lady Gilbert. "Do tell your dear mother how sorry I was that she was unable to accompany you."

"Can we see your Arabs?" asked Jinny. Really, she didn't care any more, but it seemed such a waste when she had come especially to see them.

Lady Gilbert looked at her distantly. "You are a very impertinent little girl," she said. "I never allow strangers near my horses. Never."

"But you said you'd asked, that you'd asked her on the phone if I could see them and that she'd said I could." Jinny's hands were clenched into fists, she was sitting on them hard as Clare drove back to Craigvaar. "You said we'd see her stallion. And foals. You told me she wanted to hear about Shantih!"

"Well, I did warn you that she was rather eccentric," said Clare.

"I wouldn't call her eccentric. She seemed to me to know exactly what she was doing. I would never have come if you hadn't promised we'd see the Arabs. I wanted to see the stallion." But the only thing Jinny wanted now was to get back to the hide before Ken arrived. "Can't you go any faster?"

"No, I cannot," said Clare. "One thing's certain, if we're copped for speeding you certainly won't be back in time."

Jinny stared through the windscreen, willing the car to greater speed. She kept glancing at Clare's watch, seeing its hands creeping steadily to three and then down towards a quarter past.

240

"I should never have come. I knew I shouldn't have left the nest."

"Oh, dry up," said Clare. "I never met anyone who made a fuss about every single thing the way you do. If you'd been at my boarding school you'd jolly soon have learned to do things that the mistresses didn't know about. What does it matter what your precious Ken says? He won't jolly well eat you, will he?"

At last the car reached Craigvaar. Jinny wrenched the door open. She saw to her surprise that Spencer was standing at the front door, but she hadn't time to think about it, hadn't even time to go and see Shantih. The minute Jinny was out of the car she was running full speed over the moors in the direction of Loch Varrich. She had half an hour in which to reach the hide.

Stumbling and breathless, Jinny raced across the moors. "If Ken is there I'll tell him that I was feeling sick, that I just went for a walk to get out of the hide for a bit." The rough going slowed Jinny to a walk. She fought her way on up the hillside, panting for breath, pulling herself up, using her hands as well as her feet.

She was mad with herself. Why had she told the Burnleys about the ospreys? Why had she gone with Clare? Jinny didn't know.

Getting her second wind, she broke into a run again. "Oh, please don't let him be there," she thought. "Please let me get there first."

Jinny staggered over the hilltop above the loch. She paused to look quickly round for any sign of Ken approaching on one of the ponies but there was nothing. Jinny gasped with relief. She freewheeled down to the hide, and ducked in at the doorway. It was empty. Everything was exactly as she had left it.

Jinny collapsed on to the box, and sat for a few moments until she got her breath back. She was there before Ken. No one would ever know she had been away.

She looked out through the slit in the hide. Both ospreys were flying above their nest. Jinny had never seen them behaving like this before. She snatched up the glasses, focused them, and saw the ospreys wheeling round the nest in obvious distress. Jinny froze with horror. She could see nothing that could be disturbing them. Then she saw that part of the nest seemed to have been broken off. She could see the sticks lying scattered at the foot of the tree.

Jinny dropped the glasses. She ran down the hill to the pine trees. The ospreys' cries of distress and alarm were loud in the still air. As Jinny reached the nest one of the birds swooped towards her. Jinny caught a glimpse of its gaping beak, the useless, wordless strip of its tongue, before it flung itself upwards again, screaming with fury.

A great lump had been broken out of the side of the nest. It lay scattered at Jinny's feet. Close beside the sticks was a smashed egg. The yolk had already begun to knot itself into an osprey embryo.

The parent birds screamed and cried around Jinny as she stood staring down at it. While she had been away someone had destroyed the nest. No matter who had done it, it had been Jinny's fault that it had happened. If she hadn't left the nest unguarded the egg would have gone on growing until it became a great hawk, able to ride the air, to live wild and free and self-contained. But now, because she had gone with Clare, this could never happen. Jinny felt cold and sick.

She would have to go home and tell them what she had done. She turned away, and, walking very slowly, made her way back to Finmory.

CHAPTER TWELVE

Mrs. Manders was standing by the sink when Jinny walked into the kitchen. Mike was sitting at the table, cutting out pictures of space rockets from a Sunday newspaper supplement.

"You were quick," said Mike. "Ken hasn't been gone long."

"What's wrong?" asked Mrs. Manders, seeing Jinny's face. "Has something happened to Shantih?"

Jinny shut the door and leant against it. She looked at her mother but couldn't find the words to tell her what had happened.

"I didn't mean to," Jinny said. "Honestly I didn't mean to."

Her father came into the kitchen to see who had arrived.

"Something wrong?" he asked.

Jinny's face was drained of colour, her eyes huge in her pinched face.

"I didn't mean to do it," she repeated.

"Do what?" asked her mother, going over to Jinny. "Come and sit down and tell us about it. See if we can help."

"You can't," said Jinny, wishing she could cry, for that would make it easier, but what she had done was too bad to be smoothed over with tears. "I didn't stay at the hide. I went with Clare to Lady Gilbert's. And the eggs have gone. The nest's broken and one of the eggs is smashed. And I think the others have gone too."

"Oh, Jinny," said her mother. "Why did you do that? If you'd told us you wanted to go somewhere with Clare we could have arranged for someone else to be at the hide."

"I didn't know," said Jinny. "I met her on the moors."

"Better wake Brian and Peter," said Mr. Manders. "Maybe we can find the fool that took them. Just a chance that he might still be hiding on the hills somewhere."

"They'll be raving," said Mike. "After all the nights they've sat up and you had to go and do this."

In minutes, Brian and Peter came running downstairs. They pulled on wellingtons and set off over the moors. Mr. Manders and Mike went with them.

"I didn't mean to," Jinny said to her mother after they had gone.

"But you did it," said her mother. "And it can't be changed now."

"I only wanted to see Lady Gilbert's Arabs and we never saw them anyway."

"You know you were trusted to look after the nest and you left it unguarded. You knew what you were doing was

243

wrong. There's no way round that. You chose to do what you knew was wrong."

When Jinny heard them coming back from the nest she wondered if she should go and hide in her bedroom, but she knew that would be no use. She sat still and waited.

They all came into the kitchen. For a moment there was silence, then Brian and Peter began to tell Jinny what they thought about her.

"Why didn't you tell us from the beginning that you weren't interested? Of all the sneaky, rotten things to do, to pretend you were going to keep watch and then to go off and leave them. When you'd only to lift the walkie-talkie and tell us that you were going. One of us would have been up in half an hour. You could have gone for the whole day then. If you'd only waited half an hour. All bloomin' wasted now. If the ospreys have any sense they won't come back here. All bloomin' wasted because of your selfishness."

"You might as well have taken a gun and shot them," said Peter. "You killed them."

"I know," said Jinny despairingly. "Oh I do know. But I didn't mean to. If I'd shot them I'd have meant to shoot them."

"When a thing is destroyed it doesn't make much difference why it was destroyed—it's good and dead. There ain't going to be no young ospreys now, and that, sister, is that. The ospreys don't know whether you *meant* to abandon their eggs or not. Whether you *meant* to go off enjoying yourself when you should have been guarding their nest. They only know what's happened."

Jinny stared down at her hands, hating herself.

"Who could have taken them?" asked Mrs. Manders. "Who would want to destroy like that?"

"Who knew about them?" asked Mike.

"It wasn't the man from the gift shop," said Mr. Manders. "Brian knows him."

"Lives quite close to my area," said Brian. "Drops in from time to time to tell me of any rare birds he's seen. Compare notes. Not a chance on this earth that he'd touch the eggs."

244

"Who then?" insisted Mike. "We didn't tell anyone."

"You told the Burnleys," said the voice in Jinny's head.

"But they wouldn't have touched the eggs. The Burnleys wouldn't do a thing like that," Jinny replied indignantly.

"But you told them," insisted the voice. "Perhaps they told someone else and they stole them."

Jinny looked round miserably at her family. "At least they don't know about that," she thought guiltily.

"Maybe one of the farmer's pals," suggested Peter. "Though from what you said he seems the type who would keep his mouth shut."

"Well, there's no more we can do about it," said Brian bitterly. "Jot it down to experience and learn the lesson that you keep watch yourself. Or share it with experienced people you know you can trust."

"It's early enough in the season. They might find another nest site. Let's hope they do," said Peter.

"And that they've the sense to clear out of this district before the lunatic returns and finishes off the birds as well."

When Petra got back she, too, was loud in expressing her opinion about her sister's behaviour.

"I just don't know how you could do such a thing," she said over and over again, as if she was pleased with herself for not knowing.

"Well neither do I," said Jinny, probed at last into answering back. "I expect we all do things we don't mean to do. I didn't mean to harm the ospreys. It wasn't me that took the eggs." And she went to bed to dream of the judge from the Inverburgh Show chasing Shantih up a pine tree and then catching her and breaking her like an egg.

Jinny got up early the next morning. She had breakfast before anyone else was up and walked to Craigvaar. Shantih came rushing to the box door, whinnying to her. Jinny clapped her neck, rubbed her hands lovingly over her face and breathed in the warm sweet smell of her breath.

"Oh, you'd understand how it happened," Jinny said to her. "You do things that you don't mean to do. You'd understand."

Jinny mucked out the three horses, gave them water and an armful of hay, then sat in Shantih's box talking to her.

245

Spencer came into the yard first. He looked at Jinny with unconcealed surprise.

"Good lord," he said. "Clare didn't tell me you were in residence."

Jinny regarded him uncertainly. She had managed to re-arrange the past so that it was Spencer who had galloped off leaving her lying in the road. She was almost sure now that Clare had wanted to stay and see that she hadn't hurt herself.

"How kind," Clare said when she saw that Jinny had mucked out. "But of course, now that Spencer's back, we can really manage this sort of thing ourselves. And I do wish you wouldn't give them so much hay. I know your nag needs filling out, but when we're going to exercise them straight after breakfast we don't want them stuffed up with hay."

Clare and Spencer tacked up their horses.

"Could I bring Shantih?" Jinny asked Clare.

"Shantih?" said Clare. "Oh, I don't think so. I mean to say, it isn't that we wouldn't love to have you with us, but now Spencer's back we'll be having a gallop over the moors and you don't want to damage her wind, do you?"

Jinny stood and watched them ride out of the yard to-gether, their horses stepping out, their tack gleaming, with bits and stirrups glinting in the sun. She still saw them as if they were bright with gold dust, a brightness about them that ordinary people didn't have. Anything they did must surely be right because they were the Burnleys.

Jinny took Shantih down to the paddock and concen-trated on her riding, blanking off the thought of the smashed egg and the ospreys' cries of distress. Although Shantih had several bucking outbursts Jinny didn't come off. In all the disgrace that was surrounding Jinny the thought that Shantih was improving was like a tiny chink of light in a long dark tunnel.

Later in the morning, while Clare was grooming Jasper, Jinny told her about how the ospreys' nest had been robbed while they had been at Lady Gilbert's.

"No!" exclaimed Clare, "I cannot believe it. Is no-where safe from them?"

"Them?" demanded Jinny, thinking Clare knew of some gang of international egg-collectors.

"Why, the yobs and vandals, of course. Who else would do a thing like that? But it does mean that you won't have to do any more of that dreary guard duty. Actually, Spencer and I are going out this afternoon, so I was going to say that would leave you free to watch your nest, but I suppose that will be a thing of the past now."

"They won't lay again in that nest this year," said Jinny.

"Oh, well, if you want to hang around here do, but we shan't be here so it does seem a bit pointless."

Jinny stayed to groom Shantih and then she went home. She took her drawing pad and went to sit in the ponies' field but her pencil was clumsy in her fingers. She was only wasting paper so she stopped and sat staring at the sea until it was supper time.

Peter and Brian had left.

"There was no sign of the ospreys this morning so they reckoned there was no point in waiting on here. Both had plenty of work to do," said Mr. Manders.

"They left this envelope for you," said Petra. "Said I was to give it to you when they'd gone."

Jinny took the envelope unwillingly. She couldn't think what they could have left for her. She opened it, feeling for a letter, but the envelope was empty except for something in one corner. Jinny tipped it up and a fragment of eggshell fell into her palm. She stared down at it, tears blinding her, then she turned and dashed upstairs to her room.

Lying stretched out on her bed she buried her head in the pillow and cried. She cried for the ospreys that would have hatched out of the eggs to fly high and clear over the moors and the sea, that might have come back to Finmory to build their own nests and breed their own young. But her own selfishness had spoiled it all. She might have watched the fledglings grow and fly. But now there was nothing.

Yet Jinny wasn't only crying for the ospreys, she was crying because Clare and Spencer had ridden out of the yard on their bright horses and she hadn't been with them. They hadn't wanted her.

When Mike came up to tell her supper was ready Jinny had scrubbed her eyes dry.

"That was a rotten thing to do," said Mike. "You shouldn't have left the hide but they didn't need to do that."

"I expect that's how they felt about me," said Jinny. She blew her nose hard and went down for her supper.

"But your horse just isn't fit to keep up with ours. Asking for broken wind galloping an unfit horse," said Clare the next morning when Jinny wanted to ride with the Burnleys.

"She galloped from here to Loch Varrich," said Jinny.

"Well, one wouldn't want that to happen again, would one?"

Jinny supposed one wouldn't. She knew Clare didn't want her and yet she couldn't stop herself from begging Clare to pay attention to her.

"It's so useless," Jinny thought. "When I don't like a person, the more they try to make me like them the more I can't stand them, so there's no point in trying to make Clare like me." But somehow she couldn't stop herself pleading with Clare.

"Could I come part of the way with you, and if it's too much for Shantih I'll come back?"

"Oh honestly!" exclaimed Clare. "I've told you. She isn't fit. Take her down to the paddock and do stop being such a bore. I let you use my paddock. I feed your horse. What more do you expect?"

Jinny waited until Spencer and Clare had clattered out of the yard, then she put on Shantih's tack and rode her home. Shantih was pleased to be going back to Finmory, back to her own field, to Punch and Bramble. She walked out with a long striding step, and when Jinny asked her to trot she went forward without any nonsense, going kindly into a steady jog.

"So you've had enough of your fancy friends?" Mr. MacKenzie called as Jinny rode Shantih past his farm.

"They've had enough of me," answered Jinny. "Clare's got Spencer back now."

"That'll be the way of it," said Mr. MacKenzie. "Did I not tell you it was the toffs you were dealing with when you were taking to do with the Burnleys?"

Jinny rode slowly back to Finmory and turned Shantih out into the field. The Highlands came trotting over, whinnying a welcome, and in no time they had their heads down grazing. Jinny watched them for a moment or two then went indoors.

"I've brought Shantih home," she said to her mother.

"That's good," said Mrs. Manders. "Not be long before you're back at school. You'll need to start and get your things ready. Did you thank Clare for all her help?"

"Huh," exclaimed Jinny. "Clare won't even notice I've gone. She's got Spencer now."

"Well, she is much older than you and she has been very kind."

But Jinny hadn't wanted anyone to be kind to her. She had wanted to be part of the Burnleys' life, to be Clare's friend, to ride as well as Clare, to know all the things Clare knew about horses and, most of all, she had wanted Clare to admire Shantih—to see her as Jinny saw her, a golden, magic horse. That was what Jinny wanted and that was why she had told them about the ospreys.

But now it was all over, all hopeless. Never again would Jinny ride with Clare or stand in her stable yard listening to her stories of all the cups she had won and all the horses she had ridden.

Jinny stared blankly through the kitchen window. The whole world seemed grey and empty. There was nothing in it that was worth doing when she couldn't ride with Clare.

CHAPTER THIRTEEN

"You'll be for Craigvaar tomorrow?" Mr. MacKenzie asked Jinny.

"Why?"

"Why? To wave goodbye to your friends. I was hearing they'll be off back to England."

"Will they?" said Jinny as if she didn't care.

"Aye, they will, and you'll be off back to the school. And a good job too, I'm thinking. Your head's been filled with the nonsense these holidays."

"Has it?" said Jinny.

"Indeed it has. Taking that wild horse of yours to the show—I never heard such nonsense in my life. And a fair carry-on you've had over the sea eagles. Though I'm thinking maybe that wee bit of business was not altogether your fault."

"It was," said Jinny.

As Jinny walked home with the milk she thought that she would have to go to Craigvaar tomorrow to return the martingale and drop noseband that Clare had lent her. She supposed she should have thanked Clare. Perhaps it had been rude just riding off like that. Not that Clare would have noticed, Jinny thought. She wanted to get rid of me.

Next morning Jinny rode round the back of Craigvaar and into the stable yard through the paddock. Shantih whinnied and, with a clatter of hooves, Jasper and Huston were looking out over their half doors. Jinny was pleased to see that they weren't being exercised. When they were in their boxes it meant that Clare would be around somewhere. Jinny jumped down from Shantih and waited a moment or two, hoping that Clare would have heard her and appear, but there was no sign of her.

"Clare," Jinny called, "Clare." But no one answered. Jinny hesitated, uncertain what to do next. She led Shantih into the loose box and took off the martingale and drop noseband.

"If the gift shop manages to sell my drawings and Nell takes some more, I'll buy you a martingale," Jinny said to Shantih, who was more interested in getting to the door to rub noses with Huston.

Jinny went back out into the yard and called again but still no one answered. She wondered if she could leave the martingale and noseband on the tack room table—Clare would know where they had come from. But Jinny knew this would be taking the easy way out. She had to give the tack to Clare.

Jinny stared round the yard, remembering the morning when they had all set off for the Inverburgh Show; the day Clare had said she had a good seat; the day she had jumped Huston; the days of exercising the horses with Clare when they had ridden together through the spring sunshine. Jinny heard Clare's voice in her ears telling her all about the ponies and horses she had ridden, all the shows she had been to, all the cups she had won, and the great leaps she had taken when she was giving the field a lead out hunting. For a last time Jinny looked round the yard, imagining that it all belonged to her—the loose boxes, the horse box, the tack room with its gleaming saddles and bridles and rows of rosettes pinned to the walls, and, best of all, the three horses, Huston to jump, Jasper to show and Shantih because she was herself and Jinny loved her.

Jinny gave herself a shake. She walked quickly through the shrubbery and over the lawns to the house. There was no one to be seen at the windows or at the back door. Jinny hesitated awkwardly, wondering if anyone was watching her, holding out the martingale so that anyone seeing her would know why she was there.

She decided to go round to the front door. It was standing half open. Jinny knocked and stood back, hoping that Spencer wouldn't be the one to answer it. Mrs. Burnley would be the easiest. She would tell Jinny how wonderfully pretty her hair was and Jinny could thank her and hand back the tack.

It was Heather, the Burnleys' housekeeper, who came to the door. She was a warm, kindly woman who had always made Jinny feel welcome.

"You'll be wanting to see Clare?" Heather said.

"Yes," said Jinny. "I've come to give these back to her."

"Och, come in then," said Heather. "We've all been wondering where you went off to in such a hurry. Clare was in the drawing room a minute ago. In you go and wait and I'll be telling her you're here."

Jinny rubbed her wellingtons on the mat and followed Heather inside.

"Wait you there for a moment and I'll find Clare for you," said Heather, opening the drawing room door.

Jinny stepped carefully over the pale primrose carpet on to the black hearth rug. The morning sun streamed through the double-glazed windows, filling the room with light. All the furniture was tastefully modern. You could tell that the people who lived here read the right advertisements. On top of a long, low sideboard were photographs of Clare and Spencer on their ponies. Jinny went over to have a look at them.

Lying on the sideboard was an open box. Inside it, carefully padded with cotton wool, were two cream-coloured eggs marked with brownish purple blotches—ospreys' eggs.

Jinny stared at them in disbelief. They couldn't be, couldn't possibly be . . . She felt cold and sick and wanted to run away from them. Never to have seen them. Not to know about them. Never, ever to know about them for it could not be true.

"No! Oh no!" breathed Jinny. She stretched her hand out and touched the ospreys' eggs with her finger, felt their porous texture. "No," she said again. "No," as if by denying them she could make them vanish. But the eggs were real.

Jinny stood drowning in the same horror as she had felt when she had seen the smashed egg lying at the foot of the tree. The useless, pointless killing engulfed her, this sad and stupid waste. Left in the nest the eggs would have hatched into ospreys, now they were no more than lifeless

252

objects, senseless possessions. "Oh no," said Jinny, unable to believe it.

The door opened and Clare came in. "Well, hello," she said. "We couldn't think what had happened to you, vanishing like that . . ." Then she realised that Jinny had seen the eggs. "Oh Lord," said Clare. "This jolly well would have to happen."

"It was Spencer," cried Jinny. "It was Spencer who stole the eggs. You told him about the nest and you made it all up about Lady Gilbert being interested in Shantih and wanting me to see her Arabs. You made it all up so that I'd leave the ospreys unguarded and Spencer could take the eggs."

"He is frightfully keen on birds' eggs. Always has been," said Clare. "And I mean to say, the chance of ospreys' eggs laid in Scotland—it was just asking too much of anyone not to jump at the chance."

"You came up specially to take me away from the hide. All the time we were at Lady Gilbert's you knew what Spencer was doing. And you must have phoned him. *You* must have phoned him and told him to come back here because of the eggs."

"Now look here," said Clare. "Do be sensible about this . . ."

"How could you?" cried Jinny. "How could you do such a rotten thing! They would have been ospreys. They would have been ospreys."

And suddenly words were not enough to express Jinny's disgust. She grabbed the eggs out of the box, one in each hand, and before Clare could stop her Jinny had thrown them down and stamped on them, smashing them to fragments. Then she ducked under Clare's outstretched arm, dodged through the door, ran out of the house and was tearing down the garden to Shantih almost before she knew that she intended to smash the eggs.

Spencer was standing at Jasper's box.

"You rotten thief," Jinny yelled at him and his eyes flickered over her, dry and emotionless as a lizard's. "It was my fault but you killed them."

253

Jinny tugged up Shantih's girths and raced out of the yard.

"Stop her," bawled Clare, crashing through the rhododendrons. "She's jolly well smashed the eggs."

But Jinny was through the paddock gate. She flung herself on to Shantih's back and they were galloping over the moor as fast as they had on Shantih's first mad gallop away from Clare.

When they were well clear of Craigvaar Jinny steadied Shantih to a walk. All the things she hadn't allowed herself to see before came flooding into her mind. Clare bringing expensive horses up from England to win cups at a small show; Clare riding off with Spencer, leaving Jinny lying on the road; Clare's voice saying that she wouldn't care to be seen on Shantih; Clare's temper; the speed with which she had cast Jinny off when Spencer came home and the way she had tricked Jinny over the ospreys. Jinny didn't know why she had wanted to be so blind.

For a last time she glimpsed her golden image of Clare —and then it had gone. Clare was only a lumpish girl with heavy hands who wanted her own way all the time and didn't care how she got it. The exclusive, select life of the Burnleys that had haunted Jinny since her first glimpse of it had lost its magic. They were loud and selfish and Jinny knew what she would think if any of her own family behaved the way the Burnleys did. The golden bubble had burst.

Jinny put Shantih into her box, gave her a scoopful of nuts and went in to tell her family what had happened, to tell them the whole truth.

Everyone except Ken was in the kitchen.

"I know who took the eggs," Jinny said. "Spencer Burnley. I told Clare about the ospreys and she told him and he took them."

"Oh, Jinny," said her father. "You told Clare? But why? Why?"

"I wanted them to like me," said Jinny, and she told them all that had happened. It was like taking off layers and layers of heavy clothing that had been stifling her and being able to move again, being able to breathe.

"Well, it's all over now," said her mother when Jinny had reached the end of her confession. "Let's hope you've learned something from it. You do get yourself tangled up in things."

"Oh, don't I?" agreed Jinny wearily.

She led Shantih down to the field and leaned over the gate watching her. She could see her again as her own horse and it was herself, Jinny Manders, and no one else, who had to find a way to ride her and school her and help her to understand how to live with humans.

"Nice to have you back," said Ken, coming to stand by the gate. "Mike told me."

"I didn't mean to harm the ospreys."

"They'll come back," said Ken.

"Will they?" asked Jinny, seeking reassurance.

"You know that yourself," said Ken. "Open your eyes. Summer into winter. Winter into spring. That's the way it is."

And suddenly it didn't seem quite so bad. After all, Jinny thought, there was the summer holidays when she would do better than she had these holidays. Much better.

"Perhaps if the gift shop takes some more of my drawings I'll buy a proper lunge rein," she said.

Ken laughed, throwing back his head, taken by ridiculous, total laughter, making Shantih look up, the tips of her ears pointed in surprise. She gazed steadily at them through her dark, lustrous eyes, then whisked her tail and went back to her grazing.

"Knowing you, you'll find a way," said Ken.

"I will," said Jinny. "Oh yes, I will."

The Summer Riders

CHAPTER ONE

Jinny Manders woke with the thought quite clear in her mind that today was the first day of the summer holidays.

"The summer holidays," Jinny said aloud and shivered with excitement.

She jumped out of bed and padded on bare feet across her bedroom to the window that looked out to the rolling hills and high, rocky crags that surrounded Finmory House. Nothing stirred in the grey summer dawn. Then, as Jinny stared out, the glistening golden disc of the sun began to slip up from behind the hills. The high, cloudless sky shimmered into blue.

"Going to be a smashing day," thought Jinny. "I'll go for a ride now," she decided. "Before anyone else is awake. Nobody to spoil it. Just Shantih and me."

Jinny somersaulted back across her room, past the mural of a red horse charging through a jungle of white flowers, past her own drawings and paintings pinned to the walls, under the arch that separated the two halves of her room and did a floppy cartwheel over her bed to reach her other window. It faced in the opposite direction, looked over Finmory's garden, down to the ponies' field and on to Finmory Bay and the glittering reach of the sea.

Jinny opened the window wide and leaned out, her long, red-gold hair swinging over the sill.

"Shantih," Jinny called. "Shantih."

Punch and Bramble, the two borrowed trekking ponies that Jinny and her younger brother Mike had ridden to school, went on grazing, ignoring her, but the third horse looked up, instantly alert at the sound of Jinny's voice.

"Shantih," Jinny breathed, and the Arab horse whinnied in reply, her nostrils dark pits in her delicate, dished face. Her ears were pricked above her silken forelock and her dark, lustrous eyes looked up at Jinny from under long-fringed lashes. She was a pure-bred Arab, red-gold with a white blaze and four white socks, and Jinny loved her completely, totally.

Jinny had first seen Shantih in a circus. Then she had

been 'Yasmin, the Killer Horse', being lashed into rearing viciousness by the ringmaster. But now she belonged to Jinny and was Shantih, which means peace. Ken had chosen the name, saying that names changed people and that it would help Shantih to forget the circus.

Almost a year ago, Jinny and her family—Petra who was now fifteen and Mike who was ten—had all left the city life of Stopton, where Mr. Manders had been a probation officer, to come and live at Finmory House. It was a large, grey, stone house in the Scottish Highlands. Their nearest neighbour was Mr. MacKenzie, whose farm supplied the Manders with milk and eggs, and then there was nothing but moorland until the tiny village of Glenbost where Mike and Jinny went to school. Now Mr. Manders made his living as a potter, helped by Ken, who was seventeen and was staying with the Manders.

They had first got to know Ken Dawson when he had been on probation in Stopton, charged with other boys for breaking into a warehouse. At the end of his probation he had said to Mr. Manders, "I'd nothing to do with it." "I know," Mr. Manders had acknowledged.

Although Ken's parents were rich enough to send him a monthly cheque, they wanted nothing further to do with him. "Just so long as they know I'm not starving," Ken had mocked when his first cheque had arrived direct from the bank, and he had laughed, stuffing it into the pocket of his jeans. But Jinny hadn't thought it was funny. Your own parents not loving you. She couldn't even bear to think it might be possible.

"We want you here," she had assured Ken. "I care." And Ken had smiled directly at her, his green eyes bright in his thin, tanned face. He had pushed back his long, straw-coloured hair and looked down at her from his bony height. "Thank you," he'd said and gone out to the vegetable garden he was creating, with Kelly, his grey, shaggy dog padding at his heels.

Jinny wasn't quite sure what was the best thing, Ken living with them or owning Shantih. She could never make up her mind.

Shantih whinnied again and walked towards the hedge closest to the house, her stride neat and precise through the dew dark grass.

"We're going for a ride," Jinny told her. "I shan't be long. Stay there."

A few minutes later Jinny was flipping down the steep flight of stairs that led from her attic bedroom. She ran along the corridor, down the wide staircase to the hall, and into the kitchen. She was the first, there was no one else awake. She paused for a second to choose two apples, one for herself and one for Shantih, then she opened the heavy back door, hearing its creaking echoing through the sleeping house, and she was free. In the back yard she whirled round and round, her long hair flying out about her skinny body.

"Summer," she yelled. "Summer, summer, summer." And thought of galloping over the moors, swimming Shantih in the sea, camping by Loch Varrich—if she could find a tent. Days and days of being with Shantih. "And it was summer; warm delightful summer," said Jinny slowly.

The Manders stables had once been crumbling outhouses. Now there was a place for tack and the horses' feed, two stalls for the Highland ponies and a loose box for Shantih. Jinny took down Shantih's snaffle bridle. Beside it, polished and gleaming, was the tack belonging to Bramble and Punch. Jinny swallowed hard and tried not to look at it. It wasn't that she had forgotten that tomorrow Punch and Bramble were going back to Miss Tuke's trekking centre, just that she wasn't allowing it to come up to the surface of her mind. Tomorrow would be time enough to think about Shantih being alone in the field and Miss Tuke taking back both saddles which meant that Jinny would need to ride bareback all the time. Jinny didn't mind riding bareback but she had to admit that without a saddle Shantih would be able to throw her off more often than usual.

"Nobody, absolutely nobody, could possibly say that Shantih wasn't improving," Jinny thought. Only last Easter Jinny had spent most of her rides flying through the air while Shantih bucked or reared but now she managed to stay on top most of the time.

Jinny counted on her fingers as she walked down to the ponies' field. Last week she had only been bucked off six times and Shantih hadn't really reared at all. Not what you'd call rearing. There had been rather a nasty moment

261

when they had met Mr. MacKenzie's tractor, but she hadn't actually reared, Jinny decided, just tipped up a bit, and it had all been Mr. MacKenzie's fault, coming charging round the corner when he knew he might meet them. "He does it for kicks," thought Jinny darkly. "Lurks and pounces on us."

Shantih was waiting at the field gate and whickered when she saw Jinny.

"Horse," said Jinny lovingly, "are you in a good mood or can you smell the apples?"

Jinny slipped the bridle over the Arab's head and led her out of the field. She shared the apples with her, feeling Shantih's velvet muzzle lipping her hand.

"Finished," Jinny told her. "That's all." Shantih pushed at Jinny to make sure. "Come on," said Jinny. "We're going down to the sea."

Jinny sprang up onto Shantih's back. There hadn't seemed much point in dirtying a saddle for one day, not after Mike had helped her to clean the tack. Now that Punch and Bramble were going back to Miss Tuke's trekking centre Jinny didn't suppose she'd be seeing much of her brother round the stables. Mike was easy-going and cheerful, with brown eyes and curly hair. Jinny liked being with him but she knew that although Mike was fond of Punch he wouldn't really mind not having a pony to ride. Mike's summer holidays would be full of his own things—fishing and helping Alec Clark on his father's farm, hoping that this summer he might just be allowed to drive the tractor.

Petra was even less horsy than Mike. When it suited her she didn't mind sitting sweetly on a horse with a headscarf knotted at just the right angle over her curls, but most of the time Petra wasn't in the least interested in Shantih. Really, Jinny was quite glad. Whenever Petra was around, Jinny seemed to make more of a muddle of things than usual. Sometimes Jinny thought that her sister was made up of all the opposites to herself. She was sharp and efficient and organised; her curly hair was always tidy and her clothes always looked clean and smart. "And bossy," thought Jinny darkly. "Very bossy indeed." Later in the summer Petra was going to sit an important music exam and all her spare time would be spent practising the piano. Jinny knew she would pass. Passing exams was one of Petra's things. Reading teenage fashion magazines was another. "But not helping me with Shantih," Jinny decided.

It wasn't that Jinny wanted anyone else to ride Shantih but she couldn't help thinking that it would be nice to have a friend. Someone to ride with her. None of the other children at the village school was the least interested in ponies. They thought of them as things they had kept around the crofts before the tractors came.

"What I would like," thought Jinny, "is another girl who has her own pony and knows a bit about schooling. Someone who could tell me what I'm doing wrong. Someone to help me to lunge her . . ." Jinny stopped in mid thought. Last Easter holidays she had tried to make Clare Burnley help her with Shantih and things had gone disastrously wrong. It was not something that Jinny allowed herself to think about too often.

"All past. Utterly past," thought Jinny, and she gathered up Shantih's reins and urged her into a canter. Shantih bucked. Jinny sailed over her head, landed on her feet and sprang back up, almost in one smooth circle.

"Get on with you," shouted Jinny, sitting tight and close. "On you go." And the mare was cantering smoothly. towards the beach. The sea breeze flicked back her mane and lifted strands of Jinny's red hair. Jinny laid the palm of her hand flat on Shantih's shoulder, feeling the power of the Arab's stride. "Faster," urged Jinny and the mare stretched her neck and raced over the rough grass.

Jinny brought Shantih back to a walk before they reached the beach. She slowed down reluctantly, snaking her head and jangling her bit, curtseying suddenly sideways, her tail kinked over her back.

"Don't bother showing off," said Jinny severely. "There's no one to see you. Walk now. Steady."

Shantih strode down the path between the massed boulders and out into the dazzle of the shore. On the sands Jinny stopped her and sat staring over the water. Gulls searching for an early breakfast looped the sky or squabbled at the edge of the surf, a pied squadron of oyster catchers flew low over the sea.

"Cor!" thought Jinny, glutted with the blue and silver and gold. "Just think, you might still have been in your

263

piggy circus and I might have been stuck in filthy old Stopton. You remember, Shantih Manders, how lucky you are and stop bucking me off."

Shantih flickered disinterested ears and dug impatiently at the wet sand until Jinny let her walk on along the beach.

At the far side of the bay, on the grass above the barrier of sea-smoothed boulders, was something that looked to Jinny like a bright yellow sheet hanging out to dry. She peered at it but couldn't make out what it could be, then trotted Shantih towards it, thinking that it might be some sort of shelter that Mr. MacKenzie had put up. Then suddenly she stopped Shantih and stared in disbelief at the sands in front of her.

"It can't be!" thought Jinny. "Yet it is!"

Someone, but Jinny couldn't imagine who it could possibly have been, had been schooling a horse. The wet sand was pitted with hoof prints. Circles, figure eights and serpentines were tracked out on the sand. For a moment Jinny wondered if Clare Burnley might have been riding on the shore; but Jinny knew the Burnleys were still in Sussex and their house, Craigvaar, was still empty. And it couldn't have been Mike or Petra or Ken. Even if one of them had taken a Highland for a ride they would never ever have brought him down here to school.

"Man Friday," thought Jinny, and jumped down to examine the marks more closely.

They were certainly hoof prints. Someone *had* been schooling a horse there and not so very long ago. Then suddenly Shantih jerked her head into the air, almost snatching the reins out of Jinny's hand. She whinnied with a blast of sound and was answered with a high, squealing neigh. Almost invisible against the boulders a girl in jodphurs and a yellow tee shirt was riding a skewbald pony.

Jinny threw herself back up on to Shantih, knowing that if the Arab got too excited she might not be able to get up on to her again. With neck arched and tail high, Shantih pranced across the sands towards the skewbald. The girl had seen them. She waved and walked her pony to meet them.

The brown and white pony was thick-set and cobby, with a shaving brush mane and a placid, two-colour expression. His rider looked about twelve years old, about the same age as Jinny. She had short, brown, wavy hair, a tip-tilted nose and wide-set, hazel eyes. She wasn't fat, but rather like her pony, Jinny thought, sturdy and reliable-looking.

They were within a few yards of the girl and her skew-bald when Shantih reared violently, hung poised in the air, balanced on her hind legs. Jinny clung round her neck helplessly until she touched down again.

"It's the strange pony . . ." Jinny began, her face scarlet from being scrubbed into Shantih's mane. She looked defiantly across at the girl, expecting to see her laughing at Shantih's bad manners and Jinny's rotten riding, but on the girl's round, freckled face was an expression of total admiration.

"She is absolutely super," said the girl. "She's an Arab, isn't she? Is she yours? I've always wanted an Arab. And a chestnut too! Oh, she is beautiful!"

Jinny's sharp features spread into an ear-to-ear grin. It wasn't often she met someone who said the things that she herself thought about Shantih.

"Super horse," repeated the girl, still gazing at Shantih. "Oh, how I'd love a horse like that."

"She gets a bit excited," apologised Jinny. "She used to be in a circus where they treated her badly."

"Not that I don't think Pippen is the mostest pony and I wouldn't change him for anything. But an Arab . . ."

"I'm Jinny Manders," said Jinny. "And this is Shantih. We live at Finmory House."

"You don't! We saw it last night when we arrived. Dad said he'd give anything to live there but Mum said there'd be mice. I'm Sue, Sue Horton, and this is Pippen."

"Are you staying here?" asked Jinny.

"Camping," said Sue. "All summer. Normally we have a fortnight in a stuffy hotel but with things being so expensive we bought a tent and more or less at the last minute we were able to borrow a trailer and bring Pippen with us. Thought we were going to have to leave you behind all summer, didn't we?" said Sue, ruffling the skewbald's mane. "Would you look at it?" she said. "Every spring I swear I'm going to let it grow and it goes on growing up and up and up. Then every autumn I give in and have it clipped again. Still, perhaps this time . . ." She grinned, then said, "You are lucky living here. Can you ride all over the hills?"

"More or less," said Jinny. "You have to watch out for boggy bits on the moors but there are lots of places where it's quite safe to gallop."

"Shall we go for a ride together?" asked Sue. "That's if you'd like to. I don't want to be tagging on."

"Like to!" exclaimed Jinny. "Honestly I was longing for someone to ride with. I'm the only one who's keen on horses in my family."

"Well, I'm the only anything one," said Sue.

"This morning?" asked Jinny. "We could go for a ride this morning if you like."

"Not at all today," said Sue regretfully. "We're all going to Inverburgh to stock up and Dad wants some new fishing gear—but every day after that."

"Sue! Sue! Breakfast's ready," called a voice, and Jinny, seeing a woman standing by the bright yellow sheet, realised that it was part of an elaborate tent.

"How about tomorrow?" Sue asked.

"This time," said Jinny. "Very early." And she explained about having to return Punch and Bramble to Miss Tuke.

"See you here, then. Tomorrow at seven."

"Right," said Jinny, sitting very tight on Shantih in case she reared again when Sue rode Pippen away. "'Bye."

Riding back to Finmory, squeaks of delight burst out of Jinny. "And a friend for you," she told Shantih. "Dare say Pippen can share your field. Will that be nice?"

Jinny's family were all sitting round the kitchen table having breakfast when Jinny burst into the kitchen.

"There's a family camping on the beach," Jinny told them. "And there's a girl called Sue, 'bout my age I should think, AND SHE'S GOT A PONY!"

"Oh, I'm glad," said Mrs. Manders. "She'll be company for you. I've been worrying about you riding Shantih by yourself all summer."

"Well, you don't need to now," said Jinny. "I'll be riding with Sue." All the things Jinny had been planning to do were suddenly warmer, more exciting, now that they were to be shared with someone else. "We're going for a ride tomorrow."

266

"What about the sad returning?" asked Mike.

"Hadn't forgotten," said Jinny, making herself toast. "We're going to ride early."

"The Thorpes come tomorrow," said her father.

"Tomorrow!" cried Jinny. "But I thought they weren't coming until the end of August!"

"That was changed weeks ago," said Petra, crimping at her crispbread with her front teeth. "You never listen to anything, do you?"

"When was it changed? No one told me," said Jinny indignantly.

The Thorpes were two children Mr. Manders had known in Stopton. The boy, Bill Thorpe, was thirteen and had been on probation for shoplifting. Since the Manders had been at Finmory, Bill had spent six months in hospital with lung trouble. Mr. Manders had heard from a colleague that they were trying to get Bill away from Stopton for a holiday in the country but were having trouble fixing it up because the boy's younger sister wanted to go with him. "Send them to us," Mr. Manders had offered, and the visit had been arranged.

"Well, everyone else knew," said Mike.

"I didn't. And I think someone could have told me," grumphed Jinny, sitting down beside her father with her plate of blackish toast. The very last thing she wanted was two unknown Stopton children coming to stay just when she had found a friend. Jinny hacked at the butter and spread it thickly on her toast. She gulped the coffee that her mother had poured out for her.

"Having a tiny tantrum, are we?" asked Petra.

"Well . . . I didn't know they were coming," said Jinny. "Still, I don't suppose I'll see much of them. I'll be riding Shantih with Sue."

Ken got up from the table, pushing his chair back with a sharp sound of disgust. He went silently out of the back door, his bony shoulders hunched.

Jinny ignored his departure.

"What's the sister's name?" Mike asked.

"Marlene," said Mr. Manders. "She's ten. Both lived in Stopton all their lives."

"Isn't the girl lame?" asked his wife.

267

"Lame?" said Jinny. "Then she won't want to ride, will she?"

"She was knocked down crossing the road when she was about six," said her father. "Her leg was badly broken and never set properly. Now she walks with a very bad limp." Mr. Manders went to get a sheet of paper out of his desk.

"Meant to show you this," he said to Jinny, handing it to her. "Marlene's teacher gave it to Tim Lawrence, the social worker who's working with the Thorpes. I must have mentioned Shantih to him and he must have told Marlene about her. Anyway this is what she wrote. Normally her compositions consist of one or two words. Read it."

Jinny looked suspiciously at the folded page that had obviously been taken from a school exercise book. She took it from her father unwillingly. The writing was uneven and sprawling and even Jinny could see that the spelling was terrible.

"This sumer I am to ride a arab hors. We will gallopp. When I am on the hors you wont see me leg is wonky. It wont mattar. I think the hors will be ok with me. He is spesull. I will lov the hors. When I am on the hors we will go fast as flames."

When Jinny had finished reading she kept her eyes on the paper. The girl must be daft thinking she could come and gallop Shantih. No one who hadn't been on a horse before could just get on a horse and gallop off.

"She could have had a ride on Bramble if he hadn't had to go back to Miss Tuke," Jinny muttered. "Or perhaps Sue would let her have a ride on her pony. He looked pretty quiet. But not on Shantih."

Mr. Manders took back Marlene's composition.

"I think the hors will be ok with me," he read.

"Well, I don't think Shantih will be O.K. with her," stated Jinny. "She can't ride. She can't arrive here and expect to go galloping off on Shantih."

"Fast as flames," said her father.

"Not fast as flames on my horse," muttered Jinny sullenly.

CHAPTER TWO

The next morning Shantih and Jinny careered down the track to the beach. Jinny had slept in and was still feeling cross and gritty. Shantih, catching her irritation, was playing up. She would bound forward then jerk to a sudden halt, wait with her neck arched and every muscle tensed—totally ignoring her rider, who was perched insecurely on her bare back—then with a half rear she would spin round and plunge back to her field.

"Oh, come on then," said Jinny furiously, when she had been carted back to Punch and Bramble three times. "I'll just have to lead you or Sue will be back in her tent."

Jinny dragged the reins over Shantih's head and, tugging on her bit, set off for the beach.

"Might as well be pulling a rhinoceros," thought Jinny as she plodded towards the sea. Her book on horsemanship said that you should never look back when you were leading a horse. "'Spect she has changed," Jinny decided. "Wonder what Sue will say. Expect she'll be polite. 'What strange horns your horse has got,' she'll say, and I'll say, 'All the better to charge you with'."

From the direction of the beach came a shrill whinny. Shantih froze, her eyes goggling. Just in time, Jinny lassoed her reins over her head and managed to scrabble on to her back before Shantih, with an answering whinny, was galloping down the track.

Jinny fell off when Shantih did a four hoof, emergency stop in front of Pippen and Sue.

"Hi," said Sue as Jinny picked herself up off the sand. "Wish I'd had a ciné. She looked fantastic galloping like that."

"Huh," grunted Jinny. "She wouldn't leave the Highlands. That's why I'm so late. She must have known they're going away today."

"I've been schooling him," said Sue. "Would you watch for a minute and see if he does change legs when we do a figure eight?"

"I'll try," said Jinny, who wasn't too sure what it looked

269

like when a horse did change legs, although she knew it was the correct thing to do.

Watching Pippen cantering round, Jinny grinned to herself as she imagined his legs dropping off and reassembling themselves at the centre of the figure eight.

"No good, was it?" demanded Sue when she rode back to Jinny. "He trotted."

Jinny thought it best to agree.

"Would you mind if we stayed here and schooled? It's after eight so we haven't much time for a ride."

Jinny didn't think Shantih was in the mood for schooling but she had promised Mike that she would be ready to set off for Miss Tuke's before ten.

"Even leaving at ten we won't get there much before twelve," Mike had said. "Dad's meeting us there with the car. We've to take his pots in to Miss Storr's shop and then be at the station to meet the two-thirty train. You be late to start with and the whole day will be a mess."

"That's right," Jinny had replied. "Make it all my fault. And we haven't even begun."

But Jinny knew that if they went for a ride now she wouldn't be ready to set out at ten and it would be her fault.

"Flippin' time," thought Jinny, already seeing how the day was going to be full of people telling her to hurry up.

"Well, all right," she said to Sue, "but Shantih isn't very good at schooling."

"Walk her round in a circle," suggested Sue and Jinny rode Shantih out in a wide circle.

It took all Jinny's concentration to keep Shantih going round at a walk, and each time they passed Sue and Pippen the circle bulged towards them.

"Try a trot," called Sue.

"Well . . ." said Jinny, but closed her fingers on Shantih's reins, tightening her legs against the Arab's sides.

Shantih leapt forward into a raking trot and there was a moment when Jinny felt all the pride and gaiety of her horse as she flowed round the circle, but the next minute Shantih was fighting to get to Pippen. Jinny shortened her left rein and kicked with her right heel.

"Get on," she shouted. "Get on with you," as Shantih began to buck, her head tucked between her forelegs, her

270

quarters and hind legs soaring skywards. Clinging to a lump
of hairy wither, Jinny clamped her knees against Shantih's
hard shoulders and fought to stay on. Sue was shouting to
her but Jinny couldn't hear her, could only see her mouth
opening and shutting and Pippen's bland, brown and white
face as he knitted his brows in disapproval at such behaviour.

Shantih managed to work a twist into her fourth buck
that sent Jinny sprawling towards her ears. Arms linked
round her mare's neck, Jinny slithered to the ground.

"Gosh," said Sue. "Is that what she did in the circus?"

"She is much, much better than she used to be," stated
Jinny firmly. "She didn't feel like schooling. It was my fault.
I should have known better. She hardly ever mucks about
when we go for a ride. I don't blame her for bucking. If I
wanted to go over the moors and some stupid human tried
to make me go round in circles I'd buck them off." Jinny
rubbed Shantih's neck and stroked her hand over her
muzzle. "She gets excited, that's all. I don't mind."

"She looked terrific," said Sue. "All mane and tail and
hooves. I'd be scared stiff to ride her. Bit of a coward,
that's me."

"Me too," said Jinny in surprise that anyone
should think of her as brave. "Only it's different with
Shantih."

"You don't use a stick, do you?" asked Sue. "Mrs. Ross
at our Pony Club would say that she needed to be taught a
lesson."

"Clare Burnley thought that too. But it's no use. The
ringmaster at that circus whipped her. It only makes her
go mad."

"Well, I think I'd ride with a saddle."

"Well I did," said Jinny. "Haven't got one now. I used
one of the ponies' saddles but it goes back to Miss Tuke
today." And guiltily Jinny remembered about the time.
Her watch said ten to twelve which Jinny considered
unlikely.

"But I can lend you one!" said Sue. "I thought you were
improving your seat. Come up to the tent and we'll see if
it fits."

"Oh, but I couldn't take that," cried Jinny when Sue,
after a car key sortie into the tent, unlocked the boot of

their car and took out an almost brand-new saddle. "It's far too good."

"Try it on," said Sue, ignoring Jinny's protests.

Sue fitted the saddle on to Shantih's back. "There," she said, tightening the girth. "Seems perfect. Get up. I must look under it while you're sitting on it to make sure I can see daylight under the channel."

"Perfect," said Sue, squinting under the saddle when Jinny was mounted. "Not touching her spine."

"But I can't just take it," gasped Jinny. Her knees were tucked against the knee rolls and she sat with a new sense of security in the deep seat of the saddle. "It's too good. I mean, you don't really know me. And it's such a smashing saddle."

"Please borrow it," said Sue. "I'd be glad to see someone using it. Perhaps it will stop Dad moaning. My cousin, who is completely spoiled, thought she wanted to ride. They bought her everything, including a beastly show pony. Of course she fell off, broke her arm, and that was that. No more ponies. Screamed if she saw one. They had to sell the lot. I persuaded Dad to buy the saddle for Pippen. And he's too broad for it. 'Course I really knew that, didn't I, but I so wanted to have it. It gave Pippen a sore back and I can't use it. We brought it with us because Dad thinks this holiday will slim Pippen down. If it doesn't he's going to sell it. Now if you were using it you'd be doing me a favour. It upsets Dad when he sees it lying around."

"He didn't buy it for me to use," insisted Jinny. "Perhaps seeing me using it would upset him more." She couldn't believe that a more or less complete stranger was offering to lend her the kind of saddle that she had always dreamed about but known she could never afford.

A stoutish woman with long, dark hair came out of the tent.

"Mum," called Sue. "Here. This is Jinny who lives at Finmory House."

The woman pulled a heavy sweater over her head and came towards them.

"Hullo," she said, smiling with Sue's smile and holding her hand out to Jinny. "Just crawled out of our burrow. Shocking lying in bed until this time on a camping holiday."

"Time!" remembered Jinny.

"I'm lending Jinny *the* saddle," said Sue.

"Grand," said Mrs. Horton. "Glad to see someone using it. Gave poor old Pippen a bad back, didn't it, son? I'm about to brew up. Will you two have a cup?"

"Is it nine o'clock yet?" Jinny asked, wondering desperately if she could just ride off with Sue's saddle; just turn round and ride off with a brand-new saddle or whether she should offer to sign some sort of agreement or even leave a deposit—not that she had any money.

"Twenty past," Mrs Horton told her.

"Oh no," cried Jinny. "I'll need to go."

"You will," said Sue. "I'd forgotten all about the time."

"They'll be mad with me," said Jinny, already beginning to turn Shantih towards Finmory. "Are you sure it's O.K. for me to take the saddle?"

"Certain," said Mrs. Horton.

"I told you," said Sue.

"Well, thank you very much indeed," said Jinny. "I mean thank you isn't enough but I will need to go."

"Then go," said Sue, giggling. "Don't keep on telling us."

"See you tomorrow," Jinny shouted back as she cantered off. "Come up to Finmory."

Half-way across the field, Shantih's head went down and she began to buck.

"Ah, no you don't. Not this time." And Jinny, bracing her knees against the knee rolls and sitting deep in the saddle, was able to pull Shantih's head up and send her on.

"This saddle," Jinny told her horse as they cantered home, "is going to make a great deal of difference in your life. See if it doesn't." And she thought that she would do some drawings of Pippen and give them to Sue. As Jinny rode home she could see quite clearly how she would paint the skewbald pony. She knew the way his hooves had to be round and settled into the ground, his neck bulky and his ears thickly rooted into his head. She could feel how she would draw the corners of his smug lips. Jinny didn't understand how she knew these things. They came welling up inside her and then she was able to draw them.

The ponies' field was empty, and as Jinny took off Shantih's tack and turned her loose, she supposed that Mike must have taken both Highlands in to their stalls.

273

"You're late," shouted Petra's voice.

"Surprise, surprise," shouted back Jinny, running up to her bedroom and setting the new saddle carefully in a corner. She paused for a second of utter disbelief and then ran out to the stables.

"Thought you were going to be back before nine," said Mike, who was grooming the white Punch. "I've brought them in and given them a last feed. We don't want to arrive at Miss Tuke's with them covered in sweat. She'll think that's the way we've been treating them all year."

"Well, we haven't," said Jinny, grabbing a dandy and starting to groom Bramble. Under the strokes of the brush Bramble's summer coat gleamed like jet, dapples spangled his quarters and broad barrel. Jinny ran her hands down his flat knees and strong-boned legs. She brushed out his feathery fetlocks and tipped his haystack mane from one side of his neck to the other as she tried to brush it flat.

"I shall miss you terribly," she whispered to the pony, remembering all the wild gallops they had shared, all the journeys to and from school. Jinny buried her face in Bramble's mane. She wanted to keep him, wanted to find her parents and try to persuade them to buy Bramble. Punch could go back to Miss Tuke's, but Bramble belonged to her.

"No time," said Mike. "Don't start to cry. You should have been earlier if you wanted to go on like that."

Reluctantly Jinny supposed so. She put on Bramble's tack and went inside. Her mother caught her and made her drink a cup of coffee and gobble down a bacon sandwich.

All the family came to say goodbye to the ponies.

Ken, his hands encrusted with clay, held his face out to them and breathed in their nostrils. "Been nice having you with us," he murmured, rubbing his face against their fumbling lips.

"He'll be back in September," said Petra, seeing her sister's red eyes. "You'll still need him to take you into the village."

Next term Jinny was to go to the new comprehensive school that was still being built in Inverburgh. She would ride Bramble into Glenbost, leave him there and catch a school bus. Jinny was sorry to be leaving the village school. Trailing in and out to Inverburgh every day wouldn't leave

274

her much time for Shantih. But it was so much better than going with Petra to Duninver school where you had to spend the week in the school hostel that Jinny had hardly grumbled at all.

"But I don't want him to go," said Jinny obstinately. "Couldn't we keep Bramble, even if we have to pay for him? He would be just right for this Marlene to learn on."

"I'll be at Miss Tuke's for half-past twelve," Mr. Manders said, ignoring Jinny. "We must be away from there before one if I'm to get my pottery delivered."

"Oh, O.K.," said Jinny. "Don't go on about it. We're going."

But they had to wait in the farm yard while Mr. Mac-Kenzie found a bit of turnip for the ponies, said they had been like hairy vacuum cleaners when it came to the oats and that it hadn't taken Jinny long to be scrounging her way down to the tent.

"Scotland Yard needs you," said Jinny. In all the months she had known Mr. MacKenzie she had never managed to discover how he managed to know about things almost before they happened.

By the time they had waited for the ponies to scrunch their way through the turnip they were even later.

"Come on," said Mike, when they had escaped from the old farmer. "We're not even going to be in time to meet Bill and Marlene at this rate."

"Fuss, fuss, fuss," said Jinny. "You're growing up just like Petra," but she urged Bramble on along the road to Glenbost.

They clattered through the village, past the school, the garage—encrusted with wrecked, rusting cars—Mrs. Simpson's sell-everything shop, past the crofts and the two churches and turned left to jog on towards Ardtallon.

At last they reached the track that took them over the hills to Miss Tuke's.

"Remember the day we brought them home?" asked Mike. "They kept on stopping dead and we had to shout, 'Trek forward,' to make them move."

"I expect they'll be as bad when we get them back in the autumn," said Jinny despondently.

About a mile from Miss Tuke's Bramble's head went up and he began to walk out excitedly. By the time they'd reached the drive that led to the trekking centre he was bouncing along, whiffling to himself and making sudden dives to smell the piles of droppings on the hoof-pocked ground.

"They don't half know where they are," said Mike. "I've never felt Punch like this before."

Miss Tuke was waiting for them. She opened the yard gate and the ponies bustled through.

"They are looking well," she said. "You've done them proud. I shall need to find two trekkers who can ride to take them over for next week."

"They're pleased to be home," said Jinny while Bramble clomped around her, whinnying to a bunch of ponies standing at a gate leading on to moorland.

"Right," said Miss Tuke when they had taken off the ponies' saddles. "Here we go. Be heels and teeth," she warned, as Mike and Jinny led Punch and Bramble through the gate on to the moor and unbridled them.

"Look out!" she warned, as Bramble plunged away from Jinny.

"But I'd got an apple for him," exclaimed Jinny, staring in dismay as the mob of Highlands went hightailing off up the hill.

"Too late," said Miss Tuke. "That's one of the things I like about native ponies. Independent little blighters," and she laughed as she shut the gate tightly.

"Your Dad says you'll be wanting them back in September."

"There is just a chance that I might be riding Shantih to school next term," said Jinny, admitting it to herself now that she had seen Bramble happily reunited with his mates.

"That red squib you had at the show?" demanded Miss Tuke. "I shall reserve Bramble for you."

"Has Dad been here long?" asked Mike.

"Quite a wee while. Seems in a hurry. Not his usual self."

They thanked Miss Tuke again for lending them the ponies and went to find their father. Seeing his face, Jinny got into the back of the car and thought hard about her saddle.

It was two o'clock before they reached Nell Storr's craft shop. Jinny and Mike helped their father to carry in the crates of pottery.

"Oh, lovely," cried Nell Storr, bearing down on them from a cloud of chiffon that seemed to be floating around her rather than being worn by her. "Thought you weren't going to make it. I've to be off in a min. with someone who's starting up a weaving centre on one of the islands. Free trip to inspect the goodies. As you can see, your shelves are nearly empty again, so fill them up and I'll take another lot as soon as you like."

"Bless you," said Mr. Manders. "You do realise that you are the mainstay of all my family."

"Nonsense," said Nell. "I do it for the money. These matching mugs and plates have been madly popular. I know a bod who's branching out into Europe. Shall I send him samples?"

"They're Ken's," said Mr. Manders. "Do send them."

"Wonderful glazes he gets," said Nell, picking up one of Ken's mugs that they had just unpacked and rubbing her hands over the scarlet glaze as she spoke to Mr. Manders about special orders.

"Now, Miss Manders," she said, turning to Jinny. "What about you? Have you brought me some more drawings?"

Jinny hadn't. Since Easter Nell had been buying Jinny's drawings and selling them in her shop.

"More of that Arab horse. She's their favourite."

"Well, maybe one lot more," said Jinny grudgingly. "I still need more money for my lungeing rein but now I've got the use of Sue's saddle I might buy a martingale."

"Live dangerously," encouraged Nell. "Bring me more drawings and buy both."

"I'll see," said Jinny. At first it had seemed a wonderful idea selling her drawings to Nell, but when it actually came to parting with them Jinny wasn't so sure. Sold to Nell they had gone forever. "I'll see," she said again.

It was half-past two before they reached Inverburgh station.

"Platform six," Mr. Manders shouted, running across the crowded station. Jinny and Mike sped after him, dodging in and out between luggage and trollies, passengers and rooted, old men.

They reached platform six just as the Stopton train came in.

"Too late. Here they come," said the ticket collector, so

277

they had to wait by the barrier, craning their necks to see if any of the people flooding out of the train looked like Marlene or Bill.

"That's them," cried Jinny. "Bet you."

"It is," said her father, recognising Bill, and then they could all see that the girl beside Bill dragged her left leg as she walked.

Both children were wearing jeans and black nylon anoraks. They were both pale with thick, white, city complexions and spikey, short, brown hair. The boy was slightly taller than his sister. His lower lip stuck out in a defiant, down-turning pout, and even walking along the platform his thick brows were clamped into a scowl. His sister was looking about her anxiously, her face working and her lips twisting as if she was carrying on a conversation with herself.

Mr. Manders waved. "Bill," he shouted. "Bill."

The boy heard him. He looked up, glowering under his fringe of greasy hair, and without changing his expression he spoke to his sister. She dumped the large, tartan shopper she was carrying on to the platform and waved with both hands. Then, clutching the bag in her arms again, she began to half run, half limp, towards them.

Marlene reached the ticket barrier and produced two tickets from her shopper, "I ain't half glad you're here. Didn't know what we'd do if you weren't. Them's two tickets, one for me and one for him." Marlene pointed out Bill to the ticket collector, then she pushed her way through the ticket barrier, holding her shopper well clear of the turnstile.

"Me Mum would have us bring a bag each. Said it wasn't decent unless. One each, like. Pleased to meet you," Marlene said, holding her hand out to Mr. Manders. "I'm fair dying for a cup of tea. Parched I am with that train. And I need the toilet. Didn't fancy going on that train."

Mr. Manders shook Marlene's hand. "I'm Mr. Manders," he said. "And this is Jinny."

"Pleased to meet you," said Marlene again.

Jinny grasped the small bony hand with its gnawed fingernails.

"How do you do," said Jinny distantly, her voice sounding cold and polite.

278

Marlene's black eyes beetling up at Jinny were hard as chips of flint. Her thin lips over her decayed teeth were laughing at Jinny. Jinny tried to make her mouth smile but it stuck in a half grimace and she stared across the busy station trying not to show what she was thinking—that already she didn't know how she was going to stick living with Marlene for a fortnight.

"Glad you could come, Bill," said Mr. Manders and introduced Jinny and Mike. Bill grunted, standing behind his sister, not looking up.

"Eh now," said Marlene, "now that we've got the la-di-dahs over how about the toilet and a bite of food?"

She grinned round, her eyes plucking at each person's face until she made them respond to her.

"Then it's me for the rodeo, ain't it? I'm proper churned up about it. Me on that fancy horse," and Marlene clutched up her tartan shopper and slapping her hand on her thigh she limped off to the Ladies.

"Better go with her," said Mr. Manders.

Cold with embarrassment, Jinny turned to follow Marlene, trying not to see the people who were staring as she gave Wild West whoops and hirpled her way through the crowds.

CHAPTER THREE

"Have you seen Marlene?" Mrs. Manders asked Jinny when she came down for breakfast the next morning. "We thought she must be with you."

"Well, she's not," said Jinny, glancing quickly round the table and realising that there were only two empty places—her own and Marlene's.

"We thought you might have been out with Shantih," went on Jinny's mother.

"You were wrong. I haven't seen her."

Yesterday, when they had got back to Finmory, Marlene had demanded a ride on Shantih.

"I'm not taking her out again today," Jinny had stated. "I was riding her this morning. She's not a bicycle, you know."

279

"Never thought he was," Marlene had replied. "Ain't never seen a bicycle that looked like that. Don't see why I can't have a ride now. He's walking round the field, ain't he? Why can't I sit on him?"

"Because," said Jinny finally and took herself off to her bedroom to clean her saddle.

"Bill, have you seen your sister?" persisted Mrs. Manders.

"Naw," said Bill, a slice of thickly-buttered toast in one hand a forkload of tomatoes and bacon in the other.

"Jinny, go and see if she's in her room."

"Why can't Petra go?" complained Jinny automatically but without hope.

"Marlene," Jinny called as she ran upstairs. "Marlene." But there was no reply. Jinny knocked on her bedroom door, then opened it. Marlene's bed was neatly made, her tartan shopper sitting on top of the quilt. Propped up on the dressing table was a blurry photograph of Marlene, Bill, a thin woman with a wintry face and a large, bleary man. Jinny looked at it intently, then, remembering what she was meant to be doing, went back down to tell her family that Marlene wasn't there.

"Try the garden," said her mother.

"I haven't had my breakfast and Sue's coming up to ride."

"It won't take you a second," said Mrs. Manders.

"Jinny," said her father, and Jinny went.

"Some holiday this is going to be," she thought rebelliously. "I'll bet she's with Shantih. I'll bet they make me give her a ride and when she falls off and hurts herself it will be Shantih's fault."

There was no sign of Marlene in the garden and Jinny went on past the stables, down to the ponies' field.

Marlene was sitting on top of the field gate. In the middle of the field Shantih was standing, watching her warily. Marlene looked quickly over her shoulder at the sound of Jinny's approach, then dropped down into the field. She landed on her hands and knees, scrambled up and began to run towards the Arab.

"Look out," yelled Jinny. "She'll kick you. Don't run at her like that."

Marlene paused to scowl at Jinny then went on limping across the field towards the horse.

280

Shantih's front feet were planted close together, her neck stretched out, her pointed ears nearly touching. Jinny knew that when she stood like that, she could swing round and whirl away in a split second, hooves flying as she galloped off.

"Be careful," shouted Jinny, but Marlene paid no attention to her. She was holding out a sugar lump to Shantih. Half limping, half running she blundered towards the Arab.

"Stop running," Jinny shouted. "Walk!" But Marlene went on stumbling and tripping in her haste to reach Shantih.

"Have a sugar lump," Marlene was saying. "Sweeten you up so it will."

As Jinny reached the field she paused uncertainly, knowing how Shantih's hooves could flash out quicker than lightning when she was frightened, and not wanting to risk chasing Marlene.

"Oh, slow down," she cried.

"Shut up. I'm giving him a sugar lump, ain't I," Marlene yelled back.

"Her," said Jinny, and to her horror she saw Marlene's lame foot catch in a tussock of grass, saw her go falling, sprawling towards Shantih, her arms outstretched, catching at the Arab's shoulder and legs as she fell.

The shoes on Shantih's hind feet glinted in the sun as she lashed out, missing Marlene's head by inches as she lay in the grass.

Jinny vaulted over the gate, ran at Shantih, shouting, chasing her away, but already the mare had thundered off to the far corner of the field, where she waited, quarters turned against the girls, the whites of her eyes rolling wildly.

"Are you all right?" demanded Jinny, helping Marlene to her feet. "I told you to stop running at her. That was enough to frighten any horse."

Marlene shook herself free.

"Get off me," she muttered. "I only fell, didn't I? Where's me sugar? I'm going to give it to the horse."

Jinny picked up the sugar lump. "You've to come in for breakfast," she said.

"Give us me sugar," said Marlene. "I'll just pop it in first," and she set off again towards Shantih.

Jinny grabbed hold of her arms. "You were nearly

281

kicked," she exclaimed. "Don't you realise that if Shantih had got you she could have killed you? You can't treat a horse like that."

"Give over," said Marlene, "pulling at me."

"You've got to come in to breakfast NOW," said Jinny, keeping her hold on Marlene's arm.

"What about the old horse? Got to get his sugar lump, ain't he?"

"She doesn't care whether she has a sugar lump or not. She doesn't want your sugar."

Marlene's black eyes bulleted into Jinny.

"Let me go," she demanded. "I got to give the horse his sugar. Like it says in the papers—'Be kind to a little donkey' —well, I'm being kind to a little horse if you'll only let off holding me."

"But she doesn't . . ." words failed Jinny. She let go of Marlene. "Well, wait there till I get a halter," she said.

"Halter?" said Marlene.

"Rope," said Jinny, "to hold her with while you give her your precious sugar lump. Now promise, stand there till I get back. Promise?"

"Get a move on then," grinned Marlene.

Jinny caught Shantih with a handful of oats and led her towards Marlene.

"Hold your hand out flat," said Jinny irritably. "And put the sugar lump on it."

"Bit dirty that," said Marlene, holding out the sugar lump between finger and thumb.

"No," said Jinny. "Not that way."

Shantih made a grab at the sugar. Marlene dropped it and Shantih snuffled it up and crunched it.

"Now," said Jinny. "Let's go and have our breakfast while you are still in one piece. She nearly took your fingers off that time. Not that you'd notice."

Jinny took Shantih's halter off and the horse walked beside them to the gate.

"See, I was right," said Marlene. "He right enjoyed that sugar. He's after more."

Mrs. Manders suggested that Marlene should wash her hands before she started on her cornflakes.

"They don't need it," said Marlene sitting down. "I held the sugar lump out ever so dainty. Old horse didn't muck me up at all. If I'd done it the way she told me I'd have been in a right mess then."

Jinny, sitting slumped in her chair, groaned to herself. Already Marlene had nearly been kicked to death and almost had her fingers bitten off. "And whose fault would it be?" thought Jinny. "It would all be Shantih's fault."

"And what are you doing this morning?" Mrs. Manders asked.

"Mike and I are going for a walk up the hill," said Mr. Manders to Bill. "Some wood to chop first. How about helping and then coming up the hill?"

"Naw," said Bill.

"Not after being in hospital he ain't. Doctor wouldn't have it," Marlene explained. "He can come and watch me riding. Be some fireworks when I get up on the old horse, I bet."

"Will you stop calling Shantih an old horse," cried Jinny.

"Didn't mean no offence," said Marlene. "Bit touchy, ain't she?" Marlene winked at Ken.

Jinny took a deep breath and another slice of toast.

"I'm just telling you," she said. "Just so that you'll all know, that I don't think Marlene is fit to ride Shantih. I think she'll get hurt. And it won't be my fault when it happens."

"Don't listen to her," said Petra. "She's got this thing about Shantih. Has to keep her all to herself."

"I've told you," repeated Jinny. "It will not be my fault when she hurts herself."

"I'll come and help," offered Petra, smiling at Marlene. "I'll hold you on. You'll be quite safe."

"That," said Jinny, "is all I need. Two of you who know nothing about horses."

When Jinny had groomed Shantih and put her tack on she led her down to the field with Petra and Marlene walking beside her. Mike, Ken and Bill were waiting at the gate.

"I'll ride her round first," said Jinny, mounting, and easing her fingers on the reins she let Shantih walk forward. The Arab was uneasy about the group watching from the gate and still troubled by the strange disappearance of Punch and Bramble.

"There's the horse," murmured Jinny. "Gently the good horse."

Shantih mouthed at the snaffle and Jinny let her trot on. They crossed the field and trotted round in the other direction. Riding Shantih, Jinny was aware of nothing but the rhythm of her horse; the brightness and freedom of riding her.

Jinny sat down and asked Shantih to canter. She was ready when the mare plunged and shied. Sitting deep in her new saddle, Jinny gathered her together between seat and fingers and sent her on, flowing round the field at a steady canter.

As they passed the gate Petra shouted that it was Marlene's turn, distracting Jinny, and at the same moment Kelly emerged from the hedge. Shantih reared. Jinny, secure in her saddle, hardly moved. Shantih reared again, without much enthusiasm, and Jinny sent her on to canter for a last time round the field.

While Shantih had been rearing, Jinny had caught a glimpse of Marlene's face. It had been clenched tight with fear. "Why does she want to ride when she's afraid?" thought Jinny. "And with her leg!"

"Are you sure you do want to ride?" Jinny demanded when she got back to Marlene. "You don't have to, you know."

But already Marlene was limping towards her.

"Thought you weren't never going to give me a shot," she said as Jinny dismounted. "Poor old thing'll be worn out by the time it's me turn."

Petra had brought a length of rope from the stables and was knotting it efficiently through Shantih's bit ring.

"Better put the stirrups down," she told Jinny. "Now, reins in your left hand and face her tail," she instructed Marlene.

Marlene grabbed a bundle of reins with a shaking hand.

"Left foot into the stirrup," bossed Petra, "and spring up into the saddle."

"She can't . . ." began Jinny, who was holding Shantih's head.

"Me wonky leg," said Marlene. "No use this side," and she ducked down under Shantih's neck and before Jinny had realised what was happening she had pulled herself up on the off side and was sitting astride Shantih.

"Eh, he ain't half high," squeaked Marlene. "When we going to get moving, eh? Gee up, old horse."

"Don't hit her," cried Jinny desperately as Marlene flapped Shantih's reins on her neck, but her warning was too late. Shantih, terrified by anything that reminded her of the circus master's whip, had flung away from Jinny in bunching, twisting fear.

"Hold the saddle," Jinny yelled and grabbed at the rope to help Petra to control Shantih.

"Whoa. Steady, steady," Jinny soothed as she caught at Shantih's bridle. "Steady now. It's all right."

At last Shantih stood still. She was tense and shivering, her nostrils wide, her eyes bulging from her head and, somehow, Marlene was still on top.

"What did you have to go and do that for?" Jinny demanded. Her hands gentled Shantih as she glared furiously at Marlene's white face. "Giving her a fright like that."

Mike had come dashing across to help. Only Ken still leaned on the gate, his face calm, his eyes unconnected to the turmoil in the field.

"How was I to know I shouldn't hit him? You want to see them on the telly. They wallop them good. Thought I was doing it right."

"Well, you weren't," snapped Jinny.

"I think you were wonderful staying on like that," praised Petra. "Wonderful. I'd have been off."

Marlene beamed. "Perhaps it's going to be me thing, this horse-riding. Got to get him moving though, ain't we?" And for a horrible moment Jinny thought she was going to slap the reins down again on Shantih's neck.

"Don't," cried Jinny.

But suddenly Marlene seemed to have lost interest in Shantih.

"Where's our Bill?" Marlene demanded, straining forward. "He ain't there."

They all looked at the gate and realised that she was right. Bill wasn't there, only Ken.

"Gone off somewhere on his own, I suppose," said Mike.

Marlene slithered to the ground and limped to the gate.

"Our Bill," she said. "Where's he off to?"

"Why?" said Ken.

"You know," said Marlene.

Ken eased himself off the gate. "I'll find him," he said.

"Proper decent of you," said Marlene. "It's O.K.," she said to Mike, "Ken'll keep an eye on him." And she ran back to Shantih.

There was the sound of trotting hooves, Pippen's squealing whinny, and Sue rode up.

"Morning," she said, smiling round.

"Come on," said Marlene. "Let's get on with me riding. We've been mucking round here long enough."

"Honestly!" exclaimed Jinny in disgust, wanting to introduce Sue to her family, not wanting any more to do with Marlene's riding. "Can't you wait a minute? Perhaps Sue will let you have a ride on Pippen. He'd be much more suitable."

"Ride that fat old thing?" said Marlene. "I wouldn't have it at me funeral." And she hoisted herself determinedly back on to Shantih. "Gee up, then," she said. "Gee up."

CHAPTER FOUR

Pippen snorted, digging his toes into the peaty hillside, bumbling along as he tried to keep up with Shantih's long stride.

"Look at that!" exclaimed Sue, turning to gaze back the way they had ridden. Rolling moorland fell away beneath them, hummocked with sheep and jagged with rocks. Finmory House and Mr. MacKenzie's farm were toy buildings standing in patchwork fields. The sea crinkled between the black jaws of Finmory Bay, then stretched out, a shimmering, flickering blue, to the far horizon.

"Uh huh," agreed Jinny. Normally a day like this made her frothy with delight at living surrounded by such wide freedom; at riding Shantih over the moors; at having escaped from the dirt and traffic of Stopton, but today she hardly noticed it. She had Marlene on her mind.

"There's our tent," pointed Sue.

Jinny supposed it was. Marlene had had two more rides on Shantih and was becoming bored with being led round the field. "We've been stuck in this old field for two days," she had said to Jinny earlier that morning. "Might as well be on a roundabout. When we going to go a proper ride?" she kept demanding.

"Can't you see I'm having a job keeping her quiet enough for you when we're in the field? If I took you on to the beach and she started playing up there I couldn't hold on to her, what would happen then?"

"How about Petra? She could hang on too."

"You seem to think that everyone should spend all their time running after you. How about Bill helping for a change?"

"Not with his lungs," warned Marlene. "Doctor wouldn't have it."

Jinny had not been surprised to hear that. It seemed to Jinny that the only thing that Bill was allowed to do was to sit around reading his pile of American comics under Marlene's protective eye.

"And," Jinny told Sue, "she won't leave Shantih alone. Keeps on wanting to give her sugar."

"Marlene?" asked Sue. "She's O.K. I like her."

"You don't know her," retorted Jinny indignantly. "It's not your horse that she's messing about with. When she falls off and breaks her back they'll say it was because Shantih is wild and uncontrollable, and it won't be that at all. It will be all Marlene's fault."

Sue laughed at Jinny's expression of gloom. "Shantih hasn't bucked once today," she said, hoping to cheer Jinny up.

"Pollyanna," said Jinny scornfully and she glowered over the bright sunlit moor, seeing nothing but Marlene annoying her horse.

"We can canter here," Jinny called back when they reached a flat stretch of moor, and she let Shantih plunge forward into a gallop.

Pippen's hooves drumming behind her filled Shantih with a sudden excitement. She stretched her neck and raced forward. Jinny felt her hair banner out behind her with their speed, the whole moorland blurred as Shantih scorched over it. Jinny crouched forward, her knees secure against the knee rolls, her knuckles digging into her horse's shoulders. Normally when Shantih took off like this Jinny

287

was completely out of control, being carted wherever Shantih cared to take her, but now, with Sue's saddle, Jinny had the purchase to collect her horse and feel her respond to the bit's pressure even at a flat out gallop.

They reached the end of the canter, where normally Jinny had to fight Shantih, turning her uphill into the boggy hillside to steady her up. But today Jinny sat down deep into the saddle and was able to use her reins and seat to bring Shantih back to a trot. Within a few strides they were walking again.

Exultant, Jinny turned to see Pippen rocking sedately along at a collected canter.

"Did you see that!" Jinny cried.

"She's like a racehorse," exclaimed Sue, catching up.

"Oh, not that," said Jinny. "She can go faster than that. I mean the way we stopped. And it's all your saddle."

With Sue telling tales of her Pony Club at home, they rode towards the standing stones.

"Wish there was a Pony Club here," said Jinny.

"Don't be daft. We just make up things to do," said Sue, "because we don't have anywhere real to ride. I'd swop all Mrs. Moss's instruction for even the littlest bit of this moor."

And Jinny knew that what Sue said was true.

They dismounted at the standing stones and, holding their horses' reins, sat down in the sun to share a bar of chocolate.

Jinny shuddered as she looked at the sun-glossed moorland and the floating, mauve-shadowed mountains, remembering how it had been in the winter—a terrifying desert of snow.

"What's up?" asked Sue.

"Some day," said Jinny quickly, to drive the snow ghosts away, "I'm going to ride up here and camp." She imagined herself curled up, warm and safe, in her sleeping-bag while Shantih grazed close by.

"Oh yes!" agreed Sue.

"That is," said Jinny, "when I can find a tent. *If* I ever can find a tent."

"But I've got one."

"You're all sleeping in it. You can't expect your mother and father to sleep in the car while we take their tent!"

288

"Not that one, stupid. We've got a small one. Plenty of room in it for us."

"Could we?" said Jinny. "Now, while the weather's good?"

"Why not?"

"Yes, let's. Let's."

"Tomorrow," suggested Sue.

"We wouldn't need much," said Jinny.

"A kettle and a pan," said Sue. "We could have a camp fire and cook our food on it. Pippen can be a pack pony."

The two girls grinned at each other.

"If we camp here we can ride further into the hills," said Jinny. "Further than I've ever ridden before."

"Pippen's been to Pony Club camp," said Sue. "He's used to being tethered."

Jinny wasn't so sure about Shantih, but she pushed the doubt hurriedly to the back of her mind.

"We can camp for as long as we like," said Sue. "We'll send up smoke signals to let them know we're surviving."

"Go wooding," said Jinny. "There's plenty of dead branches from the pines round Loch Varrich."

Then suddenly Jinny thought about Marlene. Marlene would want to come with them. Jinny got up to make sure that Shantih's girth wasn't too tight, which she knew it wasn't because she had just loosened it a minute ago. Whatever happened Jinny didn't want Marlene spoiling their camp. She fiddled with the girth buckles, trying not to think how Marlene would stand watching them ride off to camp in the hills. "I don't care," Jinny thought. "She's not coming with us," and she sat down again beside Sue.

"What about Marlene?" asked Sue, knowing Jinny's thoughts.

"Oh, she wouldn't want to come," cried Jinny, defending herself. "She couldn't possibly come all this way when she's lame. And I don't suppose she'd want to sleep in a tent."

Sue twisted the buckle on Pippen's reins, not looking at Jinny.

"I'm sure she wouldn't want to come," insisted Jinny. "She can't come, anyway, and that's that."

Sue didn't answer and for a moment there was only the sound of their horses cropping the short moorland turf, the high, twittering lark song, and, far off, a curlew's liquid, bubbling notes.

Jinny jumped to her feet.

"Come on," she said. "If we're camping tomorrow we'll need to get a move on. I think Mum's going to the shop this afternoon so she could buy some tins for us."

"Couldn't we each put a pound into the kitty and buy our own food?" Sue asked as they remounted. "I can afford it because I've got my holiday money."

Jinny thought of saying that she couldn't afford a pound and that she'd bring some food from home, but it sounded so much more independent going to Mrs. Simpson's to buy their own food. She would need to open the tin box where she kept the money she was saving towards a lungeing rein for Shantih.

"And I've some money from the drawings I sold to the craft shop," she admitted.

"We'll need to make a list," said Sue as they rode home.

"Bread, dried milk and butter," said Jinny.

"A raspberry jelly," suggested Sue. "To eat not make."

"Dried apple rings. They swell up inside you in case we're starving."

"And marzipan," said Sue.

Sue's parents were quite agreeable for her to camp at the standing stones but felt that it would be rather nice if she spent the rest of the day with them, so Sue gave Jinny her pound, telling her to be sure to buy marzipan if she could possibly manage it.

When Jinny got back home she tipped some oats for Shantih on to the grass and left her eating them. She hung her bridle on its hook and carried the saddle up to her bedroom.

"Had a good ride?" asked her mother, who was vacuuming the landing. Jinny said she had and went on up to her room. She stood on a chair to reach the top of her wardrobe and lifted down her cash box. Originally it had belonged to Petra, but when the lock had broken she had abandoned it to Jinny who swathed it in sellotape to stop herself getting into it.

Hesitating, Jinny thought of asking her father to give her the money, then jumped down off the chair and ripped off the sellotape in a scrumpled, sticky mess. "You are getting too mean to live," she told herself. "You'll be hiring out Shantih next." And she opened the box and took out a pound.

The sellotape was too messed up to be used again. Jinny considered putting the box back as it was, but she knew that if she did the money left in it would soon be spent.

"Need to find some more," she thought. "Better stick it up again." And she remembered seeing a roll of sellotape in the pottery room.

Ken was working at the wheel.

"Hi," he said, looking up at Jinny and smiling his slow smile that seemed to light up his green eyes and spread easily over his whole face. He set you before him, making space for you to be yourself. Not the quick, half-afraid twitch that most people made at you. "Bit of a stranger," he suggested.

" 'Spose so," agreed Jinny, looking round for the sellotape, "and you'll be seeing less of me. We're going to camp at the standing stones."

"We?"

"Might camp for nights and nights if the weather stays fine."

Jinny's eyes flicked over the bats of pots waiting to be fired, over the glowing rows of glazed pottery and the plastic bins of clay. She searched the mess of the window-sill with its frosting of powdered clay, jars of glaze and bits of broken pots. The table, too, was littered. Jinny moved things about, searching.

"Have you seen that roll of sellotape?" she asked.

"We?" said Ken again.

"Well, you're bound to find out," said Jinny in exasperation. "We means Sue and myself and *not* Marlene. She couldn't come all that way. Not with her lame leg."

"You have to camp as far away as the standing stones?" said Ken, treadling the wheel, doodling the clay between his long, gentle fingers, but Jinny could feel his eyes on her.

"Yes," she said. "We have to camp at the standing stones. We've arranged it." And to her relief she spotted the sellotape.

"Feel free," said Ken. "Do what you like."

"Will do," said Jinny, already half way out of the door.

Jinny told them at lunchtime that she was going camping. Eating stew and potatoes gave her hands something to do while she was telling them.

"What about water?" asked Mr. Manders, and Jinny's mother wondered about warmth and having enough to eat.

"I'm coming with you to Mrs. Simpson's this afternoon," said Jinny. "I've got a list of supplies and we're only camping while it's fine, so we will be quite all right."

"What'll we take for the old horse?" asked Marlene. "Won't be much grass up on them mountains for him. I'd better take him plenty of sugar lumps."

For one moment Jinny hadn't been able to stop herself looking up at Marlene. Just long enough to see her face brighten with expectation at the thought of going with Shantih over the moors.

"Oh, we'll take oats for the horses," Jinny said, staring down at her plate. She was being polite and brisk. Not using her own voice. For that was the way you dealt with situations like this. You were polite but firm, and then everyone knew where they stood. "I'm going with Sue. We'll only be away for a night or two. It's too far for you, I'm afraid."

"Oh, Jinny!" cried Mrs. Manders in dismay. "Of course Marlene can go with you. Of course you can, dear."

Jinny forced herself not to look up.

"Don't 'Oh Jinny' her for me," shrilled Marlene. "I wouldn't want to go trailing up them mountains, not for nothing. I just pity that poor old horse, that's all."

"There you are," said Jinny. "I knew she wouldn't want to come." But she kept her eyes clamped tight on to her hands, gripping her knife and fork until her knuckles shone through her skin and her nails bit into her palms.

Mrs. Manders cornered Jinny as she finished washing up.

"I am thoroughly ashamed of you," she said. "Really I am. How could you be so cruel?"

"I'm being kind," said Jinny. "If she goes on making me give her rides on Shantih she's going to fall off and hurt herself. So I'm being kind to her, taking Shantih away so that she can't ride her."

Mrs. Manders turned her back and walked away. Every bit of Jinny ached to run after her and try to explain how it really was true; that Marlene really would be hurt if she went on riding Shantih; that it was dangerous; that Shantih wasn't a pony like Miss Tuke's trekkers who would plod along with beginners on their backs not caring what their riders did. Shantih was a highly-strung Arab horse. You couldn't mess about with her. She could so easily be frightened and then it would be too late, Marlene would be injured.

But Jinny couldn't make herself move. She stood fiddling with her hair.

"When are you going to Mrs. Simpson's?" she called after her mother, her voice flat as if she was speaking to a stranger.

"About three," replied Mrs. Manders without stopping.

Mr. and Mrs. Manders, Jinny and Marlene, taking an unwilling Bill with her, all packed into the car.

"After we've done the shopping we'll drive on for a bit. Let you see the country round about," said Mrs. Manders to Bill. "We'll go round by the Crawlin rocks. Fantastic scenery there. Black gaping caves. You can stand on the cliffs and hear the sea booming under your feet."

Bill didn't bother to reply. Since he had arrived Jinny had hardly heard him speak at all. The only time he showed any enthusiasm was when Mrs. Manders called him for his meals and whenever he had stuffed the last bite in his mouth he went back to reading his comics and scratching his head.

"Anything special you'd like to do, Bill?" Mr. Manders asked. "We're open to suggestions. There's a wildlife park about thirty miles away. We could go there for the day? Or a sail?"

"Doctor wouldn't have that," said Marlene. "He's O.K., ain't you, Bill? He's better taking it easy like. Doctor said he wasn't to strain himself. Couldn't go pulling up anchors and all that."

"Not a yacht," Mr. Manders assured her. "A sail on a steamer. Bill could sit in an armchair as we sailed along."

"Naw," said Bill.

"Better not," said Marlene.

"Perhaps Mrs. Simpson will have some comics you haven't read," suggested Mrs. Manders.

"He likes the ones he's got, thank you all the same," said Marlene.

Mr. Manders trod on the accelerator and wondered what they were doing wrong. He knew what Jinny was doing wrong—smuggling Shantih off to the hills so that she didn't have to share her with Marlene. Part of him was furious with his daughter for being so selfish, part was standing back waiting to see what would happen next and part of him wasn't even surprised. To possess a loved one; to possess completely and absolutely, so that you didn't care what you did as long as you could say MINE, seemed to be deep at the centre of every human being. Except the few. The very few.

"Tom!" shouted his wife. "Look where you're going. We were right off the road then."

And Mr. Manders remembered he was driving.

"Come away in with you now," Mrs. Simpson said, as they all crowded into her shop.

Mrs. Simpson's was the only shop in Glenbost and it sold everything. Slippers and paraffin heaters, cheese and liqueur chocolates, pork chops and cabbages, men's long winter drawers and women's Sunday hats, stamps and pensions were all to be had at Mrs. Simpson's. Some of her stock had taken up more or less permanent residence, some had lodgers. Petra had found a dead mouse in a net of oranges. "Wasn't that the lucky thing now that the wee fellow died in the oranges," Mrs. Simpson had said when Petra pointed it out to her. "And them done up so tidy in their skins. I'd have been worried myself if he'd been living in with the sausages."

Mrs. Simpson leaned over her counter and examined Bill and Marlene with a hard stare. She had almost accepted the Manders as harmless lunatics but she was still suspicious of any of their visitors. She feared that the families she referred to as heathen hippies, who had lived at Finmory before the Manders, were still lurking in the hills ready to make a comeback.

"It's the beautiful day," she admitted grudgingly. "But I'm thinking myself it won't last much longer."

"See you've been branching out into a new line," said Mr. Manders.

"Indeed I have. Not new because we were having them before, but perhaps you wouldn't be here then."

Jinny couldn't think how her father could possibly notice

whether Mrs. Simpson had anything new or not since all
her stock was scrabbled and jumbled together. Then she
saw what he meant. On the counter was a smart perspex
case with about a dozen watches in it. On top of the case,
displayed in its own box, was a man's gold watch. Mr.
Manders picked it up.

"Very nice," he said.

"Now there's the coincidence," said Mrs. Simpson.
"When the traveller showed me that very one, it was yourself I saw walk into this shop, Mr. Manders, put it on, and
walk out a man with the pride about him."

"Joke taken," said Mr. Manders. "How much?"

"To you, eighty-two pounds. It has the wee bookie with
it to tell you the value of it. Jewels like Aladdin's cave and
the everlasting calendar so that you need never be wasting
your money on the paper rubbish ever again."

"Yes. Well," said Mr. Manders putting the watch back
in it's box. "How much do I owe you for looking
at it?"

"Eh, give us a see," said Bill, snatching the watch from
Mr. Manders. "That's what I call a watch, that is. I'll have
one of them. You'll see."

Mrs. Simpson swiftly removed the watch from Bill, put
it back in its box and replaced it reverently on top of the
case.

"How much did you say?" demanded Bill.

"Who will ever buy that here?" exclaimed Mrs. Manders.
"It's a beautiful watch," she added quickly, in case Mrs.
Simpson should take umbrage and plunge the Manders
into sudden famine. "But eighty-two pounds!"

"Goodness yes," stated Mrs. Simpson coldly. "It's five
hundred pounds they're paying for them in the cities."

"It's a tourist trap," guessed Mr. Manders.

"You could be saying that, but if there's not a tourist in
my trap by October I'm thinking eighty-two pounds is
about the exact sum the congregation will be giving to the
Reverend James when he comes to the retirement in
November. And him poor man without a watch to his
name."

Mr. Manders burst out laughing.

"Laugh you may," said Mrs. Simpson, not even smiling,
"but that's the good business sense." And she took the

watch away again from Bill. "Leave it be," she said sharply. "Keep your fingers to yourself in my shop."

Quickly, Mrs. Manders began to read out her order.

When her mother had finished Jinny fished out her list.

"I want some things too," she said, and began with the bread and butter essentials.

On the wall behind Mrs. Simpson was a mirror hung round with pairs of wellington boots on a string so that there was only a small space left to reflect the front of the shop, but enough for a movement in it to catch Jinny's attention. In the mirror she saw Bill reaching up for the watch again, saw Marlene catch hold of his hand and snatch it away from the case. There was a tightness at the corners of Marlene's lips. a pinched, indrawn shadow at her cheeks and nostrils, her black, bead eyes were narrowed and her brows knotted down. Jinny hadn't seen her looking like that before but she had seen that look somewhere, that cold, defeated, bitterness.

"You'll be setting up your own establishment with all this food?" said Mrs. Simpson, waiting to be told why Jinny was buying it.

"We're going camping on the moors," said Jinny.

"With that terrible wild horse?"

"And a friend," said Jinny.

From the mirror, Marlene's indrawn mask stared straight at her and suddenly Jinny knew where she had seen that look before. It had been on the woman's face in the photograph on Marlene's dressing table.

CHAPTER FIVE

Just after ten the next morning, Sue led Pippen towards Finmory, and Jinny, watching from the stable doorway, thought that he looked like the original clothes horse or the White Knight's horse from Alice.

"Even the kitchen sink," Sue yelled, waving a plastic bucket. "Did you get the supplies?"

"Couldn't afford marzipan," Jinny told her. "Anyway, the lump Mrs. Simpson had looked mousley. She'd had it since Christmas. But I got two jellies. A lemon and a raspberry."

"Same to you," giggled Sue. "Are you nearly ready?"

"I've brought Shantih in," Jinny said, "and I've packed all the things in a rucksack. I think she'll let me tie my sleeping bag on to the front of the saddle but not much else. Just need to hang them on to myself seeing Pippen is fully occupied."

"Isn't he?" said Sue lovingly. "Took me ages to pack him. It's times like this, when he's so totally obliging, that I try to remember when we're last in races. Mummy says they will be coming up the mountain to borrow back their stuff."

"You've even brought a kettle," said Jinny, examining Pippen's load more closely.

"Do not look down the spout. It has white furry knickers all over it."

"Yuch," said Jinny. "Thanks for the warning."

She put Shantih's tack on, then, very cautiously tied her sleeping bag to the front of the saddle. Shantih rolled her eyes back suspiciously, but apart from this didn't object.

"She was O.K.," Jinny announced to Sue, who didn't seem to care. "I expect it's being used to Pippen," Jinny thought. "If she'd known Shantih last autumn she'd realise what it means being able to put a saddle on her, never mind a sleeping bag.

"I'm going for my hat," Jinny said to Sue. "And then I think we're ready."

"I haven't got a pan," said Sue. "Could you bring one?"

"Frying?"

"That's all we'll need, isn't it? Be mostly sandwiches."

"Cordon bleu," said Jinny, "but between bread." And she ran up to the house.

"A frying pan," said her mother and found an old one.

"Matches?" asked her father, and Jinny said she thought Sue would have some because she seemed to have most things but in case Sue hadn't any she'd take some.

. "Come straight home if the weather changes," warned Mrs. Manders.

Jinny said they would. Then there was a pause when her family should have been telling her to enjoy herself, planning to join them for a camp fire sing-song or giving her a surprise food parcel to be opened at camp. Jinny would even have welcomed one of Petra's comments, but she could hear the piano and knew that Petra must be practising. Jinny hadn't seen Ken that morning. In a way she didn't mind. She didn't particularly want to see him.

"Well," Jinny said, sitting her hard hat in the frying pan and holding it as if she was entering for an egg and spoon race. "I'd better fry."

Nobody even smiled.

" 'Bye," said Jinny, not really looking at her parents, more taking them in as she glanced round the kitchen, before escaping back to Sue.

Marlene and Bill were standing at the stables.

"Oh no!" thought Jinny. "As if they haven't caused enough trouble already. Why can't Marlene leave our horses alone?" Jinny stomped down the path pulling her hard hat down over her eyes.

"This you off, then?" asked Marlene. "Going to give us a last shot before you go?" Her black eyes clawed at Jinny's face forcing her to answer. "Better have a ride now, eh? Old thing'll be worn out when he comes back from them mountains. Won't be fit for me to ride, he won't."

"She," retorted Jinny furiously. Her temper surged up, making her want to run at Marlene and shake her by the shoulders, yelling that she couldn't ride Shantih because Shantih was hers and Marlene was to leave her alone.

"Round the field, like?" said Marlene. "Go on, just once before you go off?"

"No!" shouted Jinny. "No! No! No!"

"Look," suggested Sue hurriedly, "I'll take Pippen's saddle off and you can have a ride bareback."

"Naw," said Marlene. "He's all hairy and he's too fat. I'd be split up me middle sitting on him."

"You see," said Jinny smugly. "It's no use trying to be nice to her."

But Sue didn't seem to mind. She was laughing at Marlene.

"Perhaps you're right," she said to Marlene, and then to Jinny, "Give her a ride round the field. It won't take a minute. I don't mind waiting."

"Well!" said Jinny. "Well honestly." And she banged down the frying pan, making Pippen jump.

Muttering to herself, Jinny led Shantih down the path to the field.

"Bill," shouted Marlene. "Come and watch me. I'm for the riding again." And Bill followed them down to the field, still reading his comic.

"This is bad enough," thought Jinny, "but it would be much worse if he wanted to ride too." And she imagined Bill sitting slumped on Shantih, scratching his head and reading his comic.

"Here we are old horse," said Marlene. "Up and over." Despite her lame leg, Marlene could mount from the off side without any difficulty. She swung her leg over Shantih's back, taking care not to touch the horse's quarters with her foot, found her stirrup without looking down and gathered up her reins, holding them correctly.

"Walk on," Jinny said to Shantih and led the Arab forward by the halter rope she was wearing underneath her bridle.

"Wait on me there, Bill," Marlene called, casting one last, quick look at her brother before she gave all her attention to Shantih.

Jinny walked at Shantih's side paying no attention to Marlene.

"How about some speed?" asked Marlene.

Jinny clenched her teeth and pretended not to hear. She thought hard about camping with Sue, of sleeping in the tent and riding out tomorrow to discover what lay beyond Loch Varrich. Mr. MacKenzie had told her that before the clearances there had been a village in the hills. Perhaps they would discover the ruined crofts. Jinny stepped over the moss-covered stones that had once been the walls of the crofts. Her eye caught the glint of silver and she pounced on a brooch that had fallen from a woman's shawl when she was being driven out to the ship that had waited in Finmory Bay to take the crofters to America.

Jinny had completely blocked out Marlene.

Suddenly the halter rope scorched through her hand as Shantih leaped forward at a ragged trot. Just in time, Jinny managed to hold on to the tail end of the rope and to dash forward beside her. For a second Jinny thought that

299

Shantih had bounded forward by herself, and then she saw Marlene's face. She was grinning with delight, her bullet eyes sparkling, her mouth laughing. "Gee up," she shouted as she bounced enthusiastically up and down in the saddle.

"Right," thought Jinny. "I'll show her. I'll teach her a lesson." And instead of trying to slow Shantih back to a walk she went on running at her side, keeping her trotting, urging the Arab to go faster.

"Eh, watch out, I'll be off," gasped Marlene.

"Good," thought Jinny. "Serve you right."

Marlene grabbed at the pommel of the saddle. Her shrill sounds of alarm coming out in sudden jerks as she bumped about.

Back at the gate Jinny checked Shantih to a sudden halt. "That's it," she said. "Get down."

Marlene slithered to the ground.

"Did you mean to trot?" Sue asked. "Marlene nearly fell. She'd no idea how to post."

"She wanted to go fast so I let her," said Jinny.

"Oh," said Sue.

Jinny ran up Shantih's stirrups, took her reins over her head and swung the loaded rucksack on to her own back. She knew what Sue was thinking but she didn't care. Jinny hoped that she'd given Marlene a fright. She hoped it would stop Marlene wanting to ride Shantih. Or, better still, make her want to go back to Stopton so that Jinny never needed to see her again.

"Gracious," exclaimed Mrs. Manders. "Are you two still here?" She looked from her scowling daughter to Marlene, who had collapsed flat on the grass.

"Jin was giving Marlene a last ride," explained Sue. "We're going now."

"We hope," said Jinny. "That is *if* we can get away."

"Marlene and Bill," said Mrs. Manders, paying no attention to Jinny's grumbling. "We're going down to the shop. Would you like to come for the drive."

Bill stuffed his comic into his trouser pocket with untypical haste, pushed the hair out of his eyes, and said, "Come on then if you're going."

"What d'you want to be going back to that shop for?" Marlene demanded, sitting up. "You was there yesterday."

"I forgot the sugar," said Mrs. Manders.

"Me and Bill, we don't need sugar. We don't want it. No need to fetch it for us."

"Afraid Tom does," said Mrs. Manders. "You can stay here though. Just as you like."

"Naw," said Marlene. "I've got to go if our Bill's going."

Jinny shrugged her rucksack impatiently. She was ready to go. She wanted nothing so much as to get away from them all. To get away from her family and most of all to get away from Marlene.

Jinny stared at Marlene resentfully. The enthusiasm that had lit up Marlene's pale face when she had been riding had vanished. As she struggled to her feet, Jinny could see the pinched, withered expression clamped at her mouth and eyes.

"Wait on me, Bill," Marlene shouted and limped after Bill, who was already striding up the path. "Wait on me."

Mrs. Manders, speaking more to Sue than to Jinny, hoped that they'd remember to brush their teeth if not their hair and that the sun would go on shining for them.

"The moon will be shining if we don't get a move on," Jinny muttered as Shantih pranced impatiently at the full length of her reins.

Mrs. Manders said goodbye and went up the path after Bill and Marlene.

"At last," said Jinny. "At flippin' last." And, leading the way, she turned Shantih towards the moors. "We could have been away an hour ago if it hadn't been for her. I don't know what she thinks Shantih is. Some kind of sea-side donkey. Always wanting rides on her. Always going on at her the way she does. Stupid nuisance!"

"Marlene's O.K.," said Sue, leading Pippen behind Shantih. "She's just keen. And you never hear her complaining about her leg."

Jinny snorted. "She complains enough about Shantih. Always wanting to ride her. Wanted to stand in the field holding the halter. Just stand there holding the halter!"

"I was like that about Pippen."

"That's different. That's quite different. Shantih could have kicked her or anything. Reared up and kicked her. Marlene wouldn't even have noticed until her head was rolling on the ground. And then what would have happened to Shantih?"

301

Jinny's bad temper was set, hard and furious. She had to keep on telling Sue how impossible Marlene was, how incredibly stupid, how she had absolutely no right to even touch Jinny's horse.

"Cooee, cooee. Wait a minute. You two wait on me. Cooee. Wait on me."

"Oh no!" exclaimed Jinny. "What does she want now?"

Marlene was running after them, her arms swimming through the air to help her to keep her balance. She limped right up to Jinny.

"Here you are," she said, tugging at something in her pocket. "Nearly forgot, what with all that banging about you made me do. Bashed me brains. Them's for the old horse," and she thrust a paper bag full of sugar lumps into Jinny's hand, and before Jinny could say anything she was hirpling back to Finmory.

Jinny stared at the sugar lumps in disgust.

"What did she want to give me these for? Shantih doesn't want them," and Jinny almost threw the sugar away, but something in the way Sue was looking at her made her keep them. "Stupid thing," she declared and marched on with Shantih jogging at her side.

The sun blazed down and the flies zooming round Jinny's head made the day seem hotter than ever. The metal frame of the rucksack hurt her back, its straps gnawed into her shoulders. It seemed to grow heavier and heavier at every step she took. She tried balancing it on Shantih's saddle and holding it there as they walked along, but the Arab sprang away and the pack went crashing to the ground.

Sue stood watching, without offering to help, while Jinny tried to hoist the rucksack on to her back again and hold on to her skittering horse at the same time. Sue waited without speaking until Jinny had reorganised herself and then followed on behind her.

"Not going to be much of a camp if Sue's going to be like this," thought Jinny. She'd given up trying to make conversation. No matter how often she'd pointed out to Sue how hopeless Marlene was, Sue hadn't joined in. As she plodded on, Jinny could feel the bag of sugar lumps in her pocket and hear Marlene's voice telling her to give them to the old horse.

"Old horse, indeed," thought Jinny. "She is just so stupid.

302

It's a good job I'm taking Shantih away from her," and she wondered if they could possibly go on camping until the Thorpes went back to Stopton.

As she trudged on, Jinny's mind bubbled and boiled, full of all the things that made her hate Marlene. She had to keep on telling herself how dangerous it was for Marlene to be near Shantih, telling herself over and over again that Marlene was too stupid to ride Shantih, for no matter how hard she tried to block it out she kept seeing Marlene's white pinched face. She couldn't stop herself remembering the dirt and noise of Stopton and the decaying slums where Marlene and Bill lived. Worst of all was the thought of Marlene's delight when she had started to trot, the way she had lit up with excitement.

"You could have steadied Shantih. Held Marlene's leg against the saddle. Shown her how to post. And what did you do? You tried to make her fall off."

"But she knows nothing about horses!"

Jinny shouted the words inside her head. But it was too late. She had allowed herself to listen to the voice.

"How could she know about horses?" demanded the voice that was her parents and Ken, and Jinny herself, really. "There's not many Arabs in Stopton."

"I'm telling you she could hurt herself," yelled Jinny in silent self-defence.

The voice that couldn't be silenced now that Jinny had started listening to it laughed scornfully. "Is that so?" it said. "How convenient." And resentfully Jinny knew what she was going to have to do.

"Pippen is sweating like anything," Sue called. "Can we have a stop?"

"O.K.," said Jinny and collapsed on to a handy boulder.

Sue sat down on the grass. Neither of them spoke. The silence was filled with waiting for who was going to speak first.

"Go on," urged the voice in Jinny's head. "It's all your fault. Sue would have brought Marlene with us." Jinny drew in her breath and said, "We can't, can we?"

At the same moment Sue looked round. "Let's go back for Marlene," she said.

CHAPTER SIX

Shantih and Pippen trotted back side by side to Finmory.
The two girls had unloaded Pippen and deposited the
rucksack, frying pan and Jinny's sleeping bag on the
ground.

"May as well camp here," Jinny had said. "It's not too
bad a place. Quite close to the burn."

"It's great," agreed Sue. "A wall to shelter us and that
old sheep pen to tie the ponies to. And a smashing view. We
could never take Marlene all the way to the standing
stones."

"This isn't really very far from Finmory," Jinny had said
regretfully. "There's a short cut through Mr. MacKenzie's
yard, but the last field gate is sometimes locked, then you
have to trail back and come round this way."

As Finmory came into sight, Jinny said, "I expect they'll
all come and visit us, now that we're camping so close to
the house." She wasn't looking forward to telling Marlene
that she was sorry for being so mean, and was trying to
keep her thoughts on other things. "Your parents could
come to."

"They'd like that," said Sue. "Mum plays the guitar.
She'd bring it with her."

And Jinny imagined them all sitting round a blazing
camp-fire, singing, while the horses listened, ears pricked,
eyes glinting in the firelight.

"I'll hold Shantih," Sue offered when they reached Finmory. "You go and find Marlene."

"Say she doesn't want to come?"

"You know she does."

"Oh well," said Jinny and went off to look for
Marlene.

There was no one around the stables, no one in the
garden, and then Jinny noticed that the car wasn't there.
"Can't be back from Mrs. Simpson's," she thought and
drew in a gasp of relief. It would be a few minutes at least
before she had to apologise to Marlene. She thought of
going back to tell Sue to put the horses in the stable and

304

come in for lemonade but decided not to bother. If she could manage to speak to Marlene without Sue listening Jinny felt it would be easier.

She leaned against the back door, the sun burning down on her. "Jinny Manders," she told herself. "You very nearly ruined your summer holidays too. Just saved yourself in time." And she went over in her mind what she would say to Marlene.

There was a noise in the kitchen. Too definite to be Kelly or one of the cats. It was a person. Jinny heard them draw back a chair and sit down at the table.

"Ken," thought Jinny. "May as well tell him first." She pushed open the back door and ran inside.

Bill was sitting at the table, hunched over something he was holding in his hands. Blinded by the dark kitchen after the bright morning, Jinny couldn't see what it was.

Bill jumped up when he heard her come in, fumbling to hide what he had been looking at behind his back.

"What you want?" he demanded, glaring suspiciously at Jinny.

"Sorry," said Jinny. "I didn't mean to give you a fright. I'm looking for Marlene."

"She ain't here."

"I can see that," said Jinny. "Is she still at Glenbost?"

"Naw. She's out at them vegetables with the hippie," Bill told her as he backed away.

"Thanks," said Jinny and went off to Ken's kitchen garden.

She made herself walk steadily—left foot, right foot. Her mind too full of apologising to Marlene to leave any room for wondering why Bill had looked so guilty.

Just before she reached the kitchen garden, Jinny hesitated behind a screen of rhododendrons. She could hear Marlene's high-pitched voice rasping at Ken.

"We had a little pup once but me Mum got sick of it, messing the floor and eating all her good things. She was having a tea party for her friends, like, and she had it all laid out nice with a fancy cloth covering it all and when her friends came they lifted up the cloth and there were only the pup there. He'd eaten all the cakes and things. Didn't take me Mum long to get shot of him after that. But he were a nice little thing. He were brown with a bit funny tail. Used to push him round in a pram, all tucked in proper nice."

"Oh no," thought Jinny. "Days of listening to that; of listening to her talking nonsense and having to watch her ride Shantih." Then Jinny thought of going back to tell Sue that she had changed her mind. "Bear up," she told herself. "It's only for a day or two," and she stepped out from behind the bushes.

Marlene was making a daisy chain. Kelly, lying beside her on the grass, was already wearing one round his neck. Ken was standing between his rows of vegetables, the hoe he held in his hands seemed almost to be working by itself, moving slowly but rhythmically. He looked up, saw Jinny, but didn't speak.

Jinny swallowed hard and marched on towards them.

"Well, look who's here," said Marlene. "You'll be in that book for records, you will. Shortestest camp in the world, that's what you'll be."

"We've come back for you," said Jinny. "Come and camp with us. I'm sorry I didn't ask you before. I thought it would be too far for you."

"Eh, get her," said Marlene. Her black eyes glistened without expression in her whitish-yellow face. "Want me to come running now do you? What's up? Can't neither of you do the cooking?"

"We were going to the standing stones but it was too hot," lied Jinny. "So when we decided not to go as far as that we came back for you."

Marlene went on with her daisy chain.

"Sue wants you to come," said Jinny.

"May be," said Marlene. "But what about you? You think I'm not posh enough for your horse, don't you?"

"She doesn't," stated Ken. "Things have just got a bit twisted between you."

"I'm asking you," said Jinny. "I wouldn't have come back for you if I hadn't wanted you to come."

"That'll be it," said Marlene.

"Go on," said Ken. "Don't hold on to that nonsense."

Marlene grinned quickly at Ken.

"What makes you all so sure that I'd want to give up me comfy bed to sleep on dirty old ground, eh? I ain't daft."

306

"It'll be fun," said Jinny. "An adventure. Something new. Exciting."

"Exciting!" scoffed Marlene. "Reckon that's the last thing our lot needs. Anyway, can't go all that trail with me leg."

Jinny stared at her in despair. She was sure that Marlene could walk over the moor if she wanted to. Jinny wanted to shout, "All right, then, stay where you are," but heard her own voice saying, "You can ride Shantih."

Marlene's mouth twitched, she kinked a quick look out of the corner of her eye at Ken.

"Need to get me bag," she said, scrambling to her feet.

"You won't need it," said Jinny.

"That I will," said Marlene.

Jinny went to find Mike's sleeping bag for Marlene to use, then she waited in the garden for Marlene to return with her shopper.

"Didn't they go with Mum and Dad?" Jinny asked Ken.

"To the shop? Yes. They've all been to the village. Think your parents went in to the farm and the kids came on here."

"That's me," said Marlene, clutching her tartan shopper to her stomach. "Now mind," she said to Ken. "We made it a promise. You keep an eye on him or I ain't going."

"All the time," confirmed Ken.

"What?" said Jinny.

"Me brother. Ken there'll watch him while we're up at the camp. We arranged it."

"You did, did you?" said Jinny, realising that if Ken and Marlene had arranged it they must have been expecting her to come back.

"Knew it wasn't you," said Ken.

"Nearly was," Jinny said to Ken. She told Marlene that Sue had been waiting ages for them, and they all went down to join her.

"Right pleased you came back for me," Marlene said to Sue.

More than she said to me, thought Jinny darkly.

"Where is the camp now?" Ken asked. "Dare say your mother will feel safer if she knows."

"Not far," said Jinny. "By the old sheep pen. That's where we've left the stuff so that's where we'll camp. If you go up the hill for a bit, you'll be able to spot the tent."

"Bright orange," said Sue. "So that helicopters and St. Bernards can spy us out."

"Mind and tell Bill where I'll be," said Marlene. "In case he wants me or anything, like. I've told him I won't be gone long."

"Only a day or two," said Jinny, taking Marlene's bag while she mounted. "No. I'll hold it while you're riding. No, I shan't drop it."

"Take joy," said Ken, and went back to his hoeing.

"What about the short cut you were talking about?" Sue asked.

"It's much quicker," said Jinny, seeing herself battering through bogs and bracken, trying to control Shantih and keep Marlene on top. "But no," she decided. "The gate might be shut and it's so maddening when you have to turn round and come all the way back."

"Couldn't we jump?" asked Sue.

"On Shantih?" demanded Jinny, feeling her stomach tighten—half nerves, half excitement. "But I've never jumped Shantih!"

"First time," suggested Sue.

"No chance," said Jinny. "It's a five-bar gate and the walls are built up to keep Mr. MacKenzie's cows in. It is HUGE."

"In that case," agreed Sue, turning Pippen round the way they had come, "old man Finnigin begin agin."

After ten minutes of trying to answer Marlene's questions, Jinny stopped listening to her and Marlene went on chatting to Shantih. Jinny had made a rule. Hold on to the pommel with one hand. She had used her father's no non-sense voice and Marlene was doing as she had been told.

Jinny smiled to herself as she plodded along behind Pippen's brown and white bottom. She could see the moor-land again, the shimmer of the sea; the black cliffs, the hazy, summer mountains. They were all part of her again. In-stead of hating Marlene she was alive again, and Jinny glanced up at Marlene to make sure she hadn't abandoned her firm hand hold.

"Eh, this is smashing," beamed Marlene. "Even the old horse is enjoying hisself, ain't he?"

Jinny agreed.

308

Sue pulled Pippen back to ride beside them.

"Have you ever jumped?" she asked Jinny.

"Once," said Jinny. "On Clare Burnley's showjumper."

"Not on Shantih?"

"No! I'm just reaching the stage where I can control her at a canter."

"There's lots of places here where you could jump," said Sue, pointing to the low, broken-down walls that criss-crossed the moor. "We could easily clear away the fallen stones and make a place for jumping. Shall we?"

"Now?" said Jinny in alarm.

"Why not?" challenged Sue.

"Not with me on horse," cried Marlene and instantly began to dismount. Shantih shied, depositing Marlene on the ground. "Getting as bad as you," Marlene said to Jinny. "Neither of us much good at this old riding."

"Really!" said Jinny in disgust. "You've got some cheek!" Then she realised Marlene was laughing at her.

The thought of jumping made Jinny curl up inside. She had read books about training horses to jump and none of them had suggested just suddenly starting to jump over stone walls.

"I don't mean great enormous jumps," declared Sue. "Well, if you don't want to jump, I do. Here," she said to Marlene, "hold his reins." She jumped down from Pippen and walked across to the wall.

Jinny, on Shantih, and Marlene, being led by Pippen, followed her across.

"This would do," said Sue, lifting fallen stones out of the way. "Good landing. No holes. And that couldn't be too high for anyone."

Jinny regarded the wall with a measuring eye. If she thought of having to jump Shantih over it, it looked about three feet; if she saw it as just an old wall, it probably wasn't even two feet high.

"Shouldn't we start with a pole on the ground and things like that first?"

"Oh, come on," said Sue. "This is fun. Not Hickstead. I'll go first."

"If she gets too excited I'm not jumping," said Jinny, feeling her mouth go suddenly dry. She certainly wasn't afraid, but . . .

Sue gathered up Pippen's reins, trotted him in a circle, turned him to face the wall and cantered him straight at it. With a gay flick of his tail, Pippen bounced over.

"Now me," thought Jinny as she eased Shantih into a slow sitting trot and took her round in a circle. She turned her horse to the jump, and Shantih, her ears pricked, raced at the wall. Jinny was only conscious of a sudden blur of speed, Shantih's neck arching in front of her, her mane blown back; and then, long before Jinny expected it, Shantih had taken off. Jinny jack-knifed over her shoulder, caught a vivid glimpse of Shantih's white legs tucked up close to her body, and then they had landed, far out on the other side of the wall.

"Whee!" exclaimed Sue.

Marlene clapped her hands above her head and stamped her foot, making Shantih shy and whirl round. "Nice one old horse!" she shrieked.

Jinny was too delighted to care. Her face had almost disappeared behind its ear-to-ear grin.

Pippen bounced back, popping obediently over the wall, and Shantih cantered behind him. Again she spread herself over the wall in a flowing arc.

"Jump back over again," said Sue, "and then we'll try something higher."

At the other side they searched for a higher bit of wall that was safe to jump.

"That's enormous," said Jinny in delight.

"Might be two foot six," deflated Sue. "Watch her this time. Be ready for her 'cause she'll really need to jump." Sue sat down in her saddle and rode Pippen determinedly at the wall. He cleared it with hardly an inch to spare.

Shantih plunged to follow him. Jinny checked her, trotted her in a circle, then, controlling her between her seat and hands, cantered her at the wall. She felt her horse rise up and over, then they seemed to come soaring down as if they had just cleared a steeplechase fence. Jinny was thrown forward when Shantih landed, lost a stirrup but stayed on top.

"That was super," she cried and threw herself over Shantih's neck, arms outstretched round her, praising her horse.

"Has she really never jumped before?" asked Sue.

310

"Not with me," said Jinny. "She flew over that. I didn't have to make her jump. She wanted to."

They went on jumping low bits of the wall until Marlene said to give the old horse a chance and when were they coming to this tent because she was starving, so they said now and went on to the camp site. Marlene led Shantih by the reins because she thought she needed a rest and Jinny held on to the halter rope in case a sudden grouse flew up under Shantih's nose or she saw an tiger lurking in the bracken.

As they walked up the hillside Jinny was suddenly aware of walls. They had always been there but she'd never really noticed them before. Now she was looking for places where she could jump; thinking of bringing a can of paint up the hill with her and marking suitable places with splodges of white paint so that she could canter over the moors and jump the walls without stopping to check whether they were safe to jump.

The tent, sleeping bags, rucksack, pan and their other things that had been stacked on Pippen were still lying obediently where they had left them that morning. It seemed to Jinny as if she had left them there in another life. Then she had been thinking about nothing but Marlene and now Shantih could jump. Jinny was lost in a dream of taking Shantih over Badminton-sized fences, over drop jumps and even possibly round the red and white show jumps at the Inverburgh Show next year.

"First thing," said Sue, "is to get the tent up."

Reluctantly Jinny abandoned the applause that followed her out of the ring after Shantih had jumped her clear round.

"Shall I tie him to the fence?" Marlene was asking, and Jinny realised that Sue had taken Pippen's tack off and tied him up to the most solid-looking bit of the sheep pen.

"Aren't you going to tie her up?" Sue asked.

Jinny looked dubiously at the sheep pen's rotted wood. Shantih would never stand tied to that. In fact, Jinny wasn't too sure that Shantih would stand tied to anything in the open.

"Think I'd better hold her."

"You can't hold her all the time," Sue said. "Who's going to help me with the tent?"

311

"Me," said Marlene.

"Well, I can't just let her go," said Jinny, seeing Shantih careering back to Finmory or running wild with Mr. Mac-Kenzie's herd of Shetlands.

"What about tonight?" Sue asked. "You can't hold her all night."

"But I'll hold her just now," said Jinny.

CHAPTER SEVEN

Sue and Marlene put up the tent, arranged the sleeping bags and laid out their food while Jinny, leading Shantih, brought a bucket of water from the burn and gathered dried bracken and heather. She found flattish stones and laid them in front of the tent to make a fireplace.

"We'll need to go wooding to Loch Varrich," Jinny said. "We could light a fire with these bits but we'll need branches to keep it going."

"What d'you want a fire for?" demanded Marlene. "Right hot up here. We don't need a fire."

"For the water," Jinny told her. "You can't drink it unless it's boiled."

"I can," said Marlene. "Bit brown, but it's not that bad."

"Further up the hill," said Jinny, "there might be a dead fox or a dead sheep lying in that burn and all the water that flows past here has been over it—that's why we need a fire. You can catch terrible diseases drinking burn water if you don't boil it first."

"Should think I've had them all," said Marlene, unimpressed by Jinny's warnings. "You want to see our water. Real green."

Unwillingly, Marlene agreed to stay at the tent while Jinny and Sue went wooding on their horses.

"You be back before it's dark," Marlene said. "Don't want them wolves eating me, do I?"

Jinny rode Shantih as fast as she dared to Loch Varrich, galloping over any flat stretch of moor, keeping at a steady trot even when her horse was stumbling into holes and over hidden stones. Jinny could hear Sue urging Pippen on as they tried to keep up with Shantih but Jinny didn't slow down. She closed her legs against Shantih's sides and forced her on.

"One minute mile?" asked Sue crossly, when they reached the pines above the loch. "What was all the hurry for?"

"In case the wolves eat Marlene," replied Jinny, not looking at Pippen's bellowing sides and sweat-streaked neck and trying not to notice Shantih's gulping nostrils Jinny was planning to make her horse so tired that she would be glad to stand tied for some of the night at least.

They gathered dead pine branches, tied them into bundles and took them back to camp. Sue rode Pippen and dragged her bundles behind her. Jinny clutched Shantih's reins with one hand and the string tied round her branches with the other. She had fallen off twice before Sue had decided that it would be quicker if Jinny walked. As the bundles of wood bounced along, Shantih pirouetted and shied, high trotting in panic at the terrible creatures bounding behind her.

"Good," thought Jinny. "After all this carry-on she'll not have the strength to break loose."

Marlene was watching out for them.

"Where you been then?" she demanded. "I've been that scared, left here on me own. There weren't no noise. Thought it was a trick you were at. Taking the horses and leaving me here. Been much longer I'd have been for off."

"Gosh," exclaimed Sue. "We couldn't have been much quicker."

"I got a bit bothered about our Bill," said Marlene. "Should I go down and look at him, like, and see how he's doing?"

"You can't go back to Finmory tonight," said Jinny. "Bill's O.K. He's with Ken."

Marlene looked blankly at Jinny, as if she hardly heard what Jinny was saying, or if she did hear knew that it didn't matter, and Jinny recognised the look. It was the way she had looked at people when Shantih had been starving on the moor and they kept telling her that the Arab would be all right.

"Just nip down?" pleaded Marlene.

313

"Goodness," said Sue, taking Pippen's tack off and leading him to the sheep pen. "He's older than you, isn't he? I should think he's perfectly all right."

Jinny hesitated, torn between admitting to herself that she knew what it was like to be worried about something and surrounded by people who didn't understand, and because she knew this knowing that she had to try and help Marlene; and the more pressing need of deciding whether she could risk tying up Shantih.

"Tie her up here, next to Pippen," Sue called. "This bit here is strong enough. You can't hang on to her all night."

"I could scoot down," said Marlene.

"Of course you can't," Jinny snapped, worried about Shantih. If they'd camped at the standing stones Jinny had been planning to tie her up to a tree that grew close by. Shantih might have pulled against the tree but she couldn't have pulled it up by the roots. Looking at the grey, weather-gnawed wood of the sheep pen, Jinny knew that Shantih could drag herself free from it in seconds. "I'll wait until later in the evening," Jinny told Sue. "She'll settle better then."

Jinny took Shantih's tack off, rubbed her down and fed both horses from the bag of nuts and oats that they'd brought with them. She would decide later what to do with Shantih. Later was always easier.

Sue was organising Marlene into opening tins and filling the kettle while she blew at the flickering tendrils of flame that bloomed along the dried bracken.

Jinny crouched on the grass, holding Shantih, the Arab looming above her. Shantih's head with its delicate bones, silken skin, great liquid eyes and flimpering muzzle swooped down for a mouthful of oats, then up again, silhouetted above Jinny as her horse stared out over the pearly-grey, luminous space.

"Must be quite late," Jinny thought. The sun that had blazed above them all day had sunk into a neat, glowing disc touching the distant glint of the sea with one golden finger. The cliffs were smudgy black and the reaches of moor had softened from their sun-chiselled enamel into pastel shadings that glowed more warmly than the greying sky.

314

Sue placed branches carefully over the core of fire. Tongues of flame licked greedily, crackled and bit, and Jinny smelt the itchy wood smell at the back of her nose. The flames spawned shadows. Suddenly it was almost night. One minute grey, stretching evening, the next minute night. Shadows had crowded Sue, Marlene and the tent into a centre of golden security. Jinny moved closer to the fire.

"Beans?" said Sue as she tipped baked beans into the frying pan. "With sausages and, when Marlene finds them, eggs."

"Gone proper dark, ain't it," said Marlene. "Better get me torch." She burrowed into her tartan shopper.

"Forgot!" said Jinny.

"Never thought," said Sue.

"You see," said Marlene. "Can't do without me." She shone the torch to and fro in the dark. "It's me mum's. She'd have a canary if she could see me sitting out here with her good torch."

Marlene began to laugh and suddenly they were all laughing—infectious giggling that brought them together and made them all forget that only a few hours ago they'd left Marlene behind.

Still giggling, Marlene found the eggs.

"One day at school," Marlene told them, "we had this student teacher and we all had to take a turn round the class at being Noah, getting them all into the ark, like. We had to say, 'forward the elephants', or 'forward the horses', but you hadn't to say an animal any of them others had said. Well, when it were my turn they'd had all the animals I knew, so I said . . ." Marlene doubled up at the memory. "I said . . . I said, 'forward the eggs!'"

"Forward the eggs," choked Jinny in delight. It seemed the funniest thing she had ever heard.

Outside the circle of firelight, Pippen clattered the sheep pen, disturbed by the din and Shantih pricked curious ears, staring in uneasy suspicion at the three girls rolling on the ground shouting, "Forward the eggs!"

Sue ate her nosh out of the frying pan because she'd only brought two bowls and there were three of them now. They ate jelly cubes as they waited for the kettle to

315

boil and when it did they drank tea bag tea and ate wedges of Sue's mother's fruit cake.

Sue held Shantih while Marlene and Jinny washed up in the burn.

"My hands!" cried Jinny, flapping her frozen hands as she tried to bring them back to life. "I've got burn bite."

"What a fuss," said Marlene. "Where we lived once we only had the one tap and it was always right freezing."

"But you could boil kettles," said Jinny.

"Not likely," said Marlene. "Them rotters had cut us off."

"You'd no electricity?" asked Sue incredulously. "Or gas?"

"We'd bloomin' candles," said Marlene. "Didn't even give enough light to scare off them rats." She flashed quicksilver glances at Sue and Jinny, mocking them.

"Well, anyway," said Sue a shade too quickly, not believing Marlene, "what are you going to do with her ladyship? Is she coming into the tent with us?"

"Is there a sleeping bag for her?" countered Jinny. She had seen the Stopton slums. In her mind she understood that people who lived there had rats in their houses. But she didn't know it. Couldn't believe it really possible. To open a door and see rats in your house.

"Better to tie her up now," decided Sue. "While we're still up. She will be all right. Pippen'll keep an eye on her."

Reluctantly, Jinny led Shantih across to the sheep pen. It was really dark, now that she was away from the fire. "But there'll be a moon later," Jinny thought as she tested the wooden bars, trying to find the strongest place. She imagined herself lying warm inside her sleeping bag and being able to look through the flap of the tent and see Shantih.

"Stand quietly now," Jinny murmured, clapping Shantih's sleek neck. She ran her hand over the mare's withers, stretched her arm over Shantih's back to clap her hard side and quarters, waited a moment leaning against the warm, safe bulk of her horse, then she tied her up with a quick-release knot to the strongest part of the sheep pen. "You've got Pippen," Jinny told Shantih. "You're perfectly safe. Stay there till the morning. I'll be in the tent. You don't need to be afraid."

316

Jinny took a few steps away from Shantih and waited. Pippen went back to his dozing, his round bulk tipped to one side by a resting hind leg, his head hanging. Shantih's neck was arched, her head high, sniffing the breeze from the night moors, and Jinny wondered if she might be smelling the Shetlands, wondered if she remembered when she had roamed the hills with them. Shantih stepped back, testing the rope that held her. She whinnied—a shrill, sudden sound—and Pippen wuffled back to her.

"He's telling her not to be so silly," Jinny thought, as she saw Shantih relax.

"There," said Sue, coming over to inspect. "She'll be all right. Stop bothering her. Come back to the fire. Marlene's making cocoa for us. We'll need to get more wood tomorrow, we've nearly used up the lot we brought today."

Jinny shivered, realising how cold it was away from the fire. She shone the torch beam for a last look at Shantih, trying not to notice the rusty nails sticking out of the planks of wood or the sheets of corrugated iron that still clung loosely, here and there, to the pen. It wasn't the place to tie up a horse and Jinny knew it. Maybe all right for Pippen but not for Shantih.

"Come and get it while it's hot," shouted Marlene, and Jinny went unwillingly over to the fire.

"You're the old cow's tail so you'll need to have the bowl," said Marlene, handing Jinny a bowl of cocoa. "But you can have all the sugar you want, nobody here won't be counting." Marlene gave Jinny the bag of sugar with a spoon stuck in it. "We're right comfy here, ain't we? Once you brew up you can make any old hole proper nice. That's what me mum says." Marlene beamed at Jinny. "Guess I'll be for the old horse again tomorrow, won't I? Can we do some more of that trotting bit?"

Jinny nodded, hardly listening. Her ears were tight to hear the least movement from Shantih. Drinking her cocoa, Jinny was ready to spring up and run to Shantih, ready to grab the tail end of the rope and set her free.

"That bloke Ken—reckon he'll watch our Bill?"

"I'm sure he will," said Jinny and far below them she heard the wind moan with a low movement of sound.

"It were strange the way he knew you'd come back for

317

me. I were crying a bit when he found me, bit lonely like being left, and he said you'd come back for me."

Jinny heard the wind again. It came blowing in from the sea, lifting the tent flap, scurrying paper bags they had left lying about, gusting the camp fire.

"It's proper knacky that trotting," said Marlene. "Guess me wonky leg won't help."

Sue told her she had known a man with an artificial leg who had hunted, never mind posting.

"Wouldn't want none of that rubbish, killing them little foxes, but I guess I'll need to get this, what d'you call it?"

"Posting," said Jinny. "Stops you bumping about." But she was listening to the wind, hearing it surging up from the sea, a sudden, howling voice gathering strength as it roared at them over the moors.

"What a wind," said Sue as the fire smoked and flamed. "We'll be blown away. And what about Mummy and Dad? They'll be afloat."

Shantih trampled restlessly back and forward. "If it's going to be a wild night I'll need to sit up and hold her," Jinny thought. She zipped up her anorak and stood up to go to the horses.

There was a sudden clattering rattle of corrugated iron, a stampeding panic of hooves and Jinny, running flat out to the horses, saw the whitish gleam of the corrugated iron sheet lifted by the wind. Sue had snatched up Marlene's torch and was running behind her. By its light Jinny could make out the frantic shape of Shantih fighting to escape—her head wrenched upward, the rope taut, her eyeballs white glisters in her head, the skin of her face drawn tight with terror. Her forelegs were splayed out and she pivoted from her crouching quarters as she fought to free herself.

"Pull the end of the rope!" Sue yelled, but already Jinny had ducked past Shantih's straining chest and was tugging at the end of the rope. The pressure of the struggling horse held the knot tight as Jinny jerked it helplessly.

"Can't get it loose," she screamed, as the sheet of corrugated iron was caught by another gust of wind and flung up again to rattle and crash above their heads.

With a rending, splintering crash, the bar to which Shantih had been tied broke. The mare plunged back, and the rotted lump of wood, still attached to her halter rope, whammed past Jinny, hitting her behind the knees and knocking her down.

"Catch her," Jinny screamed as she fell. She had seen the rusty nails sticking out of the lump of wood and in her imagination saw the wood entangled in Shantih's legs, the nails ripping and tearing. "Catch her! Get hold of her!"

As Jinny fought back to her feet she saw Sue grab at the halter rope, miss, and duck away from Shantih's plunging hooves.

"Shantih," cried Jinny in despair, "Shantih stop! Stop!"

Then, black against the camp fire, Jinny saw Marlene crouch close to the ground, leap up and throw herself at the jolting, leaping, jagged chunk of wood—not thinking of herself first, the way Sue had done, but with a movement so concentrated and direct that she seemed dragged on to the lump of wood as if it had been a magnet. Splayed over the wood, grasping at the rope, Marlene hung on while Shantih plunged above her.

In seconds Jinny reached her, grabbed at the rope, and struggled to calm her horse, to bring sanity back into Shantih's nightmare of terror.

At last the Arab stood still, her flanks heaving, her belly curded with sweat, eyes rolling and her ears pinned back to her neck.

Blood was running down Marlene's face. "Eh," she said, "that were a right to do. Poor old horse, he don't much fancy being tied up."

Jinny stared at her, speechless. It was Sue who came to worry about Marlene's cut face; demanding to know if she was all right; to praise her for holding on to Shantih.

"Weren't you scared?" demanded Sue. "I was. I thought she was going to kick me."

"Scared? Me?" said Marlene, dabbing at her face with a grubby ball of paper hanky. "Not likely. That don't stop me."

Jinny had unknotted the wood from Shantih's halter and was looking in horror at the twisted nails sticking out of it.

"If she'd gone galloping over the moor her legs would have been torn to ribbons," Jinny said. "If you hadn't caught her . . ."

"Eh, but I did, didn't I," said Marlene and told Sue to stop fussing about the scratch on her face, that it were nothing.

Jinny couldn't speak, couldn't find words to thank Marlene for what she had done.

They all had another cup of cocoa while the wind gusted about them and Pippen, hardly disturbed by all the commotion, returned to his doze.

"I can't tie her up again," stated Jinny. "I'll stay up and hold her."

"We'll take turns," said Sue.

"No," said Jinny. "I'll be O.K. She is mine. There's no reason why you should have to sit up." Sue watched Shantih, who was standing, still fleer-nostrilled and wide-eyed, the wind scattering her mane into wisping strands. Jinny's stomach tightened with love for her horse—the beauty and fire of her. Not for all the world would she have exchanged her for the placid Pippen. But as well as love there was fear, fear that one day Shantih would really hurt someone or damage herself. Jinny imagined her horse's legs torn and bleeding, or Marlene's face if she had fallen against the nails in the wood. "No," said Jinny again. "I'll hold her."

"Don't be silly," said Sue. "Of course we'll take turns. Nothing can happen if we're holding her."

They argued but Sue won. She held out two blades of grass to Jinny.

"The shortest bit holds first."

"What about me, then? Suppose I don't matter no more, eh? I'm the only one that was quick enough to catch her. Don't that matter now?"

So they had three pieces of grass. Jinny was first.

"Guess what time it is?" Sue asked when she'd looked at her watch to arrange shifts.

"One o'clock," guessed Jinny, whose own watch, as usual, wasn't going.

"Quarter to one," said Sue.

So Jinny took Shantih for the first shift from one to three o'clock. Marlene had drawn second and then Sue was third.

Wrapped in her sleeping bag, her hands inside her anorak sleeves, Jinny held Shantih while the mare grazed.

320

High above them, a wind-scoured moon darted in and out behind billowing clouds. The voices in the tent stopped. The torch was switched off. Jinny and Shantih were alone. Soon it was too cold for Jinny to even think. She waited, frozen, for the hands of Sue's watch to reach three o'clock. At first Jinny decided not to wake Marlene, but Marlene had made her promise and now Jinny wouldn't have cared who she woke as long as she could get in from the cold.

Just before three o'clock Jinny thought she heard some-one moving quite close to her. Shantih, too, had looked up suddenly. Jinny swung round, the skin on the back of her neck prickling, but there was no one there. She couldn't see anyone. She tried to listen but the wind made it impos-sible to make out any movements.

At three, Jinny hobbled on numb feet to wake Marlene. A touch on her shoulder made Marlene spring upright.

"What's up?" she cried. "What's the matter?"

Then remembered where she was.

"Gone proper perishing," Marlene said as she wriggled into the extra clothes she had brought in her shopper.

Jinny waited until Marlene was settled with Shantih, then went back to the tent, too cold to do more than hope they would be all right.

She squirmed down into her sleeping bag, pulling it over her head. Sue was snoring and what felt to Jinny like a force ten gale seemed to be blowing into the tent. She waited, hoping she would fall asleep, but the ground was knobbly and most of the gale seemed to be finding its way into her sleeping bag. Reluctantly Jinny poked her face out into the cold. The flap of the tent was gaping open.

Jinny reached out to tie it together again. Then she looked out for a last check on Shantih.

Her horse wasn't grazing but standing with her neck stretched and her ears sharply pricked. Marlene was hold-ing her halter but paying no attention to her. Jinny had been right. She had heard someone else on the moor and whoever it was they were standing talking urgently to Marlene.

CHAPTER EIGHT

For a moment Jinny wondered if she should wake Sue. She thought of horror films and night attackers and getting to Pippen so that she could ride for help. But Marlene didn't seem to be afraid. As far as Jinny could make out it looked as if Marlene was holding on to the stranger's arm.

Jinny wriggled out of her sleeping bag and crept out of the tent. Keeping to the pools of shadow by the side of the wall, she moved silently towards Marlene. Shantih saw her. She swung her head round to watch Jinny but Marlene didn't notice the horse's movement. Jinny edged her way closer and realised that the second figure was Bill.

Instantly Jinny felt as if she were spying. Whatever it was that had brought Bill out on to the moors to find his sister had nothing to do with Jinny.

"Say they see me," Jinny thought. "They'll think I've been standing here listening to them, that I'm the kind of fungus who would want to watch other people when they think they're alone." Jinny screwed up her face in total disgust. "Yuch," she thought and half turned to go back to the tent. A branch cracked beneath her foot. Jinny froze as both Marlene and Bill looked sharply round in her direction.

Jinny waited, her heart leaping in her throat, to be discovered. But although they both seemed to be staring straight at her they obviously couldn't see her and after a moment went back to their discussion. Jinny couldn't make out what they were saying, only the sound of their urgent whispering.

She eased her foot over the ground again, trying to get away before they found her; again the dried heather twigs crackled under her weight.

Jinny held her breath but this time only Shantih heard. Bill was trying to make Marlene take a small, flat parcel and Marlene was pushing it back at him. They were both too involved to have heard Jinny.

Suddenly Bill threw the parcel on the ground, spun

round and was off down the hill. Marlene had grabbed at his sleeve but he had been too quick for her. Left alone, she stooped to pick up the parcel and Jinny thought she could see tears glistening on her cheeks.

Marlene walked across to Shantih and stood whispering to the horse, as she looked down uncertainly at the parcel in her hand.

"Right bloomin' idiot," she was muttering. "Stupid bloomin' nit." Then she scrubbed the sleeve of her anorak over her eyes and began to lead Shantih towards the sheep pen.

For a second Jinny thought Marlene was going to try and tie Shantih up again.

"I'll need to pretend that I've just come out to see how she's managing," Jinny thought, watching anxiously.

But Marlene didn't tie Shantih up. She stopped by the wall at the side of the pen and began lifting down the stones.

"Now's your chance," Jinny told herself. "Get back to the tent now."

Jinny took one last look at Marlene working at the wall, then satisfied that, whatever she was doing, she wasn't going to tie Shantih up, Jinny crept back to the tent and crawled into her sleeping bag.

"Is it my turn?" Sue asked sleepily.

"Not nearly," said Jinny.

"Are you O.K.?"

"Yes."

Sue grunted and curled back down. "Wake me when it's time," she said and almost before she had finished speaking was asleep again.

Jinny lay flat on her back trying to sort out what she'd seen. She was almost certain that the parcel that Bill had left with Marlene was the same one as he had hidden behind his back when she had surprised him in the kitchen that morning. Why had he brought it to Marlene? What was in it? Why was it so important that he had come over the moors at night to give it to her? Jinny couldn't find the answers.

Before it was Sue's turn to hold Shantih, rain was drumming on the canvas. Marlene's voice woke Jinny. "Proper pouring," she said.

Jinny switched on the torch and saw Marlene's rain-sodden hair and pale, wet face looking in at her.

"Better get the old horse home, eh?" stated Marlene. "No point in hanging about in this?"

Sue emerged to organise an extended halter rope for Shantih made up of stirrup leathers, so they could sit inside the tent holding the end of the halter while Shantih grazed outside.

"Pippen is a very no-trouble pony," said Jinny, feeling guilty about all the fuss that Shantih was causing.

"Isn't he," agreed Sue. "And the thing about him is that he really doesn't mind. He's not just putting it on." Sue gazed contentedly at Pippen still dozing by the sheep pen, his tail plastered flat over his hocks and quarters by the driving rain.

It was nearly morning and they were all crouched inside the tent, saddles and bridles, rucksacks and food packed in around them.

"I'm asking you," said Marlene. "When are we going back down?"

Neither Jinny or Sue were answering.

"We're going to have breakfast soon," Sue said, consulting her watch. "Nearly six. We'll have breakfast at six."

"Then back down?" insisted Marlene.

"It's only a shower," said Sue irritably.

"Some shower," said Marlene, and Jinny, looking out at the louring, grey sky and the visible sheets of rain gusting over the moors, had to agree with her.

Pretending to be checking on Pippen, Jinny had taken a quick look at the wall where Marlene had lifted down the stones during the night. At first she hadn't been able to see any signs of Marlene's activities. Whatever she had been doing she had built up the wall again so that no one could tell that the stones had been removed. Then Jinny had noticed several long hairs from Shantih's tail caught between the stones just where Marlene had been standing. "So I didn't dream it," Jinny thought and went back quickly to the tent in case Marlene should be watching.

At six they had breakfast—bread and butter, cold baked beans and a tin of peaches. They drank the peach juice instead of water because Jinny refused to let anyone drink unboiled burn water.

"No chance of lighting a fire in this," said Sue.

"So no one drinks it," said Jinny flatly.

"When are we going down?" demanded Marlene every few minutes.

"You don't go running home just because it's raining," Sue told her.

"Do what I bloomin' like," said Marlene. "Only loonies sit out in the rain."

But Jinny didn't think it had anything to do with the rain. She thought that even if the sun had been shining Marlene would have wanted to go back to Finmory to find out what Bill was doing. Jinny hadn't told Sue about Bill's night visit. She wished that she had never seen him herself.

By nine o'clock, Marlene's patience had worn out.

"I ain't waiting no longer," she announced. "I got to get back. No use sitting here." Before Sue or Jinny realised what was happening Marlene was out of the tent.

"Poor old horse," she said, pausing to clap Shantih's spongy side. "You ain't half drowned." And Marlene limped off over the moor.

"Come back," yelled Jinny. "You can't go off like that. Come back!"

Hunched over her tartan shopper Marlene didn't even look round.

Sue ran after her. They stood in the grey downpour arguing with each other until Sue, her arm round Marlene's shoulders, began to steer her back to the tent.

"Oh well," thought Jinny. "Home we go."

She didn't mind. Rain had seeped through her jeans, her feet were sodden, her hair heavy with the rain and her stomach hadn't thought cold baked beans and peaches were the ideal breakfast. To be dry and warm in Finmory kitchen would be quite pleasant, Jinny decided, and with numb hands she began to fumble things back into her rucksack.

"She says she MUST go back NOW," announced Sue. "So I suppose we may as well pack up. Looks as if it's going to rain all day. And I don't fancy another night holding Shantih."

"Next time," said Jinny, "we'll need to find something solid to tie her to."

Shantih's chestnut coat was darkened with the rain.

Dark streaks of water ran down her white stockings. It was bad their camp whimpering out like this but it would have been much, much worse if Shantih's legs had been torn by the nails; if Marlene hadn't held on to her. Jinny shuddered at the thought. She looked at Marlene standing in the rain holding Shantih. If Marlene hadn't been there . . . Hadn't . . .

"If you'd not caught her last night . . ." began Jinny, desperately wanting to thank Marlene.

"What?" demanded Marlene. "Eh, don't start on about that now. Come on. Let's get on down quick."

Marlene's black, bullet eyes glinted in her pàle face. She was tense as a coiled spring. Her whole self set on one aim. Last night it had been to hold Shantih. Now it was to get back to Finmory as soon as possible.

Sue loaded up Pippen, tying the soaking tent, sleeping bags, bucket, pans and kettle on to his saddle. Jinny heaved her rucksack on to her back and stared round their campsite, making sure that they hadn't left tins or plastic bags lying about. She scuffled the ashes of their fire, knowing it wasn't really necessary. They were cold and dead with the rain.

It had been good in the evening when they were all sitting round the fire. That had been really nice. But it was over now.

"Eh, come on," said Marlene.

"Do you want to ride?" Jinny asked her, pulling down Shantih's stirrups, soothing her restless fretting.

"Might as well. Be a bit quicker." Fingers slipping on the wet leather, Marlene pulled herself into the saddle.

"Thought you'd want to ride," said Jinny.

"Don't mind. Be quicker."

"But I thought you wanted to learn to post?"

"Eh, well. Don't matter now. Too late for that. Got to get a move on." Marlene's knuckles shone through her skin as she gripped the pommel, and from Shantih's back she looked tensely over the moors. "Gee up," said Marlene. "Gee up, old horse."

Jinny led Shantih down the hillside. pushing with all her strength against the mare's shoulder, fighting to control her as she plunged forward, bounding downhill in great leaps that splashed peaty water into Jinny's face. Jolting back and forward in the saddle, Marlene stared straight ahead.

"Don't fuss on about me," she said. "Let him hurry up if he wants. Best get out of this rain, ain't we?"

"Doesn't it get boggy?" Sue shouted as Pippen suctioned soup plate feet through the mire.

"It's the green bits that are dangerous," Jinny shouted back. "Suck you down and drown you."

"Eh, hope our Bill didn't get stuck in one of them," said Marlene. "I mean if he were out for a walk, like. He's not used to all this nothing."

"Hot coffee," said Jinny as Finmory came into sight.

"Glad to see our tent's still there," said Sue, looking at the fluorescent patch of colour still perched by the shore.

"Do you want to come up to Finmory?" Jinny offered. "All of you, I mean."

"Not likely," said Sue. "Dad's got it all fixed up for rain. More like a caravan really than a tent."

Excited by the sight of home, Shantih broke into a pounding canter. Jinny dug her elbow sharply into her shoulder, yelled at her to behave, grabbed her bit ring and pulled up her head to stop her bucking.

"Stop fussing at him," ordered Marlene. "Doing his best to get us back, ain't he?"

So Jinny, splodging at Shantih's side, let the mare surge forward. Marlene's hands were welded on to the pommel and her eyes fixed on Finmory. "Even if I let go," Jinny thought, "she'd still be on top when Shantih reached home."

As they came closer to Finmory, Jinny thought there seemed something strange about the house. No lights in any of the rooms although the morning was dark; no one in the yard or about the stables; no sign of smoke from a fire; not one of her family watching their approach from a window.

"Odd," thought Jinny, and even as they reached Finmory there was no one to be seen. "Must be the bad weather," she decided, but knew that couldn't really be the reason. The Manders had lived long enough at Finmory to have stopped staying indoors when it rained.

Down past the ruined outhouse they went and into the yard. Still no one opened the door to welcome them. Even when Jinny called, announcing that they were back, there was no reply.

"I'll go on to our tent," Sue said. "May as well dump all this clobber. See you later."

"Right. Come over whenever you like," Jinny said, but she was thinking how strange it was that all her family should be away from home in the morning. It certainly wasn't the day for a picnic or a drive.

"Let me off here," demanded Marlene.

"Wait," said Jinny, "until we get to the stable."

"I got to get off now," cried Marlene, but Jinny ignored her and let Shantih jog on down to the stables.

The second Shantih reached the stable door, Marlene dropped to the ground. She snatched her shopper from Jinny and began to run back to the house.

"Good job," said Jinny to Shantih, "that you've got me to look after you."

In the loose box Jinny's numb fingers couldn't unbuckle the girth. She put her hand in her mouth, blowing to bring her fingers back to life and then tugged at the buckles again and managed to loosen them. She took Shantih's tack off, fetched an armful of hay for her and then stood pulling the mare's cold, wet ears through her hands to warm her.

"Jinny! Jinny!"

Marlene's voice made Jinny dash out of the stable. It linked with her own uneasy feelings about the strange emptiness around Finmory.

"He's not there," Marlene cried. "There ain't no one there. And our Bill's gone. He's taken his case and done a bunk. I shouldn't never have left him to go with that horse."

Marlene wasn't crying but her face under her rain-flattened hair was peaked and drawn, her mouth twisted into a lipless knot.

"There must be someone in the house," said Jinny. "Or a note to say where they are."

"There ain't," said Marlene. "He's gone."

CHAPTER NINE

"We're back," Jinny shouted as she ran along the landing. There had been no one downstairs and no note to say where they had all gone to. "They wouldn't be expecting us," Jinny thought, trying to reassure herself. "That's why they haven't left a note." But she knew that whenever her mother saw the rain she would have been expecting them to come home.

"Anybody there?" called Jinny, her voice echoing through the empty house.

"No need to panic," Jinny said when she was back in the kitchen with Marlene. "They've just gone somewhere for the day, that's all."

"I'm telling you, our Bill's taken his case. That means he's off. And his old books. He ain't coming back, not when he's got his books."

"There's nothing we can do," said Jinny. "We'll just need to wait until someone comes home. I don't suppose Mike is with them. He hates going for drives. Or Ken."

"I got to find Bill," said Marlene.

"How?"

"I don't know, do I? I don't know where to look, not here. I'd know in Stopton. Know all the places he goes there. I'd find him there. I think he's gone back home. That's where he's gone."

Jinny thought it likely. Perhaps that was what Bill had told Marlene last night—that he wanted to go back to Stopton.

"There's nothing we can do until the others come home," repeated Jinny. "You can't go off to Stopton by yourself. We'd better change out of these wet clothes and have some coffee. Shall I lend you a pair of jeans?"

"Got me good ones," said Marlene, and they went upstairs to change.

When Jinny got back to the kitchen, Marlene was wearing black velvet trousers and a lacy, lurex jumper. She had brought her tartan shopper down with her.

"When's this rain goin' to stop?" she demanded as if

Jinny were in control of a rain tap. "I got to get going. Can't muck about here when Bill's off on his own."

"Have a cup of coffee," said Jinny. "You'll look daft if you go tearing off to Stopton and Bill's only away for the day. Then you'll be in Stopton and he'll be here."

Marlene considered this while Jinny made the coffee.

"How we going to find out?" she cried. "I got to know."

"Don't worry," said Jinny. "Bill wouldn't go without you."

"Not much," said Marlene. "Not bloomin' much."

There was a sound of footsteps outside. Marlene rushed to the door and flung it open. Ken came into the kitchen, his hair sleeked back, his oilskin dripping.

"Hi," he said.

"Where's Bill?" demanded Marlene. "Thought you was keeping the eye on him? You let him go off, didn't you?"

Ken hung up his oilskin, asked Jinny if there was a cup of coffee for him and sat down at the table before he answered Marlene.

"Mr MacKenzie phoned up this morning about seven, said he thought we should check up that Bill was O.K. He was up with a sick cow and saw Bill going past his farm at about four o'clock. Said he had a case with him. Wondered if we knew."

Marlene's black eyes stared unblinkingly at Ken as she chewed at her nails.

"We checked Bill's room but he wasn't there. Your Mum and Dad have gone into Inverburgh. Tom thought he might have hitched a lift, trying to get the train back to Stopton. I've been up the moor. Petra and Mike have gone down to the shore, just in case. He might have fallen and hurt himself."

"Thought you promised," Marlene accused bitterly. "You ain't no better than the rest. Thought you understood. I'd have heard him. I'd have stopped him. It's me that's to blame. Shouldn't have gone off with that old horse."

The sound of a car interrupted Marlene's reproaches.

"That be them?" she cried. "Think they've got him, then?"

330

Jinny knew that it wasn't their car. It was too powerful. "Might be news," she said.

There was a heavy banging at the front door. Jinny went to answer it. A policeman stood there with Mrs. Simpson standing behind him.

"Good morning," said the policeman. "Is Mr. Manders in?"

Jinny said he wasn't.

"We'll be coming in to wait on him for it's the urgent word I'm for having with him," said Mrs. Simpson, and, pushing past the policeman and Jinny, she walked into the hall.

The policeman took off his hat, stroked down his sandy hair with a calloused hand and followed the shopkeeper into the kitchen.

"Would you be looking at the state of that one," said Mrs. Simpson, meaning Ken. "I tell you, Donald," she said to the policeman, "they're all tarred with the same brush. Nothing but layabouts has there been in this house since the last of the MacCraes was taken."

"It's your brother I'm wanting," she said to Marlene, "though I daresay you'd be having a hand in it yourself. Be telling me now where's the boy?"

Jinny saw Marlene's shoulder stiffen, her hands clench under the table.

"Do you mean Mike?" Ken asked.

"I mean that one's brother, as you know very well. The one that stole the watch from my shop yesterday."

Events linked together like jig-saw pieces in Jinny's mind—Bill in the shop holding Mrs. Simpson's eighty-two pound watch; Marlene snatching his hand away from it; their second visit to the shop; the flat parcel Bill had hidden in a guilty fumble when Jinny found him in the kitchen; the same flat parcel he had left with Marlene at their camp.

"And she buried it in the wall," thought Jinny and sat down suddenly, pretending to tie her shoelace, so that she could keep her head down and stop the kitchen sliding about.

"You ain't got no right to say that. Our Bill never touched your old watch."

But Jinny knew he had. She felt sick at the thought of

331

it. What good was a gold watch to Bill? Bill would be charged with stealing it but Marlene would be hurt as well. She would feel that it was her fault because she had left him to go camping.

"You could be had up for saying those things about Bill. You ain't got no proof. You're just saying lies to get him into trouble. When me mum hears she'll sort you out. 'Cause our Bill, he didn't never touch your watch. He didn't have nothing to do with it."

Words sputtered out of Marlene. Her back eyes darted hate at Mrs. Simpson.

"You leave our Bill alone," Marlene threatened. "You leave him alone."

"Would the boy be in the house?" the policeman asked Ken. "I could be asking him a few questions."

Ken said no Bill wasn't and the phone rang in the hall. Jinny's feet took her to answer it over a floor that felt as soft as sponge rubber, past walls that breathed in and out.

"Hullo," she said.

"Jinny," said her father's voice and Jinny felt tears prick in her eyes, wanted to tell him what had happened but didn't know how to begin.

"Were you washed out?" Mr. Manders asked but didn't wait for a reply. "Tell the others we found Bill at Inverburgh station. Sudden bout of homesickness. He wanted back to the city but he missed the train so he's coming back with us until tomorrow."

The sound of pips interrupted Mr. Manders' voice. "Sorry, no more change," he said and the line went dead.

Jinny went back to the kitchen. They all looked round at her, their faces turned on her. She had to tell them.

"Bill was at Inverburgh station," Jinny said. "He's coming back with them."

"Did you hear that, Donald?" Mrs. Simpson demanded of the policeman. "Is that not his guilt clear now! Off to England with my watch." She stroked her flowered nylon overall down over her knees with both hands. "And we will be staying here, I'm thinking, until he walks through that door."

"If you think Bill took the watch yesterday morning," Ken asked. "Why weren't you up here yesterday?"

Mrs. Simpson regarded him coldly. "It's no business of

332

yours," she said, "but I'll be telling you. Mr. Simpson was away on the wee visit to his brother and I was thinking he had the watch with him."

"He didn't?" asked Ken.

"He did not," said Mrs. Simpson.

Petra and Mike came in and stared in amazement to see Mrs. Simpson and a policeman in the kitchen.

"Not surprised," stated Petra when she understood what was happening. "He'd been in trouble before, you know. I think it was shoplifting then, as well. Dad'll know. If you ask me they get away with these things once and they just go on doing them."

"You wait," thought Jinny, glaring at her sister. "You wait till something like this happens in our family. You'll not be so sure then."

"Is that a fact, now," said the policeman, and Ken said that if it was true it was over and done with.

"I'll be telling you this," said Mrs. Simpson. "I knew there was bad in that boy the minute I saw him. Couldn't keep his thieving hands off that watch. Up to no good. Nothing but a yob."

"We'll soon be at the truth," said the policeman soothingly. "I have the questions ready. Wait now until we see the boy."

Since Jinny had told them that Bill was coming back to Finmory with her parents, Marlene had sat silently hunched into herself, nibbling at her fingers and picking at a thread in her jumper.

"You don't need to do no more waiting," she announced suddenly. "Because I told you, didn't I? It wasn't Bill who took your old watch. It were me. I took it. Me you got to get at. Not our Bill. Me."

A moment of absolute silence followed Marlene's words.

"I don't doubt you'd the hand in it," declared Mrs. Simpson.

"Where is the watch?" asked the policeman.

"But that brother of yours, he was the one taking it from my counter," said Mrs. Simpson, not believing Marlene.

"You never saw him," stated Marlene. "And he don't know nothing about it 'cause I took it, see. You come back up them moors with me and I'll get you the watch."

I'll show you where I hid it." And Marlene stood up, hitching at her good velvet trousers, dragging the kirby grip out of her short hair, opening it with her teeth and jabbing it back more securely. "Come on with me and I'll get your bloomin' old watch for you."

Jinny's voice that had been stuck in her throat came out in a croak.

"You didn't take it," Jinny cried. "I know you didn't. I saw . . ."

Marlene's hands gripped the edge of the table. For a moment, as she realised that Jinny must have seen Bill giving her the watch, Marlene's face lost its mask and Jinny saw her as she really was—desperately vulnerable, powerless against them and terrified that Bill should be charged with stealing a second time.

For that moment it seemed to Jinny that they were alone in the kitchen and Marlene's true face made the false things vanish. Because she had seen Bill, Jinny had the power to break Marlene, to tell them all how Bill had come up to their camp at night to leave the watch with his sister, how Marlene had nothing to do with stealing it. This time Bill might be sent to a remand home.

"If it were Shantih," Jinny thought. "If they wanted to take Shantih away from me and shut her up . . ."

Jinny couldn't bear to look at Marlene, yet there was nothing else she could do. To see Marlene as she was now was to know what it was like to live in the Stopton slums; what it was like to come to a strange place and be treated the way Jinny had treated Marlene. "Oh no," cried Jinny. "No! I didn't mean it." But the moment was naked. The easy words of polite apology weren't there to cover it up. Jinny had been rotten to Marlene. Words couldn't change that. And Jinny saw Marlene throw herself at the bar of wood ripped from the sheep pen, grab Shantih's halter and hold on. "Oh no," cried Jinny, but the words had no sound.

Then the mask slipped back into place. They were back in the familiar kitchen.

Marlene turned furiously on Jinny.

"Shut up!" she shouted. "Shut up! Don't you come messing me up. This ain't got nothing to do with you, Miss La-di-dah Manders. So you shut up."

334

"Officer," said Marlene to the policeman. "Come on with me up them hills. I'll show you where it is."

"And what would a watch be doing out on the hills?" asked the policeman suspiciously.

"They were camping up there," Petra explained. "Where were you? By that old sheep pen?" Jinny nodded. "But Marlene can't walk all that way," continued Petra. "She's a bit lame."

"I ain't a bloomin' cripple," spat Marlene, putting on her soaking anorak. "That's me ready. Come on."

The policeman hesitated.

"Have I to be going myself?" demanded Mrs. Simpson.

"Hadn't you better wait until Dad gets back?" suggested Mike.

"Naw," said Marlene. "Come on with me now."

The policeman settled his hat back on his head. "Does the lassie know the way?" he asked.

"I'll come with you," said Ken, but Jinny, catching his eye, shook her head at him. She had to tell Ken what had happened. There must be some way of stopping Marlene taking the blame for Bill's stealing. And if anyone could help her Ken could.

Realising that Jinny didn't want him to go with the policeman, Ken asked Mike if he would go and reluctantly Mike agreed.

"A wee bitty thing her age," clucked Mrs. Simpson with satisfaction when the policeman, Marlene and Mike had set off. "Who would have thought it. Though I'm telling you that nowadays the lassies are as bad as the boys."

"I know," agreed Petra. "The things some of them do at our school."

Jinny hurried Ken out of the room.

"The pottery," he said, and impatiently Jinny followed him into the pottery. Its window looked out on to the hills at the back of the house. The rain had changed to a smirring drizzle and through its grey mist Jinny could see the three shapes walking up the hill, heads down, shoulders hunched against the rain. Mike was taking them up the hill the way they had ridden to their camp.

"It wasn't Marlene," Jinny told Ken. "It was Bill. He brought the watch up to her during the night. She hid it up there. She's only saying she took it to protect Bill."

335

Ken listened to the details.

"We've got to get the watch back to the shop," he said. "Make the Simpsons believe that it wasn't stolen."

"But how? If Marlene takes the stones off the wall and the watch is there, they'll never believe that it wasn't stolen. We've got to take it away before Marlene gets there. But how?" Jinny cried.

She didn't really know about courts or Children's Panels but she pictured Marlene, in her lacy jumper and good trousers, standing in the witness box telling the jury how she had stolen the watch, her bitten fingers clutching the rail of the box, her bullet eyes defying them—not caring what they did to her as long as they left Bill alone.

"They'd guess what you were up to if you rode past them."

"Marlene would," said Jinny, and suddenly she thought of the short cut, the way through Mr. MacKenzie's farm yard, on over his fields and out on to the moor. *If* the gate wasn't padlocked.

"I could try the short cut," Jinny cried. "I'd make it that way." And she knew she had to try. The gate had to be open. That way she could take the watch out of the wall before Marlene got there.

"Right," said Ken. "I'll go after them and do my best to slow them down."

They raced out of the house together. Ken turned to run up the hill. Jinny tore through the garden and down to the stables. She grabbed up her tack from where she had left it to go with Marlene. Shantih clattered her box door, expecting to be taken out to her field.

"It's for Marlene," Jinny explained as she put her bridle on, slid the saddle on to her back and tugged up the girth. "We've got to get there first."

In the yard, Shantih flung herself away from Jinny as she tried to mount.

"Whoa, steady, stand still," Jinny pleaded.

She sprang up, threw herself over the saddle and wriggled upright. Shantih plunged and reared but Jinny hardly noticed. She turned Shantih's head towards the path that led to Mr. MacKenzie's farm, kicked her heels against the mare's sides and sent her on at a splattering canter.

336

Shantih caught Jinny's urgency, knew that this was no ordinary ride, and Jinny felt her respond willingly, with a gay eagerness that matched her own determination to reach the wall first.

Sprays of muddy water flew up from Shantih's hooves as she galloped down the path to the farm. Jinny swung her round into the farmyard and saw to her relief that there was no sign of Mr. MacKenzie. Only his wife pulled aside the lace curtain of the farmhouse window to see what was causing the disturbance, but by the time she came hurrying to the door Jinny was across the yard and out of sight.

The gate into the first field stood propped open. Jinny crouched over Shantih's withers as they galloped through and flared over the field. She didn't know where her own body ended and her horse began. The piston beat of Shantih's hooves was the beat of her own heart.

"Let the gate be open," cried Jinny, mouthing the words. "Oh please, please, let it be open."

CHAPTER TEN

Shantih galloped across the last field before the gate. The ground was more broken here and Jinny eased her horse to a steady canter as she rode towards a rise in the land. From the top of the slope Jinny would be able to see the gate.

"It must be open. It MUST," thought Jinny desperately. She hadn't allowed herself to consider what she would do if the gate was shut.

As Shantih cantered the last few strides to the crest of the hill Jenny screwed her eyes shut. At the top of the hill she opened them. For a split second she was still sure that the gate was open, she had seen it so clearly inside her head, but instantly she knew that it was shut. She made a gulping, strangled noise in her throat and thought, "Don't let it be padlocked," as Shantih plunged downhill towards it.

The padlock was made of whitish, blue-grey metal. It

held together the links of a stout chain that encircled the gatepost and the gate, and it was locked.

In front of the gate Shantih whirled and fretted. Excited by her wild gallop, she refused to stand still. Jinny had gone cold inside. Had stopped feeling anything. She just didn't know what she could do now.

The gate was a strongly built, five-bar gate. On either side was a four-foot stone wall. At intervals, upright iron bars had been driven into the top of it and three strands of barbed wire strung through them. There was no way for Jinny to get Shantih through to the other side. If she left her horse here and ran to the sheep pen Jinny was certain she would be too late. All the time she had been galloping she had felt the approach of Marlene, the policeman, Mike and Ken; had tried to guess where they would be; how far on they were; had thought of the gold watch lying inside the wall, drawing the others and herself towards it as if it were a magnet; and now they would reach it and she wouldn't.

But there was one way. One way she could reach the watch before Marlene. Jinny hadn't dared to think about it until now. She could jump the gate.

Jinny sized up the jump. The gate was about four and a half feet high but appeared lower because of the high barbed wire on either side.

"Shantih could jump it," Jinny told herself.

"But she's never jumped anything like that height. She's hardly ever jumped anything. Nor have I. Not really," Jinny pleaded with herself. She had done her best. It wasn't her fault the gate was locked. She'd tell the police how Bill had left the watch with Marlene. They'd question Bill, find out for themselves and nothing would happen to Marlene. But Jinny knew that if they sent Bill to a remand home it would be worse for Marlene than anything they could do to her.

She had to jump the gate. There was no other way.

"We've got to get to the other side," Jinny told her horse. "You've got to jump it. You can do it easily, easily."

She cantered Shantih in a circle. Her legs seemed loose against the saddle and a hard choking lump somewhere inside her was stopping her breathing properly. "I'll hold on to her mane," Jinny thought, "and then I'll be all right."

She turned Shantih and rode her at the gate. To Jinny's magnifying eye it seemed to have grown to an enormous size. She crouched stiffly in the saddle, a lump of mane knotted between her fingers.

"Jump!" she shouted at Shantih. "Jump!" But Jinny's mind was filled with the thought of Shantih hitting the gate, crashing down and lying unable to get up because her leg was broken.

"Jump," cried Jinny again as she clung nervously to Shantih's mane. "Jump it!"

Shantih slid to a halt in front of the gate. Her eyes rolling, her tail switching, she swung round and charged away. Jinny grabbed up her reins, hauled her round and rode her at the gate for a second time.

Jinny's voice said words that were meant to urge her on but Shantih only heard her nervous, high-pitched tone. Jinny's clinging hands and rigid body held her back. Shantih stopped dead in front of the gate and Jinny went on thumping into it.

"We're going to be too late," Jinny thought as she remounted. "Are you afraid?" she asked herself and knew that the answer was yes. She was afraid.

"Then be afraid," said the voice in Jinny's head. "Be afraid but don't let that stop you." Jinny remembered the look on Marlene's face before she had ridden Shantih for the first time. Marlene had been afraid then but it hadn't stopped her. "And now," Jinny thought, "telling them she stole the watch, she's afraid of what they'll do to her. And she was afraid when she caught Shantih but it didn't stop her."

Jinny took off her hard hat, shook her hair back and settled it more firmly on her head. This time she would jump the gate. This time Shantih wouldn't refuse.

Jinny gathered up her reins, steadied her horse, cantered in a circle then rode her at the gate for a third time and this time Jinny wasn't thinking about holding on to Shantih's mane, or of Shantih falling. The only thought in Jinny's head was to be on the other side. Sitting tight in the saddle, Jinny drove the Arab at the gate, left no doubt in Shantih's mind about what she was to do. Jinny held

339

her together, waited for the moment when Shantih must soar into the air if she was to clear the gate safely, kicked her on at that exact moment and Shantih leapt from her hocks, struck upwards, sailed high over the gate and landed far out on the other side.

"You did it!" cried Jinny. "You jumped it! Oh horse! Horse! Horse!"

As they galloped on, Jinny glanced back once to see a rather low gate just being there between the walls, totally unperturbed by all the commotion, then she set herself to ride as fast as she could to the sheep pen.

Tensely, Jinny searched the moor, knowing where the others would first come into sight, but there was no sign of them, no crows flew up, cawing a warning of their approach.

Jinny reached the sheep pen, threw herself off Shantih and searched the wall for the chestnut hairs from Shantih's tail. She found them and began to topple the stones to the ground. She had to remove about a dozen stones before she found the parcel. A plastic bag was wrapped round the box, but the long, flat shape of the box was unmistakable. Jinny grabbed it up and stuffed it into the pocket of her oilskin. She lifted the stones back on to the wall, scraping her knuckles in her haste to rebuild it and be away. A gull rasped the moorland silence with a harsh cry. Jinny froze. What would she say if they caught her? Then she realised that it was only a bird and went on struggling to make the stones balance on top of each other.

"You could tell," Jinny thought, surveying the wall, "but you couldn't be certain it had been a person. A sheep could have rumpled it." She jumped back on to Shantih.

Jinny didn't stop galloping until she was absolutely certain that she was well out of sight of the sheep pen, then she stopped Shantih and sat slumped in the saddle, took her feet out of the stirrups, dropped her reins. They had done it! Shantih and herself.

" My horse without peer," quoted Jinny, achievement overflowing in her. "Leaned, patted her ear, called her my Shantih, my horse without peer," she cried, throwing herself over Shantih's neck, clapping her, praising her.

340

When Marlene got to the wall there would be no watch for her to find. Mrs. Simpson and the policeman would be annoyed, thinking she had tricked them, but Marlene would be safe.

Jinny sat up and took the watch out of her pocket. She put one arm through Shantih's reins to stop them vanishing over her head while she was grazing, and then Jinny unwrapped the box. She opened it and looked at the watch. It seemed to Jinny a clumsy lump of metal, a single handcuff. She shivered, closed the box, wrapped it up again and put it back into her pocket. Now she had to get it back into Mrs. Simpson's shop where it belonged.

Without a second thought, Jinny rode Shantih at the locked gate; grinned with delight as her Arab soared effortlessly over it and cantered on to the farm.

Jinny avoided the farmyard. Even if Mr. MacKenzie wasn't there, Jinny felt that Mrs. MacKenzie would be more prepared to pounce. She walked Shantih down the edge of a sown field, by the side of a wall that bounded a hayfield, and then trotted her out on to the road to Glenbost.

She had to get the watch back before the policeman had the chance to question Bill. From what Jinny knew of Bill she had no confidence in his being able to outwit even the Glenbost police force.

As she rode she eased the watch out of its plastic wrapping. Jinny wasn't too sure how she was going to get it back to the Simpsons but there was a chance that if she lingered over the shop's pile of paperbacks, Mr. Simpson, who would be in charge of the shop while his wife was at Finmory, would leave her alone while he attended to another customer.

"Need to find someone to hold you," Jinny told Shantih as the shop came into sight.

Dolina, who had attended the village school and was going with Jinny to the new Inverburgh Comprehensive in September, was standing in front of the garage.

"Is it the mud pack you've been giving her?" Dolina asked, coming to meet them.

Jinny dismounted. "Looks like it," she agreed, seeing Shantih's mud-splattered legs and sides. "Could you hold her for me? I've got to go into the shop."

341

Dolina regarded Shantih warily. "If she's at her nonsense I'll let her go," she stated.

"She'll be fine," said Jinny. "She'll eat the grass. Don't think I'll be long." She handed Shantih's reins to Dolina and hurried into the shop.

There were two women at the counter. Jinny knew them both by sight, the way she knew everyone in Glenbost. They both looked round at Jinny who was sure that they could see into her pocket and would think that she had stolen the watch.

"And what can I get for you?" Mr. Simpson asked in a distant polite voice. Normally he teased Jinny about her red hair.

"I want a book," Jinny said. "Can I have a look at them?"

"Don't be soiling them, now," Mr. Simpson cautioned and went back to his other customers.

Jinny rubbed her dirty hands down her wet oilskin, then dried them on her jeans.

There were about twenty children's paperbacks sitting next to a pile of murders, westerns and romances. Jinny looked through them slowly. Mr. Simpson resumed his conversation with the two women and Jinny, pretending to be reading one of the books, let her gaze wander round the shop. In front of the counter, quite close to the perspex case of watches, was an open crate of apples. It wasn't absolutely underneath the watches, but close enough to make it possible for the gold watch to have fallen in amongst the apples from the top of the case.

"But," thought Jinny sharply, "the apples would have had to be there before Mrs. Simpson noticed that the watch was missing or it couldn't possibly have fallen amongst them."

Jinny tried to remember if the apples had been there when she had bought their camping supplies. At first she wasn't sure. She could picture them there, or not, whichever way she chose. Then she remembered her father filling a bag with apples from the crate before Mrs. Simpson weighed them. The apples had definitely been there on Thursday.

Jinny slid her hand into her oilskin pocket. The box was closed. When it had been sitting on top of the case

342

the lid of the box had been fitted on to the back of the box to display the watch. Still pretending to read her book, Jinny opened the box in her pocket and fitted the lid on to the back.

One of the women went out, making Jimmy start guiltily. "I should have fixed the box before I came in," Jinny thought and wondered what other stupid mistakes she had made.

When the box felt all right Jinny palmed it up into her sleeve; holding it there, secret and hidden by her oilskin, while she waited for her chance to put it into the box of apples.

Another woman came in and Mr. Simpson began to serve her. She asked for butter and Jinny knew he would have to go into the back shop to take her pound of butter from the great mound that was kept there.

Still reading her book, Jinny moved across to the counter. Mr. Simpson went into the back shop, leaving the two women gossiping together. Jinny balanced her book on the very edge of the counter, put her right hand into the right hand pocket of her oilskin and help out her un-buttoned coat so that the women couldn't possibly see what she was doing with her other hand.

Jinny tipped the book so that it fell to the floor. The women glanced in her direction then paid no more atten-tion to her. Jinny crouched down, still shielding her left hand with her coat as she placed the watch delicately amongst the apples. Then, without looking at the women, she made sure that the fruit was covering the watch. She picked up her book and stood up. Her hands were shaking so much that she had to let the book flop on the counter and bury her hands out of sight in her pockets.

Jinny let her eyes flick down over the crate of apples. The watch was almost completely hidden. Only a tiny patch of its red box was visible. Yet to Jinny it seemed the most obvious thing in the whole shop, as if anyone coming in would instantly stop and point to it, asking what on earth a gold watch was doing in a crate of apples.

"Now to make Mr. Simpson find it," Jinny thought. Everyone must know that the watch had been recovered before the policeman had a chance to question Bill. Jinny drew in long slow breaths, let the air flow slowly out of her nose, as she tried to calm herself.

"Have you decided, then?" demanded Mr. Simpson when the two women had left the shop. "Is this the one you're taking?"

"Yes please," said Jinny. "And could I have a pound of eating apples?" To her relief her voice sounded as it always did; as if it was an ordinary day and she was just shopping for her mother.

"You'll have heard about that boy you have with you stealing the gold watch from us," said Mr. Simpson, coming to the front of the counter to fill a paper bag with apples.

Jinny said yes she had.

"It's the sorry day when you've strangers on your doorstep bringing thieves into your shop."

Mr. Simpson had put three apples into the bag and was going back behind the counter without noticing the watch.

"Do I only get three?" cried Jinny in alarm. "Could you make them small ones, please? Could I have four or five small ones, please?"

Mr. Simpson glared at her sourly but he tipped the three apples back into the crate and began to hunt around for smaller ones. The movement of the apples pushed the watch to the surface.

Mr. Simpson swore in gaelic as he grabbed it up.

"If it isn't the very watch the boy stole," he exclaimed. "Was it yourself put it there?"

"If you say Bill stole it, how could I have put it there?" Jinny said indignantly, hoping she was looking sufficiently surprised. "It must have fallen. Dropped down and got mixed up with the apples."

Mr. Simpson's eyes totally disbelieved her.

"Gosh, I bet you're jolly glad to have got it back. Is it O.K.?"

As Jinny left the shop, Mr. Simpson was on the phone to Finmory, telling his wife that the watch had been found.

When Jinny got back to Dolina and Shantih she couldn't stop shaking. She leant over Shantih's withers and shook. Her teeth chattered and her hands twitched.

"Are you feeling fit?" asked Dolina.

"Having one," said Jinny.

Her legs weren't strong enough to get her back on to Shantih.

"I'll walk beside her and lean," Jinny said, refusing Dolina's offer of a hoist on.

Gradually, as she walked back to Finmory, Jinny began to calm down. She shared the apples with Shantih as they went along.

"Shoplifters should get medals," Jinny thought. She was feeling as exhausted as if she had been galloping for hours on a runaway Shantih.

First the police car, with Mrs. Simpson sitting next to the policeman and staring straight ahead, passed them, and then the Manders' car, with Bill in the back, drove up and stopped beside her.

"Jinny," said her mother in a surprised tone of voice. "Are you all right?"

"Perfectly," said Jinny. "We were rained off so I thought I'd go for a ride."

"But you're not," said her mother. "Where's Sue and Marlene?"

"Her tent and our kitchen, I should think, and I am having a ride, only at this particular moment I'm not."

"I see," said Mrs. Manders. "'Bye then," and they drove on.

It wasn't until her parents had driven up and Jinny had seen Bill slouching in the back seat that she had given a thought to the rights and wrongs of covering up for Bill when, after all, he had stolen the watch. Until that moment all Jinny had been thinking about had been stopping Marlene taking the blame.

Jinny knew that Ken would think that for anyone—Mrs. Simpson or Bill—to own a watch that cost eighty-two pounds, when human beings were dying because they hadn't enough to eat, was so disgusting that it didn't matter who took the watch. But Jinny wasn't so sure what her parents would think. Her father might feel that Bill shouldn't get off without some form of repayment for all the trouble he had caused. It was, Jinny decided, one of the things that it might be better for her parents never to know about.

345

It was easier to think about Shantih. Jinny swung herself back into the saddle and, letting Shantih walk on at her own pace, she relived the thrill of sailing, high, wide and handsome over the gate. The more she thought about it, the higher the gate became.

"Next autumn the White City and then the Olympics," thought Jinny, wondering what she would call Princess Anne when they were riding together in the British cross country team, and she laughed aloud at herself.

They were all having a late lunch when Jinny got back. Ken looked up when she came into the kitchen, and Jinny signalled to him that she had managed it. Marlene, as silent as Bill, was bent over her plate of tomato soup.

"Where have you been?" cried Petra. "Mrs. Simpson and I thought another one of you had run off."

"Mrs. Simpson said you were in the shop when her husband found the watch," Mike said, wanting to know the details.

"It had fallen into a crate of apples," said Jinny. Marlene's beady eyes chiselled into her, but twitched away if Jinny tried to look directly at her. "And I was buying apples for Shantih, so he found it."

"You'd think they'd have found it before today," said Petra. "Lots of people must have bought apples before you."

"It had sort of worked its way down between them," said Jinny, and her father said that one thing certain was that they wouldn't leave it on top of the case again.

When she had finished her lunch, Jinny went up to her bedroom. She shut the door firmly behind her. She felt like being alone. She took out a drawing pad and pencil and sat on the floor opposite her mural, thinking that she might do some drawings of Pippen for Sue but she couldn't even start. The pencil in her hand was a dead lump of wood and lead.

Jinny stared up at the mural of the red horse. It had been on the wall before the Manders had come to Finmory and often Jinny wondered who had painted it. The horse's yellow eyes blazed light. It was a nightmare that came charging through the blue green foliage of Jinny's wondering.

"What could it be like?" she wondered. "To love

346

someone else so much that you said, 'do it to me, not to him'."

Footsteps came along the landing towards Jinny's attic stair. She heard them pause, then limp slowly up towards her. Marlene's clenched fist banged on the door.

CHAPTER ELEVEN

Jinny opened the door and Marlene limped in. She stood staring round the room.

"Eh," Marlene said. "You're a lucky thing, having a place like this for yourself. You ain't half spoilt, you ain't." Marlene sat down on Jinny's bed. " 'Spect you took it. Come on, tell us."

"I rode Shantih round by the short cut," said Jinny. "And took the watch out of the wall. Then I put it in the crate of apples when Mr. Simpson wasn't looking."

"What you want to do that for? Wasn't none of your business."

"It was," cried Jinny. "I saw Bill bring it up to you last night. "I didn't mean to spy on you. I thought he was a stranger and I was coming to see what he wanted and then I couldn't get away. That's how I knew you hadn't done it."

"He was scared they'd find the watch on him. That's why he left it with me. Thought they wouldn't search me. Said he'd tell them that he knew nothing about it. But see our Bill, he's proper soft. The minute they started with those questions he'd be in a mess."

"I couldn't let you take the blame for something you hadn't done. I'd have told them it was Bill, only I knew you didn't want that either. The only thing I could think of was to get there first and take the watch back to the shop."

Marlene was fiddling with the fringe of Jinny's bed-spread, plaiting it into little pigtails which sprang out as soon as she let go of them. "Thanks," she said without looking up. "They might have put him away this time."

"I didn't do it for Bill," said Jinny. "I just didn't see why you should say you had stolen it when he did it."

"Like I love him," suggested Marlene. "Not what he does, not what he looks like—same as me, bit of a mess. But he's O.K. He's Bill. Me mum's right fond of him too. Thinks the world of him, she does. She don't believe he does any of these things. Thinks he wouldn't steal nothing, not if you dropped a thousand pounds at his feet. She thinks our Bill would hand it in."

"I bet he would," said Jinny sarcastically.

"What do you know about it?" demanded Marlene, turning on Jinny. "You just keep your mouth shut because you don't know nothing about how it really is, you don't."

Jinny felt her skin creep, a cold shiver run over her scalp. It was true. She lived wrapped round in layers of cotton wool. It had all been an adventure to her. If Bill had gone to a remand home it wouldn't really have made any difference, not to her, not to her safe, secure little world.

"So you keep shut up," warned Marlene again.

"Of course," said Jinny. "I wouldn't tell anyone."

"Not that sister of yours."

"Ken knows."

"Argh, that don't matter. But mind, no one else." Marlene stood up. "Best be going to say goodbye to the old horse," she said.

"Goodbye?" echoed Jinny. "It's only Friday. You've got another week. Don't you want any more rides?"

"Naw," said Marlene. "Too late. We're for off tomorrow."

"Not you," exclaimed Jinny. "Bill's going but you don't have to go."

"Not much," said Marlene scornfully. "I'm for Stopton tomorrow. Can't let him go off without me."

"But can't your mother meet him?" argued Jinny. "You can't spend all your life looking after Bill."

But Marlene wasn't listening to her.

"Just say tarrah," she said as she went towards the door, "and that'll be that." Then she stopped and looked through the archway into the other half of Jinny's room.

"Proper art gallery you got here, ain't it," said Marlene and she went through to look at Jinny's pictures that were pinned on the wall opposite the mural.

348

Reluctantly Jinny followed her through. She hated other people looking at her drawings. Couldn't bear the things they said, even when they were trying to be pleasant. Once, years ago, her mother had made her show some of her drawings to a friend, the friend had said how nice it was for Jinny to have such a happy hobby. The phrase had stuck in Jinny's mind—always there when Jinny made a mess of a drawing.

"Did you do them? The big one and all?" demanded Marlene.

"Not the mural on the wall," said Jinny. "But the rest."

"Eh-h-h-h!" Marlene let out her breath in slow admiration. "That's Shantih, ain't it? That's smashing, that is. Eh, that's proper smashing." She stood staring at a painting that Jinny had done for a competition.

"See, d'you know what I'd have done if I'd been like you?" Marlene turned her bright face on Jinny, her eyes sparkling, her mouth smiling. "Like you've drawn Shantih, well I'd have written it. Did a composition about the old horse. Before I knew, like, and it made me feel real happy. As if I was going in on a Saturday night and finding them all settled round the fire. Me dad there too, and Bill, and me mum cooking something up for us all."

And suddenly Jinny remembered Marlene's composition that her father had shown her before the Thorpes arrived.

"You see," went on Marlene, "I didn't know then about all the fuss you have with this riding business. I thought you just sat on like a chair and that were it. Eh, didn't know much then, did I? Thought me leg wouldn't matter, that I'd just sit there and gallop off. Fast, like I can't with me leg."

"But it is like that," cried Jinny. "Once you've learned."

"I were scared at first, but once I was on it were O.K. Felt like I knew the old horse, somehow. Having written about him and all."

"But you've done very well," cried Jinny. "Lots of beginners would never have gone near a horse again after the way Shantih bucked with you. You only need a bit of practice."

"Don't have time for that," stated Marlene. "Got to go back to Stopton."

349

"You don't!" raged Jinny. "Of course you don't! You can stay and I'll teach you to ride. I will. I promise. Just because Bill wants you to go back you don't need to. They can't do any more about the watch now."

Marlene shook her head. "Be proper good," she said, "but I ain't staying."

Jinny listened as Marlene's footsteps limped down the stairs.

"But it's not fair," she thought. "Why shouldn't Marlene stay? She can't spend all her life looking after Bill. If he wants to steal things, that's what he'll do, whether Marlene is there or not." Jinny wondered if she should follow Marlene down to Shantih's field and try again to persuade her to stay, but reluctantly she supposed that it wouldn't make any difference. If Bill went back to Stopton Marlene would go too.

Jinny sat down, picked up her pencil and got on with drawing Pippen.

"Happy hobby," she thought when she had finished. Her drawing might have been any plump, skewbald pony. It didn't look the least bit Pippenish. Jinny tore the sheet off her pad, screwed it into a ball and threw it furiously into the corner of the room.

"It's so unfair," she thought. "Why shouldn't Marlene stay if she wants to." But Jinny knew that if Bill left, Marlene would go too.

"I've got to make Bill stay," cried Jinny. She jumped to her feet and clattered downstairs in search of him.

Petra said no she hadn't seen him but had Jinny tried Mrs. Simpson's?

Mr. Manders and Ken were loading their kiln and were not pleased at being disturbed. They hadn't seen Bill either.

"Well, I can't tell you where he'll be," said her mother, "but I can tell you what he'll be doing. He'll be reading his comics. When we found him at the station he was sitting in a waiting room reading them. What did you want him for?"

"Just something," said Jinny.

She met Mike carrying full cans of milk from Mr. MacKenzie's.

"Seen Bill?" she asked him.

350

Mike shook his head. "What were you up to this morning?" he asked.

"Getting back from our camp," said Jinny, wondering suddenly if it should have been her turn to fetch the milk.

"I mean after that," said Mike. "While I was having to trail over the moors with that policeman and Marlene. What were you doing then?"

"Went for a ride," said Jinny, edging away from her brother. "I didn't want to stay with Mrs. Simpson and Petra."

"And," persisted Mike, "I think it's very odd the way you just happened to be buying apples when Mr. Simpson found the watch in amongst them. That's what I think."

"Don't think too hard," warned Jinny.

"Tell me," said Mike.

"Some day," said Jinny, grinning at her brother, knowing that he would leave it at that, wouldn't go prodding and prying. Some day she would tell him. Show him the gate that Shantih had jumped.

"Look for Marlene, if you want Bill," Mike suggested as he walked on to the house.

"Of course," thought Jinny and ran down to the ponies' field.

Bill was standing by the gate with a comic in his hand. Marlene was in the field feeding bits of bread to Shantih.

"Come and help me clean Shantih's tack," Jinny called to Bill.

"Naw," said Bill.

"We're going to clean Shantih's tack," Jinny called to Marlene. "We'll be in the stables."

"I'm not," said Bill.

"I want to talk to you," said Jinny, lowering her voice so that Marlene couldn't hear.

"What you at?" asked Bill.

"Come on," said Jinny and led the way back to the tack room. Bill followed her, unwillingly.

Jinny hung up Shantih's bridle from a hook, found a sponge and a bucket half full of oldish water and began to wipe down the bridle. Through the open door Jinny would be able to see Marlene approaching.

351

"What?" asked Bill, leaning against the saddle horse. "What?"

Jinny tossed back her hair, dragged the sponge down the leather with all her strength.

"You're not going back to Stopton tomorrow," she said. "Marlene wants to stay until your fortnight's up. She wants to learn to ride. If you go she'll go with you. She won't stay here and let you go. So you're not going."

"Am that," said Bill.

"Please," said Jinny. "For Marlene. Don't be so mean. You can easily stay for a few more days, only another week."

"Naw," said Bill and opened his comic again.

Furiously Jinny snatched it from him and threw it on the ground. Bill swung his fist at her. Jinny ducked and felt the rush of air over her head as he missed her.

"Listen," she threatened. "Listen to me. If you go back to Stopton tomorrow I'll tell the police you stole the watch."

Bill took a step back from her.

"What you talking about? What watch?"

"I saw you giving it to Marlene last night. I found it in the wall where she had hidden it and I took it back to Mrs. Simpson's shop this morning."

Bill's normal putty-coloured complexion had turned dark red.

"Marlene will be here in a second," said Jinny, "and she's not to know anything about this. Nothing. So listen, so that you know what to do. You've to tell Dad at teatime, when we're all there to hear you, that you want to stay. And there's to be no more stealing, see? Not while you're here. You've to stay with Ken. In the pottery with him. Be keen on pottery so that Marlene doesn't worry about you. See?"

Bill didn't answer.

"That's Marlene now," warned Jinny. "You know what to do. Tell them at teatime. Or I'll tell the police. And don't think I don't mean it because I do." Jinny scrubbed at Shantih's bridle.

"He didn't half eat up that bread. I don't think you feed him proper. It's hens you feed on that old corn and he ain't no hen."

352

"You can send her food parcels," suggested Jinny.

"Eh, O.K., I'll do that," said Marlene. "What's he been at ?" she asked suspiciously, looking at Bill.

Jinny thrust a sponge into Bill's unwilling hand. "He's helping me to clean tack," she said and gave Bill Shantih's grass-encrusted bit to clean.

Marlene, planning ways in which they could posh up Shantih, helped Jinny to clean the saddle.

"Them old brushes don't get at the deep down dirt," she said. "You got to get with it. Try the Hoover on him. Or like they do with cars—a horse wash."

"Set the table for tea," said Mrs. Manders when they got into the house. "What did Sue do with all her wet clothes?"

"Took them back to their tent," said Jinny, taking knives and forks out of the drawer.

"She should have left them here," said Mrs. Manders. "You could go over and ask her if she wants to bring them up here to dry off."

"O.K.," said Jinny. "Though she didn't seem very keen on charity. I offered them all instant Dr. Barnardo's when it rained but she didn't want it."

"I won't see the fat horse again," said Marlene. "Eh, it were that podgy. What she wants to stick with that old dough ball for when she could have one like yours?"

"Bet she wouldn't change Pippen for Shantih," said Jinny.

"Like she loves him," said Marlene, grinning.

When she went to tell Ken and her father that their tea was ready, Jinny paused by Bill's side. "O.K.?" she said. "I mean it." She went on to the pottery.

There was only Ken there.

"Tea," said Jinny. "Where's Dad?"

"Bathroom," said Ken. "You managed it this morning?"

And Jinny told him about Shantih jumping the gate and how she had hidden the watch in among the apples.

"Marlene wants to stay," said Jinny. "She wants to ride Shantih. So Bill's got to stay too or she won't. If he stays, can he be with you in here? I told him that he's got to tell us at teatime that he wants to stay."

"Does he want to?"

353

"He can make clay monsters," suggested Jinny. "That's what his comics are full of—monsters from the dawn of time, monsters from the centre of the earth, deep sea monsters, space monsters—I had a read at some of them. Well, he can make them in clay. Be a bit of a relief seeing them solid rather than just reading about them and having them prowling round in your head."

"*If* he stays," said Ken, and suddenly he crashed his clenched fist down on the table, filling the air with white, clay dust. "The mess we've made of a kid like that! Where's he going to go? What's he going to do now? Back to Stopton with his monsters until he picks up some more of their trashy bits of obscene rubbish and then they'll shut him up and we'll all be able to forget about him."

"Well it's not *my* fault," said Jinny.

"You reckon?" said Ken. "Not your fault?"

"Well, it's not!" repeated Jinny indignantly. "I don't make him steal things."

"What a nasty thought," said Ken. "Tuck it away out of sign. Got nothing to do with you, has it?"

"Oh, come on for tea," said Jinny. "I don't know what you're talking about." She pushed the thought to the back of her mind that in any way she, Jinny Manders, might be responsible for Bill Thorpe.

Bill was sitting at the table having a pre-tea slice of bread and jam. Jinny gave him another hard look as she sat down but didn't risk saying anything more in case she aroused Marlene's suspicions.

If he didn't tell them that he wanted to stay would she phone the police? Jinny knew she wouldn't, but she knew that Bill couldn't be certain of this.

Jinny smiled at Petra, asking her when her music exam was, how long it would last, whether she would need to stay overnight in Inverburgh when she sat it. When Mike put down her plate of grilled tomatoes and ham pie, Jinny thanked him sweetly. This was the way someone would behave who was the sort of person who would phone up the police and tell them that Bill had stolen the watch.

Jinny stared hard at Bill, hoping he was noticing her.

They had reached the cake and second cup of tea

354

stage. Ken had finished. Since he never ate anything that was connected with animals, not even cheese or milk or eggs, Ken's meals, mostly of raw vegetables, fruit, wholemeal bread and brown rice had their own timing, didn't fit in with the Manders' pattern of meat and veg., chips and eggs. Quite often Ken had days of not eating—to make him aware of the gift of food, he said. He was watching Jinny now, knowing that she was up to something.

Bill took his fourth piece of cake and Mrs. Manders removed the plate.

"Need to leave proper early tomorrow?" asked Marlene. "Best not sleep, eh?"

Petra said she would set her alarm, and as she always heard it, she would wake Marlene.

"But you're not going," Jinny thought desperately and glared at Bill. She had tried kicking him under the table but had kicked Kelly instead, making the dog remove himself with wounded dignity to the far corner of the room.

"Tell them! Tell them! Go on, tell them," Jinny thought at Bill, but Bill was stuffing the last piece of cake into his mouth.

"That policeman who was with Mrs. Simpson," Jinny said, "does he live in Glenbost?"

"Police cottages at Ardtallon. There's two of them," said Mr. Manders.

"Could you phone him there?" asked Jinny.

"Oh yes," said her father. "It's really the police station."

"Is the number in the book?" asked Jinny.

"Will be," said Mr. Manders.

"Whatever do you want to know that for?" asked Petra.

"Handy," said Jinny. "Handy to know."

"What you on at?" asked Marlene suspiciously.

But Bill pushed his chair back from the table. Before he stood up he looked across at Jinny, mocking her. He knew she would never phone the police. He knew that Marlene cared more about him than learning to ride. And he knew that Jinny knew this. He wanted back to Stopton and he was going.

"Beast," thought Jinny helplessly. "Selfish, pigging beast."

He'd called her bluff. She wouldn't phone. There was nothing more she could do. Marlene wasn't going to get her chance to go fast like flames on Shantih. It was all hopeless.

Ken stretched out a long arm and caught hold of Bill.

"Sit down," said Ken. "No hurry." Jinny saw Ken's bony fingers biting into Bill's wrist as he forced him to sit down again.

"I was having a chat with Jinny," said Ken, and Jinny saw the red flush creep up Bill's neck and redden his ears. He shifted uneasily in his chair.

"Jinny said she'd had a word with you." Ken's green eyes had set as hard as stones. He forced Bill to look at him. There was no softness in Ken. He was contained in himself. Independent. Lived from his own centre. "Jinny said you'd something to tell us."

Everyone was looking at Ken and Bill, wondering what Ken was talking about. But no one interrupted. Not Mr. Manders, or Marlene.

"Now," said Ken, and they were all waiting for Bill to speak.

"I changed me mind," said Bill. "We ain't going to-morrow."

"Oh, grand," said Mr. Manders. "Great."

"More food," thought Mrs. Manders and hoped that Mrs. Simpson wouldn't hold the matter of the watch against her.

Marlene had sat without moving, so drawn into herself that she hardly seemed to be breathing.

"That what you really want?" she asked Bill.

"Yus," said Bill and Marlene exploded from her chair like a rocket. Stamping her lame leg, clapping her hands, she danced round the kitchen.

"Eh, ain't that right smashing?" she cried. "That's right proper smashing, that is! Jin's going to learn me to ride the old horse, ain't you? To sit on him proper so we can go galloping off, him and me. for miles and miles. Eh, I'm right pleased, Bill. I'm right proper pleased you want to stay!"

Jinny blew her nose hard but didn't feel so bad about it because her mother had suddenly found it necessary to start and collect up the tea plates.

"Come into the pottery, now," said Ken, "and I'll show you round. You can try the wheel."

Bill went with him.

"When we going to start?" Marlene demanded.

"Ride down to Sue's," suggested Mrs. Manders. "See if we can dry out anything for them."

"Want me to wipe up first?" asked Marlene.

"Don't think you'd be safe," laughed Mrs. Manders.

"It's Petra's day," said Jinny. "We'll go and find Sue."

"Take the old horse?"

"But of course," said Jinny.

"Got to start and learn how to do things, ain't I? Now that I'm going to be doing the proper riding."

CHAPTER TWELVE

"Give us the halter thing," said Marlene the next morning. "I'll do the catching bit."

"Well, take care," said Jinny, handing Shantih's halter to Marlene. "Don't rush at her."

"Eh, give over fussing. Here, how's that then?" and Marlene placed a sugar lump on the palm of her hand and tucked the halter, more or less out of sight, behind her back. "That do? Like you showed me?"

"A scoop of nuts would be easier," suggested Jinny. "Then there'd be more than one mouthful. You could put her halter on while she's got her head down munching."

"He's right fed up with all those old dried things you're always giving him. Enjoys a sugar lump he does. I've got more in me pocket." Marlene set off confidently across the field.

Jinny watched, biting her tongue to stop herself interfering, as Marlene advanced on Shantih.

"Here you are, horse," Marlene said and let Shantih lip up the sugar from her hand.

"Now for this rope thing. Let's be having your head down. End of that rope round your neck and that's me got you. Now this bit round your face."

Marlene struggled to get the halter over Shantih's ears

357

then announced triumphantly, "That's the job," and remembered to knot the halter rope. "That deserves another sugar lump, that does."

Marlene produced her bag of sugar lumps, and was just placing one correctly on her outstretched palm, when Shantih snatched it up. Without a second's hesitation, Marlene smacked Shantih hard across the muzzle. The Arab sprang back to the length of her rope, rearing away from Marlene. But Marlene hardly noticed. "You need sorting out, you do," she threatened darkly and turned to lead the prancing horse back to Jinny.

"D'you see that?" Marlene demanded when she reached the gate. "Had to give him a bat on the nose."

"I saw," said Jinny, who had been watching helplessly. "I told you not to hit her. She's scared of being hit because of the circus."

"Garn," said Marlene. "He ain't scared. He's having you on, he is. Any road I didn't hit him, just gave him a bit bat. Cheek of him snatching at me sugar lumps."

"I told you you'd be better with a scoop of nuts," said Jinny, opening the gate, but Marlene wasn't listening.

"What's next?" she demanded. "Going at him with the brush, ain't it? Keeping all them hairs lying nice and flat. Then on with the saddle and that's me set for the riding. 'Spect I'll be proper good today."

An hour later Marlene wasn't feeling so confident.

"Up, down. Up, down," chanted Jinny as she ran at Shantih's side.

"Eh, that were awful," lamented Marlene when they stopped. "I just go bump, bump, bump, bump. I ain't never going to be much good until I get the hang of this, am I?"

Reluctantly Jinny had to agree.

"Come on then," said Marlene. "Let's have another bash."

"Wait till I get my breath back," gasped Jinny. "Here's Sue," she added, spotting Pippen's skewbald shape bumbling over the fields towards them. "Perhaps Sue'll know what we're doing wrong."

"Hullo," said Sue, opening the gate without dismounting and riding into the field. "You both look like the end of the world. What's wrong?"

"I'm trying to teach Marlene to post," said Jinny. "But I'm not doing very well."

"Took me weeks," said Sue.

"And me," said Jinny, remembering the hours she had spent bumping round Major Young's paddock at the riding school in Stopton.

"Well, I ain't got weeks," said Marlene. "Come on. Give us another go."

Jinny set off round the field again, holding Shantih's bridle with one hand, the other pressing Marlene's knee against the saddle and chanting, "Up, down. Up, down," to the rhythm of Shantih's stride, while Marlene bumped around.

"Do you want a try on Pippen?" Sue offered when they got back to her. "He might be steadier."

Marlene shook her head stubbornly. "Ain't the old horse, it's me," she said.

"Try holding on to the front of the saddle," suggested Sue, "and sort of push yourself up from your hands."

Next time round Marlene tried it. She was crouched forward trying frantically to push up at the right moment when Shantih tossed her head and caught Marlene a crack on the nose.

"S'all right," Marlene assured them, staunching the flow of blood with an inadequate paper handkerchief. "I'll have it stopped in a moment. I'll not bother getting off."

Jinny insisted that Shantih needed a rest and made Marlene dismount. Sue provided her with a bigger hanky.

While Marlene mopped at her nose Jinny made a hopeless face at Sue. She didn't know how else she could teach Marlene to post except by going on making Shantih trot and hoping that eventually Marlene's bumping would change into posting.

"That's it stopped," Marlene announced, sniffing experimentally. "Let's get back to me bumping. Can't go fast, can I, until we get this up and down business right."

They spent all afternoon in the field. Sue and Jinny taking it in turns to make Shantih trot round; but by five o'clock, although Marlene could control Shantih at a walk, her bumping was showing no signs of changing into posting.

"We'll try again tomorrow," said Jinny. "Shantih's had enough for today."

Marlene didn't argue but slid obediently to the ground.

"I ain't no good, am I?" she said, looking despondently from Jinny to Sue.

"Of course you are," cried Jinny. "I told you, it took us ages to learn."

"Ain't never going to learn to go fast," despaired Marlene. "Better go and see how Bill's doing," she mumbled and limped quickly away from them.

"Come for a gallop on the sands," suggested Sue when Marlene was out of sight.

Jinny hesitated, then said no, for she knew there was just a chance that Marlene might be watching from a window and would see them doing what she dreamed of doing, going fast as flames, and Jinny was beginning to think that Marlene wasn't going to manage it in the five days she had left.

Next morning Marlene brought Shantih in and groomed her before she had her breakfast.

"Give us that bit longer for bumping," she said to Jinny.

Jinny supposed it would.

"We'll try up and down the path to the shore," Jinny suggested after Marlene had tacked Shantih up. "Perhaps that will be better. You'll have longer going straight. Maybe that's what was wrong yesterday, having to go round the field."

But going along the path didn't make any difference to Marlene's bumping, it only gave Shantih more scope for sudden shies, fly canters and head tossing. By the time they had been up and down the path a few times, Jinny knew it had not been a good idea to leave the field.

"It's your fault," she said to Shantih. "Why can't you trot smoothly and give Marlene a chance?"

"Eh, don't be blaming the old horse."

"Well, it is her fault," repeated Jinny. "We'll go back to the sea once more and then I think we'd be better in the field. And you calm down," she added severely to Shantih.

"Ready? Off we go. Up, down. Up, down."

Jinny had knotted a rope to the bit ring to make leading Shantih easier and when her horse shied at absolutely nothing at all she tugged at the rope, spoke sharply to her, feeling as irritated with her as she had with Bramble when he was having one of his spooky days. Normally Shantih could do no wrong in Jinny's eyes. On the surface she was annoyed when the Arab misbehaved, rearing or bucking her off, but underneath Jinny thought up excuses for her wild behaviour, and loved her so much that it didn't really matter to Jinny how wild she was. But now Jinny was thinking about Marlene, desperately wanting her to be able to ride before she had to go back to Stopton, and so much depended on Shantih.

"Trot on," said Jinny crossly as Shantih flung herself sideways in a sudden canter. "How is Marlene ever going to learn to post if you go on mucking about all the time?" She gave Shantih's rope another sharp tug.

"Up, down. Up, down," Jinny chanted as they trotted back to Finmory.

Sue rode up later in the morning to find Jinny holding a glooming Shantih while Marlene pressed a paper hanky to her bleeding nose.

"Knew you needed me," said Sue, handing up a larger handkerchief. "What happened?"

"Same thing," said Jinny. "And Marlene was *nearly* posting, weren't you?"

"No," said Marlene from behind Sue's handkerchief. "I were just at me bumping."

"Well, you might have been posting in a minute," snapped Jinny, "if she'd been a bit more sensible. You idiot horse."

The Arab swung away from Jinny, her ears pinned back, her eyes rolling, as she pawed at the ground with a front hoof.

"Behave yourself," Jinny told her. "You think you can do what you like, don't you?"

Shantih tossed her head, jangling the bit and narrowly missed hitting Marlene in the face for a third time.

"If I were you," said Sue, "I'd ride her in a martingale."

"I did," said Jinny. "When I had one. Clare Burnley lent me one. She was better behaved with it on. It stopped her getting her head up."

361

"Why don't you buy one? Can't be very expensive."

Jinny thought of the money in her tin box, of the lunge-ing rein she was going to buy with it. She saw herself standing in the middle of the field and Shantih cantering smoothly round on the end of her new lungeing rein.

"Don't think I could afford a martingale," said Jinny.

"Pity," said Sue. "I don't think Shantih tossing her head up the way she does helps Marlene to post. And it would stop her rearing with you."

Jinny groaned inwardly. If Marlene was ever going to go fast, she would have to control Shantih by herself and it certainly wouldn't help her if Shantih reared.

"Oh well," said Jinny, reluctantly abandoning the dream of the lungeing rein. "I suppose I could sell a few of my drawings."

"Would we need to go into Inverburgh to buy it?" Sue asked.

"Yes," said Jinny brightening at the thought. It was going to be a very hot afternoon and she was beginning to be a bit fed up with running beside Shantih, chanting her 'up, down,' refrain. "Might as well go this afternoon. If I can persuade Dad to run us to the main road we could catch a bus at two o'clock and there's one back at six."

Marlene said she would stay with the old horse and Jinny said she most certainly would not.

"Got to practise," Marlene insisted. "Ain't got much time left."

"We'll practise again this evening," Jinny promised. "And then we'll have a martingale and you can hold on to the neck strap."

"What?" said Marlene. Then, giving her nose a final dab, decided that it didn't really concern her. "Just have one more bump round the field," she said and gathered up Shantih's reins.

Jinny left Sue and Marlene to take off Shantih's tack and went in search of her father.

"Could you run us in for the two o'clock bus?" she asked.

Her father said he would and Jinny climbed up to her bedroom and reluctantly chose six drawings to take to Nell Storr. They had to be good ones. Nell knew the difference.

Jinny put the six drawings in a brown envelope and laid it carefully on her bed. She took down the cash box, pulled off the sellotape and took out the five one pound notes that were left in it. It didn't look much for months of saving, but Jinny had had to pay for Shantih's shoeing which had used up quite a lot of the money that Nell Storr had paid for her drawings.

"A pound each for six drawings," Jinny thought. "That's six pounds and five, that's eleven pounds. That should be plenty for a martingale."

Standing in her bedroom, eleven pounds had seemed hordes of money, but somehow, as they stood looking in the window of the saddler's shop, it didn't seem quite so much.

"Pretty expensive-looking," said Sue doubtfully.

Jinny agreed, but as far as she knew it was the only saddlers in Inverburgh.

"Should we go and sell your drawings first?" Sue asked.

"Let's find out how much a martingale will cost," said Jinny. "Perhaps I'll not need to sell them."

"Come on then," nagged Marlene. "We going in then? Got to have plenty time to pick a present for me mum. She likes something real nice does me mum. Proper fussy she is."

Jinny scowled at Marlene. At that particular moment she couldn't have cared less how fussy Mrs. Thorpe was.

"Shall I lead the way, seeing you're a bit shy like," said Marlene, pushing open the saddler's door. Jinny and Sue followed after her.

"Can I assist?" asked a slim young man, emerging from behind a glass counter.

Jinny was gazing entranced at saddles and bridles, horse rugs and numnahs, black jackets and breeches, and, best of all, hanging in a corner, a bunch of lungeing reins.

"We want to buy a what-do-you-call-it," said Marlene. "One of them things to stop me bumping."

The young man raised elegant eyebrows.

"We want to know how much a standing martingale would cost," said Jinny quickly.

"Pony size?"

"Arab size," said Jinny.

363

The assistant brought a standing martingale and laid it on the glass counter.

"Six pounds fifty," he said.

"Eh!" exclaimed Marlene. "For a bit belt!"

"We'll come back later," said Jinny.

"Certainly, Madam," said the assistant, putting away the martingale.

"Nell Storr's," said Jinny when they were out of the shop.

"Best be quick," said Marlene. "I've got to pick me mum's pressie."

But Nell Storr wasn't in her craft shop. She was away for a week. The girl behind the counter offered to keep Jinny's drawings until Nell came back but said that only Nell herself could pay Jinny for them, so Jinny said that was no good and kept her drawings.

Jinny stared gloomily across the road. Now that she couldn't afford to buy it a martingale seemed the most important thing in the world; the only thing that could ever teach Marlene to post.

"If we'd known I could have lent you the money," said Sue.

"Well, we didn't know, did we?" snapped Jinny.

"It don't matter," said Marlene. "Bloomin' well too much money. I'll just look for something for me mum and then we'll get back to me trotting."

"How about something from Nell's?" suggested Jinny.

Marlene regarded the pottery, glass, wood carvings and woven goods that filled the craft shop window.

"Naw," she said disdainfully. "Me mum likes pretty things, not that junk."

An hour and six ice creams later, Marlene found a pawn shop.

"Eh, we'll get something here," she cried. "People have to pop right pretty things sometimes."

The dirty window was filled with old clothes, watches, vases, jewellery, ornaments and all the other belongings that people had brought to the pawn shop, borrowed money on and never bothered to buy back.

"That's proper pretty," said Marlene, pointing to a small china posy of flowers. "She'd fancy that."

Jinny and Sue followed Marlene into the pawn shop.

Jinny looked round curiously at the clutter of abandoned possessions.

"It's all rubbish," said Sue.

Jinny nodded but she supposed that all the things her family owned would look much the same if you brought them here.

Marlene bought her posy bowl from a toothless young woman.

"Right bargain for fifty pence," she said, carrying it proudly out of the shop.

"It's a bit dirty," said Sue.

"Give it a right scrub up and it'll be real nice. Bet you'd have paid five pounds for it in one of your fancy shops. Saw one of those things we were going to buy. Be cheaper in there."

"What things?" said Jinny. "A martingale? In there?"

"Don't believe you," said Sue flatly. "You wouldn't know what a martingale looked like."

"Just seen one, ain't I? Come back in and I'll show you."

"Let's see that leather belt thing," Marlene said, pointing it out to the woman in the pawn shop.

"Would it be this you're meaning?" the woman said and laid a standing martingale on the counter.

"Wherever did that come from?" Jinny demanded in amazement.

"Came with a job lot from a sale," said the woman. "Lot of old junk out of the stables. Had to take it to get a chest our Jim had his eye on."

"It's not really a martingale," said Sue critically. "Only a bit of one. Someone's made up the neck strap from two stirrup leathers."

"Oh, but it would do," gasped Jinny. "It would be fine. How much is it?"

"One pound and fifty pence," said the woman. "Beautiful leather, it is."

Jinny still hadn't recovered from her surprise by the time she was standing in the stable fitting the martingale round Shantih's neck. She had cleaned it thoroughly and it seemed perfectly good. It was, thought Jinny, a bargain.

"Eh, this is it, ain't it?" said Marlene, as Jinny led

365

Shantih down to the field. "I'll be able to do the up and down now, won't it?"

"At least she'll not be able to bash you on the nose," said Jinny, tightening Shantih's girth and holding her while Marlene mounted. "Walk her to the hedge and back by yourself and then we'll trot."

Jinny watched as Marlene rode Shantih away from her. She sat very straight in the saddle, Jinny's hard hat firmly on her head, her heels pressed down, her elbows tucked in. Marlene was in charge of Shantih. She wasn't going to let any old horse boss her.

When they reached the hedge and Marlene turned back to Jinny, Shantih broke into a jog. Instantly, Marlene had checked her and brought her back to a walk.

"Grab hold," said Marlene to Jinny, "and off we go."

But by the time they were half way round the field both girls knew that the martingale wasn't going to work a miracle with Marlene's posting. Clutching the neck strap, she continued to bump.

As they walked back to Finmory through the summer dusk Marlene said, "It's me leg, ain't it? I ain't ever going to be able to do anything but bump."

"Don't be daft," said Jinny loudly, because she had been thinking the same thing herself. "Of course you'll be able to post. It takes time to learn, that's all. Of course you'll be able to do it."

"Some hopes," said Marlene.

"And you're doing really well controlling her and riding her."

"Riding?" exclaimed Marlene in disgust. "You can't ride when all the old horse is doing is crawling round. I don't call that riding, I don't."

They weren't any more successful the next morning, although both Sue and Jinny had spent all morning making Shantih trot round the field. Marlene went on bumping.

"While we're getting our breath back," said Sue, "try standing up in your stirrups."

Marlene did so.

"Now sit down and stand up. Go on, do it several times."

"Now," instructed Sue, "don't sit down in between,

hardly touch your seat on to the saddle and stand up again quickly."

Marlene tried but each time she sat down with a flop and had to reorganise herself into standing up.

"Don't *sit* down," said Jinny. "That's why you get bumped."

"Can't help it," said Marlene. "I ain't trying to get bumped am I?"

Ken appeared at the field gate.

"Eh," cried Marlene, all her attention riveted on Ken, "he ain't got our Bill with him." She swung Shantih round and urged her to the gate.

"Where's our Bill?" Marlene shouted as Shantih trotted forward.

"Make her walk," yelled Jinny as Marlene bumped precariously from side to side.

And then, to Jinny's and Sue's delight, Marlene was posting. She went up too far and came down with a flop but she was most definitely and decidedly posting.

"She's done it," cried Sue.

"Look at me," Marlene yelled. "I'm trotting proper. I can do it!"

Sue on Pippen led the way round the field and Marlene trotted behind her, posting most of the way. She returned to the gate, her face glowing scarlet with effort and success.

"Couldn't do it before," Marlene told Ken. "Right down in the dumps I was. Thought it were me leg mucking things up. Here, I'll do it again. You watch me."

Marlene and Sue trotted round again. This time Marlene posted all the way.

"How were that?" she demanded triumphantly. "I'm doing proper good now, ain't I?"

"Nearly as good as Bill and his pots," said Ken. "Come into the pottery after lunch and he'll give you a demo."

Marlene clapped her hand to her mouth.

"He went right out of me head with all that posting," she admitted.

Sue stayed for lunch and afterwards they went into the pottery.

"Bit squint, that one," said Marlene, looking critically at Bill's pots.

"Ain't easy," said Bill. "Watch this." He sat down at

367

the wheel and began to shape a pot out of a lump of wet clay.

"How's that?" he asked when he had finished.

"Smashing," said Jinny. "You've learned jolly quickly."

"Our Bill was looking right pleased, did you notice?" Marlene asked as they went back to the field.

Jinny said she had.

"You sit there and watch us," Marlene said as she mounted Shantih. "Sue and me'll have a bit trot round."

Jinny sat on the gate and watched as Marlene trotted round the field behind Sue. There was no doubt about it, Marlene had learned to post.

"Shall we have another go after tea?" suggested Marlene when Sue said it was five o'clock and she would have to go.

"No," said Jinny. "Shantih's had enough for one day."

"Tomorrow then," said Marlene, dismounting.

Jinny took Shantih's reins, rubbed her hand down her horse's neck, straightening her mane," said, "Yes. Tomorrow." Then she took Shantih into the stable while Marlene went to see how Bill's potting was getting on.

"You're being very well behaved," Jinny said to Shantih as she watched the Arab eating a small feed of oats and nuts. It might be the martingale that was stopping Shantih rearing, but in the whole afternoon of walking and trotting about the field, Shantih had only bucked once.

"Expect you like having Pippen for company," said Jinny, but she knew that it couldn't only be that. Shantih had often had the Highland ponies with her when Jinny had been trying to school her before. Reluctantly Jinny had to admit to herself that it must be something to do with Marlene. It wasn't that Marlene knew anything at all about how to treat horses, just that when her mind was set on a thing there was no room in it for anything else. When Shantih had tried to buck, Marlene had slapped her hard on the shoulder and told Shantih to stop his old nonsense, that if he started that mucking about she'd be bumping again. Shantih had given another protesting hitch of her quarters and trotted on.

They all spent the next afternoon on the shore. Mr. and Mrs. Manders, Mike and Petra, Ken and Bill, brought down a picnic. Sue's parents joined them. Jinny spent her time keeping an eye on Marlene and Shantih, watching anxiously as Marlene rode Shantih about. Tomorrow was Friday and then Saturday, when Marlene and Bill would go home to Stopton. Jinny didn't want anything to happen to spoil Marlene's confidence before that.

The afterglow of sunset turned sky, sea and wet sands into a glowing sapphire. We must be breathing blue air, Jinny thought. Sue and Marlene were walking the horses at the water's edge and the spray from their horses' hooves glittered ice blue, diamond, aquamarine. They were held in a jewelled paperweight of sky and sea.

"Home," said Mrs. Manders, beginning to gather up the remains of the picnic, and arranging with the Hortons to come up for supper on Saturday evening.

"Marlene will be in Stopton then," Jinny thought. "Everything will be the same for us, but not for her."

Mr. and Mrs. Horton began to walk back to their tent. Jinny's family, Ken and Bill, wandered raggedly back to Finmory.

"Don't be long," Mrs. Horton called to Sue.

"Coming now," replied Sue and turned Pippen to follow her parents. Shantih went with Pippen. Jinny ran over the sands towards them, took Shantih's bridle to turn her back to Finmory.

"Eh, let's go with them," pleaded Marlene. "Just along a bit and then I can have a last trot back."

"O.K.," said Jinny and walked between the two horses. She felt soaked through with the day's sunlight, warm and contented. She glanced at Marlene sitting very correctly on Shantih and thought that tomorrow Marlene could have a canter. If Sue rode with her, Shantih would behave, would stop when Pippen stopped. Jinny thought Marlene would manage.

Sue rode off to her tent and Marlene turned Shantih round and began to trot back. Jinny ran beside them.

"Got the knack of that posting now, ain't I?" Marlene asked as they walked up the path to Finmory.

Jinny agreed that she most certainly had.

"Reckon I'm good enough now, ain't I?" demanded Marlene.

There was a tense, strained quality in her voice that made Jinny look up at her.

"Good enough for what?" asked Jinny.

"You know," said Marlene. "To go fast."

"Yes," said Jinny. "You can have a canter with Sue tomorrow. I was thinking about it. There's a good canter on the moors. We can go up there tomorrow. I'll wait at the end and you and Sue can gallop up to me. Shantih's bound to stop. She knows that bit. She'll stop when she reaches me."

"Eh no!" exclaimed Marlene. "I don't want you lot there. Just me and the old horse, that's what I mean."

"But you can't," said Jinny. "You couldn't manage Shantih by yourself."

"I could that. We get on right good. I don't put up with none of that nonsense you have."

"Yes, but . . ." began Jinny, then changed what she had been going to say into, "We'll see tomorrow."

She didn't think she could possibly explain to Marlene the difference between riding Shantih by herself and riding Shantih with herself and Sue looking after her.

"Really Marlene knows nothing about controlling horses. Most of the time she doesn't even notice what Shantih's doing," Jinny thought.

"That's fixed up about me riding," Marlene said, before she went to bed. "I'll take him down to the sands and have a bit ride on him tomorrow, by myself. That's it, ain't it?" and she was through the door before Jinny had time to protest.

"Could she manage Shantih by herself?" asked Mike doubtfully.

"Of course not," said Jinny. " 'Course she couldn't. She's just talking nonsense. Of course I shan't let her gallop Shantih by herself."

CHAPTER THIRTEEN

In her dream, Jinny was running through Stopton streets, chasing Marlene and Shantih. The faster Jinny ran, the faster Marlene galloped Shantih away from her. "Stop!" Jinny screamed. "Stop! She's mine!" But Marlene only laughed and rode faster than ever between the roaring

370

traffic. "Stop!" screamed Jinny again and woke herself back into her own bed at Finmory.

She lay, the dream still vivid in her mind. It was daylight, early morning blue. Jinny got up and looked out of the window to make sure that Shantih was still in her field.

The Arab was grazing peacefully by the far hedge. Being herself in the field, untroubled by humans. Perhaps Ken was right, Jinny thought, when he said that horses should be left alone to be horses; that they didn't need humans to ride them.

Shantih flicked her tail, lifted each foot in slow, deliberate steps as she grazed along the hedgerow. Jinny hesitated, unwilling to break into the secret horse world in which Shantih moved. Not calling her name, not yet, but knowing that in a minute or two she would, just for the joy of seeing Shantih look up and know her.

But before Jinny had time to open the window and call down to her horse, something startled Shantih. She jerked her head up, ears pricked, neck arched. From her window, Jinny couldn't see anything that might have disturbed her. She thought that it might be Ken and Kelly out for an early morning walk, or Mr. MacKenzie taking a short cut down to his fields by the sea.

Then Jinny saw who it was. Marlene was standing at the field gate. She had Jinny's hard hat on her head, Shantih's halter in one hand and a sugar lump on the other.

"Well," thought Jinny, "of all the cheek. She's going to ride my horse. Good job I saw her."

Jinny lifted her hand to open the window, to shout at Marlene and tell her to leave Shantih alone; but somehow she couldn't do it. She watched as Marlene limped across the field, saw Shantih take a few strides towards her, then wait. Marlene fumbled with sugar lumps and halter and although Jinny couldn't hear her she could see her mouth moving as she talked to the horse.

Confidently, Marlene led Shantih back to the gate, manœuvred her through it and closed it behind them. Shantih pranced at the end of her halter rope, fretting to reach the stable, but Marlene paid no attention to her

371

impatience. She checked that the gate was shut and then led Shantih out of sight.

"I'll go down to the stables," Jinny thought, scrambling into her clothes. "Stop her there. Go with her if she wants to ride."

Jinny ran lightly through the garden and down to the stables. She hesitated at the stable doorway. Inside she could hear the sounds of Marlene grooming Shantih.

"Come on, now. Stand still when I'm brushing you. Got to get you right shiny. Can't have you looking a mess. Not when we're going galloping. Got to be all sparkling, you have."

"Go in and stop her," Jinny told herself. "You know she can't manage Shantih. She could fall, jam her foot in a stirrup, be dragged. If Shantih got a fright, Marlene wouldn't know what to do. Anything, anything could happen to them. She doesn't mean to go back to the field."

Jinny knew quite certainly where Marlene meant to ride. She was going to take Shantih down to the shore and gallop her over the sands.

"She won't be able to control her," Jinny thought. "Won't be able to stop her." For Jinny knew how Shantih could become so excited that unless you stopped her she would go plunging over the boulders that made a barrier between the fields and the sand. To cross them safely you had to bring your horse to a slow walk. Even to trot through them was dangerous.

"Go on in and stop her," Jinny told herself.

But Jinny couldn't; couldn't make herself march into the stable and spoil everything for Marlene.

Jinny knew that it was what she would have wanted to do if she had been Marlene. If she had had to leave Shantih tomorrow and go back to Stopton, Jinny would have wanted to gallop by herself over the sands of Finmory Bay; to be alone with Shantih, sharing the ecstasy of galloping together—the freedom, the joy. To hoard the moments in her mind so that she would always have them there, to bring them out, to re-live them during the black times.

"Eh, you look proper nice," Marlene told Shantih. "Now for your bridle and the martingale thing. Watch

372

that big tongue of yours, I ain't made for licking. You put this in your mouth, that'll sort you out."

But if Marlene fell off . . . If Shantih hurt herself . . . Jinny *had* to stop her, couldn't take the risk of letting Marlene harm Shantih.

Jinny took a step towards the stable door. She had to go in, had to stop her. "Be sensible. Be responsible," she told herself. "You know best."

Marlene's white, pinched face swam into the front of Jinny's mind, as she had seen it reflected in the shop mirror, as she had looked when she had realised that Jinny knew the truth about Bill.

And Jinny knew that she couldn't do it. She couldn't bear to stop Marlene, couldn't bear to go into the stable and spoil it all.

"But Shantih . . ." thought Jinny, yet it made no difference.

"Now your saddle," said Marlene. "And heave ho the old belly band."

Jinny bit hard on the knuckles of her clenched fist, flung herself away from the stables, left Shantih to Marlene, and went running as fast as she could through the garden and up the hillside behind Finmory.

Not looking back, Jinny climbed steadily until she was sure that she was high enough up to be able to see the sands and the path leading down to the bay. Then she turned, crouched down by a boulder and picked out the grey stone stable buildings.

Marlene was leading Shantih into the yard. They were tiny, puppet figures—a girl with a lame leg and a chestnut Arab, her mane and tail blown out by the breeze, lifting her white legs impatiently high as she danced out of the dark stable doorway into the sunlit yard.

Three times Marlene tried to scramble up into the saddle and three times Shantih sprang away from her.

"Don't hold the reins so tight," Jinny thought. She itched to be there in the yard, to put out her hand and hold Shantih still for Marlene. "Don't dig your toe into her side."

Then, at her fourth attempt, Marlene made it, and was sitting in the saddle, while Shantih plunged forward and trotted down the path to the sea.

A kind of stillness came over Jinny as she sat, remote and high, crouching by the boulders, her eyes held to the figures of the girl and the horse. No matter what happened Jinny couldn't have taken her eyes away from them. If Shantih went mad, raced, runaway crazy over the sands, Jinny had to watch it happening. By turning away from the stable doorway, she had said, "Yes." Had allowed this to happen and now she could only watch. Had to watch.

Shantih went trotting out, her neck arched, the sea breeze winnowing her mane, her white hooves flashing over the short grass. Marlene sat posting deligently, sitting very upright, looking straight ahead. When they reached the ridge of boulders, Marlene steadied Shantih to a walk and she picked her way through them, clipping and stumbling in her haste to reach the shore.

Then they were on the sands. Shantih gave a half rear, leapt forward and raced away. She stretched her neck low, thundered the beat of her hooves against the glimmering drum skin of the wet sands. The track of her hoof prints flared out behind her.

For a minute Marlene lost her balance, was thrown forward over Shantih's withers but somehow, her hands grabbing at the neck strap, her knees held against the knee rolls, her feet wedged crookedly in the stirrups, she stayed in the saddle.

And although Marlene was still crouched over Shantih's neck Jinny knew that she wasn't going to come off. She had found her balance against the speed of the horse. Her hands low on Shantih's neck, her knees pressed into the knee rolls, Marlene was looking straight ahead as Shantih stormed the white brilliance of sea dazzle and gleaming sands. They went like flames, the flickering, burning, chestnut mare and the brightness of her rider laughing aloud into the silence of the morning. No longer lame.

As the Arab flew over the beach towards the first black shards of rock at the far side of the bay, Marlene was completely out of control. Tight as a limpet she clung on to the horse's back as they swerved between the rocks.

When they reached the cliffs and Shantih could gallop no further, she skidded to a violent halt, flung up her head

374

and in a split second had plunged round and was galloping back across the sands to Finmory. Marlene lost a
stirrup, slipped dangerously to one side but somehow
managed to stop herself falling off. In one hand she
clutched reins, martingale and a lump of mane, while her
other hand was clenched on to the pommel of the saddle.
She was crouched over Shantih's withers but her eyes
were bright with excitement and her face open and laughing with sheer delight.

Yet still Jinny didn't move. She sat hardly breathing,
her long hair shielding her expressionless face as she
watched this stranger riding her horse.

Before they reached the barricade of smooth pebbles
Shantih broke into a ragged trot. She clattered her way
through the stones at a walk and Marlene was able to push
herself upright in the saddle. She found her stirrup and
fumbled to reorganise the lassoos of reins, so that by the
time they reached the path Marlene was in control again.

Alert and gay, Shantih trotted back to Finmory.
Marlene posted. She had done what she had set out to do.
Not once did Marlene look back at the sea.

Jinny saw Marlene reach the stable yard, drop down
from Shantih and take her back out of the sun through
the dark doorway.

Jinny had no words for it but she knew that something
had changed. By her own choice she had let Marlene ride
Shantih, had shared with this girl, whom she hadn't liked
much, her most secret possession—what it was like to
gallop alone on Shantih. The part of Jinny that clutched
tight and hard on to anything that belonged to her had
released its hold, just a little bit. She jumped up from the
hillside, stretching her cramped legs as she went leaping
down the hill. Her hair blew out behind her, her feet
found their own way. Her arms outstretched to keep her
balance, Jinny half ran, half flew down to Shantih and
Marlene.

By the time Jinny reached the stable Marlene had
taken Shantih's tack off and was leading her out to her
field.

"You just up?" she asked Jinny.

"More or less," said Jinny.

"Eh, we'd a right proper ride. It were real great it were.

375

Me and the old horse, just us two on the beach. And whee! We didn't half gallop."

"Good," said Jinny. "I'm glad." And she meant it.

Later in the day when Jinny asked Marlene if she wanted to ride Shantih in the field, Marlene shook her head.

"Ain't got time," she said. "Got me packing to do."

"Don't be daft," said Jinny. "All you've got is that tartan shopper and that's been packed all the time you've been here."

Marlene grinned. "Got to be ready," she said.

"Don't you want another ride?"

"Naw," said Marlene. "I can ride now, don't need no more learning, do I? I got me own things to see to."

In the afternoon Marlene checked to see that Bill was still working in the pottery, then went off by herself. Jinny didn't see her again until teatime.

"Where were you?" Jinny asked her. "I couldn't find you anywhere. Sue's mother was teaching me how to play the guitar but there's not much hope. I can't hear the difference in the notes. What were you doing?"

"Minding me own business," said Marlene. "But I'll show you when I've got it fixed up."

The evening was overlapping, evanescent shades of grey, the sea a distant snail trail glimmer, the last of the day drained out of the sky. Jinny was sprawled in an armchair, half reading a book, half holding back the thought that first thing tomorrow Bill and Marlene would be going back to Stopton.

"Psst!" said Marlene, appearing at the side of Jinny's chair. "Come on out with me. I've got something to show you."

"But it's nearly dark," said Jinny. "Can't you show me here?"

"Got me mum's torch," said Marlene. "Come on."

Jinny followed her out to the stables.

"Now," said Marlene, opening up the plastic carrier she had been holding. "Listen right careful so you understand." She emptied twenty or thirty small knobbly parcels on to the tack room table.

"What on earth are they?" demanded Jinny.

376

"Sugar lumps, of course," said Marlene. "For the old horse. To say thank you, like. He can't half gallop, he can't. Eh . . ." Marlene's black eyes sparkled in the torchlight as the thrill of her morning's gallop filled her memory. "It were right proper good. Now you listen careful. I've done them up for him. One for each week. Don't want him having rotten teeth."

"Is that where you were this afternoon?" Jinny asked. "Buying these?"

"At Mrs. Simpson's. She gave me a right sinker, she did."

Marlene arranged the bags in rows. "Last him for ages, them will. Come on and we'll give him one lot now."

The torch turned the grey light into darkness so Marlene switched it off, and they walked together to where Shantih waited by the gate.

"That's your lot," Marlene said when Shantih had crunched her way through the last sugar lump. "Bet you don't meet anyone as soft as me for all the rest of your life. This has been your lucky summer, this has."

Jinny heard the catch in Marlene's voice, heard her swallow hard.

"You'll come back," stated Jinny.

"No chance," said Marlene.

She laid her hand with its bitten nails against Shantih's flat-boned cheek, straightened the silky fineness of Shantih's forelock, and held out her hand letting Shantih lip at her palm.

"You ain't a bad old horse," she said, and with a last rub at Shantih's velvet muzzle, Marlene left her and walked back to Finmory.

"But of course you'll come back," insisted Jinny.

"I'm only here with Bill. We won't neither of us be back."

"You'll come back even if Bill doesn't want to. We want *you* to come back. Dad will write to your parents. Next Easter or next summer, you'll see."

But there was a hollowness about Jinny's assurances. They both knew it couldn't be certain. Marlene would go back to Stopton tomorrow and probably they would never see each other again.

They stopped outside the back door. Marlene looked

round the darkening garden and up to the high reaches of the moor.

"You ain't half spoilt, you ain't. Having all this."

"I know," said Jinny.

"It's not the horse, or living here. I'd be right bored here after a bit. Like me fish and chips, I do. It's your family. Your Mike, he ain't never going to go pinching stuff. And your Dad, he doesn't go off much does he?"

"No," said Jinny, and she struggled to find words to tell Marlene that she knew how spoilt she was; knew she had far too much, but just now there was nothing she could do about it. She had to go on being Jinny Manders.

Suddenly Jinny grabbed Marlene's hand.

"Come on," she said, hurrying her indoors and up to her room.

For a second Jinny stood staring at her competition painting, trying to fix it forever in her mind's eye. It was only about six months since Jinny had painted it but already Shantih had changed. When Jinny had drawn her for the painting she had been wild and free, roaming over the moors, part of the freedom. Now she shared her life with humans. Answered to her name. Knew Jinny.

Very carefully Jinny unpinned the picture. She rolled it up quickly, found the cardboard tube in which the magazine had returned it to her, and fitted her painting into it.

"It's your share in Shantih," said Jinny, holding the painting out to Marlene. "Your share in Finmory for always."

"That's your good painting," said Marlene. "I can't take that. It ain't right."

"Please," said Jinny desperately. "Please. It's the best I've got."

Marlene hesitated, then took it from Jinny. "Thanks," she said. "I'll keep it proper careful. Always."

Next morning Mr. Manders drove Bill, Marlene, Ken and Jinny into Inverburgh in time for the Stopton train. In the station buffet they made stiff polite noises at each other, Mr. Manders assuring the Thorpes that they must come back to Finmory whenever they wanted to. Any time during the school holidays, they had only to phone him and he'd meet them at Inverburgh. In the draughty,

378

echoing, morning station, waiting for the hands of the station clock to jerk round to the figures that would let Mr. Manders say, "Better be getting on to the platform," it sounded to Jinny more unlikely than ever that Marlene would come back to Finmory.

"Back to the la-di-dahs," said Marlene, mocking them. She was clutching her tartan shopper, thinking about Stopton. "Been proper posh staying with you lot."

Marlene handed the ticket collector the two tickets she had been holding in her hand since they left Finmory. She went first through the barrier.

Bill nudged Jinny. "Here," he said. "I left something for you with Ken." He followed his sister on to the platform.

"I am not crying," said Jinny as they drove back to Finmory because both Ken and her father couldn't possibly not have noticed that she was. She had reached the red-eyed, gulping stage.

"Bill made a mug for you," said Ken.

"He told me," said Jinny.

"He was really keen on the pottery once he got going," said Mr. Manders.

"Gave him the address of a mate of mine who has a pottery in Stopton," said Ken. "I'll phone him up in a week or so and if Bill hasn't got in touch with him, he'll look Bill up. See he gets going on with it."

"A chance for him?" said Mr. Manders hopefully.

"A chance," said Ken.

"But Marlene," said Jinny. "Why should she have to go back to Stopton?"

"Because she wants to," said Ken. "Her whole life is there. All the people she loves. She's O.K., is Marlene."

"Tough as old boots," smiled Mr. Manders.

But Jinny didn't think she was, not underneath. She remembered something she had heard Ken say once—the skin beneath the skull.

Mrs. Manders was baking when they got back to Finmory.

"Run over to the farm and see if Mrs. MacKenzie can give you some eggs," she said to Jinny, and without even bothering to protest that Mike and Petra could have gone, Jinny took the money and went.

She caught Shantih, put her bridle on, and rode bareback along the track to the farm. It was odd to be riding without Marlene. She felt cold and empty inside, strangely lost without Marlene's company.

Why had Marlene had to go back to Stopton? Why couldn't she have stayed at Finmory, shared Jinny's family? Why couldn't it be like that? thought Jinny bitterly.

But she knew it would have been no use. Ken had been right. The people Marlene loved were all in Stopton and Marlene had to be with them.

Round a bend in the track came Mr. MacKenzie, driving his tractor. Jinny felt Shantih stiffen, and drop behind her bit as the tractor snorted and clattered towards them.

"Get on old horse! None of that nonsense," Jinny said, and she slapped Shantih hard on the shoulder.

"You're not to go jumping my gates," Mr. MacKenzie shouted at her. "Now I'm warning you, lass, I'll not be having it."

"It was an emergency," Jinny shouted back.

"Well, don't be having another one."

"I won't," said Jinny and rode on.

Then suddenly she realised that Shantih had passed the tractor without bucking or rearing. Her mouth spread into a wide grin, for that was exactly how Marlene would have ridden past the tractor, her mind fixed on where she was going, looking straight ahead.

"Eh," praised Jinny, clapping Shantih's neck, "that were proper good, that were."

"I'll write and tell Marlene," Jinny thought. "Tell her that she's taught me to ride." And Jinny flicked her hair back behind her ears, deciding to go and find Sue after she had got the eggs.

"Forward the eggs," thought Jinny, and laughed. There were weeks and weeks of holiday still ahead of her and Sue to ride with.

"Be right proper good," she said aloud. "Be right proper good, eh, old horse?" and Jinny let Shantih canter on through the bright morning.

380